GIDEON

GIDEON

ALEX GORDON

HARPER Voyager
An Imprint of HarperCollinsPublishers

Harper Voyager and design is a trademark of HCP LLC.

GIDEON. Copyright © 2015 by Alex Gordon. All rights reserved. Printed in the United States of America. No part of this book may be used or reproduced in any manner whatsoever without written permission except in the case of brief quotations embodied in critical articles and reviews. For information address HarperCollins Publishers, 195 Broadway, New York, NY 10007.

HarperCollins books may be purchased for educational, business, or sales promotional use. For information please e-mail the Special Markets Department at SPsales@harpercollins.com.

FIRST EDITION

Designed by Paula Russell Szafranski

Library of Congress Cataloging-in-Publication Data has been applied for.

ISBN 978-0-06-168737-2

15 16 17 18 19   OV/RRD   10 9 8 7 6 5 4 3 2 1

TO ABSENT FRIENDS

✣

Midway in our life's journey,

I went astray from the straight road and woke

to find myself alone in a dark wood.

—INFERNO, DANTE

✣

THE FAMILIES OF Gideon

1836

Thomas Blaylock
(m. Eliza)

Jacob Cateman
(m. Ann)

Henry Mullin
(m. Eliza)

Joshua
Corey

George Hoard
(m. Maude)

Hiram Cateman
(m. Barbara)

? ? ? ?

Micah
(m. Ruthie)

Millie

Samuel
(m. Alice)

Dorothy
(d. 1836)

1871

Amos Cateman
(m. Alice)

Mark
Mullin
(m. Becky)

1978

Leaf Cateman
(m. Emma)

Matthew

Thad Trace
(m. Susannah)

Deena Trace

2015

(m. Jorie)

Dylan
Corey

Jerome
Hoard

John
Hoard

William Petrie
(m. Nan)

Eli Petrie
(m. Jane)

William Waycross
(m. Katherine)

John Petersbury
(m. Laura)

Timothy   Edward   James
*(m. Millie
Corey)*

Joseph Petrie

William Petersbury
(m. Susan)

Michael Waycross
*(m. Virginia
Howell)*

David Petersbury
(m. Deborah)

James   Constance
(m. Norma)

Emlyn
Howell

James Jr.
(m. Ashley)

Saul Petrie
(m. Epiphany)

Amanda
Petrie

Bella   Alice

- - - - - **INDIRECT DESCENT**
————— **DIRECT DESCENT**

PART ONE

GIDEON, ILLINOIS

20 DECEMBER 1836

*And the Lady gathered her followers, all who
called themselves, and bade guard the places
that bordered upon the wilderness. For their
enemies would summon demons to do battle
against the world of men, and theirs was the
only power that could hold them.*

—ENDOR 1, 14–15

1

The day the men of Gideon burned Nicholas Blaine dawned warm. Tom Blaylock worked in shirtsleeves for the first time since the autumn, binding straw and kindling into loose bundles, then dipping the ends into the bucket at his feet. It held ground herbs, a king's ransom worth, a special blend that Master Cateman himself had procured from family back east. *A combination of things,* he'd said, *to help send the traveler on his way.* And to ensure he stayed where he'd been sent.

Tom paused to rub his eyes. The aromas from the bucket, sharp as peppercorns and cloying as syrup, drifted around him, strong enough to draw tears. He coughed, then winced as a rough burning raked his throat. Shivered, even as he felt the heat of the winter sun on his back.

It's the quiet. It unnerves. Even the crows, whose cawing had greeted the morning for as long as Tom could remember, had gone silent. What would a stranger see, who entered Gideon now? A town like unto dead, buildings shuttered, streets empty but for a young man dressed in his best Sabbath black and seated on a milking stool in the middle of the square. As they walked closer, they would see him stick bundles of twigs into a bucket of crumpled leaves, hear him mumble prayers. Old ones, taught him by his father and his grandfather. New ones, that he made up as he worked.

Where is everyone? The stranger would look around, until their gaze settled upon the platform in the dead center of the square, the hay bales and the piles of logs and the stake poking up through the middle like a measuring rod. *Where are the women? The children?*

Tom pondered what answer he would give. The simple one, which would make no sense? *They're in Eli Petrie's barn, two miles away.* Or the complicated one, which explained everything. *It all started late last year, when two brothers came to Gideon and asked to stay.*

"It's a great day, Tom."

Tom flinched, then looked up to find a familiar bearded face smiling down. "Yes, Master, it is indeed." He hadn't heard Jacob Cateman approach, but then, no one ever did.

"You don't sound sure." Cateman's rumbled voice took on an edge. "You've no doubts as to my decision?"

Tom shook his head, and held his tongue. Cateman had disdained the criticism that followed his decree that Nicholas Blaine be judged at the stake, and had grown ever more irritable as the day of reckoning approached and the mutterings persisted. "No doubts, Master. Fears, though. Concerns." He stopped there, even as he ached to say more. Even as his Eliza's words rang in his head. *They can't burn him, Tom. You know they can't.*

And you know why.

Cateman stared at him, the smile vanished, eyes dark and shiny as flint. "Understandable," he said eventually. "He seemed invincible. There were times I doubted we'd ever get him. Then we had him, and I wondered how we'd hold him."

"Be five months tomorrow we put his brother in the ground." Tom swore under his breath at the crackle in his voice, brought on by his irritated throat, and by fear.

"Indeed it will be." Cateman's face brightened. He turned and walked to the pyre, his step as quick as it had been on the day he wed. Like Tom, he wore his best black suit in acknowledgment of the occasion. "Old Adam." He rearranged a pile of tinder, then stood back to ponder his handiwork. "And young Nick soon to join him, in the hell of their own choosing."

"He'd get there faster if we hanged him."

Cateman turned slowly toward the voice, as though he didn't relish setting eyes on the speaker. "We've been through this, George."

"Yes, we have, to no one's satisfaction but yours." George Hoard stepped out into the square from the dark doorway of his dry-goods store. His was a big-city voice, too rapid by half, at odds with his barrel frame and round, ruddy face, his own somber black garb. "We know what he is. When you know, you hang 'em. Those are the rules. Within the host and without, those have always been the rules." He glared at the pyre as if it were an unsound horse someone had brought him for trade, a swindle in the making. "Burning's for when you're not sure. Trial by fire—if he burns, he's guilty, and if he doesn't, he's not." He walked past Tom and planted himself in front of Cateman. "What proof do we need? We found him with her blood on his hands. We found—" He stopped, eyes widening until they looked as they had on that day, blank and staring as a madman's.

Tom stirred the herbs. He knew what George saw. The same things he saw sometimes at night, when exhaustion had stripped his ability to block the memories. Of the ash leaves, gold as coin and heavy on the forest floor as a miser's prayer. Of the sky, bright as turquoise. Of Dolly Hoard's sundered body, the skin so white . . . except where it wasn't anymore.

"George." Cateman remembered as well. You could tell by the way his voice caught, and by the sluggish way he moved, as though the effort pained him. "Hanging's too clean for him. Too quick." He shook his fist under George Hoard's nose. "'He needs to see it coming.' My Ann's words, and I agree with her. He needs to feel all we felt, the pain and the anguish and the grief. For every tear you shed for Dolly, let him shed a thousand. For every second of pain she endur—" He stopped, let his hand drop, and hung his head. When he finally raised it again, his eyes shone as clear and bright as they had on the night he pronounced his decree. "He's for burning. Of that, I am as sure as sure can be. By the Lady."

"In her name." Tom inscribed the Lady's sign on his forehead with his thumb. Her all-seeing Eye, a circle centered with an X, protection against evil, whether of this world or the next.

Hoard touched his hand to his forehead. Then he stopped, sniffed, and looked down at the bucket. "That's why the wards? Because you're sure?" He pointed toward the south, and the road that led to the farms. "That's why you've sent our families to Eli's barn? Because you're sure?"

"Caution, George." Cateman straightened, his voice returned to its Sabbath strength. "That's why I've led this host for thirty years. That's why the Council leaves us to manage ourselves, and allows me to pronounce decrees without awaiting their approval. Caution." He quieted. "Even when I'm sure." He looked up at the bright, still sky. "It's near time." He started across the square toward the squat, windowless meeting hall. The sole building in Gideon with only a single level above the ground. The sole building in Gideon with three levels below.

Tom watched Cateman until he disappeared around the corner of the weights and measures office, and sat silent as Hoard kicked at a stone, sending it flying. It struck the side of the pyre platform with a sound like the crack of a pistol—the noise echoed, underscoring the silence.

"You're quiet, Tom Blaylock." Hoard shook his head, and paced. "We know what he is. He spelled the river this summer so it would flood the low fields and ruin the corn. Made it so wells went dry no matter how much it rained. Got us back for Adam, he did. Turned the earth against us because we buried his brother in it." He stopped to stare at the pyre, and passed a hand over his face. "Now we're giving him a chance to show us what he can do with fire."

Tom bound the last handful of kindling, and set it atop the stack beside his stool. "As Mistress Cateman said, hanging's too clean for him."

"But a broken neck is a broken neck. Hard to ward against." Hoard turned to him, eyes blinking like shutters, his breathing quickening. The first signs of fear, breaking through the anger that had consumed him since his daughter's murder. "Fire is an elemental, and he calls them his own."

Tom stood, wincing as his right knee cracked. *Change comin'.* He damned the horse that had with one well-placed kick turned him into a human barometer as he looked up at the sky and tried to get a sense of the air, a feel for impending storm. *Still warm.* And barely enough breeze to ruffle a ribbon on his wife's bonnet. "Eliza thinks he gave us Adam to throw us off his scent."

"For all he begged us to spare him? For all he railed against us that we had condemned an innocent man?" Hoard's eyes sharpened, his speech slowing. "Why would he do that?"

Tom bought his own time by focusing on the kindling, picking up the bundles one by one until he held all he could carry and the herb stench enveloped him like a foul haze. It all made so much sense when Eliza said it. At times, he wondered how he could doubt her at all. "So he could buy time. Build his power."

"What for?" Hoard eyed Tom sidelong and leaned against the pyre, his weight on one elbow, like he did when he stood at the bar at Petersbury's saloon. "If you believed that, why didn't you say something at last convocation, when Jacob asked those who objected to speak out?"

Tom trudged to the pyre, and set down the stack of kindling. *Because Mistress Cateman came to see me at the stables that afternoon.* She warned him that the women of Gideon had taken against Eliza Blaylock. That she was arrogant. That even though she had not been born in Gideon, she thought she knew the ways of the host better than anyone, and refused instruction by those more learned. *She behaves in a manner above her place, Tom. You know she does.* And that manner had become more pronounced after the execution of Adam Blaine.

Think on it, Tom. Mistress Cateman's eyes had glittered with tears. *I tell you this as a friend. Think on it.* She hadn't had to say what "it" was. The women of Gideon thought that his wife had allied herself with the Blaines, with "allied" taking on as many meanings as a human being could imagine.

And Tom had imagined. In the hours between Ann Cateman's visit to the stables and the gathering that evening at the meeting hall, he had imagined too much and too well. And so it went that, with Eliza's stare drilling the side of his face, he sat quietly as Master Cateman asked for objections to his condemnation of Nicholas Blaine for the murder of Dorothy Hoard, and said nothing.

Tom collected another stack of kindling, and tried not to think. Of Mistress Cateman, youthful face aged with worry. Of Eliza's throaty laugh, unheard these past weeks, that hit him in the pit of his stomach and sent his mind a-tumble. Of her hair, dark as mink and heavy as a summer night, spread across a pillow not his own.

Think on it. . .

Hoard watched Tom heft the last armful of sticks and set them on the pyre, then shook his head. "Your problem, Tom Blaylock, is that the more you have to say, the less inclined you are to say it." He flinched when he heard the distant slam of a door, straightened as the voices drifted from the direction of the meeting hall. "They're coming."

Tom stifled a cough as he stacked the last of the kindling. His throat ached in earnest now, a combination of nerves and the damned stinking herbs. He had never heard of this particular curse, but even at age twenty-four, he was still young in the arts. If anyone could concoct a spell that would send Young Nick into the bosom of Old Nick and keep him there, Master Jacob Cateman could.

"There they stand!"

Tom breathed yet another prayer, and turned.

"Two more members of Gideon's illustrious host!" Nicholas Blaine stood half a head taller than any of the scores of men who surrounded him like a phalanx and maneuvered him down the empty street toward the pyre. "Come to once again dip their hands in the blood of an innocent man."

"I told you we should've gagged him." John Petersbury prodded Blaine in the back with the blunt end of a pike.

"Let him yell." Jacob Cateman brought up the rear, his expression solemn, his Master's copy of the Book of Endor tucked under one arm. "He'll be silenced soon enough."

Tom watched Blaine approach, and tried to see him as Eliza would. He was twenty-seven, or so he claimed, ten years younger than his late brother. He was taller than Adam as well, and thinner, with pale skin and black hair that fell into his eyes. During friendlier times, Mistress Cateman had once called him "Lord Byron," whoever he was. *He never worked.* Never plowed a field or shoed a horse or felled a tree. *Not like his brother.* Adam Blaine had worked harder to win the trust of the citizens of Gideon, and had paid for his crimes by being pressed under the weight of the same rocks he had helped clear earlier that summer.

But Master Cateman declared that you were for burning, Young Nick. Tom clenched his own callused hands, then shifted his weight to ease the pain in his knee. *Because Adam stole, and lied, and betrayed.* But the one thing he hadn't done was kill. *Not like you.* He took his place next to Hoard, and tried not to think of all the other things the man had done. Things that had not ended life, yet destroyed it just the same.

"And where are the women?" Blaine looked from one end of the square to the other. "Fine young flesh that wants more than Gideon can provide." He fixed on Tom. "Where's your beauteous Eliza, Blaylock? I'm surprised you let her out of your sight." He jerked his head back, in the direction of Cateman. "Ask the good master how one keeps a young mistress in line—"

"*Shut up!*" Petersbury rapped Blaine across the back of the head with the pike butt, sending him stumbling into Frank Mullin and Bill

Waycross. They shoved him upright, Waycross elbowing him in the gut for good measure.

Blaine regained his balance and straightened slowly, breathing ragged and eyes watering from the blows. He remained silent until they reached the pyre—as he took it in, his eyes widened. "So, this is it." His voice emerged soft. "The means of a poor witch's destruction." He hesitated as his escort parted to allow his passage, then squared his shoulders and mounted the stair, Waycross and Mullin closing in behind to prevent his bolting. He still wore the clothes in which he'd been captured, a white shirt gone gray with prison grime and open at the neck, and checked brown trousers, one leg torn, courtesy of Hoard's tracking hounds.

Tom followed close behind, picking up an armful of the kindling along the way. He waited until Mullin and Waycross bound Blaine to the stake, then set about his own assigned task, tucking the warded kindling into Blaine's pockets, under his arms, into his waistband, and down the front of his shirt. He sensed the man's eyes on him as he worked, did his best to avoid them, yet felt the pull. *He's powerful, darling,* Eliza had said on more than one occasion.

So am I. Tom stopped, stood up straight, and looked Nicholas Blaine in the face.

"Do you think this will save you?" The past weeks had taken their toll on Blaine, the days spent in the wilderness evading capture, followed by his seizure and confinement while the host debated his fate. His eyes glittered fever-bright, while the skin of his face showed sallow and blotted with razor scrape. "Do you think this will preserve the life in this pathetic little place?"

"Whatever life we have, it'll last longer than yours." Tom forced himself to stare into the man's red-rimmed eyes. "And each year hence, the host of Gideon will celebrate this day."

"You think so?" Blaine arched his brow. "Well, it would give you something to do." He rested his head against the stake. "By all means, then, let's get on with it."

Tom shoved the last of the kindling into the spaces around Blaine's feet while other men dragged bales and bundles of hay into a ring around the stake, stacking them until only Blaine's face remained visible through a small gap. When they finished, they stood aside as Jacob Cateman mounted the stair.

"Nicholas Blaine." Cateman took the Book from under his arm and held it out so that Blaine could see it. "Do you have any last words before we carry out the will of the host?"

Blaine studied the tome for a moment. Then his gaze moved to Cateman's face and settled there, a smile playing at the corners of his mouth.

Cateman's face reddened. "Very well, then." He motioned to Mullin, who hoisted a small bundle of hay and inserted it into the gap, hiding Blaine from view.

Tom's knee complained as he and Mullin and Waycross stacked more logs large and small around the hay. Then Waycross hefted a bucket of spirits from a corner of the platform. He slopped most of the fuel over the logs and hay, then held the bucket out to Mullin, who shoved the end of an unlit torch into the dregs.

"Let it be written that on this day of the new calendar, the twentieth of December in this year eighteen and thirty-six, justice was done in the town of Gideon." Cateman nodded to Mullin, who struck a match on the seat of his pants and lit the torch, which sputtered for a moment, then burst into flame. Mullin then handed it to Cateman, who turned to the other men standing around the pyre. "George?" He held out the torch to Hoard.

Hoard stared at the flame. "Fire's his, Jacob."

"I don't see him putting this out, do you?" Cateman walked down the stair toward him. "The pyre's yours to light. No one here has a greater right."

"I'd have gladly sprung the trapdoor at his hanging." Hoard stood his ground as Cateman approached, the other men backing away to allow the pair some room. "I'd have gladly done that."

"Do this." Cateman's voice emerged low, level, a voice for an old friend. "You have my word, it will have the same effect."

Hoard looked from the torch to the ground at his feet, then back to the flame, his lips moving as if to speak even though no words came. Then he looked to the pyre, and his eyes narrowed. He took the torch from Cateman, and mounted the steps to stand beside the hay-walled stake.

"*Curced in kirc an sal ai be,*" Cateman said in the old language, "*wid candil, boke, and bell.*" He walked around the pyre until he stood directly in front of Blaine. "Nicholas Blaine," he continued in the modern tongue, "we the sons of Gideon separate you, together with your accomplices and abettors, from the precious body of the host and the society of the children of Endor." He opened the Book, and held it out before him. "We exclude you from our Body in this life and the next. We exile you outside the border that divides we the blessed from the ruined and the lost, and cast you into the wilderness. We declare you anathema and judge you damned, with the Devil and his angels and all the reprobate, to eternal fire until you shall recover yourself and return to amendment and to penitence. This sentence I pronounce upon you, by the Lady."

Tom and the other men signed themselves as they answered with one voice. "*In her name!*"

"Ring the bell." Cateman nodded to Petersbury, who took up a cowbell and jangled it, while down the street, untouched by mortal hands, the bell outside the meeting hall entry pealed in counterpoint, sounding the death knell of thirteen rings.

After the last reverberation ended, Cateman held up the Book, balancing it atop his open hands. "Close the book." He slammed the cover closed, and separated Blaine from the host from that moment until the end of time. Then he looked to Hoard, who stood still as a statue beside the stake, the torch aloft. "Light the candle."

Hoard brought the torch down, touching it to the turpentine-wetted hay at the base of the stake. The fire licked around, then traveled upward as Hoard circled the stake, touching the torch to the kindling, the logs. As the flames rose and strengthened, he walked down the steps, stopping along the way to snuff out the torch in a bucket of sand. "So be it," he said under his breath.

Tom followed Hoard down from the platform, and went to stand with the other men. The sun still warmed and there was no breeze worth mentioning, the only sounds the crackle and hiss of the growing blaze.

How long will it take? It was Tom's first burning, and all he knew was what he had heard from the older men. If Blaine were lucky, which no one hoped, the smoke inside the hay would suffocate him in a few minutes. If not, he would burn from feet to face, with death claiming him at some point along the way.

"It's a day of salvation for us all." Petersbury removed his hat, in deference to the occasion if not the man. "I remember—" He fell silent as a low sound drifted from the pyre.

" '*O let me in this ae nicht, this ae ae ae nicht . . .*' "

"He's still breath enough to sing." Cateman snorted, a laugh with no humor in it. "Good. He'll use it up that much faster."

" ' *. . . O let me in this ae nicht . . . And I'll never seek back again . . .*' "

"He always could carry a tune." Petersbury placed his hat over his heart. "Let him carry this one to hell."

" ' *. . . But when he got in he was sae glad . . . he knockit the bottom-boards oot o' the bed . . . he stole . . . the lassie's maiden . . . head*' "—Blaine coughed, once, then again.—" '*and the auld—*' " Another cough, then silence. The flames shot up to the top of the hay mound, roaring as though stoked by a bellows, glowing to rival the sun. The minutes passed, the men marking time's passage by watching the fire, as somber as surgeons observing a procedure.

We've removed a disease from our midst. Tom scuffed the toe of his boot into the dirt. *Now we can heal.* He thought of Eliza, waiting for him in Petrie's barn, as the fire died and the stake and what remained bound to it became visible.

Petersbury strode up the steps, pike in hand. He poked at the dark, smoldering shape, then turned to Cateman. "We can bring Maude Hoard here to declare matters proper, but I'd say it's dead."

Cateman nodded. "Wait till it cools. Then we'll cut it down, take it to the lowest level of the hall, lay it out."

"Better to smash it to powder and spread the ashes hither and yon." Hoard shook the smothered torch. "Why keep him here? It makes no sense."

"Because that which we sundered could be made whole again with the right spell." Cateman paced, his chin high and his step quick, his earlier energy returned. "Better to keep him here, intact, where we can keep an eye on him." He stopped, and turned to face them. "Ann has seen it done. Says it's common practice back east."

"The cellars of the Boston host must be sights to behold." Hoard looked at the spent torch he held as though he'd never seen it before, and tossed it aside. "A corpse in each, laid out next to the coal and the preserves."

"Be quiet, George." Cateman looked up at the sky, and took a deep breath. "Let's get—" He fell silent, and stared toward the northwest.

Tom followed Cateman's gaze, and saw the heavy gray line of cloud where just a few moments before there had been clear blue sky. "Change comin'." He flexed his knee, felt it crack.

"Comin' in mighty fast." Cateman's voice emerged quiet.

"It does, sometimes." Tom watched the clouds tumble toward them, as dark as the pyre smoke. "One hour, it's bright and sunny, and the next—" He stopped as a gust of wind slapped his face, cold as sleet and just as sharp.

"*Inside!*" Cateman turned and ran as above them, the sky filled and blackened. "*Into the nearest shelter and bar the doors!*"

Hoard pointed to the pyre. "The body—"

"*Leave it!*" Cateman stumbled, the Book flying from his grasp. He fell to his knees, and scrambled on all fours toward Hoard's store.

Icehouse cold. Blizzard freeze. It washed over like a wave and struck like a blow, an invisible avalanche that stopped them in their tracks and drove them to the ground.

Tom looked toward the pyre in time to see Hoard collapse, clutching his left arm. Watched him shudder, then lie still. He saw Petersbury sag to the ground, Mullin slump against a water trough.

He won't kill by fire, my love—he'll leave the fire be. He wants to die—I don't know why, but he wants to. He has to.

Tom looked overhead, saw nothing but swirling blackness, and started to run—

But he won't stop there. Tom, he won't stop there. He's more powerful than the host—

—felt his knee crack, the pain shoot like roaring flame. His leg buckled, and he grabbed the edge of a trough to break his fall. But it proved near empty, and he pulled it over as he fell.

—and he's had help. And you know who that is, Tom. She's tried to drive a wedge between us since we wed.

"Darling." Tom tried to rise, but a spasm of shivering took him. *You were right, dear Liza.* Shaking like a newborn calf, he rose onto his elbow as the storm darkened the day to night and the water that splashed his skin and clothing froze. "I love you. Forgive me. Forgive . . ." He caught a glimpse of his reflection in a puddle, and saw the slack features of a dead man. Felt his heart shudder as his face altered, the bones narrowing as the hair lengthened, until his wife's face formed. "Eliza? Can you see me . . . hear . . . me . . ?" Then her face vanished, leaving only his reflection, which hazed and faded as the ice skinned over the water. "Eliza . . ." He laid down his head, shivered again, then stilled as the pain of freezing subsided. He no longer felt the ache in his knee. He no longer felt cold. Only tired. So tired . . .

2

Eliza Blaylock hunched over the mirror, the scream rising in her throat as she watched Tom's face fade. She prayed again, every visualization she could remember. But still the surface of the mirror continued to lighten, until she could see nothing but her own face in the silver.

Around her, the wood of the barn creaked and thumped, battered by the wind and the sudden drop in temperature. She could sense the change in the air, even from her place among the stalls. Through a gap in a wall, a finger of wind found its way to her and brushed her face, cold as death and just as pitiless. *Are you trying to tell me something, Young Nick?* As if in reply, her mirror fogged, threads of frost radiating across the surface. *I thought you might be.* Horses and mules whinnied and stamped, and hard cracks sounded as Eli Petrie's prize stallion kicked the wall of his loose box.

"Damned beast will bring the barn down on us." Maude Hoard dragged a stool beside Eliza and sat, tucking her skirt around her and tugging at her cloak. She wore her graying hair in a braid that coiled her head like a crown, white strands catching the light of the scattered lanterns and shimmering amid the brown. "See anything?"

Eliza had dropped the mirror in the folds of her skirt as soon as she sensed the elder woman approach. She rested her hands on her knees, spread her fingers, tried not to look at her wedding ring. "I don't know what you mean."

"Don't give me that, Eliza Blaylock. You've been espyin'." Maude paused as the wind rose again, as the barn shook and rattled. "Did something happen?"

"Can't you sense it?"

"Sense what? Master Cateman himself warded this place. Swaddled us like babes, he did, and crippled us in the process, the damned fool." Maude leaned close, hawk face set in grim lines. "Except for you, Eliza. The Lady herself touched you with her power, and no mistake. What happened?"

Eliza dug out the mirror, wiped away a drop of ice melt, and held it so Maude could see the reflective surface. "Tom's dead."

Maude's breath caught. She looked away, swallowed hard. "Likely George is, as well." She fell silent for a time, then sniffled. "Likely they all are." She pulled a handkerchief from inside her sleeve and wiped her eyes. "Did you see what happened?"

"I couldn't see anything. It was all black and swirling, like the bottom of a well." The ache took hold of Eliza's throat, like a slow strangling. "I shall die."

"No, you will not." Maude gripped her hand and squeezed. "You will hold your head up as you have these past months, and you will give them no reason to think you know anything of this."

"But I must tell them. Their husbands—"

"Are dead. And there are two miles of witchstorm between us and them. What can we do?" Maude gave Eliza's hand another squeeze, then let go. "You knew something would happen. So did George. 'Blaine was for the rope, Maude.' He told me that just the other day. 'But Jacob deemed that he will perish by fire. You grant a witch an elemental death at your own peril.'" She fingered her own wedding ring, a heavy silver band, its beaded border long since worn away. "He warned me—" Her face screwed up as though she would burst into tears, but she breathed slowly and steadied herself. "It will end badly. That's what George said. 'Gideon is one of the thin places,' he said. 'The wilderness is closer here, and Blaine knows the way.'" She glared at the wall at the far end of the barn, hard enough to bore through it to the outside, to what lay beyond. "But even he couldn't see what really went on. Sometimes men can be so blind."

"Are women any better?" Eliza looked up at the heavy oaken beams that ran the width of the barn. "They would string me up from one of those if they had their way. The only thing preventing them is the word of our dear mistress, and how long will she hold her tongue?"

"Your presence buys her time. As long as you live, those fools won't see her for what she is." Maude patted Eliza's knee. "But if they do try to hang you, they'll have to hang me first, and good luck to any who try." She tensed, head raised like an animal sniffing the wind. "She's coming." She sat up straight. "Hide your mirror, and clear your mind." She folded her hands in her lap, as prim and collected as if she sat in convocation.

"It's snowing hard. We will be here for some days." Ann Cateman walked past as if she intended to keep going. Then she stopped and turned, her skirts swirling. "But we've food enough for a fortnight, and I've invoked the essences in the wood to strengthen the barn." She paused as the wind rose, shaking the double doors and rattling windows. "Eli built it as a refuge, a place of safety, and Jacob's warding has made it even stronger." She smiled. "As has my own. It will stand."

"We hope." Maude fussed with the hem of her cloak.

The blush rose in Ann's fine-boned face. *"It will stand."* She turned away from the elder woman and fixed on Eliza, eyes narrowed and gauging.

Eliza felt the tingle at the base of her skull, the rough probing of an arrogant talent. She made herself look Ann in the eye, and met the lifeless gray of old ice. *Did poor Jacob ever see himself in your stare, Mistress? Did he ever wonder at the misbegotten thing that his old man's lust drove him to marry?* Had he realized the truth in the end, or had he gone to his frozen death still believing in his wife's fidelity, her goodness?

"We must be strong." Ann allowed Eliza the barest of smiles.

Eliza smiled in return, cheeks aching from the effort. "Yes, Mistress." She winced as the first needles of a headache prickled, brought on by her struggles to keep Ann Cateman from divining her thoughts. She lowered her head and covered her eyes, and prayed that the woman would mistake her pain for worry, and leave her be. Felt a soft hand caress her shoulder, and forced herself not to flinch.

"Courage." Ann fingered the edging of Eliza's collar as though judging its workmanship, then slowly pulled away. "You will see your Tom soon."

"Not her Tom she wants to be seein', is it?" A sniff from a dark corner, the rustle of a skirt.

"Shut your mouth, Nan Petrie." Maude stood and turned toward the voice. "You keep carrying tales, you'll grow one of your own."

"Stop defending her, Maude." Nan stepped out of the shadows, followed by some of the other women. "She's his and you know it. My Will said—"

"But was he sober when he said it? That's the question." Maude's voice was deceptively quiet, calm. "That would make for a change."

"How can you say such things?" Nan's face reddened. "Her lover did this." She pointed to Eliza, then overhead as the wind battered. "Nicholas Blaine."

"Blaine? Raise a storm?" Maude's voice dripped mockery. "Do you remember the last harvest dance, when he tried to light the bonfire with his touch. He failed there, didn't he? The task fell to my George and his flints and spirits, as usual." She lowered her voice, playing it like an instrument. "But this powerful witch who could do nothing while he lived but take our hospitality as his Lady-given right and give nothing in return but pain and grief can compel the weather to do his bidding after he dies." She tsked. "Such power."

Nan looked back at her friends, but they had returned to the safety of the shadows. Maude Hoard had midwifed their children, doctored them in sickness, and to go against her was like going against Gideon itself.

"Couldn't light a fire." Maude snorted. "And yet you believe that that excuse for a man, that soft-handed fop, could command the weather like a god."

Take care, Maude. Eliza kept an eye on Ann Cateman as Maude ranted, caught the flicker in the cold gray eyes as the insults to her lover struck home.

"How can you talk like this, Maude?" Nan shuffled her feet. "After what he did to your Dolly."

Maude nodded. "Yes, I lost my darling to him. My beautiful, beautiful—" She pressed her hand to her mouth, then slowly lowered it. "This is why you will listen to me. He killed her as an animal would. What magic in that?" She breathed out with a shudder, hung her head. "Our men are in town, with more shelter and sustenance than we have, my girl. If you wish to ponder something, ponder that. We'll be crammed together cheek by jowl until this storm subsides, and there'll be enough upset in that without looking for more. Go to your children. See to their feeding." Her voice came exhausted now, colored by age and grief. "Then see to your own business."

"One could say the same to you, Maude." Laura Petersbury stepped into the light, her mending still in hand. She was an elder and Maude's oldest friend, and all but Ann Cateman bowed their heads as she spoke. "Defend her if you will. It's your choice." She looked past Maude to Eliza, and her expression hardened. "Although one could ask why she doesn't defend herself."

"What have I done that needs defending?" Eliza's voice came thin and ragged, her throat aching, the barn dust burning like ash. "Nan's had her turn—who's next? Speak your accusations to my face."

"You saw fit to visit Adam Blaine in his cell on the day of his execution." Laura Petersbury smoothed a hand over the shirt she mended, and all could see it was one of her husband's. "He stole money from Joshua Corey and goods from just about everyone else here. Frank Mullin's best horse. With him began the story that Will didn't father Nan's youngest—a vile slander. He turned us against one another, friend against friend, neighbor against neighbor, and yet you gave him comfort."

"I sat with him, yes, until the men came for him. Unlike his loving brother, who couldn't be bothered even once to cross the prison threshold to visit him." Eliza looked them in the face, her accusers, at least the ones she could see. The others remained just beyond sight, in the darkness, their whispers as soft as the rustle of rats in the straw. "So Adam died. And nothing changed."

"He was guilty!" Nan cried.

"He was a distraction!" Eliza hesitated as she realized that all watched her, that even the animals had gone silent. "The money was found in his rooms. The clothes. Jane's locket and Kat's silver. Under his mattress, where a child could find them. He was smarter than that." From the corner of her eye, she saw Nan sneer. Heard the mutters of the others. Felt Laura Petersbury's level examination. "As for gossip, when do any of us recall him saying more than three words together. Our lives held no interest for him. He didn't care."

"Interesting." Laura had resumed her mending. Even during convocation, she had to have something in her hands. "So, who committed those crimes against us? And why?"

Eliza felt Ann Cateman's dead stare. "The one who did it burned today." She saw the tension leave Ann's shoulders, sensed her relief. But she also sensed watchfulness, a renewed sense of alertness, and knew she needed to take care as well. "Discord was as meat and drink to Nicholas Blaine. Our pain sustained him. But like a glutton, he required more and more nourishment as time went on, and that led to his downfall." She thought back a year, to a party held in the very barn in which they stood, the dancing and the laughter. "Life here was good. We didn't all love one another as sisters, but we got on.

Then he came." She looked at her jury now, and found a little soften-ing, a slight bend in the rod. "We were played by a master. But now he's dead."

As one, all turned to Laura. Even Mistress Ann, who for once seemed almost deferential in her silence.

The woman worked the needle. Then she tied a last knot, cut the thread with her teeth. "You've stated your case, Eliza Blaylock, such as it is." She folded the shirt over her arm, stroking it like a cat. "Time will tell, won't it?" She turned, the hem of her skirt kicking up dust. "Time will tell." The others followed her, the mutterings more muted, the animus in backward glances tinged with doubt. Then came the cry of babies, the rattle of pots.

"It's your turn to choose the afternoon's reading, Eliza." Ann Cateman picked up her skirts and followed the rest. "Something hu-morous might be welcomed, I think. A light tale."

"Yes, Mistress. Thank you, Mistress." Eliza kept her eyes lowered until she heard Ann's footsteps recede. The prickling had deepened to a throb, like a harbinger of a summer storm, and she raised her head slowly to thwart any dizziness.

"You bought yourself a little time. At least until Nan decides her grievances require another airing." Maude's voice crackled like straw. "You think the truth will save you?"

Eliza tried to nod, stopping as her head pounded and the floor seemed to shift. "Truth always comes out eventually."

"Yes. After the lie gets you hanged." Maude's gnarled hand shook as she pointed to the departed women. "I will see to you, Eliza Blay-lock. I will keep them from you as best I can." Her hand dropped. "But in return, you will see to Nicholas Blaine."

Eliza shivered as the wind once more rose and another draft brushed her cheek. She imagined Blaine's face and form, saw him as clearly as if he stood before her in the flesh. Tall and slim, his hair blacker than Tom's, his eyes the dark blue of deepest seas. He had cut a fine figure, yes, but his had been the surface beauty of a statue, all marble hardness and chill, a façade behind which lurked cruelty of a sort that Gideon had never experienced. *But he's dead now.* And with his dying breath he had struck down Gideon's menfolk. Surely he had nothing left. Surely his strength had been spent. "The men saw to him. He's dead."

"You don't believe that." Maude lowered her voice as Timothy Waycross, a half-grown gangle a-swim in his father's hand-me-down coat, ambled past with a bucket of slop. "And neither do I. It will take more than a lick of flame to vanquish that demonspawn. You told me yourself that he planned this, that he needed to die by fire in order to work his spell."

"I said so many things." Memories returned before Eliza could close them off, of the silence that had grown and deepened between her and Tom, until she had felt like a spinster in her own house, untouched and unloved. "Sometimes I think I spouted crazy talk just to goad Tom into speaking to me."

"You saw him at the end." Maude's eyes flickered as the barest hint of envy showed through, the wish that she'd been allowed her own farewell. "He came to you as he died, and that means his last thoughts were of you."

"I heard him. He asked me to forgive—he asked—" Eliza choked back a sob.

Maude took her hand, squeezing it hard enough to hurt. "Tom was a good man, but his love for you was his weakness as well as his strength, and they turned it against you both." Shadows hollowed her cheeks and shaded her eyes, rendering her thin face hard and skull-like, a face of judgment. "Think on that, while the storm winds blow. Mourn your Tom while one who helped plan his death doles out your biscuit and salt pork." She tugged her cloak tighter as another gust shook the walls. "You are the only one of us she fears. Show her that her concerns are not unwarranted. Show her, for your Tom and my George and all the rest. Because she chose that murdering degenerate over her husband, and felt our mourning a fitting dowry." She turned and strode toward the other side of the barn, where the rest of the women had gathered.

Eliza watched Maude fade into the dimness. Her throat still ached, her limbs felt chill and heavy as stone. She recalled Tom's voice as she heard it through the mirror, weak as a whisper.

Forgive me.

Eliza closed her eyes and cursed Tom's weakness even as she longed to see his face, feel his touch. *Instead of your own wife, you believed them.* She felt it form then, in the center of her heart, like a crystal of ice. The hatred, fed by misery and loss and anger as frigid and raging as Blaine's magicked storm.

Think on that. Maude Hoard's voice in her ear.

"I will." Eliza stood in the darkness as around her, wood walls shuddered and groaned, and Blaine's winds blew, and Blaine's snows fell.

THREE DAYS LATER, the storm ended.

Eliza pushed open one of the barn's side windows and stuck her head through the gap. The cold, fresh air stung her eyes, but she breathed deep even as the tears ran, felt the chill wash away the stink of animals and slop and stale bodies. She had always been sensitive to odors. Pleasant aromas like baking bread turned to songs in her head, soft tunes sung by gentle voices. But strong smells, bad smells, changed to shouts and screams, the clatter of metal and breaking glass. Weeping. The snarls of wild animals.

Eliza had suffered from the affliction for as long as she could remember. As a young girl, she had tried to explain it to her parents more than once. But her mother had scolded her for lying, and her father had warned her never to tell other people such tales lest they call her a witch. *And you know what they do to witches, don't you, my girl?* He had towered over her, dark eyes alight with the truth as he knew it to be. *They light them like kindling, and laugh as they burn.* When he had learned that the traveling farrier who seemed so taken with his only daughter had come from Gideon, he forbade the relationship. A place of strange doings it was, he declaimed, and no child of his would take part in such a sinful exercise.

So we eloped. Eliza had confessed her strangeness to Tom Blaylock, and he called it a gift from the Lady, then asked for her hand. When he told her about Gideon, she thought that at last she would be with people who understood her, that she had found her true home.

Could I have been more wrong? She had been branded an outsider from the first, accused of plundering Gideon's men and flouting their traditions, their sacred trust. The arrival of the Blaines only sealed her fate.

Eliza rested her elbows on the sill and buried her head in her hands, which already ached from cold. She dreaded what the day would bring, even as she realized that she, that they all, had no choice but to follow the path to the painful end. For a mad moment, she debated crawling out the window and walking to Gideon on her own, even though the cold burned and the wind bit like fangs and she would meet the same fate as Tom before she had gone a half mile.

"At least we won't have to listen to little Ginny Blake's incessant howling any longer."

Eliza flinched, banging the top of her head against the window frame. "Is it time already?" She eased back inside, and massaged her scalp in search of splinters. "How will we get there? There aren't enough wagons."

"The older girls will stay behind with the youngest." Maude Hoard had already donned her coat and muffler. She now pulled on thick gloves, eyes on the task. "The rest of us will head out as soon as the boys clear the way in front of the main doors. Laura and I tried to move the snow ourselves, but we had trouble concentrating." She turned and started to walk away, then stopped. "You best get ready yourself."

Eliza pulled shut the window. "I'll never be ready for this." She followed her friend to the other side of the barn, and gathered her things.

As the boys cleared the area in front of the barn's double doors, the women hitched Eli Petrie's mules to a trio of buckboards, then loaded all the spades, rakes, and hoes they could find. Wheelbarrows. Buckets. Anything that could be used to move snow, clear doorways and alleys so that buildings could be opened, damages assessed.

But there'll be no graves dug until spring. Eliza fastened her coat, then wrapped her muffler around her neck. *The ground is frozen now.* At best, they could move the bodies into the meeting-hall catacombs, then spell the rooms so that the temperature remained below freezing until the first thaw.

The bodies. . .

Eliza's eyes filled. She gripped the skin of the back of her hand and twisted, as she had so many times over the past days. Gasped at the pain, and concentrated on it. Anything to keep her tears from spilling.

But it found her anyway, the image of what awaited her somewhere in Gideon. The body of a black-haired young man bedecked in his Sabbath best, frozen in a witch's snow.

"*Tom.*" Eliza's chest heaved, the first sob escaping.

"Save your tears."

Eliza turned to find Maude standing in the half dark, watching her.

"Keep your face dry, or the wind and cold will chap your skin." Maude held a dried apple, a bribe to quiet a child or coax a stubborn beast. "Let him see you at your best, one last time."

"I shall break down when I find him." Eliza wiped her eyes. "Will that give her joy, do you think?"

"Let her rejoice as she will. It will make her downfall that much sweeter." Maude glanced around, then beckoned Eliza closer. "She bit into this." She held out the apple. "You can see the marks of her teeth."

Eliza shivered as her hand closed around the dried fruit, its surface as smooth and leathery as old skin. She turned it over, saw the gouging and the ridges. "Why didn't she finish it?"

"I willed it turn bitter in her mouth. She spit out what she'd bitten, and threw this to the floor." Maude smiled. "I thought you might find it useful."

Eliza tucked the apple in her coat pocket. Then she wiped her hand against the rough wool until her skin burned, pulled on her gloves, and swept past Maude while avoiding her eye. If anything angered her more than Ann Cateman's smug dominion, it was Maude Hoard's equally smug assurance that Eliza Blaylock could vanquish it.

I can do nothing. Eliza stepped through the barn door into the winter brightness. The sun hit her full in the face, and her eyes stung as though someone had flung acid into them. She had tried to find the words, the strength. She had focused her hatred, probed every part of the shield that Ann Cateman had constructed around the barn, but could find no gap, no weakness. *It's not her power alone.* That, she knew as well as she knew what awaited her in Gideon. *Blaine gave her something.* His talent. His knowledge. Sustenance to see his mistress through until they met again.

Eliza heard the creak of wheels, and stepped aside just as one of the buckboards emerged from the barn. The mules whinnied and snorted, breath shooting from their nostrils like kettle steam, harness bells jingling.

"Eli loved the bells." Jane Petrie, Nan's sister-in-law, reined in the beasts while Maude gave Eliza a hand up into the back of the wagon. "I want him to hear us coming." She twitched the reins as soon as Eliza sat down, and the buckboard lumbered forward, snapping crunches sounding as the wheels broke through the snow crust. "Work your will, my ladies. Lighten this wagon. I don't relish the thought of spending the morning digging us out of a snowbank."

One of the boys piped, "I can dig!" The eldest Waycross but one, cheeks reddened and nose like a beet.

"You'll need your strength to help your mother, James." Maude leaned close to the boy and tucked the ends of his scarf inside his coat.

"James could dig all day." Kat Waycross, his mother, forced a smile.

"All the way to China and back." She tugged at the brim of her son's cap, then ruffled the hair that stuck out from beneath. "All the way to China." She looked up the road, then closed her eyes and draped her arm across her stomach, six months big with her and Will's fourth.

"Can we hold firm until we reach town, Janie?" Maude looked over the side to the snowpack beneath, the narrow grooves cut by the wheels. "Two miles is a long way. We've never attempted such a distance before."

"We will hold." Jane Petrie guided the wagon to the road's center, well away from the ditches that lined either side, the fallen trees and buried rocks. "If you concentrate, we will hold." She looked back toward the barn as the second buckboard broke into the light. "We are weightless as feathers, and so we'll ride atop the snow to Gideon. By the Lady."

"In her name," Eliza called out with the rest.

In response to their words, the crackling crunches of hooves and wooden wheels against snow ceased. One of the mules tossed her head as she sensed the sudden lightness, and danced off to the side until Jane reined her in.

Eliza pulled her coat tight around her. A light breeze wafted, but the dry and the cold gave it the bite of a gale. She glanced back at the third and last buckboard, and saw that Ann Cateman had taken the seat next to Nan Petrie. She sat straight and silent, her hands clasped in her lap, expression blank.

Eliza felt in her pocket for the dried apple, clasped it, tasted the bitterness that Maude had willed into it. *May you know our grief. May it clothe you like a coat that gives no warmth.* As the last words of the curse settled like the snow, she sensed a glimmer of bewilderment, and looked back to find Ann staring at her. She forced herself to nod a greeting, to hide her loathing behind a veneer of regard. Felt the other woman's probing, hard as a slap, and allowed it in, clearing her mind ahead of it like a bird taking wing ahead of a marauding fox.

As though reading her thoughts, a crow burst out of a thicket, wings beating like a broom against a carpet. It flew alongside the road, coursing the buckboard until they reached the pile of stones that marked the outer boundary of Gideon. It veered off then, and Eliza watched it vanish into the trees. Then she settled back, concentrated on the to-and-fro waft of the buckboard, and tried not to think of what awaited her at journey's end.

3

Gideon stood wrapped in silence, a doll's town swaddled in cotton and packed away. No hoofprint or wheel rut marred the blanket surface of the streets, the alleys between buildings, the wooden sidewalks. Nothing had walked there, on two legs or four, since the day of Blaine's death.

The buckboards pulled up near the edge of the square as all stared at the stake and the thing tied to it, the only dark amid the whiteness. Any snow that had touched the corpse of Nicholas Blaine had melted, or blown away, or, Eliza suspected, never lit upon it in the first place.

He controlled it all, even after death. The water that formed the snow. The air that formed the wind. *Even as he let the flame consume him.* Eliza stepped down from the buckboard, which shuddered as the women and boys disembarked and the spell that had lightened it dissipated.

"*Eli!*" Jane Petrie's shout was muffled by the snows. "Where are you?" She headed toward the pyre, Maude at her heels.

"*Wait.*"

They all stopped, and turned.

"There is a proper way for things to be done, Jane Petrie!" Ann Cateman stood atop her seat, hands on hips.

"We have more pressing matters than propriety, Mistress." Jane gave the younger woman a look of disgust, then turned back to the square. *"Eli!"* The other women chimed in, calling their husbands' names until the air shook with their cries. Then they fell silent. Some looked to Eliza, their expressions hard. Others looked lost, as though they wandered through a place they'd never seen before.

Ann waited until everyone else had disembarked from the buckboards before stepping down. "We must find the Book first." She strode toward the pyre, brushing past Jane. Then she stopped, surveyed the expanse of blank whiteness before her, and spread her arms wide. "Show me."

The air, already still, seemed to freeze. Then a pinpoint of light formed near the pyre, shimmering like a star. Ann headed for it, so intent that she lost her power over the snow and sank into it up to her knees. "The one who holds the Book controls Gideon." She stopped when she reached the light, then knelt and commenced digging with her gloved hands, plunging her arms into the snow to her shoulders. "I am Mistress of Gideon, and the Book is mine to protect. Mine to—" She gasped. "I have it!" She struggled to her feet, the tome in her grip. "I have it!" She raised it above her head, eyes bright. "I will take it for safekeeping." Before anyone could interfere, she darted atop the snow to the far side of the square, like a water bug across a still stream, and disappeared into Petersbury's saloon.

"She has the right to it," Maude said as the saloon door slammed closed. "I'm sure her concern for its safety is what led her to hunt for it before searching for her husband." She scraped up a handful of snow, and patted it into a ball.

"Maude?" Laura Petersbury walked to her friend, boots sinking into the snow as her emotions overtook her. "What are you doing?"

"The snows hide them." Maude held up her hand, the snowball resting on her palm. "Let the snows find them." She tossed the orb into the air, and it flew apart with a sound like a sigh. The flakes remained still for a few moments, suspended, catching the sun and flashing it back like flecks of diamond. Then they spun off in all directions, one swirl after another. Toward the pyre, the doorways of buildings, down alleys, flitting back and forth like dragonflies before finally stilling at scattered points above the square, glistening like ripples in a sunlit pond.

Nan Petrie screamed.

Eliza counted the lights, even though she knew there would be one for each of their men. Grave lights. Markers.

When the last light halted, Maude made as if to speak, then stopped. Laura took her by the hand, and said something to her in the old language. They both stood silent for a time, heads bowed. Then Maude looked up, her eyes glittering. "Call to us."

And the lights sent out streamers, links from the dead to the living. One finger licked out from a place beside the pyre and whipped around Maude Hoard's wrist. She reached out her free hand to Sam, her middle boy, and together they walked to uncover their own private piece of hell.

Eliza watched as the other lights found other women. Laura. Kat. Alice and Nan and Peg and Carrie. She waited, counted the passage of time, and felt her heart lift. Hoped that by some twist, some unimaginable blessing, Tom had managed to flee. That he had found a place to hide, sanctuary from Blaine's wrath. She prayed, and prayed harder, even as the other women's grief sank its claws into her, brought tears to her eyes and an ache to her chest.

But the hope shriveled as her own light found her and coiled around her wrist, tingled and sparked along her skin, filled her nose with the metallic tang of the air before a storm. Eliza let it lead her across the square, walked as best she could on legs gone to wood. Her light had settled above a squared-off mound the length of a man, and she brushed away snow to reveal the edge of a water trough.

She fell to her knees and dug with her hands. The wet chill soaked through her gloves. Thrown snow sprayed across her face, melted into her skirt, her coat. The light had let loose her wrist and shimmered around her head now, dipping in front of her eyes, swirling and eddying with her every movement.

Then she struck something hard yet soft. Brushed away snow, and saw the rich black of fine wool.

She kept digging. Uncovered a leg, a booted foot. An arm, encased in the sleeve of a white shirt, the cloth too thin to provide any protection against the wind and the cold.

"Mistress Blaylock?"

Eliza looked up into a round, pale face, cheeks red with cold and speckled with the first hints of beard.

"Ma sent me to help," Sam Hoard said as he hefted a small spade and started to dig. Behind him, a wheeled cart settled into the snow, its magic spent, weighted down by its blanket-wrapped burden.

"Thank you, Sam." Eliza kept digging, even as she edged away to give the boy room to work. Uncovered a collar, a neck. Held her breath, and scooped enough snow to expose a cheek, an ear, hair as black as the wool.

"They all just fell asleep, Ma said." Sam's voice came light, as though they dug in his mother's garden. "She said she could tell from the way Pa lay on his side, all curled up. By the look on his face. So peaceful. 'Just like he fell asleep, Sam,' she said. 'No need to worry 'bout him having felt any pain.'"

Eliza's hand hovered. Then she flicked lightly, as though brushing away a fly—

"'Just like sleeping,' she said."

—and uncovered Tom's eye. It was closed, dark lashes stark against his skin. He looked as he had in the hours toward dawn, when he slumbered so still and deep that Eliza wondered if he would ever awaken.

"See, Mistress?"

Eliza looked up to find Sam staring at her.

"Sleeping. Just like Ma said." His voice held a brittle edge, as though he forced words he didn't quite believe yet needed to say. "Just like."

Eliza looked back down at Tom. Ran a finger over skin sallow and stiff as wax. "Just like." She smoothed a lock of her dead husband's hair, then resumed digging.

DUSK HAD SETTLED by the time they moved the last of the bodies into the catacombs. It proved to be Carrie Tuckwell's Simon, which caused Maude to remark that he brought up the rear as usual. And they all laughed, because it reminded them of a time they would never know again, and because it was either laugh or go mad.

Eliza tied one last knot in the cord that bound Tom's shroud, then wiped a small puddle of snowmelt from the top of the bier. She knew that she would visit him many times over the course of the winter, but at that moment she could not connect the blanket-wrapped form with the man she had awakened beside only a few mornings before. *He didn't speak much.* She managed to draw only one-word answers to her questions about the burning-to-come, and they had ridden in silence to the Petrie barn. His kiss good-bye had held no trace of warmth. *He believed her.* Her breath caught. *Instead of me, his own wife, he believed—*

"—not right!"

Eliza started, her heart thudding, as more voices, sharp with anger, rose from below. The third level beneath the meeting hall, a place of meditation and sacrament, of baptism and final rites.

Eliza whispered farewell to Tom and hurried down the narrow, crypt-lined corridor. She descended the packed-dirt stairway, one hand braced against the damp wall. The flames from oil lamps cast shadows that flickered across every surface, altering with the movement of the air. She ran past the baptismal cistern, the roughhewn altars, to find the other women crowded near the opening to the largest chamber.

"It's not right." Carrie Tuckwell pointed to the bier on the far side of the crypt, the sheet-draped object that lay atop. "That thing doesn't belong under the same roof with our men."

"Jacob decided this was the place for him." Ann Cateman stood in the opening, and held the Book against her chest like a shield. Like the rest of them, she looked exhausted, bedraggled, dirt smearing her face and clothes. "It's my duty as his widow to see that his wishes are carried out."

Laura Petersbury stood slumped against the wall, face gray and drawn. "I don't believe Jacob expected to—"

"His last words to me. 'Annie, see to it. Even if I die.'" Ann made a show of looking around the room. "He told me this was the only safe place. We know Blaine had followers. If we put him anywhere outside Gideon, shattered his bones to dust, and spread them far and wide, they'd divine a way to bring them back together." She stroked the Book, as though it were a baby needing comforting. "Great men keep their friends close and their enemies closer. We must keep Nicholas Blaine as close as our hearts." She stared down Laura, then Carrie, then the other women in turn, her gaze sharpening as it settled upon Eliza.

Eliza met the woman's stare with a cool smile. The grief that had consumed her since the day of the burning had ebbed since she had entered the catacombs, replaced by something harder. She had always felt at ease here, hemmed in by rock and dirt, the spring that fed the river close under her feet. She had never been one for the light. Darkness cleared her mind.

"Let her have her way," Maude Hoard said softly, to no one in particular. "For now." With that temporary reprieve, the women dispersed, leaving the Mistress of Gideon alone with her Book and the remains of Nicholas Blaine. They mounted the stair in silence, some stopping on the second level to bid tearful good nights, others continuing upstairs to the meeting hall.

Eliza returned to Tom's small crypt, lowering to the floor and hugging her knees to her chest. "Can you hear me?" She waited for a sign, a whisper of air or any errant sound. "Darling, why didn't you trust me? We could have stopped them." She huddled in the dark and waited for steps to die away and voices to fade. Reached into her pocket, and felt for the dried apple. Waited longer, and finally heard the quiet crunch of Ann's boots on the stair. Held her breath as the steps paused at the entry to the second level, and exhaled ever so carefully as they resumed, grew softer, faded to nothing.

Eliza waited, until the silence pressed like a weight. Then she rose. "Watch over me, love." She left Tom's crypt and wended her way once more down the narrow corridor, the curving stair. This time as she entered the lowest level, she detected things that she had missed before. The gentle movement of the air. The lap of the water in the baptismal cistern. The barest whiff of burned flesh.

Eliza entered Blaine's chamber, pausing as the scorched smell strengthened and a whisper of heat brushed her cheek. Then she approached the body. So withered, the form beneath the shroud. Shrunken, as though a child lay there instead of a grown man.

"Hello, Young Nick." Eliza detected no movement. Even so, she heard the softest rustling, like autumn leaves lifted by a breeze. "You can hear me. That's good. It would be a waste of time, me standing here talking to a bucketful of charcoal, wouldn't it?" She felt another waft of ovenlike air. Hotter, this time, the smell stronger.

"I'm not the one you expected, am I? She's gone above with the others, but I'm sure she'll return. Ann Cateman. Gideon's mistress"—Eliza smiled—"and yours." She laughed as the rustling intensified. "Did you think you kept your secret so well? Did you truly believe that no one suspected? Or had you grown so arrogant that you didn't care?" She stepped closer, but the heat flared as though she'd opened a furnace door, and she stopped. "You should have been hanged. We knew what you were. Trial by fire was not necessary. But you had to burn for this spell to work. What would it have brought you? Eternal life? Unimaginable power? Whatever it is, it demanded you die by fire, by something you could control. Hanging wouldn't have served your plan. So Ann convinced Jacob that you had to burn, and you had to be interred within Gideon, and he fell for it. Poor, stupid cuckold."

She paused. The rustling had ceased. There was a sense of listening now, of waiting.

Eliza's smile faded. Her hands clenched. "Do you remember the harvest gathering, late last year, when we officially welcomed you and Adam into the body of the host? It began there, after you had been here but two days. Your plan to cleave me from Tom. The night was so clear and the stars so bright, and you asked Tom's leave to dance with me. You swept me around the bonfire once, then again, making sure everyone saw us even as you steered me away from them. Away from the light and warmth, into the darkness and the cold. Then you stopped, and bent close enough to kiss me. Before I could back away, I heard a cough, and when I turned there was Tom, watching us. You stepped back so quickly, stuttering as you spoke. You couldn't have looked more guilty." She brushed a finger along the earthen wall, and felt the stiff chill of Tom's cheek. "Did you ever read Milton? 'Better to reign in hell than serve in heaven.'" She spread wide her arms. "You'll do neither after I've finished with you." She drew strength from the darkness, found the words, stood her ground even as the thing beneath the sheet groaned through a throat gone to ash and tried to sit up.

"Dead by fire, by water be bound. Held within earth, by air be bound—" Eliza gasped as heat enveloped her. From the corner of her eye, she saw flames flicker along the wall, knew that Blaine would trap her within an inferno if she let him, that she'd burn like tissue if her nerve failed and her spell with it. *Water feeds earth and air feeds fire.* Her voice rose as hellfire pressed in from all sides. *Let them form thy eternal mire. Thy binding circle.*

The flames roared around Eliza as though she stood in the center of a firestorm. Then, like a loving hand, she felt coolness through the heat. The magicked blaze vanished. She looked to the bier, and saw that Blaine had lain back, grown smaller, as though the conflagration he had willed on her had consumed him instead.

Eliza lowered her arms. Every spell demanded a price and she felt her debt now. Weakness as the sweat bloomed and trickled beneath her clothes. The dull ache in her limbs, as though she had hiked for days. "You shall never leave this chamber." Her voice rasped like a crone's, her throat battered by heat. "Dormant as you are now or alive as you plan to be, someday. Until the end of time, never will you know the sun's warmth. Never will you feel the breeze, or the rain on your face, or the drift of a snowflake." She closed her eyes, and remembered the snow. How it had fallen steadily for three days. How it had settled on Tom's face. "Damn you, Nicholas Blaine, and damn her who aided you. You two will never meet again, in this life or the next." She fell silent, savored the cool, the quiet. The damp mustiness of the air.

And she waited, for the sound she expected, the soft footfall.

"Eliza?"

Eliza turned. Saw the slender form in the shadows. "Mistress."

"I heard your voice." Ann Cateman stepped into the lamplight. Her arms were empty, her prized Book of Gideon left above. "Why were you talking to Blaine?"

Eliza felt the probing in her mind, and closed herself off to it, brushing it away as easily as a greedy child's hand. "Why did he kill Dolly?"

Ann watched her for a time, head cocked. Then she looked past her toward the bier. "He offered his brother first, but Adam proved too tainted. The spell required a cleaner gift."

Eliza felt her strength return, the ache in her limbs ease. "You wept at her funeral."

"I will weep at Jacob's." Ann smiled. "We study the Book all our lives, but do we understand what it means? The possibilities it offers?" Her face looked like a young girl's, the dim light softening the feral edge. "The Lady teaches us how to fight demons, but that same power may be used to summon them and bind them to our will. That knowledge is there, for those with the courage to use it."

Eliza stepped out of Blaine's crypt. "We guard the borderland, and protect this world against the demons that roam the wilderness. That is our meaning. That is our possibility."

Ann laughed, the sharpness of the sound muffled by the dirt walls. "Nick thought you different. He feared you. But you're as stupid as the rest of them." She pointed to her lover's remains. "When he returns, I'll see that he casts you out with them. You'll toil in his fields, and build his temples, and worship his greatness." She circled Eliza and approached the crypt. "You will—" She stopped, and stared into the dark. Then she turned to Eliza, eyes wide. "What did you do?" She tried to step through the entry, but stopped short, as though she met a wall. Passed her hands over the invisible barrier, then backed away. *"What did you do?"*

"What the Book commands. Which you would know, if you read it as it was meant to be read. We guard the border between this world and the next, we who serve the Lady." Eliza turned so that she faced Ann. "We vanquish the demons—"

"No!" Ann hurtled toward her, hands out, fingers curled.

Eliza braced for the impact. She pushed Ann's arms out of the way with her left arm as she drove her right fist into the woman's stomach, a lesson learned from a youth with four brothers and honed by every fight they had ever teased her into. She grabbed Ann as she crumpled, stumbled herself as she felt the knifing in her mind as her foe scrabbled for purchase. Fought off dizziness and confusion as she dragged her burden to the edge of the cistern. Smelled smoke and burned meat in the woman's hair, the tainted remains of Blaine's touch.

"Nicholas!" Ann wheezed, coughed, twisted and writhed like a beast in a trap. *"Nic—!"*

"He can't give you his power." Eliza pushed Ann's head into the water. "He can—never help you—again." She steeled herself to the tumult of sensation that the woman hurled. That fistfuls of snakes sank their fangs into her hands. That the water into which she had plunged her arms boiled, and that her skin blistered and peeled. She struggled to block the pain, held on for dear sanity to the reality that she fought Ann Cateman, who had killed Tom as surely as if she had buried a knife in his back. Told herself that the water that splashed her face and clothes was cold, and that she was strong, and that vengeance for Gideon was hers.

"By the Lady." Eliza pressed a knee between Ann's shoulders. "In her name." She leaned with all her weight, pushed Ann's head deeper into the cistern. The woman's thrashing slowed, then ceased. The bubbles from beneath the water's surface stopped.

Eliza waited. After a time, the pain in her hands broke through, the ache from immersion in the frigid water. She tasted the dank air, saw the flicker of the oil lamps, and knew her mind had cleared. Knew that Ann Cateman could no longer reach her. That Ann Cateman was dead.

Eliza stood, then dragged the woman out of the water and flipped her on her back. Studied the blued lips, the skin pale as parchment. Heard the sounds behind her, the rustle of skirts and the squeak of leather boots.

"Is it finished?" Maude Hoard drew next to the body, knelt beside it, pressed her fingers to wrist, then throat. "I knew you could do it." She looked up at Eliza, and smiled. "You were the only one strong enough." She struggled to her feet. "He didn't help her?"

"He couldn't." Eliza looked to Blaine's crypt, sensed the finger of hatred that labored to push through the barrier of her spell.

"Did you hear it all, Laura? Jane?" Maude Hoard turned to her fellow elders. "Do you all know the truth now?"

More footsteps followed, hushed voices murmuring prayers.

"We heard." Laura Petersbury offered Eliza a grudging nod, then stepped around her and prodded Ann's body with the toe of her boot. "Drowning. An elemental death. She could come back."

"Only if she managed to spell herself as she died, and Eliza didn't give her the time to think that through." Maude put her arm around Eliza's shoulders and hugged her close. "You freed us. Who knows what awaited us if she'd brought him back. What horrors he would've subjected our sons to. Our daughters."

Eliza shivered. "Someone else will have to inter her. I cannot."

"We will." Maude gestured to the others, and as one they bowed their heads to the woman who had saved them from Nicholas Blaine's wrath. "Mistress Blaylock."

THE WINTER CONTINUED hard, as the remnants of Nicholas Blaine's rage spent themselves over Gideon. The women and children housed together, pooled their food and fuel, stripped bare the shelves of Hoard's dry-goods store and burned any spare wood they could lay hands on.

All but Blaine's pyre. That remained in place through storm and sun and thaw, water swelling the boards until they creaked like footsteps, the fire stain dark as blood. No one touched it, not even the rowdiest children. Even the crows stayed away.

In the spring, men arrived from the East, brothers and uncles and cousins, to marry the widows and adopt the children, to plow and plant. To guard the border, and watch over Blaine's body.

A year to the day after Tom's death, Eliza accepted Henry Mullin's proposal. He was a skilled carpenter, and he was kind, and she came to like him well enough. But she kept some of Tom's hair in a locket pinned over her heart, and when Henry reached for her at night, she closed her eyes and saw Tom's face.

Years passed. Eliza bore Henry two sons and two daughters. A few considered her Mistress of Gideon no matter which poor unfortunate the Boston Council sent to assume the official title. But most others did not, and the rumors persisted. That she had been Nicholas Blaine's lover. That she had helped Blaine do murder on the twentieth of December in the year eighteen and thirty-six. That she killed Ann Cateman when the woman discovered her plan, and now bided her time and awaited the call of her dark master.

Henry Mullin heard the rumors, too, of course, as did the children. The daughters married outside Gideon in order to escape and the sons simply fled, leaving no one to inherit the family business. The chill with which Henry Mullin met the outside world gradually worked its way into his home, and when his heart finally failed him, his widow mourned a man but not a husband. Whatever affection they had felt for each other had died years before.

As for Eliza herself, she turned aside every challenge, every insult. The truth, she said, would come out, eventually.

And every so often, when her senses bade her, she went down into the catacombs beneath the meeting hall with her own blend of herbs, and ensured that Nicholas Blaine stayed where he'd been sent.

PART TWO

GIDEON, ILLINOIS

8 OCTOBER 1871

For they will entreat, and bargain, and promise you all manner of things, and your desire to aid them will be great. But you must steel yourself to their pleas, and never forget that which defines the demon.

—ENDOR 2, 7–8

4

Joe Petrie held the wet blanket in front of him like a shield and ran into the burning house. Smoke already filled the entry, clawed his throat with every breath.

He crouched below the level of the suffocating cloud, until he could see the floor and baseboards and legs of furniture, the first steps of the staircase. Caught motion from the corner of his eye, and turned in time to see the hem of a skirt vanish, a door close.

"No. Mistress." Petrie scuttled like a crab to the door. Pressed his hand to the panel to make sure it still felt cool, then turned the handle. Tried to turn the handle. Swore.

Then he closed his eyes and concentrated. Locks. He had a gift for locks. A minor talent, but his own. He bent close to the door, and held his breath. Pressed fingers to metal and willed the movement of slides and bolts.

Silence, at first. Then he heard the scrape as the key turned, then worked out of the keyhole, followed by the muffled thump as it fell to the carpet. He gripped the handle again, twisted and pushed with all his weight. The door flew open, and he tumbled through.

"Mistress?" Petrie stayed low to the floor, even though the smoke had yet to enter this interior hallway. "I'll get Billy and Ed and we will carry you out if we have to." He waited, the only sounds the crackle of the flames and his own ragged breathing. "Mistress Mullin?" He looked into the gloom lit only by the faint flames of oil lamps, and imagined them exploding when the fire found them, shattered glass turned into shrapnel that would slash him like claws.

He felt the growing heat at his back. Too late now to leave the way he had come. He closed the door just as the first tendrils of smoke drifted in.

"Mistress Mullin?" Petrie set forth on his hands and knees. He peered under doors, alert to any sound, any movement. "I know you're back here." His heart pounded as panic tested its grip. "Please come out." Sweat dripped down his nose, trickled down his back. The hall had grown hot as a smithy in summer, the air thick enough to cut. "We need you here, Mistress. Gideon needs you." He stilled and listened, heard nothing but the growing roar of approaching death, and hammered the floor with his fists. *"Mistress!"*

Then it came to him, faint as a breath, a low voice that set his teeth on edge even though he couldn't pick out words or even tell whether it belonged to a man or woman. It came from the small storeroom at the hallway's end, and he rose and walked toward it even as fear took hold, the urge to turn and flee even if doing so meant running through the flames. Death would be better than meeting the owner of that voice—worst witch in Gideon, Joe Petrie was, and even he could sense it.

Petrie dropped the wet blanket to the floor, and drew his Army Colt from his belt. As he edged nearer the door, he finally heard Mistress Mullin's chanting cadence, a slow, steady rhythm of words that continued even as the other voice grew stronger, harsher.

A man's voice. Petrie could hear it better now. *Oh, my Lady.* Memory charged up from the depths, images of storm and snow. His gun hand shook as he crept to the door and looked inside.

"—I can return your husband to you. Not the one you married out of duty, but the one you loved. Yes, I can give Tom Blaylock back to you, as young and handsome as he was on the day he died." The man stood in the center of the room, his back to the door. "No one will question your standing as Mistress of Gideon then. Barbara Cateman and her flock of twittering hens—I can help you silence them all. Those who plot against you, who seek to blame you for their crimes—I will expose them." The weather had been brutally hot and dry for weeks, yet he had dressed as if for winter in an old-fashioned greatcoat and top hat. "I will be the friend you never had. I can grant you the respect you have always deserved. Be silent and think on it—you know I possess the power."

"I don't care what Barbara and the rest of them say. I care even less for your power or anything else you offer." Eliza Mullin paced the length of the room, right hand tracing sigils in the air. "You murdered my Tom. His soul has moved on. Whatever you brought back from the wilderness, it wouldn't be him." She had been a beauty once, tall and slender and dusky-haired. But now, in the half-light and shadow, she looked a crone, shoulders hunched, face lined and hair gone white as summer smoke.

Petrie stepped closer to the door, then choked back a cry as something in another room—a lamp, a bottle of liquor—exploded with a sound like gunshot. He still had time to get Eliza Mullin out of the house. But he had to walk past the man to do it, and if he did, the man would see his face, and know him. *Say his damned name.* Petrie cursed his fear, even the hated appellation stuck in his throat. *Young Nick.* Nicholas Blaine, son of the Devil himself.

Petrie had been but a boy when it happened, but he remembered it all as though it occurred yesterday. The murder of Dolly Hoard and the manhunt and the trial. The mounting tension as the day of the burning approached. The stink of his father's barn and the waiting and the praying. Then, finally, that silent ride into Gideon, and the tears that coursed down his mother's cheeks as they dug Eli Petrie out of his snowy grave.

But how did he—? Petrie gripped the Colt more tightly. Cocked the hammer. What did it matter? However Blaine magicked his return to the land of the living, Petrie's own path showed clear. *Kill him.* He had a clear shot. *Kill him.* One pull of the trigger and it would be over and he could rescue Mistress Mullin and flee this hell. *Kill him.*

"But tell me, Joseph Petrie, son of Eli. How can you kill what's already dead?" Blaine turned, and smiled.

Petrie froze, Colt half raised, his cry silenced before it could escape. So many battlefield horrors he had seen, the damage that shrapnel, shot, cannon, and sword could inflict upon a man, but all were as nothing compared to this. How could Blaine talk with a face like raw meat, without flesh covering his cheeks and jaw? How could he see, with eyes bulged and split and leaking fluid that ran like thick, pale tears?

Blaine doffed his hat in greeting, revealing a peeling scalp dotted with yellowed patches of exposed skull. "It appears you have a savior, Mistress, come to free you from my dire clutches." He held a walking stick in one gloved hand, polished black wood capped with a silver ferrule that twinkled like a star. "Assuming he is able." He raised the stick and pointed it at Petrie. "Assuming he can find the courage."

Eliza Mullin stopped pacing and turned to Petrie. "Get out, Joe." Another sigil, the very air rippling with the movement of her hand. "Go. Now."

"I can't leave you with him." Petrie tried again to aim the Colt at Blaine, but his hand shook like palsy, too weak to pull the trigger. "I can't."

"But you will." Blaine wheeled, coat swirling like a mage's gown. "Because you can smell the smoke and hear the flames roaring into the upper floors. The attic. The roof." He took a step toward Petrie. Another. "Leave the lady behind, Joseph, as you left so many men behind on the battlefield. Men you called friend until you learned the coward's truth, that friends are nothing more than bodies to hide behind."

"*Don't listen to him.*" Eliza Mullin's voice rose above the growing din. "He'll fog your mind and turn your fears against you." Her voice softened, a mother's comforting murmur. "It's all right to be afraid, Joe."

Petrie snorted. "You're not."

"Shows what you know." Eliza Mullin smiled sadly. "This is my fight to see through, not yours. Get out while you can."

"You heard your mistress, Joseph, son of Eli." Blaine grinned, the ravaged remains of his face twitching as blood dripped like sweat. "Run to the others. Tell them who you saw. I'm sure they'll believe you, just as they've believed all your other whiskey-sodden tales."

Petrie raised the Colt again, took aim at the flame-blackened smile. Then he sniffed and smelled the smoke, turned, and saw it seep beneath the door through which he had passed just a short time before, a door he knew would now be too hot to touch.

Then came the licks of flame, like cats' paws feeling for prey. In another room, a shatter of glass, followed by a crash.

A sob rose in Petrie's throat. He looked to Eliza Mullin, who now stood still, hands folded like a mourning angel.

"Go, Joe." Not a request this time. An order.

"Yes, go, Joe!" Blaine clapped his hands, the sound muffled by his gloves. "Run, run, run—"

Another crash sounded. It drove Petrie like a whip—he hurtled down the narrow hallway as the ceiling rained fire and Nick Blaine's laughter rang in his ears. As he reached the rear door, he looked back in time to see flames shoot out of the parlor like the exhalation of a dragon. In the space of a heartbeat, the hallway became an inferno.

Petrie fled into the night, past the other burning houses, through the ring of fire that had been Gideon's town square. He ran past old men, women, and children, ignored the shouts and cries for help, the calls for missing loved ones.

Run, Joseph Petrie. It's what you do best.

Petrie ran into the woods that encircled Gideon, and kept running even as the darkness deepened and the trees pressed close. He stumbled over a root, pitched headfirst into the mess of the forest floor, curled into a ball, and clapped his hands over his ears.

But the cries of Gideon still found him. They tapped a well that had never run dry, released memories of other fires, other cries. The booms of cannon and rifle. His mother's sobs as she wiped the snow from his father's face.

It's all right to be afraid, Joe.

Eliza Mullin's gentle words, like acid in his ears. He muttered prayers, spells, gibberish, anything to drown them out. But still they burned.

"JOE?"

Petrie opened his eyes to find Edward Waycross standing over him.

"Figured you'd be out here." Ash and dirt blackened Waycross's long face, his once-white shirt. He wore his own Army Colt stuck in the waist of his dungarees and leaned heavily on a shovel, as though he needed the support.

Petrie stared up at his friend, then at the blue sky that showed through the trees. "It's morning?"

"Yup." Waycross dug into his pocket and pulled out a flask. "It's all over." He uncapped it and took a long swig, then held it out.

"What's all over?" Petrie sat up slowly. "Where's your uniform?" He took the flask, tossed back a healthy slug, shuddered as Waycross applejack seared its way down his throat and settled in his gut like live cinders.

"No uniform." Waycross shook his head. "We're not in uniform anymore, Joe. We're home. Been home for a while now."

"Home." Petrie stared at his reflection in the side of the flask, his dirt-smeared face warped by the curve of the metal so that one eye bulged while the other shrank to nothing. "Home?" Then the smoke stench found him and the scenes of the night before flooded back, Mistress Mullin's face and Nicholas Blaine's laughter and how he ran so fast.

Friends are just bodies to hide behind.

"Gideon, Joe. Remember? You're in Gideon, Illinois." Waycross sighed. "What's left of it."

Petrie struggled to his feet. "Is anyone looking for me? Does anybody know—?"

"Nobody knows you're out here." Waycross wiped his sleeve across his brow, leaving a pale streak amid the grime. "Billy Petersbury asked where you were around dawn. I told him I sent you to check the Corey place. He was so rattled, he didn't think to ask which Corey." One shoulder twitched. "They all had enough to keep busy without worrying about you."

Petrie leaned against a tree. Took another swallow from the flask, then handed it back to Waycross. "Fire's out?"

"Yup. Master and Mistress Cateman got us settled, and we formed the circle and said the words. A wonder to behold, it was. The flames just . . . died. Like turning down an oil lamp." Waycross drained the last drops of liquor, then capped the flask and shoved it back in his pocket. "Not that it mattered by that time." He poked at the ground with the shovel. "What happened, Joe? Last I saw, you were headed to the Mullin place." A pause. "We found her. Rear of the house. Room near the kitchen. Not much of her left. Must have been bad, where she was. Flame burns hottest at the source." He poked the ground harder, and the shovel blade struck a rock with a sound like snapping bone. "What did you see, Joe? You know it goes better when you talk about it."

Petrie picked a leaf out of his hair, laid it out on the palm of his hand and examined it, bought time as he tried to figure out how to answer. "Did you find anyone else?" He tried to tear the leaf down the middle, but it proved too dry and crumbled to bits. He tossed away the mess, wiped his hand on his dungarees. Felt Waycross's stare, as steady as a judge. "In the room with her. Did you find anyone?"

"Why? Did you see someone?" Waycross struck the ground again. "Who? She lived by herself. Never wanted no one around, not even a maid." He hoisted the shovel to his shoulder and started back toward Gideon. "She lived alone, and she died alone. Lady's justice, if you ask me."

Petrie stumbled after his friend, and kept his protests to himself. They had been through hell on earth together, he and Ed. Chickamauga. Kennesaw. Dozens of nameless skirmishes in between. Others might call Joseph Petrie soft in the head. A coward, even. But not Edward Waycross, who remembered what fear felt like, and who had lost both a father and an uncle to Nicholas Blaine.

I can tell him. He'll believe me. I can tell him who else I saw. But the others would find out, as they always did. Their voices sounded in Petrie's head, sharp as snakebite, the hectoring of Hiram and Barbara Cateman, Alice Hoard, and the others. *You had your gun, Joe—why didn't you shoot him? You're a witch—why didn't you spell him? How could you let him get away?* And as the questions piled one atop the other, he knew he would crumble like a dead leaf, and then even Edward Waycross would wash his hands of him. "No." The word stuck in Petrie's throat so that he had to cough it out. "No. I didn't see no one else." He trudged after Waycross.

"Wouldn't surprise me if those husbands of hers come to collect her. I imagine they would have a lot to talk about." They had reached the edge of the wood, and there Waycross stopped, lowered his shovel, and plunged it into the drought-hard dirt. "Look at it." His voice cracked. "Look at it."

Petrie drew alongside, shoving his hands in his pockets to still their shaking. He had seen before the devastation that fire wrought. In his nightmares, he relived the times he had set loose the beast himself.

But this place of smoke and rubble, this was Gideon. Petersbury's saloon, gone. Hoard's dry-goods store. Corey's smithy. Some of the finest houses in the county, columned and balconied merchant palaces, now nothing but a forest of bare brick chimneys. The dead had been moved to the center of the square, row after row of blanket-covered mounds, most so small that you would think only children had perished if you had never seen what savage heat could do to a full-grown body. Among them walked the living, heads bowed, hands slowly tracing sigils through the leaden air, the only sounds the crunch of footsteps on dead grass and the rise and fall of murmured prayers.

Petrie held his breath, and listened. Yes, even the crows had gone quiet. The Lady's birds, Eliza Mullin had called them. They flew between this world and the next, bearing news to the Lady, and returning with her wisdom and her grace. *Listen to the crows,* Mistress Mullin had said. *Rough and wild, yet they speak with the Lady's voice.*

"Master Cateman said the new meetinghouse is a pile of ash. The official Book of Endor is gone. All our history. All the Lady's words." Waycross's voice emerged winter-cold. "She did this. Every time you seen her, she'd be walking down along the river or standing where the old meetinghouse used to be, talking to someone no one else could see. Who the hell knows what she got up to in that house, all by herself." He hoisted the shovel to his shoulder and started walking. "She did this, to get us back for killing Blaine."

"But she died. What's the point of revenge if you have to die to get it?" Petrie scanned the rows of bodies, in search of something from the Mullin house that he had seen before. A curtain. A blanket. A familiar object that marked the resting place of the only Mistress of Gideon he had ever known. "Besides, you found her alone. You said weren't nobody else—" He quieted when Waycross stopped and nailed him with the look he had brought home from the war, the look that made even Alice Hoard flinch.

"We found a body of a woman. It had a wedding ring, and that locket she always wore. Alice Hoard said it was her." Waycross resumed walking, the slow step of a man headed for a place he didn't want to go.

"So she's gone." Petrie hurried after him, that final horror of the hallway explosion echoing in his head. No one could have survived that. No one.

Not even a dead man.

5

told you, Joe." Alice Hoard pulled the blanket back up over the sere remains of Eliza Mullin. "They found her in the room near the kitchen, just as Edward said." She smoothed the rough wool with a veined hand. Then with her thumb, she inscribed an *X* enclosed in a circle across the nubby brown. The Lady's sign, a plea for mercy and protection. A gesture of farewell to a departed soul.

"You blessed her." Petrie smiled for the first time in days. Not many in Gideon cared for Eliza Mullin, even though they all called her Mistress. He had heard the stories same as everyone, but he had never believed them. Eliza Mullin had always been kind to him, even when that kindness opened wounds. It was that kindness, along with the grace, the quiet dignity and lack of self-pity, that convinced him. He could never reconcile the woman he knew with the one the others talked about.

Petrie felt a tingle along the side of his face, and looked up to find Alice regarding him, brown eyes dull as mud.

"She was my mother-in-law's friend, not mine." The woman straightened, then wiped her hands on an apron streaked with blood and ash. "Maude set great store by her. Most of us felt different."

"She took in Sam and Janey after Maude died, and raised them like her own." Petrie knelt beside Eliza Mullin's body, stomach clenching as he caught a meaty whiff of burned flesh. "And after you and Sam married, she helped bring you into Gideon's ways. Taught you spell-craft."

"Wouldn't be the first time a guilty conscience made for a generous heart." Alice leaned close and her lips drew back, snaggleteeth as pointy as fangs. "I know you thought well of her, Joe. She treated you kind and gave you work. But to call herself Mistress after what she did? To put herself above the wife of the Master of Gideon?"

"It happens sometimes, when the wife of the Master isn't skilled enough or another woman is just plain more powerful—"

"A scandal—that's what it was. A pure disgrace." Alice turned and swept past the rows of covered corpses, the hem of her skirt dragging along the parched ground and sending puffs of dust and ash into the air.

"She was a good woman." Petrie lowered his voice when the others turned to stare. "Never asked me to do nothing improper." He placed his hand on the blanket, the barest touch. "A good woman." He bowed his head and prayed for Eliza Mullin's safe passage across the border between this world and the next, the demon-infested wilderness beyond. If her soul survived that journey, if the Lady deemed it pure enough, it would live out eternity in a place of fertile fields and sparkling streams, a land of peace and plenty. A refuge that offered freedom from pain and hunger and illness, and nights of dreamless sleep.

Dreamless sleep. How often had Petrie considered self-destruction in order to obtain that precious gift? He had spoken of it with Mistress Mullin more than once, and had been shocked when she told him that she had pondered it as well.

Suicide. Petrie straightened a corner of the blanket that now served as Eliza Mullin's shroud. He would never forget the smell that filled the sitting room that day, the skunklike stink of strong coffee boiled almost to syrup. The sick thinness of Mistress Mullin's face, and the way her hands shook. It was the evil, she told him. It permeated Gideon, grew stronger with each passing day. She could not fight it anymore. It invaded her every waking thought. Her dreams. Oh, how she dreaded the night, the things she saw every time she closed her eyes. *None of the others sense it, Joe. Because it comes from within. And it will destroy us all.*

"It was the heat caused the fire, Mistress. Been so dry." Petrie whispered to the form beneath the blanket, tried to comfort a soul long past such mortal kindness. "Blaine turned up because, well, fire was his, wasn't it? It was what killed him, and it called to him. That's why he showed up. It called—" He fell silent as the sounds of soft pounding reached him, a rapid thrum like a racing heart.

Hoofbeats.

Petrie stood, turned this way and that, tried to fix the direction of the approaching rider. Ed Waycross soon joined him. Billy Petersbury. Master and Mistress Cateman, Alice Hoard and Millie Corey and the rest of Gideon's survivors, emerging from the ruins swift and silent as revenants from their tombs.

First came the crash of underbrush. A cry followed. *"Lady help us all!"* A man's voice, tight with panic.

Then they burst out of the woods, horse and rider. The horse slid to a stop on the rock-hard ground, sending ash and dust roiling into the air. It wheeled in a tight circle, eyes rolled back in its head, flanks heaving, chest coated with a mess of blood-streaked foam.

"It burns! It burns!" Micah Corey slid off the beast to the ground. "Chicago." He staggered, arms flopping like a scarecrow's in the wind, until Waycross and Petersbury grabbed him and held him upright. He wore heavy boots and the rough clothes he saved for the smithy, a homespun shirt and trousers from his old army uniform, faded and mottled with patches.

Shed of its rider, the horse stilled, head hung low, every breath a rale. Micah's gelding, it was, the calm old bay that pulled his farrier's wagon. It took a step forward, and stumbled. Then it let loose a thin, horrible wail, and crumpled to its knees as the stuff that flowed from its mouth and nose turned thinner and redder.

Petrie ran to the animal, reaching it just as it collapsed onto its side. He touched its neck as it closed its eyes, as its breathing slowed and the flow of blood from its nose and mouth stopped. It shuddered once, then again, tail flicking as though warding off flies. Then it stilled.

"I spelled him. I witched him. I drove him to his death. Poor old Bob. Lady forgive me." Micah Corey struggled in his friend's grip. Then he quieted, eyes widening as he took in the blasted scene around him. "It is hell upon the earth."

"Micah?" Master Hiram Cateman strode forward, hair and beard bright as polished silver. "What has happened?"

"Master. I come from the Raleigh place, outside Sycamore." Micah straightened as Cateman drew near, and shook off the other men's hands. "I'd just started work when Andrew's son came from the telegraph office." His voice cracked. "Chicago. It's still burning as I speak."

"Chicago?" Master Cateman took a step back, then pressed a hand to his heart as his wife gripped his arm. Mistress Barbara, her hair as black as her husband's was white, her face as smooth as his was lined. They looked at each other, wife and husband, her fine brow arching as his drew down.

Then Master Cateman shook his head and turned back to Micah. "Are you certain of this?"

"I swear by the Lady. I do swear. It began last night. The city still burns. It still—" Micah squinted past Cateman to the sparse crowd surrounding them. "Millie?" He held out a hand to his younger sister, a slight figure in a filthy dress, then looked toward the burned-out stores, the bare chimneys. "Where's Ruth?" When Millie hung her head, Micah ran in the direction of his house and the new bride he had taken leave of six days before. "Ruth? Ruthie!"

Ed Waycross and Billy Petersbury ran after Corey, took hold of him, and led him to the bodies. They walked along the first row, stopped before a form covered in blue damask, and steadied the new widower as he sagged to the ground.

"She did it." Alice Hoard shook off her husband Sam's restraining hand and stepped out in front of the crowd. "Eliza Mullin. She brought the fire down upon us just as her foul lover brought the snows down upon you thirty-five years ago."

"Alice speaks truth." Ed Waycross stood over the mourning Micah Corey like a guardian spirit. "It took her years, but she finally got her revenge." One corner of his mouth turned up as a rumbling passed through the crowd, and he nodded toward Alice Hoard.

Petrie caught the look that passed between the two, the shade of a grin that Alice offered in return. "It's not true!" He struggled to his feet. "Mistress Mullin was afraid. She couldn't sleep for the dreams. She knew that evil had come to Gideon, but she lacked the strength to stop it."

"So speaks her champion." Alice Hoard shook her head. "What sort of witch would use such a poor, addled soul as a confidant?" She paced back and forth in front of the others, pointing at each in turn. "A witch who knew no one else would believe her." She used her convocation voice now, a schoolmarm scold that brooked no argument. "A witch who knew that she had lost her hold over us."

"So what she could no longer hold, she destroyed." Ed Waycross left Micah Corey's side and stepped to the edge of the gathering. "Took her a while to get us, but get us she did." He scanned faces, narrow-eyed gaze fixing on Petrie for the briefest instant before moving on.

"Mistress Cateman is our rightful Mistress." Millie Corey's voice piped, high as a child's. She wiped her eyes with her sleeve, then walked to her brother and knelt beside him. He leaned against her hard, almost toppling her, and she wrapped her spindle arms around him and held him as he wept.

"Yes, Millie, yes. You are so right." Alice Hoard folded her hands and nodded. "But the wrongful Mistress is still among us. What are we to do?"

"Get rid of her." Billy Petersbury stepped over corpses until he came to Eliza Mullin's body. "She'll find a way to get at us from the grave if we don't." He grabbed the ends of the old brown blanket, hefted it, and tossed it over his shoulder. "Break her up and scatter the pieces. Grind her bones to dust."

"Grind them to dust!" Alice Hoard shouted, and the survivors of the flame answered her as one.

"To dust!"

Billy Petersbury strode toward the woods, the rest of Gideon hooting and hollering after him, his burden jostling against his back as though struggling to escape.

Then one flame-blackened hand fell out through a gap in the woolen folds, open, pleading.

"No!" Petrie ran after Petersbury, but stopped when Ed Waycross stepped in front of him.

"Choose your side, Joe." Waycross held him with a cold stare. "The living or the dead."

Petrie started to argue. Then long-banked anger filled him, rage he had spent so many times against strangers, but never against someone he called friend. He lowered his shoulder to bull past Waycross and knock him to the ground, clenched his fists so he would be ready when the man rose and came after him—then felt a tug on his sleeve, so strong that it yanked him backward.

He will kill you, Joe. A gentle voice, but strange, like a buzzing in his ears. *Protect yourself. Nothing they do or say can hurt me now.*

"Mistress?" Petrie stumbled as dizziness swept over him, then fell to the ground as Waycross shoved him.

"Stay here, poor addled soul, or share the whore's fate." Waycross spat upon the ground, then turned and trotted after Billy Petersbury.

Petrie waited until Waycross entered the woods, then scrambled to his feet and scurried after. He stayed low to the ground, ducking behind bushes and trees and forest wreckage as every trick he had ever learned about moving soft and quiet came back to him. He tossed up what protections he could muster despite his anger and his fear, so that none could get the sense of him. Not Alice Hoard, or mouse-faced Millie Corey.

The quiet place. He knew they would gather there. A low clearing hard by a bend in the River Ann, where troubled souls went to ponder their fates and courting couples to seal theirs. The border between this world and the next stretched thin there, the darkness that seeped through, touching every Gideonite.

Petrie sensed the pull as he darted behind a rock pile that overlooked the clearing. It coursed through him like liquor, calmed and emboldened him. He could save Mistress Mullin—he felt it in his bones. He could dash into the clearing, grab her remains, and be gone before anyone could stop—

They'd kill you, Joe. Stay here.

"Mistress?" Petrie's knees shook as the surge of strength ebbed. "You'll always be here, won't you? To talk to me sensible?" He leaned against the cold stone and waited for an answer, but no sound, living or otherwise, came to him. Even the crows had gone quiet.

Petrie peered over the top of the rocks at the scene below. They stood in a circle around Billy Petersbury, the faithful of Gideon, and watched in silence as he laid the remains of Eliza Mullin upon the ground and pulled back the blanket, exposing the burned and shrunken form. A few moments passed. Seeming hours.

Then Millie Corey picked up a rock. "For Ruthie!" Her cry pierced the stillness as she hurled the missile at the body. It struck the chest dead center and stove it in, the force sending bits of rib and dried flesh into the air.

Then Alice Hoard picked up a rock and threw it. Susan Petersbury. Deborah Watt and the others. When they ran out of stones, they beat the corpse with branches, and when they ran out of those, they tore at it with their hands, kicked it and stomped on it. Eliza Mullin's arms and legs crumbled and the body broke apart as the men whooped and hollered and the women screeched and clapped.

Petrie's eyes stung. Tears spilled. He should have tried to save Eliza Mullin, and damn the consequences. He should have tried—

"Joseph?"

Petrie stiffened. Then he wiped the wetness from his face, and turned. "Master." He tried to close his ears to the roisterous hoots and chants, but they filled his head like nightmares and he knew he would hear them forever. "They're like dogs tearing apart a deer."

Hiram Cateman drew alongside and looked down at the scene below. "We will offer prayers in her name. That she find what peace the Lady allows her."

"You won't get any prayers from that crowd. Tried and executed her, they did." Petrie started to wipe his nose with his sleeve, then pulled a rag out of his pocket and used it instead, in deference to the company. "The truth will come out eventually. That's what she always told me."

"All Gideon knows the truth." Cateman sniffed. "Eliza Blaylock cleaved to Nicholas Blaine when first he arrived. It pained Uncle Jacob greatly—his letters to me were filled with self-recrimination. He begged me for counsel in spite of my youth. He wanted to know what he could have done to dissuade her, to help her."

"But she didn't—" Petrie quieted as Mistress Mullin's words filled his head, soft as a whisper yet loud as a cry. *Protect yourself.* So he bit back his arguments, met the older man's blue-eyed gaze, felt the power behind it—and something that he had never sensed before. Doubt. Uncertainty.

Fear.

Cateman looked away first. "Gideon shall begin again, Joseph." He raised his voice. "For we shall be reborn from these ashes like the phoenix of myth." He paused, and waited until the mob below stilled and fell silent. "We will forget the betrayal that brought us to this, forget the evil that birthed it and the hatred that gave it refuge." He glanced sidelong at Petrie. "Don't you agree, Joseph?"

"It's not for me to agree or disagree, Master." Petrie imagined Eliza Mullin standing next to him, guiding him, prompting him. "It's for me to obey. By the Lady."

"In her name." Cateman held out a hand to his wife, who had appeared by his side as if from nowhere, cat-quiet as ever. "For amid this tragedy, our Lady has granted us a boon. The chance to rid ourselves of evil influence. To rebuild. A new Gideon. A new beginning. We will rival Chicago, Joseph. We will, indeed."

"Yes, Master." Petrie looked down at his shirt and dungarees, filthy with sweat and dirt and ash. Felt the hatred and loss and dread that saturated the air like fog. Eventually, the activity in the clearing calmed and slowed. Men and women broke into separate groups and talked in low voices, the men passing around flasks and pouches of tobacco. As if it were a day like any other, a day without fire and death and bitter vengeance. A day that saw truth scattered to the four winds along with the sad remains of a tormented woman.

"I saw him." Petrie's voice cracked, and he stopped and swallowed hard. Alice Hoard had been right—he was the poorest of champions, and standing up for his Mistress would do nothing to make up for all the sinning he had done in his life. But someone had to speak for those who could no longer speak for themselves. "Nicholas Blaine. A face like Hell itself, and a voice to match. He tried to tempt her. Promised to bring Tom Blaylock back to her. But she said no to him." He waited for a harsh rebuke, until the silence battered harder than any storm of words possibly could. Turned, and met the questioning eyes of his Master.

"What else did he say?" Hiram Cateman spoke so softly one could barely hear him.

"I didn't hear everything." Petrie kept Blaine's mockery to himself. That was his private shame. No one else's business.

"Question is, did you hear anything? Did you really see anything? Panic plays tricks, Joseph." Cateman's voice came stronger now. "Confounds the senses. One imagines all sorts of things—"

"I know what I saw, Master."

"Yes, well." Cateman nodded to his Mistress wife, who still stood in uncharacteristic silence. Then he pointed toward the clearing, indicating that she should leave him and join her earthly charges, which she did, eventually, with many a backward glance. "So many things that seemed real at the time," he continued when she was out of earshot, "they turn to dust when exposed to the light of reason." He laid a hand on Petrie's shoulder. "Best forget what you thought you saw. What you thought you heard. In fact, best forget all that happened this day. Dwelling on the horrors in one's past does nothing but harm, as you well know. And repeating such a tale as yours, mentioning names—"

"Weren't no names mentioned, Master. Well, except for Tom Blaylock. And then your good mistress wife, because of all the talk about Mistress of Gideon and all—"

"As I said. Talk just breeds more talk. And you know the things people will say."

Petrie fought the urge to shake off Cateman's hand, which squeezed harder with each passing moment. Instead, he bowed his head and nodded. "Yes, Master," he said after Cateman released him, after his heart stopped pounding and his temper settled and he tried to erase the sensation of the man's grip weighting him down.

"You will do your duty, Joseph." Cateman drew up tall and straight. "You are a Petrie of Gideon. A child of the Lady, charged with guarding the border between this world and the next. Your duty has called, and you will answer." With that, he headed down the slope to join his wife and the others, his white hair bright against the woodland gloom.

Petrie watched as Cateman's earthly charges crowded around him like children welcoming their father, as they trod upon Eliza Mullin's ashes and ground them into the dirt. When he could no longer bear it, he slipped away, off to search for a place where he could be alone, where he could pretend that the last few hours had never happened.

Where he could begin to forget.

AFTER NIGHTFALL, PETRIE took a lantern and snuck out to the clearing. He had planned to collect what remains he could find and give them a proper burial, but the mob had been thorough, and animals had taken care of whatever had managed to survive their assault.

After a futile search, Petrie lowered himself to the ground and listened in the hope that Eliza Mullin would speak to him again. But he heard nothing except insects and the odd rustle of some foraging beastie, and knew himself to be alone. She had passed into the wilderness, his Mistress. Gone to wander among the demons and haunted dead until such time as she atoned for her sins and was accepted by the Lady into the peace of paradise.

Petrie pulled his knees to his chin and rocked back and forth as his tears fell and the darkness swaddled him. He did not see the glitter at first for what it was, passing it off as a trick of lantern light or the reflecting eye of a raccoon or possum that watched him from the edge of the woods.

Then it flickered again, hard gold against the darkness of rock and tree and bush. Petrie scrambled toward it on hands and knees, then slowed as he drew close. They set traps sometimes in the thin places, those who inhabited the wilderness, to lure the careless living into the realm of the dead. He would be imprisoned there for eternity if he succumbed, and for all his life had been one horror after another, he was not prepared to give it up just yet.

He felt around until he found a stick that was long enough, and used it to drag the object into the lantern's beam. A small pocket watch, he thought at first, given the round shape.

Then the light fell across it, illuminating the etched letters *EB* in the center, framed by tiny flowers.

Petrie tossed aside the stick and picked up the locket. How many times had he seen Eliza Mullin fondle it and touch the lock of black hair nestled within? He opened it now, even as heat flooded his face, as embarrassed as if he had walked in on a woman as she dressed. Found the black lock curled in place, bound by a short piece of blue ribbon.

. . . *I can give Tom Blaylock back to you, as young and handsome as he was on the day he died.* Nicholas Blaine, ugly as sin even as he promised redemption. *I can help you silence them all.* Why had Eliza Mullin rejected his offer? What had he wanted in return?

Forget. Master Cateman's voice sounded like a knell in Petrie's head. Forget the sad-eyed woman who had fed and comforted him and told him of her fears just as he told her of his own. Forget what little kindness he had known in his life.

Forget.

Petrie shut the locket, cleaned it with the hem of his shirt, and slipped it into his shirt pocket. He told himself he had no right to keep the thing, that it belonged to one of Eliza Mullin's children, wherever they had scattered themselves. *I should look for them.* Surely one lived nearby, perhaps in Chicago. He would search for them. If they had lost their home in the fire, he would help them as he failed to help their mother. For once in his damned life, he would do the right thing. For once in his damned life, he would . . . *forget.*

Petrie stood. To the east, the sky had brightened from black to deepest blue, the first faint hint of dawn, and he listened for the chorus of squawks as the Lady's crows greeted the new day. As time passed and the sky continued to lighten, he heard cardinals, jays, and even the distant cry of a hawk. All but the crows, for all that day . . . and for all the days that followed. Like the phoenix, Gideon arose from its ashes. Those who had been widowed remarried. Hiram Cateman's power grew, and his good wife, Barbara, took on the mantle of Mistress of Gideon, as was rightful and just.

But still the crows failed to return. *It was Mullin's doing,* everyone said, because for all Master Cateman's talk of forgetting the sins of Eliza Mullin, folks never did. Instead, they forgot other things, like how she had helped them when they had taken ill or needed counsel, or what they had done to her body.

Joe Petrie forgot a few things as well. He forgot all about journeying to Chicago, tracking down one of the Mullin children, and returning their mother's locket.

And everyone in Gideon, even Joseph Petrie, son of Eli, forgot about Nicholas Blaine.

PART THREE

SEATTLE, WASHINGTON

2015

Demons lie.

—ENDOR 2, 9

6

The rain spattered against Lauren Reardon's umbrella, loud enough to drown out the minister, the distant chimes of the cemetery chapel. December in Seattle. A world trapped beneath a dome of cloud, and the sure and certain feeling that you would never see the sun again.

Lauren watched the minister bless the urn containing her father's ashes, a plain oak cube with only a few carved leaves for decoration. The scant remnants of a life that ended much too soon.

You never got to see the sun, Dad. Not once in the two weeks that had elapsed since John Reardon had tried to get out of bed to get ready for work, but couldn't find the strength to stand. The fourteen days since the visit to the doctor's office, and the CAT scan, and the verdict. The 336 hours it took for him to decline from living room chair to hospital bed to the quiet finality of the hospice room. Two weeks, and no sun that entire time.

You could've given him that much. Lauren berated the god who gave cancer with one hand and took away the light with the other. *One bright day.* Something to give a minute's cheer, a bit of warmth. A chance for a fifty-six-year-old man to forget, if only for a little while, as the darkness closed in.

Lauren shifted her feet to keep the heels of her pumps from pushing into the saturated sod. Dug a tissue out of her handbag, and wiped the tears as they fell. Picked out the small plaque on the site next to her father's, which bore her mother's name. Angela Reardon, who had died that past April, victim of a bad heart at the age of fifty-five. *Hi, Mom. You won't be alone anymore.*

"You okay, hon?"

Lauren caught motion out of the corner of her eye, a flash of copper hair. "Yeah."

"Paul went to get the car." Katie Westbrook peeked out from beneath her umbrella, and brushed away the drops that struck her face. "Seems strange to bury ashes. Most folks want to be scattered somewhere."

"They wanted to be cremated and buried together."

"I'm not criticizing."

"I know." Lauren touched her friend's arm. "There were one or two places where I thought they might have wanted their ashes scattered, but they didn't ask me."

Katie fell silent as the minister intoned the final blessing. Then she jerked her chin in the direction of a group of older people clustered nearby. "Are those the folks who worked with your Dad?"

Lauren nodded. "The owner gave them time off so that they could attend." She held out her hand as the minister approached, the other mourners, and dispensed handshakes and hugs and directions to her condo. Then Katie left her to join her husband and she stood alone, John and Angela Reardon's only child, shifting her feet every so often to keep her shoes from sinking. The minutes passed as she listened to the slam of car doors, the starting of engines, before finally making her way to her friends' car. She slipped into the backseat, felt the warmth like a shock, and realized how cold she was.

"Just a little while longer, hon." Katie, watching her in the visor mirror.

As they headed for the cemetery exit, Lauren laid back her head and studied the sky through the rain-spattered moonroof. Clouds like dirty cotton, sodden, low and gray. No sign of the sun.

THE MOURNERS CAME, ate finger foods, reminisced. After a couple of hours, Katie steered them toward the door, a wall of polite resolve, while Lauren took refuge in the kitchen.

"I think you should stay with us, at least through the weekend." Katie stood in the kitchen doorway, coat in hand. "The store can do without me for a few days. We could drive down to Portland and see Nance's new house."

Lauren leaned against the counter, slipped off her pumps, and pressed her aching feet against the soothing coolness of the tiled floor. "I don't think I could take Nance right now." She forced a wide, toothy grin. "A little too much perky."

"A little perky might do you some good." Katie brushed nonexistent lint from a sleeve. "I kept an eye out for him at the gravesite. He never showed."

"Jared?" Lauren's smile faded. "It's all right. You can say his name." She tilted her head in the direction of the living room. "He sent flowers. The pink tulips."

Katie sniffed. "Not really appropriate for a funeral."

"They were my favorite." Lauren thought back to the previous December, when her mother and father had both seemed in the bloom of health and she had a wedding to plan. She had gotten as far as choosing the flowers. "At one time, I liked pink tulips quite a bit." She picked up a dish towel and folded it, then shook it out and folded it again. "I didn't expect him. Truth is, I'm relieved that he stayed away. He'd have just made us all uncomfortable. I think he realized that."

"I wouldn't give him that much credit." Katie's lip curled. "What's that bumper sticker of his? 'When the going gets tough, the tough go climbing.'" She glared up at the ceiling. "I'm sorry. I just can't forget how he fled the scene when your mom died. Couldn't allow someone else's tragedy to upset his beautiful life." She groaned. "And I'm doing a lousy job of taking your mind off things, aren't I?"

"I'll be all right." Lauren set the towel aside. "I have things to do.

I may call in to the office. And I need to go to the house and pick up some stuff for Dad's lawyer."

"Can't that wait?"

"I don't need to do it today." A chill draft brushed Lauren's cheek. She checked the window above the sink, found it closed, tightened the hand crank anyway. Then she retrieved her jacket from the chair on which she had hung it and dragged it on. "He wanted me to hunt down the receipts for Dad's tools. Help with the valuation for the estate sale."

Katie donned her coat, then knotted her scarf with a few deft twists. "It still bothers you that your dad didn't name you his trustee, doesn't it?"

"No, it—" Lauren turned her back so Katie couldn't see her face. "We never discussed his financial affairs. There never seemed a good time." Not even during those last days, as her father grew weaker by the hour and she realized that he had never told her where he kept his important papers or even where he banked. The few times she tried to broach the subject, he drifted off, fell asleep. Later, when she learned that he had designated his attorney to handle his estate, she wondered if he had pretended to sleep to avoid breaking the news.

"I'd be thankful he kept you out of it if I were you. One of Paul's aunts tagged him as executor of her will, and it took him over two years to clean up the mess she left behind." Katie sighed. "Not saying your dad was sloppy. From what I could see, he was a model of organization."

"Frank Welles handled his affairs for over thirty years. It made sense to put him in charge."

"Less for you to worry about."

"Yeah." Lauren picked up her shoes, then walked over to Katie and linked her arm through hers and led her through the dining room and living room to the front door. Past the inappropriate flowers from ex-fiancés, the cards that crowded the mantel over the gas fireplace and the coffee table and the top of the rolltop desk that her father had built for her the year before. "It's just that it makes me wonder whether—"

"—whether he trusted you?" Katie patted her hand. "Speaking as someone whose childhood traumas paid for my therapist's home in Friday Harbor, let me assure you. I saw trust, and respect, and love, and believe me, I know how to tell." She pursed her lips. "I also know when I'm being given the bum's rush."

"I'm just tired."

"Still having trouble sleeping?"

"A little."

Katie fidgeted with her gloves. "Are you dreaming? Like you did that time when you were a kid?"

Lauren fiddled with the doorknob, and avoided Katie's eyes. The problem with best friends was that they remembered things you wish you had never told them. "They come and go."

"She's taking new patients. Dr. Friday Harbor. You'd like her better than the last one you tried."

"I'd like the Spanish Inquisition better than the last one I tried." Lauren opened the front door. "I'll think about it." She shivered as cold air washed in, damp and stale as the gasp from an old refrigerator. The rain had stopped, at least—she put on her shoes and stepped out into the condo's tiny excuse for a courtyard. "Tonight, I just want to sit. I'll light the fire, put on some music. Catch my breath."

Katie concentrated on pulling on her gloves. "I didn't see anyone from your mom's family."

"They never cared for Dad."

"Christ." Katie gave her a quick hug, graced by traces of a light, summery scent. "Couldn't they have set that aside given the circumstances?"

"I'll be fine. I'll call you later." Lauren waited until her friend drove away. The late-afternoon sky had darkened to dusk, the streetlights shimmering through the gloom, and if someone had demanded a thousand dollars in exchange for a ray of sunlight, she would have handed them her bank card on the spot.

She went back inside, then dimmed the lights and closed the curtains so that latecomers would think no one was home. Changed into jeans and an old sweatshirt. Turned on the gas fireplace and set the music on low. Air's *Talkie Walkie,* quiet songs to soothe her battered nerves.

She poured a glass of wine and settled in front of the fire, but after a short time restlessness overcame her and she got up and paced the room. Stopped in front of the rolltop desk, pushed up the lid, and stared at the array of drawers and cubbyholes hidden beneath, the tiny front panels centered by knobs fashioned of brass and mother-of-pearl.

It relaxes me. That had always been Dad's answer when Lauren asked him why he built furniture in the evenings and on weekends after spending his workweek repairing it. As a child, she had watched for hours as he sawed and mitered and stained. Sometimes they talked about her day at school. Friend problems. What she wanted to be when she grew up. But more often Lauren listened as her father talked about wood. Oak had been his favorite, white for the public rooms, red for bedrooms, each piece with its own personality. It needed to be handled a certain way or you would wind up with firewood instead of furniture.

Your father was an artist, one of the mourners had told Lauren. *The wood spoke to him.* An elderly lady, tiny figure clad in a curious wrap of black and brick red, hair the color of cloud twisted into a knot and held with an enameled clip. *The wood spoke to him, and he listened.* She had stroked the desk with a heavily ringed hand as a single tear tracked down a leathery cheek. *They were like brothers.*

Lauren flicked open the tiny doors one by one. She had tried storing things in the myriad compartments, but afterward forgot which one held what. Finally, after a summer afternoon spent in fruitless search for stamps bought that morning, she had cleaned out every drawer, every niche and hidey-hole. The desk had sat empty since, lovely but useless, a once-in-a-lifetime gift better suited to someone else.

I'm sorry, Dad. Lauren slid drawers off their tracks, brushed her fingers over the silken interiors, held them to her nose. Even after a year, the unfinished surfaces still exuded the scent of freshly cut wood. Memories returned with each breath . . . the old kitchen chair she sat on when she watched her father work, cracked mustard vinyl mended with duct tape . . . her mother's singing drifting downstairs from the kitchen . . . the chilly basement, barn-red floor and whitewashed walls, warmed by laughter and life. "You made this for me and I never appreciated—" She quieted, held her breath, willed her tears not to fall.

She steadied eventually. Slid the drawer back into its slot, then pulled out another. A corner drawer, impossible to see unless she pushed up the lid of the desk all the way, too small to hold much of anything. But it rustled as she pulled it out, as something inside moved.

Leaves? She fingered the blackened, withered things that filled the compartment, so desiccated that they crumbled at her touch. *Potpourri?* She sniffed, and winced at the faint foul stink of cat box. Could potpourri rot? *Apparently.*

She carried the drawer into the kitchen and tipped the leaves into the trash. As they tumbled, a flash of red caught her eye—she picked through the mess of smelly vegetation, food containers, and coffee grounds and retrieved the thing. It turned out to be a twist tie, worked into an odd shape, a circle centered with an *X*.

$$\otimes$$

Lauren smiled. For as far back as she could remember, her father had fiddled with blades of grass or bits of string or wire. He would stuff the twists and knots in his pockets, then forget about them until they liberated themselves in the washing machine, tying up the sheets and towels or snagging favorite sweaters.

Someday, John Reardon, Mom would say as she inspected the latest damage. *Someday you're going to break something you can't fix.*

Lauren rinsed the circlet in the sink, then dried it, straightening the places where the wire had bent. She tried to remember whether she had ever seen that particular configuration before, but among all the shapes and braids and knotted lengths she had seen her father fashion over the years, it was one she could not recall.

She held it up to the light, tilting it one way, then the other. Then she put it in her pocket and returned to the living room. The music had ended, silence filled the gap and settled like a weight, and she wondered if she should have accepted Katie's offer of refuge after all.

She walked to the front window and twitched back the curtain. Fog had settled thick as smoke, rendering the glow from streetlights diffuse and pale yellow as the moon through cloud, altering cars and buildings into darkened shapes that might have been man-made or other things entirely. Rocks. Cliff faces. Trees. Every so often, what wind there was caught the fog and sent it swirling, like dancers across a stage. Here was where the tales of ghosts began. In mist and wind, memories of the grave still fresh in the mind.

Lauren forced a laugh to break the silence. Maybe she should have majored in English lit, left the business world behind and studied all those rambling poems of highwaymen and wronged women and vengeful spirits. She hugged herself as she squinted into the gloom and picked out the flower planters and shrubs, the wet gleam of wheel rims and bumpers. Dull reality. Safe harbor for an anxious soul.

Then she caught movement, the shifting of a dark shape. A man, face rendered indistinct by the haze, his clothes smears of dulled color. *Jared?* It would have been like her ex to wait until everyone had left to pay his respects. Except that Jared slouched and ambled like someone without a care in the world. Whoever this was, tension wrapped around him like the mist. He paced beside one of the cars, then stopped and stood in front of it, arms folded, facing straight ahead.

Then, slowly, he turned his head toward her.

Lauren stepped back, let the curtain fall. But even though she no longer saw the man, she sensed his stare through the murk, knifing through the glass and brick and plaster. She crept to the door and rattled the knob, tested the lock, activated the alarm. Then she ran from bedroom to bathroom to kitchen, checked that windows had been closed and locked. In the kitchen, she latched the back door, her hand shaking so that it took her four tries to fit the chain into the slide.

Then she stilled, and closed her eyes. Listened, but heard nothing except her own rough breathing.

What the hell's wrong with me? The poor guy had probably stopped by to pick up his girlfriend or collect his kids for a long weekend. *Idiot.* She counted to three, then walked to the front door, deactivated the alarm, and unlocked the locks. Took hold of the knob and twisted, yanked the door open, and walked out into the cold—

The man had gone. Lauren scanned the parking lot, the entries to nearby condos, but saw no one.

She walked to the edge of her courtyard and then across the short stretch of lawn to the parking lot. Mist brushed her face, condensed on her skin, trickled like cold sweat. She stopped in front of the car, an older-model Accord, and noted the license number, the UW parking permit. Bent to touch the place where the man had stood, the damp and filthy asphalt.

After a few minutes, Lauren returned to her condo. She opened the curtains and turned up the lights, then grabbed her wineglass on the way to the kitchen and dumped the dregs into the sink. Debated making coffee, and settled for herbal tea. The last thing in the world she needed was caffeine.

As she waited for the kettle to come to a boil, she paced, turned the faucet on and off, stared out the kitchen window into the dark. Felt something in her hand, and saw that she had dug the wire circlet out of her pocket without realizing it, squeezing it so tightly that it left its imprint in her palm. She massaged the thing between her fingers, and slowly calmed. She just needed something to do with her hands. Like father, like daughter.

LAUREN WENT TO bed early, tossed and turned for an hour or so. Got up and walked to the dresser and opened the top drawer, and poked through the prescription bottles in search of something that would help her sleep.

Correction. The sleeping part had never been the problem.

Dreams. She had lied to Katie. Her dreams didn't come and go. This time, for the first time in years, they came and stayed.

Lauren emptied one of the pill bottles atop the dresser, then counted the tiny green tablets and pushed them into piles. Distraction. Give her brain something to work on in the present so that it would leave the past alone.

Except that it didn't work. Memories bubbled up from the depths of repression, burned into her brain like scars. Her cries in the night. The pound of footsteps, and the blinding flash as her bedroom lamp flared to life. Her mother's worried face.

Monsters, Mommy! The only word her six-year-old self could think of to describe the grayed faces that grinned at her with blackened mouths, and reached for her with clawlike hands.

There are no monsters here, honey. Angela Reardon, the circles beneath her eyes as dark as her hair, opening the closet door and poking at the clothes. *Look.*

They're not in there, Mommy—they're in here. And Lauren slapped her head over and over, as though she could drive the faces away if she hit herself hard enough.

And through it all, her father stood in the doorway, slack-faced, as though the bottom had just dropped out of his life.

Visits to doctors followed. Psychiatrists. And they had been investigated—Lauren realized it years later. Too many unexpected visits by serious women with clipboards. After one visit, Lauren eavesdropped on her parents as they went over each question they had been asked, and wondered if they had given the right answers. Then her mother cried. *They'll take her away. Our baby.*

One of the serious women dropped by the following week, and asked to speak with Lauren. As they sat on the porch steps, Lauren took the woman's hand as she answered her questions. When they finished, the woman spoke to Lauren's parents. She wouldn't be back, she said. Everything was fine. No one would visit them again. Lauren's mother wept with relief. But her father took her aside and knelt before her.

What did you say to her, Lauren?

What she wanted to hear.

But how did you know what she wanted to hear?

I just knew, Daddy. I held her hand, and I just knew.

And John Reardon had stared at her as he had when she told him about the monsters. *You're a good girl,* he said after a time as he held her close. *I love you very much.* He stroked her hair, one soft sweep after another, and she fell asleep in his arms. Sweet, dreamless sleep.

Maybe the relief she sensed from her parents reset something in Lauren's head. Whatever the reason, the dreams stayed away for years, all through grade school, high school, college. Then they returned after Angela Reardon's death, this time a little different. Sometimes a roaring blaze, orange and gold against a clear blue sky. Other times, falling snow, the most vivid scene of all. Lauren would feel the sting as the flakes struck her skin, the spreading chill as they melted.

Lauren opened another bottle and dumped out the pills. Mottled brown and orange this time, like tiny bundles of dried moss. She blamed grief for the return of the dreams. Work pressures. Jared. *And now Dad.* She could choose her own doctors now, and they proved about as useful as the ones her parents had taken her to. Talking about the images and what they might mean—the grasping hands, the faces—didn't help. Neither did medication. The only useful thing she ever heard had come from another patient, an older woman she met in one of the waiting rooms. They had talked about their reasons for seeking help, and the woman had patted Lauren's hand.

Dreams are our mind's way of telling us that something is wrong.

"Be nice if they could be more specific." Lauren paged through the inserts that had come with the various prescriptions, searching for some magic treatment that had eluded her to that point. But the drugs all seemed more likely to cause nightmares than stop them, so she swept the pills back into their bottles, then wrapped the bottles in their paper instructions like so much garbage. Stuffed them back in the drawer, and settled for a cup of herbal tea.

That night, she dreamed of fire, and a man's shadowed face watching her from the flames.

7

Lauren awoke before sunrise. Showered. Dressed in clothes suitable for rooting through attics and closets, khakis, a faded denim shirt, and beat-up deck shoes. Made coffee, then stood at the front window, mug in hand, and surveyed the parking lot, the morning comings and goings of her neighbors. The Accord still sat in the same space it had occupied the previous night, but soon a man emerged from a nearby unit and headed for it. A blond, short and paunchy with a plodding gait, radiating all the tension of cooked spaghetti.

Lauren watched the man toss a briefcase and suit coat into the backseat and drive off. So much for her connection between the car and last night's watchful visitor.

She yawned. Her man in the flames had hung around for most of the night. At times, he even attempted to speak, but his voice emerged muffled, indistinct. *He tried to tell me something.* Was it a threat? A warning?

Dreams are our mind's way of telling us something is wrong.

Lauren raked a hand through her hair, a chin-length bob gone shaggy from neglect. "Maybe he was trying to tell me that I need a haircut." Before her father's funeral, the idea of having her hair styled had struck her as frivolous, disrespectful. But now it seemed exactly the right thing to do.

Lauren dug out her phone and ran a search, found a downtown salon recommended by friends, and made an appointment. She would stop by her father's house, collect his papers, and drop them off at the lawyer's office. After her haircut, she would stop by Katie's store and drag her to lunch.

Lauren traded her shabby shirt for a brown cashmere pullover. Grabbed a raincoat. Katie had been right all along—she needed to break out of the dark place she had inhabited these past few weeks and reenter the world.

IN CONTRAST TO the bustle of the U-District, Wallingford proved an island of quiet. Lauren drove along streets lined with close-packed homes, some with their original plain frame exteriors, others modernized and landscaped into architectural showplaces.

Her parents' home fell in between. It had been painted the year before, cream with dark taupe trim. Over the years, John Reardon had sanded and stained the porch his favorite light oak shade, replaced the doors and windows, installed brick steps in front and a flagstone patio and small greenhouse in the postage-stamp backyard. Angela Reardon had planted flowering trees and shrubs, bulbs and bushes, so that in the spring the steeply banked front yard turned into a waterfall of hydrangea and dogwood, rhododendron and golden elderberry and rose. At the display's height, neighbors ferried houseguests to gaze in awe, while passing motorists stopped and took photographs.

Three-quarters of a million, I would say, Frank Welles told her the day she first met with him after Dad's death. *Assuming you want to sell it, of course. They paid off the mortgage years ago.*

Lauren pulled into the short driveway, got out of her silver Outback, waved a greeting to a curious neighbor. Peered through the one-car garage's narrow window at Dad's old green Forester, two hundred fifty thousand miles and counting, nestled within. Then she walked up the steps to the porch, past the dormant shrubs and winter-drab grass. Collected the mail from the box alongside the

door, sorted out the business letters, and dumped the holiday cata-
logs and other junk into the recycle bin.

As she inserted the key into the lock, she hesitated. She had not
been to the house since the day before the funeral, and her visits to
that point had consisted of quick dashes in and out to collect her father's clothes, toiletries, documents for Frank Welles.

She opened the door, lingered in the entry, listened to the lonely
silence of an empty house. The suitcase containing her father's effects
rested on the floor next to the couch, the hospice welcome packet a
bright blue splotch on the coffee table.

Lauren closed the door. Checked her watch. She had an hour until her hair appointment, just enough time to grab the receipts and
drop them off. She simply had to go downstairs, collect them, and
leave.

Instead, she walked around the living room, stopped before the
framed photographs that hung on walls and rested on tabletops, and
studied them as if for the first time. Her kindergarten class. Candid
shots at the beach, at picnics, in the stands at a Mariners game. Her
graduation from UW, fresh-faced in her cap and gown, bracketed by
Mom and Dad.

And finally, her parents on their wedding day, looking impossi-
bly young in seventies hippie chic. Angela Reardon, née Olivetti, in
gauzy white, a ring of yellow roses in her black waist-length hair.
John Reardon, steady eye on the photographer, in an open-necked
white shirt topped with a leather vest, his hair a shoulder-grazing
mass of dark ringlets.

He refused to wear a suit. Called them funeral clothes. Lauren's mother
would stand in front of the photo with a hand to her mouth, shaking
her head as though still wondering how she survived that day. *My
papa was not happy. It didn't defrost between them until you came along,
and even then. . .*

Lauren returned to her graduation picture. At some point in the
intervening years, her father had made peace with funeral clothes.

He had worn a charcoal-gray suit on that day, and looked quite dapper even though he had at some point unbuttoned his jacket and loosened his tie.

Lauren gave the photograph one last look. Then she sat on the couch, pulled a throw pillow onto her lap, and hugged it as memory tugged like a child's hand on her sleeve. If she concentrated, she could sense trace aromas in the stale air. Sirloin tip and apple pie, the last meal she and her father cooked together, on the Sunday before he fell ill.

John Reardon had been quieter than usual that day, studying his late wife's handwritten recipes as though for the first time. Every so often, Lauren would catch him staring at her, but before she could say anything he would turn his back and run the food processor or the garbage disposal, anything that made a noise loud enough to preclude talking. She sensed that something bothered him, but she didn't push. He would tell her when he was ready, when the time was right.

"But then time ran out." Lauren set the pillow aside and picked through the day's mail, tucking the bill for a magazine and a bank statement into her handbag for delivery to Welles's office. She then got up and headed for the basement. Down the wood plank steps, which squeaked and creaked underfoot. Opened the drawer of the first floor-to-ceiling cabinet, spotted the thick brown envelope tucked beneath a drill case, and grabbed it.

On her way to the stairs, she passed the old kitchen chair that had served as her perch years before. It looked even more battered now, the duct tape curled and stiff, her father's favorite jacket slung over the seat back. A rescue from a navy surplus store, weathered coffee leather, the once-rich coloring faded and scuffed. *My southpaw jacket,* John Reardon had called it, because the inside breast pocket was located on the right side, a natural fit for his left-handed self.

Lauren picked up the jacket and hugged it, then draped it over her arm. Smoothed the worn leather, and felt something hard beneath her hand. She rooted until she found it in that inner right-hand pocket, a small book, thin, the black leather binding worn to bare cloth in places, the pages edged in wine red.

Lauren checked the front cover and the spine for a title. She found nothing at first. Then she tilted the book toward the light and picked out the shallow ridges and curves of an ornate font, the scant flecks of gold leaf that were all that remained of the gilded embossing. Worked out the letters one by one. The words.

The Book of Endor

She opened the book to the inside front cover and found a printed name and date, the black ink faded to gray with age.

Matthew James Mullin
1975

A tissue-thin divider followed. Then came the title page:

The Book of Endor
As translated by Hiram Cateman
Master of Gideon, Illinois
In this the year of the Great Fire 1871
By the Lady
In her name

A few blank pages followed. Or more correctly, pages that would have been blank but for the drawings, tiny images expertly rendered. Pen-and-ink illustrations of plants and animals. Branches and trunks of trees. Ferns growing along the edge of a river.

Lauren sat down on the basement step. Her phone chimed, the hairdresser's appointment alarm sounding. She turned it off.

Another page, this one filled with printing. An old-fashioned serif font, the straight line of the text marred by the occasional misaligned letter:

*And the Lady departed as the King ordered, and with her, her
followers. And they went out into the world and battled the demons that sought to invade the world of Men. Across the seas they
traveled, to every corner. . .*

Lauren moved from the text to the page margins, which Matthew
Mullin had filled with more artwork. Very different, these drawings.
Studies of a young woman, a refined beauty of the lace-and-cameos
variety, fine features set in an oval face. Black, waist-length hair. A
narrow, dancer's body clad in seventies garb, handkerchief skirts, and
peasant blouses.

Mullin had filled every available space with her, page after page,
captured her twirling on tiptoe, standing at the edge of a stream, or
in one arresting scene, lying on her back amid a mass of wildflowers,
arms thrown wide, eyes fixed on the artist and bright with invitation.
Emma. The name in pencil beneath the image, barely visible, as if it
had been written, then erased.

Lauren felt her face heat. No letter, no poem, however explicit,
could have said more. Love, lust, rapture, and longing, inscribed in
every line and shading of face, every curve of lip and body. *What happened to them?* Had they married? Had heat faded to embers, or cooled
completely? Or had something driven them apart, some personal disaster they couldn't overcome?

She turned the page—

—and stared at the X-centered circles that filled these margins,
twins to her wire circlet, inscribed in pen with such force that the nib
had furrowed the paper. *Fear the outsider,* the text read. *Fear the one
who tells you what you want to hear.*

Lauren riffled the pages back and forth, in search of more symbols. The images of Emma flitted past, herky-jerk as an old movie.
Lines of printed letters rippled.

Then some pages flipped all at once, like in a magazine jammed
with reply cards. Lauren leafed back and found the cause, a yellowed

strip of paper wedged between two pages like a bookmark. A newspaper clipping, folded thin and tight and yellowed with age.

She extracted it, unfolded it. It was a photo of a young man dressed in shorts and a sleeveless jersey, all slim, muscled legs and elbows as he dribbled a basketball down the court. *Matthew J. Mullin, 17,* the caption read, *star point guard for the Gideon Rangers—*

Lauren studied the young man's face, half hidden under a mop of ringlets. Sharper cheekbones, firmer jawline. But the familiar stare, that steady fix, deep-set eyes locked on his task.

"Hello, Dad." Her voice shook. "I didn't know you played ball."

8

Lauren left the house eventually. Drove in a daze until she arrived at the parking garage of the building that housed the attorney's office, realizing when she arrived that at some point she had donned her father's jacket and tucked the book back into the inside pocket. She dug out the book and stuck it in her handbag, stashed the jacket in the trunk. Rode the elevator to the office and listened to the receptionist's expression of sympathy as she handed off the receipts, the image of her father's teenage face playing through her head over and over . . .

She left her car in the garage and stepped out into the downtown holiday bustle, the damp chill, the package-laden and harried crowd. It was a short walk to Katie's store, just enough time to settle down. She caught glimpses of her reflection in the display windows, coat collar askew, eyes a little too wide. Stopped to make adjustments, and felt the tingle along her spine as she sensed someone watching her. She turned, and spotted a figure across the street. A man, face shadowed despite the sunlight, standing tall, arms at his sides, radiating tension like the heat from a summer road.

Parking-Lot Man? Lauren watched him in the window. Then a large truck blocked her view—by the time it rumbled past, the man had vanished. She scanned the crowd for straight shoulders, a head held high, as she started back up the street. Quickened her step as she turned the corner and spotted the familiar blue awning a few doors down, the name KATE's printed along the edges in black block letters. She looked back over her shoulder as she entered the store, in time to see a shadow shift in a doorway on the other side of the street.

The inside of Kate's proved to be a cinnamon-scented press of shoppers hunting through racks and shelves of high-end sportswear and clerks dashing back and forth. Lauren spotted her friend conferring with a customer, and fidgeted in her line of sight until she caught her eye. "I wondered if you wanted to get some lunch."

Katie maneuvered toward her, Christmas-bright in tomato-red shirt and trousers, horn-rims perched atop her head. "I can't, hon. It's a little crazy just now." She studied Lauren for a moment, brow furrowing. Then she leaned close. "My office."

"WHERE DID YOU find this?" Katie paged through the book, eyebrows arching when she came to the drawings of Emma.

"His jacket. The old leather one that he used to wear all the time." Lauren sat in the chair across the desk from Katie, and slipped the newspaper clipping into her handbag. She had removed it before giving the book to her friend. As much as she felt the need to confide, she couldn't bring herself to admit that particular detail.

"So what are you worried about?" Katie shrugged. "It's just an old book."

"It's a weird old book. All about witches wandering the world, gathering followers."

"So it's a weird old book." Katie flipped to a page of text, then pulled down her glasses. " 'With bell, condemn them. With closing of the book, sever them. With candle, burn them.' " She chewed her lower lip. "Okay, that *is* weird." She closed the book, then examined the cover. "Maybe your dad found it in something he worked on. An old dresser he picked up in a junk shop."

Lauren felt a flicker of relief. *Commonsense Katie.* It failed to explain everything, but it was a start and it made the everyday sort of sense that she longed to hear. "But why would he keep it?"

Katie eyed her over the top of her glasses. Then she opened the book and flipped through it until she came to the first page of Emma drawings. "The other artwork is really good, but these are something else." She turned them to face Lauren, waggled her eyebrows, then cocked her head. "Okay. What are you not telling me?"

Lauren took the book from her, and flipped to the page with the symbol-filled margins. "I found something that looked like these symbols in the desk he built for me. He'd made it out of a twist tie." She dug into her trouser pocket and pulled out the wire circlet. Stared at it for a moment and tried to recall when she had put it in her pocket in the first place, then set it on the desk.

Katie glanced at the thing, then rose and walked around her desk to the door. "I know exactly who you need to talk to." She opened the door and beckoned to one of the clerks, a slight blonde in a brown knit dress. "Dilys Martin, I'm not sure if you've ever met my friend Lauren Reardon." She waved the woman into the office. "Dilys is my resource for all matters alternative spiritual." She pointed to the circlet. "Have you ever seen anything like this before?"

At a distance, Dilys had appeared younger than Lauren, athletically trim, her short hair spiked with gel and tipped in purple. Her age revealed itself in the harsh office lighting, in the lines around her eyes and her veined hands. She bent over the circlet, elbow on the desk, chin resting on her fist. Poked it with her finger. "Where did you get this?" She looked over at Lauren, a diamond-flecked nose ring flashing each time she moved her head.

"My dad put one in a desk he built for me." Lauren showed the woman the symbols in the book. "It looks like these."

Dilys nodded, then turned and rummaged through one of the many sample boxes that lay stacked against the wall. "I've never seen anything exactly like that." She pulled out a bracelet and handed it to Lauren. "This is close, but no cookie."

Lauren fingered the smooth glass beads, formed of concentric rings colored white, blue, and black. "They look like eyes."

Dilys nodded. "That's exactly what they are. *Nazar boncuğu.* Eye beads." She took back the bracelet and draped it over her hand. "You would wear them as protection against the evil eye. The charm acts as a mirror, reflecting the evil back on whoever is trying to curse you." She tapped the circlet with a manicured finger. "This may be something like that. I'm only saying that because it's round and the X in the middle makes it look like an eye." She crossed her index fingers one over the other to form an X and held out her hands as though trying to stop something from coming near. Then she crossed her middle finger over her index finger in the classic "cross your fingers" gesture. "It seems the most likely explanation, but if you want, I can take a picture and ask around."

"I would appreciate that." Lauren waited as the woman handed the bracelet to Katie, then pulled her phone from her pocket and snapped. "What about leaves? Are there leaves that protect, too?"

"Quite a few."

"Do any of them stink like a litter box?"

Dilys smiled. "Elder, maybe." She opened up an app on her phone. "Did they look like this?" She drew a short branch with five oblong leaves, one at the top and two on either side.

Lauren shook her head. "I couldn't tell. They were all dried out. They crumbled as soon as I touched them." She thought about her leaves, tossed out with the previous evening's garbage. "So they were for protection?"

"Told you she's my expert." Katie toyed with the bracelet, wrapping it around her wrist, fidgeting with the clasp. "If you find any more interesting things your dad made, bring them here for identification."

"Did I know your father?" Dilys turned to Lauren. "Did he practice?"

Lauren shrugged. "What do you mean by practice?"

"Dilys is a witch, hon," Katie said, her voice just above a whisper. "She means practice witchcraft."

Lauren imagined her father standing over a cauldron, muttering curses. "Like broomsticks and black cats?"

Dilys sniffed. "Have you ever known any witches?"

Katie put her hand over her eyes, and watched Lauren through her fingers. "When we were in school, we seemed to get a new one every year in our apartment complex. I remember a Gawain, and a Freya, and an Alastair." She met Dilys's irritated look with one of wide-eyed innocence.

"I'm sure they wore black the year round and worshiped Satan. So many of them do." Dilys sighed. "We do suffer more than our share of poseurs."

Lauren took the bracelet from Katie. "The minister who officiated at Dad's funeral was Unitarian, but that was because he didn't belong anywhere. At least, not that I knew of." She massaged the glass-smooth beads until their resemblance to tiny eyeballs started to turn her stomach. "Would he have to have been a witch, to use these things?" She handed it back to Dilys.

"No, not at all." Dilys rubbed the beads with a more gentle hand. "But anyone can buy these. You said your father fashioned his from wire. When you go to the trouble of making things yourself, that implies some background, some core belief." She looked at Lauren, and the color rose in her face. "I'm sorry—have I said something wrong?"

Katie shook her head slowly. "No, Dil. I think that sound you hear is the clatter of some pieces falling into place." She leaned toward Lauren. "You okay? You look a little shaky."

"I'm fine." Lauren fielded her friend's worried look. "Just something else to think about."

A bell sounded as the front door opened, and Dilys turned her attention to the well-dressed couple that entered the shop. "As much as I would love to continue this conversation, boss, don't you think I should get back to work?"

"By all means." Katie waved Dilys away, then waited until she moved out of earshot. "Hon, I'm sorry, but I should get back out there. Are you sure you're okay?" She stood and pushed her chair against the desk.

"I'm fine." Lauren glanced at the wall clock, and gathered up the book and the circlet. "Anyway, I need to go, too."

"You should come to dinner tonight." Katie linked her arm around Lauren's waist. "It'll be late, and it'll be takeout. But it will get you out of the house and force me to think about something besides this place for a few hours."

"Sure." Lauren checked across the street before opening the door. No strangers lurking in doorways. No shaded figures with excellent posture. "That sounds good."

"See you around eight." Katie hugged her, then released her into the lunchtime throng.

Lauren pulled on her coat, let herself be swept along by the pedestrian wave. Her stomach grumbled, reminding her that breakfast had consisted of coffee. *Lunch.* Someplace quiet, where she could sit and gather her thoughts.

"Lauren!"

She turned to find Dilys hurrying after her.

"I didn't want you to leave before I had the chance to talk to you again." Dilys stopped short. "And to apologize. I think I may have upset you."

"It wasn't just you. This entire day has been one surprise after another." Lauren rubbed the back of her neck, tried to erase the faint tingling, the sense that whoever had been watching her had returned. "Why didn't my father tell me?"

"Sometimes family members don't take it well when you leave the more accepted paths. Maybe he thought you wouldn't approve." Dilys's eyes clouded as some memory surfaced. She stared at nothing for a moment, then shook herself back to the present. "I also wanted to ask—and I don't want to impose—but I would love the chance to look at the desk your father built." She took out her phone. "If we could exchange contact info, then you could call me whenever you're ready."

Lauren hesitated. Her university experiences with those who called themselves witches had not been good. They had all seemed to radiate menace, a sense that they enjoyed upsetting and causing pain. But Dilys seemed as far removed from them as a rose was from a patch of weeds—Lauren took out her phone, saved the woman's number, and gave Dilys hers. "What do you think the desk is, some kind of charm?"

"A ward. Your father was trying to protect you from something." Dilys took Lauren's arm and steered her to the shelter of a jewelry-store doorway. "Judging from how tense you are and the way you keep looking around, it isn't working anymore. Wards often do lose power after the person who set them dies."

Lauren hunched against the cold brick of the store entry, and watched the street. Saw no sign of Parking-Lot Man, or anything else unusual, and relaxed a little. "My dad asked for his jacket so many times after he went into the hospital. That's where I found the book, in the jacket. I wouldn't let him wear it the day I took him in because I didn't think it was warm enough. I told him I'd bring it to him, but I never did." Of course, he likely wanted the jacket to keep her from finding the clipping, but the book must have worried him as well. "After that, he would ask for it every so often, but he was already slipping in and out—"

"Don't blame yourself for that. You didn't know. Katie mentioned how sick he was. He wouldn't have been strong enough to strengthen his wards—he would only have weakened himself further." Dilys stepped closer, and lowered her voice. "I don't want to push. But I wish you would think hard about things that are happening now, and be honest with yourself. What you're feeling right now, what you're learning about your father. Is it really unexpected?"

Lauren met the woman's steady gaze. "Yes."

After a beat, Dilys nodded. "Could I see that book again? I didn't have a chance to examine it before."

Lauren dug it out of her handbag, and handed it to her. "Katie thinks he may have found it in an old piece of furniture he was refinishing."

"Uh-huh." Dilys opened the book and studied the cover. Passed her hand over the first few pages, then closed it. "Do something for me?" She held it out to Lauren. "Hold it."

"I've been holding it since I found it."

Dilys shook her head. "Don't fear it, or try to figure out what your father was thinking. Just hold it."

Lauren took a deep breath, bit back the sharp *excuse me—I have to go* that fizzed on the end of her tongue, and took back the book. Concentrated on the worn cover.

After a few moments, she felt her mind drift. A lovely quiet, the first peace she had known in weeks.

Then she caught a hint of a vague smell that touched sense memory, then overwhelmed her, rendered the blare of street noise a muffled whisper. She held the book to her nose, and inhaled the soft green scent of freshly cut wood. Looked to Dilys to find her smiling with the satisfied air of a teacher who had gotten through to a problem student.

Then she clasped Lauren's hand. Started to speak, then stopped, and studied Lauren through narrowed eyes. "Sometimes those who love us try to keep us from the thing we need the most."

Lauren shook her head. "I'm not a witch."

"Of course you're not." Dilys shook her head. Then her look grew pointed. "This won't be an easy time for you. Be careful. And please, call me if you need to talk." A weak smile. Another hand squeeze. Then she released Lauren and headed back to the shop.

Lauren felt something in her hand. Looked down, and found the eye bracelet nestled in her palm. She called after Dilys, but the woman had already reentered Kate's.

Protection. A scrap of dialogue from an ancient horror movie bubbled to her memory's surface, a line from an old Scottish prayer. *From ghoulies and ghosties, and long-leggedy beasties, and things that go bump in the night.*

Lauren started to tuck the bracelet into her handbag. Then she paused, and looped it around her wrist instead, fumbling with the clasp until it shut with a *click* sharp as the snap of bone.

9

Lauren pulled into her garage, got out of her car, scrabbled for her house key with hands gone clumsy with agitation. *I am not a witch.* The words had tumbled in her head like clothes in a dryer all during the drive home, a declaration that she would have thought ridiculous only an hour before.

Why, Dad? She stabbed her key at the dead bolt, leaving deep scratches in the brass. Why witchcraft? *Why now?* Protection, Dilys had said. From what? Parking-lot lurkers? Nightmares returned? Something worse?

"Best weapons in the world, stinky leaves and twist ties." Lauren braced against the door to steady her hand and inserted the key in the slot. Unlocked the door and opened it slowly, then paused on the threshold and listened. She heard nothing but the rumble of the refrigerator, the soft flow of air through vents, and stepped inside, pulled off her coat and tossed it atop a kitchen chair along with her handbag.

Her shoulders ached, the tension like claws digging into her upper back. She longed for a glass of wine, but settled for a couple of pieces of baking chocolate mined from the depths of the utensil drawer. The way she felt, one glass of wine would lead to another, and she needed to stay sober, focused. Too much was happening too quickly. She would panic herself over the edge of an emotional cliff unless she took care.

Lauren walked through the dining room into the living room. Her home, this place, scented with lingering hints of morning coffee and the cinnamon-apple candles set atop the sideboard. Even so, she fought the sense that she had become a stranger here, an intruder, that something had invaded and supplanted her. She felt for the eye bracelet, then remembered she had taken it off during the drive home and put it in her coat pocket, along with the twist-tie circlet.

"No protection." Lauren flinched at the sound of her own voice, then swore under her breath. Katie had been right, as usual. Perky Nance and her new house were exactly what she needed right now. They could make plans tonight, and if for some reason Katie couldn't make the trip to Portland, she would go by herself. A change of pace. A change of scenery. The issues with her father, the settlement of his estate, her job, and the return to routine could all wait for a few more days.

Lauren flipped on the lights and turned on the television. A weather report in male staccato filled the room, the sanity of the world outside. She opened the curtain, and cloud-filtered daylight splashed across the leaf-patterned rugs, polished hardwood floor, her father's desk—

Lauren stared at the hulking rolltop. The finish, which John Reardon had buffed to a warm caramel, now looked grayed and faded, the brass fittings oily black with tarnish. She ran her hand across the surface and felt the dry grate of neglected wood, then examined her palm and found it coated with flecks of old stain, the powdery residue of decay.

Lauren pulled one of the small drawers from its niche. As she did, she caught its smell, stale air and mildew and the closets of closed-off rooms. She turned it over, and found an X-centered circle in one corner of the underside, the edges burned like a brand. Her father's protection. She scraped it with her thumbnail and it powdered away, as though it had been traced with pencil and not cut into the wood itself.

Lauren shot the drawer back into place and pulled out another.

Smelled the same dank odors. Found the mark again, and watched it disintegrate to her touch. She pulled out every other drawer in turn, and found them all branded, all in the same decaying state.

She backed away until she collided with the end of the couch, then lowered herself to the arm and held on. Watched as dust motes thick as fog streamed from the desk into the weak sunbeam, swirled and tumbled by the air currents. *It's dissolving.* Eroding like a stone in a stream. Already it looked duller than it had just a few minutes before, the surface whited as though coated with chalk. Dilys had been right. If John Reardon built the thing to protect her, it had stopped working.

For long minutes, Lauren could only stare at the desk, limbs frozen, mind a blank. In the background, a car commercial jangled, counterpoint to her ragged breathing.

"Dad?" Lauren imagined her father standing by the desk, polishing the hardware with his handkerchief or smoothing some scratch invisible to all but him. "What in the hell is happening?" She raised her hands and crossed her index fingers one over the other to form an X, as Dilys had done, and centered it over the desk like a bull's-eye. *That's all I have going for me.* She had to do better.

She stood, and edged closer to the desk. *It's a ward.* And according to Dilys, it had weakened because her father built it, and now he was dead. *So it's dying, too.* She ran her finger along a roughened edge. *But I'm alive.* And she was her father's daughter.

"And this is my damned desk." But Lauren had no clue what to say, or whether anything she said would even matter. The Book of Endor had contained no spells, no magic words.

Maybe the words didn't matter.

Maybe all that mattered was being angry.

"Get out of here." Lauren gripped the desk with both hands, tried to clear her head as she had when she held her father's book and smelled the wood he had loved so much. "Whoever you are, whatever you are, get out and leave me alone."

Nothing happened at first. Then the dust motes swirled like eddies in a stream, forming whirlpools that narrowed, then rounded again, like mouths working in silence.

But there were words. Lauren heard them in her head, soft as whispers.

Let me in . . . let me . . . in . . .

Keeping the desk in sight, Lauren backed out of the living room, shutting off the television on the way. Through the dining room. Into the kitchen. She grabbed her handbag and her coat and dug through the pockets for the bracelet. Fastened it with shaking hands, then fled to the one place where she still felt safe.

IN CONTRAST TO downtown Seattle, the Wallingford streets were weekday-morning quiet, commuters long departed, children sent to school. Rain had returned, a fine mist that fell from low clouds, and the sun was nowhere to be seen.

Lauren kept her eyes on the brick-and-concrete planters in the middle of the intersections. If Parking-Lot Man stepped out from behind one, what would she do? Run him over? Confront him? Call the police? Would it make a difference, whatever she did?

Only if he's human. The thought dropped in out of nowhere, unbidden and unwelcome, to join the jumble that filled her head.

She turned onto the street on which she had grown up, felt the pressure ease as happier memories returned. Sounds. Smells. The sensation of the breeze in her hair and the summer sun on her face as she raced her first two-wheeler down the sidewalk. Halloween parties, her mom filling an aluminum tub with apples for bobbing. Sitting on the front porch at night with a flashlight, sending coded messages to her friends across the street.

Home.

She pulled into the driveway, shut off her car, and stared at the house. Took out her phone and called Dilys, then disconnected after the first ring. What would she say to her? *The desk my dad built spoke to me.* She wasn't sure that even Dilys would believe that.

Lauren eventually got out of her car and mounted the steps to the front porch, disturbing a crow that had chosen the spot to pick apart a piece of bread. It hopped down to the sidewalk, then took to the air and came to rest atop a nearby spruce, squawking all the while.

"Get used to it, bird. I think I'm going to be here awhile." Lauren walked along the porch, the oak railings as firm as ever beneath her hand. Examined the front windowsill, and wondered if her father had carved protective eyes in this woodwork as he had in her desk. Would they work any better than hers did? *God, I hope so.* She unlocked the door and stepped inside. Stood with one hand on the knob, and listened.

The air was cold and still, the rooms dark. Lauren closed and locked the door and walked from room to room, turning on every light and lamp, opening closet doors, looking under beds and behind the shower curtains. When she felt certain nothing had changed since her last visit, she went to the kitchen and stood at the top of the stairs that led to the basement, flipped on the light and checked her dad's workshop. But even with bulbs burning bright, she couldn't make herself take that first step down.

She finally set a kitchen chair in front of the basement door to keep it from closing, and braved the descent. The place looked as it had the previous day, but now the smell of fresh-cut wood filled her nose. "What do I call you, Dad? John Reardon or Matthew Mullin?" She imagined him standing at his workbench, adjusting a table saw or setting up clamps. "Why didn't you tell me?" She listened to the silence, then returned upstairs.

She dragged down the folding staircase and climbed into the attic. But instead of symbols carved into the support beams and stinky elder leaves scattered in corners, she found boxes filled with Christmas decorations and chairs from an old dining room set. No signs of magic. No disintegrating wood. She returned to the kitchen, sat at the table, and pondered what to do next, drifting in and out of awareness, half conscious of the weekday noises she seldom got the chance to hear. Barking dogs. Shouting preschoolers at play. The *ping ping* warning of a delivery truck backing up.

"Child? Where are you?"

Lauren flinched. She thought at first that she had imagined the voice. But the back of her neck tingled and she sensed a change in the air and knew someone had gotten into the house. *A neighbor with a key.* The reasonable explanation. But reason had long since fallen by the wayside.

"Come out, child—I know you're here."

Lauren stood and backed toward the counter, her eyes on the entry to the kitchen. Took a knife from the block, and waited for whoever had called her to show themselves, to say something more. But the silence lengthened, and she crept to the doorway and looked toward the living room.

"There you are, child." Dilys stood next to the couch, one hand resting on the back. "I heard your call. I came as soon as I could." She wore a black coat, a baggy, hooded thing that hung to her boot tops and made her look like a medieval monk. "I'm sorry I kept you waiting."

"You didn't—how did you get in?" Lauren hid the knife behind her back. She knew she had locked all the doors and windows, had checked them again during her circuit of the house. She had wanted Dilys to contact her, maybe, eventually, but not by breaking and entering. She glanced at the living room windows, in search of any sign of movement out on the porch—had the woman brought any friends with her?

"I came in as one does. Through the door." Dilys inscribed something in the air, a letter or symbol. "One door closes, another opens. The cycle of life." She winced, then pressed a hand to the side of her face. The black coat had sucked all the color from her skin. She looked pale, ill, eyes and cheekbones shadowed with fatigue.

"Are you all right?" Lauren took one step closer. Another. No, those weren't shadows. "You're bleeding."

Dilys rubbed her cheek, stared at the dark wet that coated her palm. Then she looked around the room. "House of lies. He lied to you, but you know that now, don't you, child?" She started to say more, then stopped and squinched her eyes shut. "Please." A bare whisper. A mouthing of the words. "Please. I need more time." She wrapped her arms around her head as though warding off a blow.

"I'm going to call 911." Lauren rounded the couch and grabbed her handbag, set the knife on the coffee table, and dug for her phone. "You've been hurt. You need help."

"Too late." Dilys rocked back and forth. "Too la-a-ate." She jerked upright. Her arms fell to her sides and she rose above the floor, legs dangling, as though someone had lifted her by the scruff of her neck. She screamed, writhing as she tried to break free of whatever held her. Then her head snapped to one side, stove in like a smashed egg.

Lauren backpedaled as the mess hit her, warm-wet gobbets of brain and blood mixed with chips of skull. Bits of scalp studded with purple-tipped hair. They hit her face, slithered down her neck, spattered over her clothes and the furniture and the rugs.

Dilys dropped to the floor and stumbled around the couch toward her, arms flapping so her coat sleeves billowed like wings, the side of her head pulped and lumpy. One eye bulged, blood flowing out around it. "Child." Her jaw had dislocated, torqued to one side, and she tried to push it back into place. "You—mustn't—"

"Stay away. Lie down. Keep still!" Lauren freed her phone, but before she could key in a number, Dilys knocked it away, gripped her arm, pulled her close.

"You mustn't—go—you mustn't—that's what he wants." Dilys coughed, wet hacks that brought blood bubbling up. It coated her teeth, dripped down the corner of her mouth. "He had his reasons."

"Who's 'he'? Who are you talking about? My father?" Lauren stared into the woman's eyes. "Somebody else?" She watched clear gray dull, then grow milky as life light faded. "Let me call for help. You need help."

"I told you it's too late." Dilys pressed her ruined face to Lauren's, blood warm and wet as tears. "Take care, child." Her body twitched and shuddered—

—and vanished.

Lauren stood frozen. After a time, she touched her cheek, felt nothing but her own clean skin. She looked down at her clothes, then at the rugs, the couch. No skin or bone, no clots of blood or anything else. She lowered herself to the floor, hugged her knees to her chest, every so often rubbed away a stain that wasn't there, that had never been there.

The sound broke through eventually. *Ping-ping.* Lauren thought it another truck at first. But it kept repeating, over and over, and she realized it came from her phone. She crawled to the place by the couch where it had fallen, checked for bloodstains before picking it up. Saw the name "Paul" on the screen, and bit back a cry. "What happened? Is Katie—?"

"No, no—she's fine. She just can't talk right now." A rumbling sigh. "She wanted you to know—"

"Dilys." Lauren worked to her feet and circled the couch until she came to the place where the woman had stood. Where some part of the woman had stood. Her ghost, spirit, soul. "It's about Dilys."

"How did you—?" Paul paused. "Hang on."

Lauren heard muffled back-and-forth. Switched her phone to her other ear, almost dropping it as her hands shook.

"I can't believe this. It's too horrible." Katie, voice cracking. "She left the store a few hours ago. Right after you did. Some emergency. On her way home. Her car went off the road."

"A few hours ago?" Lauren shivered as Dilys's words came back to her. *I heard your call.* She imagined the woman's phone ringing in the wrecked car, remembered hospice workers telling her to be careful what she said in front of her father even as the end approached, because hearing was the last sense to die.

"Her partner just called me. He said it looked like she hit her brakes and swerved to avoid hitting something. They found skid marks." Katie's voice broke, and she paused to blow her nose. "But no one saw her car. They drove right past the spot where she went off the road, and no one saw her car. It was a bright red Prius, for God's sake. How could they miss it?" She sobbed. "She was still alive when they found her—she died in the ambulance."

Lauren looked across the room at the mantel clock. "About a half hour ago," she murmured.

"What?"

"Nothing." Lauren pushed up her sleeve. The bracelet Dilys had given her had already begun to deteriorate, the shiny glass eyes clouding as whatever protection it provided ebbed away. She unfastened it and tucked it in her pocket.

"I've closed the store for the day. We're all just—there are no words for this. We're meeting at our place to sort through . . . to talk about . . ."

"I'll be right there." Lauren listened to Katie ramble for a few minutes more, what-ifs and maybes and whys. Then she disconnected, still standing where Dilys had stood. She sniffed the air, expecting to smell . . . what? The metal tang of blood? The stale chill of death?

She walked to the couch, and sat. *Where now?* Where could she go? *My office.* She could stash clothes in her locker at the on-site gym, sleep under her desk. *They'd think I had lost my mind.* Word would filter to the top floors as it always did, and someone from human resources would appear bearing a folder and a card with a few hastily scribbled phone numbers. Billings-Abernathy was a conservative company. Strange behavior by program managers was not looked upon kindly.

Lauren turned off the lamp, sat in the quiet dark. She couldn't go to any other place where they knew her. Whoever, whatever, had stalked her father had turned its attention to her. It wanted her for reasons unknown, and would hurt anyone who helped her. *So what can I do?*

After a few minutes, she got up, walked to her old bedroom. She pulled together the few clothes she kept there and stuffed them into a suitcase. Returned to the living room, grabbed her handbag, and checked for credit cards, her bank card, and her father's book. Turned off all the lights, locked up, returned to her car, and fled the one place in Seattle where she'd thought she would be safe. She should have known better. Dilys had tried to help her, and had paid with her life. Safety was just a word. It didn't exist anymore.

LAUREN STOPPED BY Katie's house for as long as she dared, long enough to hear stories of kindness and silliness and words of regret at a life cut short. Then she headed to a nearby sandwich shop. Found a table in a dark corner, sat with her back to the wall, and watched the door. As time passed, she sensed the fish-eyed stare from the young woman behind the counter, and ordered coffee.

On the other side of the glass, the U-District went about its weekday December evening. No signs of ghosts. No shadowy figures lurking across the street. It would be easy to relax here, convince herself that Dilys had simply suffered a tragic accident, that stress and grief had overwhelmed her and she just needed to breathe.

On the sidewalk in front of the shop, a crow pecked at a piece of bread while dodging pedestrians, squawking when one passed too close. Lauren watched it dart and dance until it finished its meal and took wing. Then she dug her phone out of her handbag, opened a map app, and worked out the route to Gideon, Illinois.

You mustn't go. Dilys's voice, garbled by blood and broken bone. *That's what he wants.* But which "he" did she mean? Not her father—he had done his best to hide his past, along with a good part of his present. Was it Parking-Lot Man, who even now could be watching her? *Who are you, you son of a bitch?* She meant to find out.

She took out her father's book and paged through it more carefully. In addition to Emma, he had drawn a few others, their names traced beneath in the same block printing. *Jimbo,* next to the sketch of a lanky, shaggy-headed boy. *Connie,* a solemn, pigtailed girl, no more than eight or nine years old. A stocky young man named *Lolly,* crew-cut and sullen, with a face like a fist. An older girl with a long face and a self-conscious smile. *Gin.*

Another page. Amid pencil sketches of trees, rocks, and the edge of a river, she picked out a head-and-shoulders rendering that she had somehow missed before. A man, his features misshapen, knots of scar tissue or growths bulging his cheeks, forehead, and neck. *Pizza Face.* The name printed beneath. *A face to hide in the shadows.* Lauren studied the deformed visage, then hunted for more depictions.

Pizza Face finally turned up on the next-to-last page. A full-length drawing this time, tucked into the gutter margin. He wore clothes from another time, a greatcoat and top hat, and flourished a cane or tightly rolled umbrella. He gave the impression of youth with his straight posture and slim build, but his twisted face altered it into something from a horror film. A Victorian ghoul out for a midnight stroll.

PF, Mullin had penciled at the man's feet. *Connie called him Mister Lumpy.*

Lauren studied the drawing. *Who the hell are you? The town creep? A legend that everyone knew about but no one ever saw? Parking-Lot Man?* No, he had been dressed in regular clothes. Pants, shirt or sweater, a light jacket.

She opened her phone's browser and ran a search on "Pizza Face," waded through references to Italian restaurants and acne medications. The closest hit she found was a site devoted to "drive-in" movies. *Pizza Face*—the title of a cut-rate early seventies slasher film about a deformed killer who lived in the woods outside a small town. A single still frame centered the page, a low-res image of a mangled visage, eyes bulging, skin like raw meat.

You always hated horror movies, Dad. Lauren set down her phone. *You said anything that wasn't real was a waste of time.* His voice rang in her head, that man who had called himself John Reardon. His stern warnings to keep her feet on the ground, stay in the real world.

The only monsters are human, daughter. We make our own hell.

Lauren closed the book and stashed it in her handbag, saved the directions to Gideon on her phone. Then she keyed in the speed-dial sequence for Katie's number and followed with the code that sent her directly to voice mail. "Katie, I have to leave Seattle for a while. I don't know when I'll be back. Something came up with Dad's estate, and I need—I need to find out what's going on." She spoke a little longer, promises to call as soon as she could, to explain everything when she returned.

By the time she left the sandwich shop, the clouds had thinned enough to allow a few stars to peek through. Once she hit the road, she would see Mount Rainier in her rearview. The breadth of the Cascade Range. She would bid them farewell, not good-bye, and tell herself that she would see them again soon.

PART FOUR

INTO GIDEON

And the Lady entered the village and found those who lived there sore afraid, for their homes had been overtaken by demons and they did not know how to fight them. 'Do battle as you have been taught,' said the Lady. But their Master had not instructed them in the ways of Endor, for years before he had fallen under a spell. Now he lay asleep in his chamber, like unto dead, and spiders and beetles made homes in his flesh.

—ENDOR 4, 3–6

10

The clock radio lit like a beacon, filling the bedroom with a chilly blue glow. Then came the manic voice of the morning-drive disk jockey. "—and it's going to be another rainy day in north-central Illinois. But if it's snow you want, just wait five minutes—"

Jim Petersbury mashed the snooze button, then yanked the cord out of the wall. Silence settled and the display went dark, the afterimage of the hour floating before his eyes like spots from a camera flash: 4:30 A.M.

Petersbury lay on his side, blinking until the numbers faded. It was his third night sleeping on the floor, and his back ached as though he had been punched in the kidneys. The thin carpet didn't cushion worth a damn, and the old blankets he had found in the basement hadn't helped. He straightened his legs, then drew his knees up to his chest, felt the pull of tight muscles all along his spine. "I thought sleeping on the floor was supposed to be good for you, baby." He listened to the quiet, pretended that Norma would answer if he waited long enough. Reached behind him, and felt the curve of her hip. Remembered how she would stir and put her arm around him and stroke his chest and whisper *good morning* in his ear.

His throat tightened, and he drew back his hand. If he let his mind drift, he could hear Norma telling him that they had done all they could, that they had cast all the spells, strengthened all the wards, taken every step possible to protect themselves. It just hadn't been enough. Their fates rested with the Lady now.

And then he would hear Matt's voice. Like the toll of a distant bell, it was, so soft, yet so powerful. *Don't be a fool, Jim.* Thirty-seven years past, yet if he closed his eyes, he could see Matt standing in the oak-ringed clearing in the woods just west of town, his work denims whitened with sawdust, duffel bag slung over his shoulder. *It's all going downhill. Go get Connie and come with me.*

"I should have listened to you, old buddy." Petersbury wondered if his old buddy could hear him, if he could sense him from wherever he was now. "I called you a liar. I called you a lot of things. But it's happening just like you said it would. Took a while to get going, but it's like a runaway train now. Won't be no stopping it."

He paused to lick his lips. "Connie said that it served us right that you left, seeing how we treated you. You remember Connie, don't you, Matt? My baby sis. She had the biggest crush on you." He struggled for the right words as memories of the last few months came to call. "We—we had a—fight, she and I. About what to do. How to stop it. I finally told her to stay away and not come around no more." A tear tracked down his cheek, and he brushed it away. "I just couldn't make her understand. Sometimes you have to do things you could never imagine a human being doing. Just to stop the bad from taking you over."

Petersbury quieted as a wave of glitter swept across the ceiling. No magic that he could sense, just sparkles in the paint catching the headlight beam of a passing car. He had set aside the bedroom for his granddaughters when they came to visit, and left it to his daughter-in-law Ashley to decorate. She had drawn fairy-tale princesses on the walls and painted the ceiling to look like summer sky, pale blue dotted with big white clouds that went shadowed and starry at night.

Petersbury raised his head and squinted into the half-light until he picked out Ashley's form, bundled under a blanket beside Jim Junior. He had laid them out in the corner of the room near their daughters' beds, taking care to turn Ashley toward the wall so he didn't have to see her face. He hadn't wanted to hit her, but she had shaken off the sedative, and when she saw her little Bella and baby Alice lying so still, she screamed loud enough to rattle the windows, and if he hadn't stopped her, the neighbors would have heard.

Crazy old man! She had beat his chest with fists as small as a child's, then tore at his face. *Killer bastard bastard bastard!* He had slapped her once, then again, hard enough to knock her down, and still she kept coming. Junior hadn't told her, the damned idiot, even though he had promised he would. But as usual he had lollygagged, then left his old man to deal with the mess.

So Petersbury had hit Ashley one last time, good and hard, then put his hands around her neck and did what needed doing. Laid her down next to Junior, and as he did, found his boy looking up at him, eyes glassy from the dope.

Lady's will be done, Dad. Junior's voice had come slurred and hoarse. *Her will.* He had smiled then, tobacco-stained teeth in a big kid's face, while his wife grew still beside him. Always so trusting, Junior was, long past the age he should have grown up. *See you on the other side.* Then he had closed his eyes, taken one last shuddery breath—

Petersbury jerked into a sitting position, gasped as his lower back cramped, choked down a curse because he couldn't swear in front of Norma even though she was dead. Squinched his eyes shut as if that could block out things already seen. Muttered prayers and pleas to the Lady over and over as he hugged his knees and rocked like a damned baby. "All my fault—all my fault." He stuffed his fist in his mouth, bit down until he tasted blood.

Eventually, the tears stopped. The ache in his chest eased. He sat still until he heard the rattle of Po Barker's old Taurus turning onto the street, the clattery stop and start as the woman tossed newspapers up driveways. He wondered what would happen if he ran out and flagged her down, dragged her into the house, and showed her what he had done. They'd grown up together, hadn't they? She'd been born a Wickham, had been named an elder before her twenty-fifth birthday.

Then Petersbury looked around the bedroom at the blanket-covered bodies, and knew in the pit of his soul that however much Portia Wickham Barker or Virginia Waycross or any of the others understood, none of them would condone this.

"They don't know, Matt. I tried to tell them, but they wouldn't listen. They wouldn't see what was in front of them." He thought about his last visit to the Grill. How men he had known his whole life never looked at him, not once. Not even when he told them about how the space between had gotten too damned thin. Not even when he asked them if they ever stopped to think why no one ever saw crows in Gideon. They just stared down at the drinks he had bought them, their silence like dull knives.

Petersbury felt for his watch, pressed the tiny button that lit up the dial: 4:45 A.M. He knew he had to move, had to do what needed doing before the sun rose and one of the neighbors, Phil or Jeannie or old Margaret Corey, stopped by to check why the truck hadn't moved out of the driveway for four days, and ask if someone was sick.

Yeah, someone's sick, all right. Petersbury's shoulders shook, his laughter silent and bitter. This time, he stopped before the tears came. It wasn't that he feared death. Whatever dangers the wilderness held, whatever punishments the Lady meted out to him for what he had done, they were nothing compared to what he would face in this world if he stayed.

My fault. If only he had minded his own business that day. *My fault.* He should have turned the job down, told Leaf Cateman to go to hell. But the furnace needed work and the truck needed tires and it was Christmas, dammit. He had just wanted to get Norma something nice, see the looks on his grandbabies' faces as Junior and Ashley carried them into the living room and they saw the tree and the colored lights and the presents.

Besides, Leaf Cateman was his Master. Master of all Gideon. Not an easy thing for a child of the Lady to turn his Master down.

Petersbury rolled over and kissed Norma's cold forehead, then struggled to his feet. The night air had seeped in through the open bedroom window, filling the room with a damp chill that stank of wood smoke. "I'm sorry about the smell, baby. I know how you hate it seeping in everywhere. But the colder, the better." He walked to the window, took a look outside before he closed it. The bedroom faced the backyard, a bare, treeless swath that sloped down to an overgrown ravine. In the half-light, the mist played tricks, swirling to form shapes like bodies that walked up the incline toward the house. Once they reached the summit, they fell victim to the morning breeze, which blew them asunder, the fragments tumbling through the air like leaves back down to the foot of the rise, where they came together once more.

Petersbury watched the figures form, then vanish, again and again. "'By the pricking of my thumbs.'" A line from one of Shakespeare's plays, the only thing he remembered from four years of high school English because it was one of the few things that had made any damn sense. *Something wicked this way comes.*

"Too late. It's already here." Petersbury closed the curtains, then walked out of the bedroom and down the short hallway to the bathroom. Showered and shaved, maneuvering his razor around the deep scratches that Ashley had gouged into his cheeks. Put on the Sabbath shirt and pants he had laid out the night before, his best laced shoes, and the narrow black tie that had belonged to his grandfather. Time to look his best. A man only died once, after all.

He had originally planned to lay himself out with Norma and the others, but something told him that he needed to guard and protect right up to the end. So he walked past the dining room table, still laden with the spoiling remains of that last drugged dinner, and into the kitchen. From there he had a clear view straight through the house to the front door, and likewise, anything that came in through the front door had a clear view of him. It would see him first, and come for him, and leave his family alone.

He had prepared his final resting place the previous evening. First had come the ring of framed photos: him and Norma on their wedding day, Junior and Ashley and the babies on the days the little smidgens came home from the hospital. He had set the frames atop bricks so that his blood wouldn't touch them, and set a Christmas ornament before each one. Then he had retrieved a couple of drip pans from the garage, scrubbed them out, and set them on either side of the place where he would sit.

Now he filled the pans with hot water from the sink. He couldn't do the deed while sitting in a warm bath, the way the old Romans did, but he figured this was the next best thing. Keep the blood from clotting. Keep it warm and flowing.

Finally, he made coffee, black, with sugar. Because he wanted to taste it one last time.

It was still dark when Petersbury sat down on the floor, knife in hand. Before he had a chance to think, he placed the point of the knife against his right forearm down near the wrist and slashed. The pain brought tears to his eyes, but then the warmth welled up from under his skin and flowed out, and he relaxed. He cut the other forearm, let the knife slip from his grasp, then laid back his head. A couple of minutes, all the articles on the Internet said. A couple of minutes and he would be free of the nightmares. Free of the shadows that danced at the edges of his sight, flickering like dark flame. Free of the things that had dogged him these past weeks, things no human being should ever have to see.

He watched his blood spread through the water, felt the hollowness in his chest. The kitchen darkened, spots swimming before his eyes. His heart fluttered.

Then he felt . . . something through his growing daze. A sensation like wind over snow, sharp and cold. He shivered, and his gaze drifted to the drip pans, the water gone from clear to deep, deep red. Swirls formed in the liquid, like currents in a pool.

Then his blood separated from the water, combined into streams that blended together and flowed back into the gashes he had made.

Petersbury tried to pull his hands out of the water, but something held them fast, something with a grip as cold as the wind. Blood chilled by the water reentered his veins, sending them twitching beneath his skin like snakes. His life returned, but with it came pain—it racked his limbs as his muscles cramped and his gut clenched and his heart stuttered, slowed, then quickened again.

Yet through the shock and the agony and the fear, he heard a sound. It came from outside, a click like bone on bone, moving up the sidewalk that led to the house and up the steps to the front door. Quiet followed, for a few moments. Then the knob rattled, the door shaking so that the chain clattered like beans in a can. Then, again, silence.

Then it came through the closed door, a tall, slim column of darkness that flowed thick as oil. Petersbury watched it approach, picked out clothing amid the swirling blackness, pants and a knee-length coat, the cane or umbrella that swung with every stride. Again, he tried to pull his hands out of the trays, but something still held him fast. "It's you, isn't it? Did you come for them? You can't have them. They've gone over. The Lady has them. You won't get them now!"

The man-shape stopped just short of the kitchen doorway, his shadow coat floating around him as though tossed by wind. *They called to me. I heard the weeping of women and the cries of small children, and I thought, Ah, it must be a man of Gideon, doing what he does best. Murdering the innocent.*

Petersbury choked back a cry. He couldn't hear the thing speak, yet its words needled through his head and raked his soul the way Ashley's nails had raked his skin. He tried to close his eyes and turn away, but whatever spell his visitor had cast over him tightened its grip, held him fast.

Visitor. As if he didn't know who it was. "Matt tried to tell us. He tried to warn us, and we ran him out of town."

You know my name.

"Yes. Damn you."

Then say it.

"Blaine." Petersbury spoke before he could stop himself. "Nich-o-las. Blaine." Buzzing filled his ears, and his scalp crawled as though bugs scuttled across the skin.

Thank you. It has been a while since I heard you speak it aloud. The shade that was Nicholas Blaine cocked his head to one side. *Now, which one of you was Matt? Ah, the fair Eliza's descendant. Ignored just as she was. History repeats.*

"He'll know you're here, you bastard. He'll smell your stink from wherever he is, and he will lock you down."

Blaine shifted so he appeared to fold his arms, his cane dangling from one wrist. *I have felt the torment of my enemy like an old wound for so many years. An ache each time I tried to move. But something has changed of late. The prisoner looks up, and sees sunlight stream through the bars of his cell.* He chuckled. *Your savior is no more.*

"Liar!" Petersbury shook his head, neck bones crackling from strain as he fought invisible bonds. "Matt will stop you. Somehow. He will."

Would you have slaughtered your family if you believed that? Blaine straightened, then turned and started back the way he had come. *Stupid man of Gideon, you killed them for nothing. They never crossed the wilderness. They came to me. They were lost, and they begged me to help them. To guide them.* He drifted like a bobber in a slow-flowing stream, rising above the level of the floor, then dipping below. *It was your loving daughter-in-law led them to me. She is not happy with you. I fear your family reunion will not be all you hoped.*

"No! You're lying! It's been over three days. They've had time to cross the wilderness. They're innocent and they're for Paradise. The

Lady's waiting for them!" Petersbury fell silent as Blaine's shade vanished through the door. Then came the sound of the cane again, *tap-tap* on the front step and down the sidewalk, fading to nothing.

Minutes passed. Petersbury strained for any sound, heard only the hum of the refrigerator, the distant barking of a dog.

Then it drifted to him from the back of the house. Family noise. Junior's loud yawning. The babies' high-pitched yammering. Ashley's laugh and Norma's soft voice.

Petersbury started to smile, then looked down at his wrists. The deep cuts he had made had closed. The water in the pans now looked clean and clear. But he had to be dead. How could he hear his family unless he had crossed over? They couldn't return on their own.

They came to me.

Floorboards creaked. Voices grew louder.

They begged me to help them.

Petersbury tried to make out words, but whatever Norma and the others said ran together in weird singsong.

To guide them.

His family walked into the living room, Junior carrying Alice and Ashley carrying Bella and Norma leading the way.

"Norma? Baby?" Petersbury strained against Blaine's binding spell. "He came here. He's come back, just like Matt said he would. He said you asked him for help, but that can't be true. You went to the Lady. I know you did. He's a liar." He waited for his wife to answer, but she just watched him. They all just watched him, silent and motionless as dummies in a store window.

Then Norma stepped forward, and the light from the kitchen shone across her face.

Petersbury dug his heels into the floor and pushed, tried to scuttle against the wall and away from his wife. The thing that had been his wife. Gray skin and sunken cheeks and bony fingers grown too long. A smell like swamp and bait buckets. "Why, Norma? You'd have been safe with the Lady. Why did you go to him?"

Norma said nothing. Instead, she watched him while the others crowded behind her, their skin as gray, their hair as lank and stringy, their eyes as black and shiny as stone. Even the babies watched him, in a way babies never did. Focused and so still, the way cats in the bushes watched birds.

"Norma?" Petersbury struggled to keep his voice from shaking. "It's me, remember? James. Your husband."

Norma cocked her head, then uttered garble that might have been a question. For a moment, something flickered across her face. Comprehension. Recognition. The hard glitter in her eyes softened and her brow furrowed.

Petersbury tried again. "Norma? I love you. I'll always love you." But the last glimmer of what his wife had been had already vanished. She smiled like an animal now, revealing teeth gone rotted and pointy.

Then Ashley skirted around her and closed in. She had handed off Bella to Junior, and now crouched down and crawled toward Petersbury. He tried to kick her, but his legs had turned to lead and he barely managed to raise his foot off the floor as Ashley reached out and ran a clawlike finger down his leg, slicing through his pants and the skin beneath.

Petersbury gasped as the pain sang and the blood welled. The sound drew them all in as Ashley cut and cut some more, fingers flitting to his other leg, his arms and chest, and his blood flowed in warm rivers that soaked his clothes and pooled around him. Norma dipped a finger in it and drew on the floor while Junior put down the girls and Bella toddled right in to the red mess and splashed and giggled.

"Ashley." Petersbury waited until the thing that had been his daughter-in-law stopped and looked at him. "I swear, I did it to save you."

Ashley stared at him, claw poised in midair, nails dripping. Then she smiled. "Grampy Jim." Her nickname for him, in happier days.

Then she reached for his eyes.

11

O l' Tom's been fixing his signs again." Virginia Waycross cracked the thin skin of ice in the horse trough, then swept out the shards and tossed them on the ground. "Saw him limping along Old Orchard Road yesterday afternoon with his toolbox."

"He's getting started early." Connie Petersbury sank the de-icer to the bottom of the trough and attached the clips that held it in place. "He always used to wait until March, April, when it warmed up." She dried her hands on the seat of her jeans, then worked the electrical cord through the hard rubber sleeve that protected it from horse teeth and plugged it into the outlet just outside the fence.

"Couldn't get much warmer than it is now." Virginia crumpled the de-icer carton and shoved it into a trash bag with the others. "This is the latest I've installed these things since I don't remember when. We've always had at least one real frigid snap by now, but this year? A little bit of snow. A little bit of cold. Like it's teasing us." She tossed the trash bag over the fence, beyond the reach of the trio of curious horses that watched from the far end of the corral.

"It's only the middle of December. We'll be wishing for days like this soon enough." Connie buttoned her barn coat to the neck, then took her gloves from her pocket and pulled them on. Her fingers felt clumsy, stiff as the battered leather, and she told herself it was just arthritis aggravated by the cold. Fear had nothing to do with it.

Gideon nerves. "Did he say why?" She fielded her friend's puzzled look. "Tom. Did he say why he was putting up the signs now?"

"Change comin'."

"That's it?"

Virginia shrugged. "You know him. I was lucky to get that much." She trod through a small pile of snow, flattening it into the mud. "He's right, you know."

"Even a stopped clock is right twice a day. Can't think of a bigger stopped clock in Gideon than Tom Barton." Connie looked up at the early-morning sky, the smears of rose-colored cloud. "Stopped about 1960 and ain't been wound since."

"I know you don't like him." Damp breeze ruffled Virginia's steel-gray curls. From the side, she looked like a tall sliver, all muck boots and skinny jeaned legs and Mike's old barn coat, the cuffs hanging past her knuckles. "Hell, I don't like him. But he's just saying what everyone is thinking."

"And enjoying the hell out of it while he does. Plastering the Lady's words all over the roadsides. Folks driving through think we're a bunch of crackpots."

"Who cares what strangers think? Our duty is to protect them, not befriend them."

Connie turned away. One of the horses, Kermit the Morgan, had followed them, and she adjusted his blanket as he nickered and nibbled the hem of her coat. "Protect them how? We can't even protect ourselves. We can't even pro-tect—" The word cracked and her voice with it, and she pressed her face against the horse's neck as the tears fell. Felt Virginia's arms around her, the weathered softness of the canvas coat and the mingled smells of hay and lilac soap.

"I shouldn't have asked you here today." Virginia pulled her close and rocked back and forth, like she held a baby instead of a grown woman. "Dylan could have helped me—it's his job."

"I needed to get out." Connie eased out of her friend's embrace, wiped her eyes with her sleeve. "All I'd do at home is clean stuff and cry."

"Well, I'm glad I could help a little, then." Virginia cocked her head this way and that, trying to meet her eye. "Anything else happen I should know about?"

Connie sniffled, shrugged. "Saw Jorie at the post office yesterday. Mink coat and those spike-heel shoes of hers, like she was headed into the city. 'The one time I see Gideon in the papers,' she said, 'and it's for something like this.' Asked how I couldn't have seen it coming, why I didn't stop it."

"Well, damn her and all who sail with her." Virginia's eyes glinted. She hated Jorie Cateman, and had never hidden her feelings despite pressure from the other elders. "She's nothing but a spoiled child, angry with the world for upsetting her day. Not unexpected, and not important."

"She'd beg to differ."

"So would Leaf. But she's his folly, not ours, and I say the hell with them both." Virginia took a piece of carrot from the depths of a coat pocket and held it out to Kermit. "Chew on this, not on my guests." She gave the horse his treat, then patted his flank. "There's something else, isn't there?" She had switched to her meeting-hall voice, level and stern. "Constance Petersbury? I'm not asking as a friend."

"I understand, Mistress." Connie took hold of a lock of Kermit's mane and rolled it between her fingers.

"Because I hate to sound cold, but this is about more than the loss of your family."

"I know that, Mistress."

"This is about the survival of Gideon, and the world outside."

"Yes, Mistress."

"Just so we're clear." The sight of carrots had lured the quarter horses, Bert and Ernie, and Virginia gently scolded them as they closed in and waited for their snacks. "I remember how close you and Jim were. Except that for the last few months, you weren't anymore. Bella's birthday came, and you didn't go to the party. Sent a present, but Jim sent it back. Then Norma caught that bug that was going around, and you didn't stop by once to help out or even check how she was doing."

"You do have your sources." Connie struggled to keep the bite out of her voice.

"I'm Mistress of Gideon." Virginia distributed the last of the carrots, then shooed the horses with a wave of her hand. "Rank has its privilege as well as its duty." She headed toward the gate, then stopped and waited. "Now, I want to know what you two fought about."

Connie took her time catching up. She had pulled a hair from Kermit's mane when she petted him, and now she weaved it through her fingers and muttered under her breath. Just a couple of words in the old language, taught to her by her great-grandmother years before. Within a heartbeat, she heard whinnying and snapping teeth and the pound of hooves, and turned to find Kermit cornering Bert, yellow choppers bared, hindquarters tensed as he made ready to rear and strike.

Then just as quickly, he quieted, shaking his head as though coming out of a daze.

"You think you can throw me off by making my boys hurt one another? On my land? *How dare you.*"

Connie looked back at Virginia to find her red-faced and glaring. "I am sorry, Mistress." She had seen the woman angry before, but never had both barrels been directed at her. *Gone too far.* She needed to tread lightly now. "I beg forgiveness."

"You want forgiveness?" Virginia paced, back and forth, like a big cat in a cage. "Answer my questions. And tell me the truth, or I swear by the Lady, I will make you regret the day you thought you could get the better of me."

"Yes, Mistress." Connie racked her brain, tried to piece together a story that could fool Virginia Waycross. She never had thought good on her feet, and Virginia would pounce on any detail that sounded fake or didn't fit. "We argued about what we thought was happening." She paused. "We argued about Matt."

Virginia looked down at the ground, then away, her jaw working. "You been thinking about him, too?"

Bingo. Connie nodded. "Most every day, lately."

"I wonder what he would make of all this. The way things are now." Virginia stared off into the distance. "Jim never forgave him for leaving. I know that. Not sure I ever have either, for all he had his reasons." She inscribed a sign in the air, a ward against demons. "I wish he was here now, though. Lady knows we could use him." She trudged to the gate, then stopped, her hand on the latch. "You were just a kid when Matt left. What did you know about it?"

"Not much." Well, that was a lie—Connie knew a lot. *He and Emma opened a door, and left the rest of us to deal with what stepped through.*

Virginia mounted the steps to her front door, then turned and looked out over the winter-brown yard. "You know, I saw Mike for months after he died. I'd be mucking out the barn or working in the vegetable garden, and I'd look up and there he'd be, dressed in his Sabbath suit, just watching me. He never believed I could manage this place on my own, and he had to see for himself that I could. Didn't go away for good until the day I hired Dylan."

Connie stood at the foot of the steps, eyes steady on Virginia as she sifted through the truth and the lies she knew she needed to tell, as all the while the back of her neck tingled and she fought the urge to turn around. "Sometimes I dream about him. I see him bleeding all over. Like he fought with someone. Like they hurt him bad."

"Connie, he cut his wrists. Nothing else."

"All over. His chest and his legs and his—" Connie waved toward her eyes. "They're just black holes and bloody tears running down his face."

Virginia scanned the yard, then looked toward the road. "Have you strengthened your wards?"

Connie shook her head. "Why would I want to keep him away? He's my brother."

"Yes. And you know he was scared. You know how he was acting.

The things he was saying. Gideon nerves, we all thought. Same as all of us. But you're his sister and you're touchier than he ever was, and even you didn't expect him to do what he did."

Connie rubbed the back of her neck as the tingle ramped up to a poison-ivy itch. "What are you saying?"

Virginia dug a small plastic bag of protective herbs out of her coat pocket and sprinkled some of the brown fluff across her front steps. "I think you should stay here with me for a few days. I'm alone now that Dylan's moved out, and it's not like I wasn't alone even when he was here. He's a hired man. You're a friend."

Connie dragged off her glove and pressed her cold hand to the back of her neck. The itch had changed to burning now, as though she stood with her back to a roaring blaze. "Jim would never hurt me."

"I'm trying to tell you, dear. And I'm trying to be gentle, but I've never been good at it. He may not be Jim anymore." Virginia sighed, acknowledgment of the battle lost. "If you ever see him, you'll tell me."

"Yes, Mistress."

"I'm not asking. I'm ordering."

"Yes, Mistress."

"He's a tormented soul, fearing judgment, wandering the in-between, afraid to take that final walk into the pathless waste because he knows what's awaiting him there. That much anguish, it opens doors best kept closed."

"Yes, Mistress."

"By the Lady."

"In her name." Connie turned and headed to her pickup. Looked out toward the road, and saw Jim Petersbury standing just past the end of the driveway, beyond the reach of whatever wards the Mistress of Gideon had set to protect her property.

JIM HAD FIRST appeared in Connie's dreams the day after they found him and Norma and the kids. Due to the nature of the deaths and the subsequent investigation, the county coroner had delayed releasing his body. And so it was that, bloody tears coursing his cheeks, Jim had come to Connie and begged her to rescue him, to free him from the confines of the morgue drawer and bring him home to Gideon. So she had done as every good child of the Lady would have done in her stead, and asked to meet with her Master, to request that he intercede. But her phone calls to Leaf Cateman had gone unanswered, and as for her post office encounter with Jorie, to say that had not gone well was to not say nearly enough.

Jim, meanwhile, had taken to turning up everywhere she went. Friends' homes. The grocery store. Hoard's Grill. The only place he hadn't been able to enter was Virginia's property, and maybe that stood to reason. He and Virginia hadn't seen eye to eye in years, their friendship a memory, and once you lost Virginia Waycross, well, you lost her. Even after death.

"She never guessed you were there." Connie checked the rearview, and saw Jim seated behind her in the cab's jump seat, blood-rimmed eyes on her. "You were never able to fool her in life. Guess dying made you smarter." She waited for a reply, but her brother had remained mute since that first impassioned plea. "Sure did make you quiet."

She circled the village square, past Petrie's hardware store, Corey's feed store, and the grill, then paused at an intersection all but hidden by the tumbled remains of a stone gate and overgrown shrubbery. Tapped on the steering wheel, and looked toward the small cluster of Federals and Victorians where all but one of the elders of Gideon resided. *All but Virginia.* "'Air's too thin for breathing there,' she says. But it's just because of Leaf. Those two never got on."

Connie pondered for a bit, then turned onto the narrow, tree-lined street, drifting down until she came to a sprawling painted lady done up in gray, wine red, and pink. "Haven't got an appointment. Think he'll see me?" She glanced at Jim again, and detected the barest hint of a smile. "Yes, I think so, too." She pulled into the curved driveway, then stared up at the gingerbread eaves and ornate chimneys for a few courage-affirming moments before finally shutting off the truck and getting out.

Amanda Petrie, Leaf's housekeeper, must have been watching from the front window, because she opened the door before Connie had a chance to ring the bell. "Constance?"

"I need to see him." Connie tried to look past Amanda into the house, but the woman had some breadth to her and knew how to use it. "A couple minutes. That's all I'm asking."

"Master Cateman's a busy man, Constance." Amanda's wattled neck quivered. "You might have called first." She wore her usual black pantsuit and pearls, silver hair pulled into a tight bun. On the weekends she worked as a greeter at the family funeral home and behaved with the same impatient bustle, barely concealed irritation with the whole human race, living or dead.

"He's not the only person who's busy—I have things that need doin', too." Connie stuffed her hands in her pockets and drew up as tall as her bad back would allow. "I'll wait fifteen minutes, and then I'll go." She paused. "And I'll never seek back again."

"All right." Amanda backed away, hands drawn up, as though trying to protect herself from a crazy person.

"You tell him that. Those words. Just like I said them."

"You'll never seek back again. Right." Amanda stopped, and gave forth a grumbling sigh. "Well, you may as well come in. You can sit in the east parlor." She tugged her jacket over her ample backside and turned on her heel. "I'll have one of the girls bring you coffee. It's payroll day, so all I can tell you is that you're going to have a wait."

"I will wait for fifteen minutes." Connie looked back at the truck and Jim's face visible between the headrests. Then she stepped inside the house and wandered the maze of walnut paneling and flocked wallpapers that had been old when she was a girl until she reached the dark, velvet-curtained cave that was the east parlor. A few moments later, one of Amanda's many helpers came in bearing a cup of coffee and a plate of cookies. She served Connie, took her coat, then asked after her health in that low-voiced way that folks had taken to talking to her since the incident.

Connie drank her coffee, and listened to the mantel clock tick. Watched the minute hand move. Counted the seconds. At the fourteen-minute, forty-five-second mark, she set down her cup, rose, and headed for the front door. Just as the last second ticked by and she put her hand on the ornate brass handle, she heard a creak on the stair, and turned to find Amanda regarding her with head-cocked puzzlement.

"He'll see you." Disappointment made her sound kind.

THREE FLIGHTS OF stairs. They beat the hell out of Connie's back, but Leaf liked to brag that at the age of seventy-three he still took them two at a time, that it would be a bright day in the wilderness before he would have an elevator installed in his old pile. So she winced through each twinge and catch and concentrated on the paintings that lined the curved walls, the images of the wives and children and grandchildren. Of Leaf's father, Amos, and his grandfather, Hiram, who built the place after the Great Fire.

No more family for me. The thought caught Connie by surprise. *I'm the last Petersbury.* The realization made tears spring, and when one of Leaf's men met her at the set of double-wide oak panels that marked the entry to the office and asked if she wanted time to catch her breath, she told him to just open the damn doors and get out of her way.

Leaf Cateman, the Master of Gideon, sat in the middle of the room at an ornate cherrywood desk the size of a small banquet table. "Good morning, Constance." He rose, a craggy-faced, bearded patriarch, and extended his hand across the polished surface to take hers. As usual, he wore black jeans and a crisp white shirt held at the neck with a string tie. "I say so as a formality only. It isn't a good morning, is it? How are you keeping?"

"As well as can be expected, Master." Connie extracted her hand as quickly as good manners allowed, and fought the urge to wipe it on her pant leg. Leaf's skin felt rough as sandpaper, and was reddened in spots and dry enough to flake when touched. Psoriasis, Jorie called it. Soul rot breaking through, according to Virginia.

Leaf walked to a nearby conference table, and hefted one of the chairs. "The loss of the children is the most painful aspect of all this." He set it down in front of his desk, then motioned for Connie to sit.

Connie tried to settle in, but the chair was straight-backed and armless and as comfortable as a board. "I miss them all the same." In truth, she had never cared for Ashley, but now was not the time to talk about poor choices by dumb nephews.

"Of course you do." Leaf returned to his chair, sat back, smiled without showing his teeth. "Now, what did you wish to see me about?"

"I want to bring Jim home." Connie wiped away a brimming tear, catching it just before it fell. "I called the coroner's office, and they put me off. Said they had tests to run."

"Stands to reason. They're looking for drugs. Alcohol. Those tests take time."

"Jim didn't drink. And Norma had to force him to take so much as an aspirin for a headache."

"Well, we know that, but the officials do not."

"Why do they need to know? It's none of their business."

"He murdered his family and then killed himself. We want to know why."

"We know why." Connie scooted to the edge of her chair and tucked her legs beneath, lessening the pain in her back just enough so that she could concentrate. "I want him home. The end of today would be nice, but tomorrow is okay, too. That'll give Saul and Epiphany time to prepare him so he can be buried with Norma and the others. I've held off their final rest long enough. Saul says his back room is starting to get a little crowded."

Leaf's expression didn't change. Still the half smile, the kindly light in his eyes. "What do you expect me to do?"

"Call someone."

"Call someone?"

"Yes, call someone. Like you do when Jorie gets a speeding ticket or one of your men gets pulled over for driving drunk." Connie took a deep breath. "Or when you have an old shed out back that needs clearing out. A shed that's been closed up a long time." She sucked her lips between her teeth and bit down to keep from saying more. Unclenched her hands, and found that she had driven her nails into her palms deep enough to draw blood.

Leaf spent a few long minutes studying his desk blotter. Drummed his fingers on the wood. *Rat-ta-thump.* "I might give Thad Trace a call. He is only a coroner's assistant, but he has some experience in matters concerning Gideon. I am sure he can . . . do whatever needs to be done." He stood, his wooden office chair creaking like an old building in the wind. "His mother was a Cateman by marriage. That would make us kin." The smile returned, although the voice had grown cooler. "If you will excuse me." He walked to a side door that led to an adjoining room, the click of his boot heels muffled by the thick rug.

Connie tried to settle her nerves by looking around the office. Like the rest of the house, it hadn't changed in years. Still the same strange room she remembered from girlhood visits with her mother. The walls had been paneled with ancient boards salvaged from the basement. Matt had planed and prepped them, and Emma had painted them with scenes from Gideon's history. The Sudden Freeze of 1836. The Great Fire of 1871. Always researching, Emma was. *You're too pretty to sit all day with your nose stuck in books,* Connie's mother, Deborah, would say, and Emma would just shake her head and smile.

Emma. Leaf's first wife. "Didn't spend all her time reading, that's for sure." Connie spoke without thinking, then glanced around to make sure Leaf hadn't overheard. He never talked about Emma, and that meant that no one else in Gideon was to talk about her either.

Not so he can hear you, anyway. Connie looked up at the domed ceiling, decorated at the top with a round window through which the dull winter light streamed. *An oculus.* That's what the window was called—Emma had taught her the word. Matt had built it a few months before he ran off, had made it by inserting quarter-round panes into a wooden *X*, so it looked like the circles he used to weave from grass and strands of hay. *Eyes of the Lady,* he had called them. *For protection.* Connie had grown to hate him for that, for thinking that the Catemans deserved protection but none of the rest of them did.

"What are you doing here?"

Connie turned as far around as her back would allow, and saw Jorie Cateman standing in the doorway. She looked even more the child bride than usual in jeans and one of Leaf's old shirts, her feet bare and blond hair bound up in a ponytail. Little if any makeup, which made for a change. "I came to see the Master."

Jorie stepped inside the office, and the light caught the gold chain around her neck and the diamonds on her ears and fingers, the cherry-red polish on her nails. "About what?"

"I came to . . . make a request." Connie worked to her feet, more to ease the pain than out of respect for Leaf's wife.

"What for?" Jorie's was a mean girl's voice, high-pitched and sharp.

"Constance asked me to say a few words at the memorial service." Leaf had opened the side door without a sound, and slipped back into the office. "A passage from the Lady's book should suit as always." He held up the old Cateman family book, the black leather binding gone gray with age. Made a slight bow in his wife's direction, then returned to his desk.

"Thank you, Master." Connie willed daggers at Jorie, but the dense little bitch made no move to leave.

"I phoned Saul to ask a question about the time of the service, and he asked me to tell you that he will need a new shirt for James." Leaf showed teeth this time when he smiled, choppers as big and yellow as Kermit's.

Connie picked out the message between the lines, that the call to Thad Trace had borne fruit, and that Jim would soon be on his way back to Gideon. "Thank you, Master. I will see to that today." Then she looked from Leaf to Jorie, and stood frozen in place, like a rabbit caught between two foxes. "I won't take up any more of your time." She bowed toward Leaf and gave Jorie a quick nod, then left as quickly as her back would allow.

I shouldn't have threatened him. Connie angled down the stairs sideways, gasping with every step. One phone call was all it had taken. A few minutes of Leaf's time. If she had just been patient, asked nicely, it could have been settled. *And now he knows.* That Jim had told her about the shed, and what he had found.

Another of Amanda's girls met Connie at the bottom of the stairs with her coat, and she grabbed it before the poor thing could help her put it on. She struggled into it as she limped out to the truck, only to find that Jim had gone. As usual, he had run off and left her to deal with his mess.

Calm. Down. Connie looked back at the house, checked each window in turn to see if anyone watched her. Saw no one, and felt the panic lift a little. She had gotten what she had come for, and unsettled Leaf Cateman in the process. Someone like Virginia Waycross would call that a good day.

Connie got in her truck, got on her way. *Gideon nerves.* Someday they would be the death of her.

12

Jorie Cateman stepped into the hallway as soon as Constance Petersbury departed, leaned against the wall, and bent over double, hands pressed against the sides of her head. She hated everything about the office, the paneling and the oculus and the dread she claimed radiated from the very walls. Thus, she avoided entering whenever possible.

For that reason alone, it had become Leaf's favorite room in the house.

"I told you she'd be trouble." Jorie straightened slowly, and crossed her arms over her stomach.

"Nothing that can't be dealt with by trusting in simple human nature." Leaf settled back behind his desk and returned to the ledger he had been examining prior to Constance's arrival. "No one believed James when he ranted about shadowy figures and impending doom, and he was considered the rational one. Constance has cried wolf so many times that no one in Gideon will ever believe a damned thing she says."

"I can think of someone." Jorie stepped just inside the entry, and gripped the jamb with one taloned hand. "Virginia Waycross."

"Everyone knows Virginia and I do not get on." Leaf sniffed. "No one will listen to her either."

"You're taking an awful lot on faith. Let me take care of it."

"Like you took care of James and his family?"

"I had nothing to do with that. The man just snapped. How many times do I have to tell you?"

"Your problem, my dear, is that, as with Constance, your past dictates your present. You have lied so many times that your claims of truth now fall on deaf ears." Leaf took a pot of Amanda's special ointment from the top drawer of the desk and dabbed some on the red patches that dotted the backs of his hands. The condition would worsen during times of stress, his doctor had warned, but he had suffered through worse times than this with nary a blemish. Age was to blame, no doubt. The damned passage of time.

Jorie winced as she watched him minister to himself. She never bothered to hide how much his condition sickened her. "Is there something important that you're not telling me?"

"The things of importance that I have not told you could fill a book, my dear." Leaf looked across the desk, imagined Constance still seated there, and wondered what exactly she knew. So many secrets, accrued over so many years—the possibilities were endless. "I held Constance the day after she was born, you know. Deborah bled so that we almost lost her. In the hospital for five weeks, she was. So I cared for Constance and James. Took them into this house and cherished them as my own. That allowed David the chance to stay at the hospital." He glanced at Jorie in time to catch the tail end of a yawn. "Am I boring you?"

"Need you ask?" Jorie drew the band from her hair. "Connie Petersbury is not a baby anymore. She's a grown woman who thinks she has you by the balls." She shook out the golden mass, then gathered it and twisted it into a knot atop her head. "And maybe she's right."

Leaf sighed. "As I have heard you insist on more than one occasion, you've balls enough for both of us. Feel free to take up the slack. Just don't come running back to me when it blows up in your face."

"We made a deal, old man. I marry you, and—"

"And I teach you. And you did your part, and I have done mine."

Leaf sat back, chair screeching like an animal in distress. "You possess talent, Jorie. Power. That, I could never deny. But you're petty and selfish and impatient, and because of that, the ways of the Lady will never truly be yours."

"What are you saying?" Jorie walked farther into the office, anger overwhelming dread as it always did. "Don't you even think of cutting me loose. I know enough about you to—"

"To drag me down in the mud with you. Yes, I know." Leaf rubbed his forehead, watched the flakes of skin drift down and settle on his jeans, and brushed them away. "I won't cut you loose, as you so aptly put it. You will always have a roof over your head and the wherewithal to display yourself as is befitting the wife of the Master of Gideon—"

"Mistress of Gideon. I am your wife and that makes me Mistress of Gideon."

"Virginia Waycross is Mistress of Gideon."

"The title is mine."

"Title? You make it sound like Fried Chicken Queen of the county fair. It is an honor and a duty, earned by displaying leadership and extraordinary skill in times of crisis. For all her irritating ways, Virginia Waycross is an exceptionally talented and levelheaded practitioner. If I thought I still had any chance to win her over, I would not hesitate."

"Gideon had no right to select her. The Council is supposed to choose masters and mistresses, and they have always chosen married couples. I'll take my case to them—don't think I won't."

"The Council is a rule-bound collection of academics and theorists. However, if they suspect impropriety, they can be as mindlessly driven as a pack of hounds on the scent. If they investigate your charges, they are certain to uncover all manner of irregularity, most of it involving you. You'd be cutting off your nose to spite your face." Leaf pursed his lips. "All that plastic surgery wasted."

Jorie's cheeks reddened. "You're nothing but a filthy, power-grubbing old man trying to hang on to life any way you can."

Leaf slammed shut the ledger, pushed it aside, took another from the stack. "And that makes us well suited to one another, doesn't it?" He scratched a patch on his wrist that had blossomed just that morning, dug too deep, and rolled up his shirt cuff to keep it clear of the blood. "You have work to do, don't you? Helping Amanda inventory the herbs."

"Maid's work."

"Counting your bullets." Leaf shook his head. "You see? You whine and wail that no one respects you, and yet you make the same mistakes over and over again." He studied the columns of numbers until he heard the angry mutter and the pad of bare feet. The slam of his door.

He waited, until he felt sure that Jorie had either shut herself in her bedroom to pout or gone downstairs to assist Amanda. Then he pressed a small carving of acanthus leaves just under the lip of the desk, and muttered a few words in the old language. The carving popped open like a tiny door, revealing a small compartment. He reached inside and removed a key. A new purchase, it was, bright silver and shiny and as magical as a brick. Sometimes the new ways could prove just as useful as the old.

Leaf tucked the key in his pocket, then rose and walked across the office to the section of wall on which Emma had painted the tale of the Freeze. She had used Grandfather Hiram's journals as her source material, and had covered the panels with scenes of the fallen men of Gideon, the lamentations of their women, the burials.

Winter in Gideon. Even now, almost two hundred years later, the season tried the soul. It always snowed more in Gideon than anywhere else in Illinois, and in between the storms came the thaws and the mist and the mud. Never a time to rest. Always the pendulum swing from one extreme to the other.

"And so it goes." Leaf cracked the oaken door and checked the hallway for errant servants and angry wives before departing. Loped down the stairs, past the second floor to the ground floor, past the kitchen, and down a short, dark corridor that ended in the doorway to the rear yard.

Leaf opened the door, then hesitated as the damp cold wrapped around him. He thought of going back in the house for a jacket, but the sound of approaching footsteps and the pipings of a gaggle of Amanda's helpers drove him outside. Key in hand, he trotted across the browned yard to what Constance had called "the shed," the old carriage house.

He unlocked the padlock, and opened the steel door that Jim Petersbury had installed a few weeks before. Reached into the dark and fumbled for the light switch, flipping it on as the smells of damp and dirt, mold and warding herbs, enveloped him. He stood in the doorway, and envisioned the place as it had been when Emma had used it as her studio, the walls covered with sketches and paintings, the plank floor thick with rugs in brilliant Indian patterns of ultramarine and gold and scarlet. The tiny kitchen, nothing more than a sink and a two-burner hot plate. The narrow bed in the far corner hidden behind a painted screen.

It was a dank shell now. After he had discarded the furnishings and burned the artwork, Cateman had given the building over to his men for use as a break room, had even installed a sink, a toilet, a larger refrigerator. But after a few days, they had refused to set foot in the place. Voices, they said they heard. A man, singing.

So the place had sat, unused and unusable, until that summer, when James had gone poking around where he shouldn't have, his Gideon nerves driving him like a hound on the scent.

Master, there's something underneath the shed. He had run up the three flights to Cateman's office, his face red, breath coming in gasps. *Steps. Leading down.* The words echoed in Cateman's head, as clear as if the man who had spoken them stood before him now. Poor James, so eager to earn extra money for the holidays. So eager to help. And unlike his sister, Constance, so willing to believe whatever his Master told him, and to forget all that had happened thirty-seven years before.

So Cateman ordered Petersbury to board up the windows and fashion a trapdoor to cover the hole in the floor. The man had done a slapdash job, truth be told, but carpentry had never been the poor fool's talent. That skill with wood had resided with another . . .

Leaf stood still for a time, lost in memories that wiser men would have long since buried. Then he stepped inside and pulled the door closed after him. Shut off the light so that no one in the house, especially Jorie, would see it and take it into their damned-fool head to investigate. The sudden darkness hampered him for a moment or two, but then he adjusted, his witch sense guiding him now that the other five could not. He walked to the trapdoor as if he strode across Gideon's square in broad daylight, head high and step sure, pulled it open, then felt with his booted foot for the wooden steps that better hands than Petersbury's had built all those years before.

Down one short flight, then another, the stairs altering from wood to packed earth, the passageway twisting down, down, growing narrower and narrower until Leaf's shoulders brushed the dirt walls on either side. Lightbulbs swayed as his head knocked against the power cord strung overheard, throwing shadows that made it seem as though someone mounted the steps toward him, emerging from the depths of the deepest cellar in Gideon.

Leaf paused when he reached the foot of the stair. The air felt thick and wet as fog here, ventilation blocked by rubble and dirt. Once the place had been an open chamber, employed for baptisms and other rites. But the walls had collapsed after the Great Fire of 1871, and repeated attempts by his grandfather and father to reopen the chamber failed. Tools vanished. Supports toppled during the night. At one point, Grandfather Hiram ordered that a small child remain in the excavation at all times. That following morning, he found the walls once again fallen, the child curled safe asleep on the top step.

"Now's not the time, son." Leaf's father, Amos, veined hand heavy on his shoulder, after yet another failed attempt. *"There's something down there that wants what's buried to stay buried."* They never spoke the name,

but they knew what it was. Mullin magic, thwarting them at every turn.

Leaf held his breath, stretched out his hands. Near a century and a half since the fire, and still he could feel the remnants of power, like kitten claws scratching his sore skin. But here and there, he sensed the weakening, like a warm touch. "Time is the enemy of us all, old girl." He smiled. It wouldn't be long now.

He crept down the final passage, this one so narrow that he needed to shuffle sideways to wedge through. He had never been a claustrophobe, had never dreaded the dark or the unknown or the creaking sounds in the night. Even as a boy, Leaf Cateman had been fearless.

But his heart pounded now. He had traveled this path countless times over the past month, had helped Petersbury shore up the walls and shift dirt, had sworn the man to silence and taken his wife of all people into his confidence.

Leaf edged forward. As he neared the end of the passage, he felt along the wall for a niche he had scooped out, removed the flashlight he had stashed there, and switched it on. Petersbury had strung a line of bulbs along the way, yes, but they didn't always stay on. Some burned out. Others never lit at all. And others, they found on the floor, as though someone had walked along the passage and unscrewed them as they went.

This time, the bulbs remained on, so Leaf shut off the flashlight and tucked it in his pocket. Entered the tiny dirt-walled space, no more than two paces in any direction, and walked up to the waist-high bier set against the far wall.

Even with the lighting, the thing that lay atop the mound proved hard to distinguish. Leaf patted the dirt until he found the edge of the shroud, the cloth stiff with age and spotted with mold. Probed a little more, until he felt the hard length of a forearm.

"Just making sure you're still here." He stared at the form until his heart slowed. Then he peeled back the cloth and regarded the mummified face. "One hears stories." He pondered the desiccated visage, the hollowed eye sockets, lips dried into a snarl that revealed blackened teeth. "I will never understand how you survived intact down here in the damp. You should be a mess of mold and rat-gnawed bone, and yet here you are." He quieted, and listened for the odd noises that sometimes came to him in this place. A rustling like dried leaves. The crackle and spark like that of a fire. And finally, almost beyond hearing, a whisper.

Let me in . . . ne'er seek back . . . ne'er seek back again. . .

"Dear Constance, how can you know?" Leaf sighed. "Either Jim broke his vow of silence, or you've been having your feelings again." Gideon nerves, she called them, the ever-present edginess that came with living where the barrier between worlds had grown thin and the wilderness and those who dwelled there ever so close. Everyone with even an iota of talent suffered from the condition to some degree, but compared to Constance Petersbury, they were all deaf and dumb and blind, their hands swaddled, their noses stopped, as senseless as posts.

He formed a cradle with his arms, imagined the tiny body that rested there so long ago. "What have you heard? What have you seen?" He closed his eyes and concentrated, tried to reach out into Gideon, find that bright bead of light that marked the prematurely aged woman sitting behind the wheel of an old pickup truck. But he sensed nothing. Constance had shielded herself, put up barriers not even he could breach.

Leaf let his arms fall to his sides and looked down at Nicholas Blaine. "My grandfather believed you would help him usher Gideon into a new age. Unfortunately, he tried to free you while Eliza Mullin lived, and, well, let us say that plan failed miserably and leave it at that. Luckily, he had no trouble laying the blame for the Great Fire at her feet. The fair citizenry were always prepared to believe the worst about her." He pulled the shroud back over the desiccated face, while overhead, a lightbulb stuttered and hissed. "Unfortunately, while slander destroys reputations, it does nothing to weaken curses. But we will free you, and in return your knowledge and power will make us great."

Leaf watched Blaine's body as he backed out of the chamber. "James panicked. He was a fool, and he paid a fool's price. Accept him as payment. But leave Constance alone. She's a child in all this, whatever her age. I can reason with her. She's no threat to you." He pointed to the balky bulb, which flickered once, then shone bright and steady. "Leave her be or suffer the consequence. Always remember that I am Master here." Even so, he continued to face the chamber as he sidled back down the passage, and kept the flashlight with him all the way to the top of the stairs.

13

After her visit to Leaf Cateman, Connie got the call from Petrie's Funeral Home that they had Jim's body and now plans for the service needed to be finalized. So she drove to Jim and Norma's house, broke the seal left by the cleaning company, unlocked the door, and entered for the first time in weeks. Ignored the sense of death that overwhelmed her like a flood, made her way to Jim and Norma's bedroom, and took Jim's second-best suit from the closet. Turned, and found Jim standing in the bedroom doorway, blood dripping from his wounds onto the carpet.

"You're back." Connie crossed to the other side of the bedroom, dug socks out of the dresser drawer. "I wondered what had happened to you." She watched his reflection in the dresser mirror as he held out a hand to her. Funny how ghosts showed up in mirrors and vampires didn't. But then, vampires weren't real, were they? Everything real left a mark in the world. "What are you on about now? I got you home, didn't I? Just like you asked." She turned to face him. "I don't know what else you want from me, Jim. You felt you had to leave and take your whole family with you. The last family I'll ever have. Thanks for that." She shoved the socks into the pockets of the suit and hurried from the house, leaving her brother behind.

Connie dropped off the clothes at the funeral home. She didn't tell Saul Petrie about Leaf Cateman's offer to speak at the service, however, because she knew Leaf had only said it to throw off Jorie. When she got home, she would write him a note, offer him an out. It was only fair, seeing as she had threatened him into helping her in the first place.

"Oh let me in this ae nicht." Her shaky alto filled the cabin. "And I'll ne'er seek back—" She stopped, then wiped away a tear. She could hear Jim's baritone in her memory, singing the same words. He had taught her the song during the summer, before it went bad between them. It was a bawdy tune, about a man visiting a woman in the night, but for all that it reminded them both of the folk music that their mother had loved.

"Oh, let me in this ae nicht, and I'll ne'er seek back again." "The Laird o' Windywa's," the title was. Jim said he had heard Leaf sing it around the Cateman place, or someone that sounded like Leaf. *It's not a nice song, Connie,* he said after he taught it to her. Still, he had taken to singing it while he worked at the Cateman place, because it blotted out the other sounds. The ones he started hearing in the basement under the shed. The ones that came home with him, and got into his dreams.

He's in the shed, Connie. In the ground below. Just like Matt said. It's the Catemans' secret.

"The Catemans have a lot of secrets." Connie left Gideon proper and turned onto Old Orchard Road. "Probably buried one of their kin down there to save money on the funeral." She drove past acre after acre of Cateman land, until she reached her poky tan ranch, the five-acre plot bordered on two sides by the bend of the River Ann. The scant remnants of the once-extensive Petersbury holdings.

"You here? You okay?" Before Connie got out of the truck, she checked the rearview for any sign of Jim. She didn't see him, but still she paused before closing the door to give him time to exit, even though she doubted it mattered.

She didn't sense her brother behind her. Didn't feel him pass. Even so, she found him waiting for her in the backyard behind the house.

He stood in the middle of the yard next to the bird feeder, hands at his sides. This time, he looked as he did in her dreams, his eyes slashed, blood and eyeball gunk smearing his cheeks, mouth hung open in an eternal howl. Suffering, he was—she could sense it in the very air. Oh, how it broke her heart, but what could she do? He had made his choice. The Lady's price was his to pay.

"I saw a man the day it happened. The day you—" Connie shook her head. "I was here in the back trimming the crabapples, and saw him wandering through the trees out by the bend. Thought at first it might be Old Tom, but he never goes near the river." She walked to the plastic chest by the back door and took out a bucket of bird-seed and a scoop. As always, she found it easier to talk if she concentrated on something else. "I've seen him every day since. And if he's up here walking around, he can't be in the Cateman cellar, can he?" She hefted the bucket and walked to the feeder. "It's him, isn't it? Mr. Lumpy?" She winced as her brother's stink found her, the dank smell of root cellar.

Do you want to meet him?

Connie dropped the filled scoop as Jim's voice filled her head; it hit the ground, seed scattering. "Not really, if it's all the same to you." She dug a piece of cardboard out of the chest, used it to sweep the seed into piles and push it onto the scoop. "I need to tell Virginia I seen him. She's going to yell at me for waiting this long, but I wanted to get you home first. If I told her while you were still at the morgue, she'd have done something to get Leaf mad, and he would've fixed it so I'd never get you back. You need to be here, Jim. Alive or not, we're going to need you. It's just the four of us, you and me and Virginia and Lolly. We need to stick together however we can."

But I've told him about you. Jim's mouth moved now, but it was out of sync with his words, like one of those old dubbed Japanese monster movies. *He said you know him.*

"That's not true. I only know what Matt told us." Connie dropped the seed bucket and backed away as Jim circled the feeder and moved toward her. "That he was bad. Anyone who saw him would know he was bad—nobody good looks like that."

He looks like that because we hurt him.

"I had nothing to do with hurting him. Besides, Matt said that was just a story made up by the Catemans. We're supposed to think he's a good guy, but he's not. He's bad. If we release him, he'll kill us all."

Matt lied to us.

"He left us." Connie finished cleaning up the seed, then carried the bucket to the feeder. "Doesn't mean he lied. Just means he left."

"He's dead."

Connie stumbled back, caught hold of the deck railing just in time to keep from falling. Turned, and spotted a girl standing at the edge of the yard where grass merged with weeds. A young girl, age eight or nine, dressed for summer in denim shorts and a sleeveless red top, shoulder-length brown hair parted in the middle and gathered into pigtails. She couldn't see what shoes the girl wore, but knew they would be white sandals with red ladybugs embroidered on the straps because they'd been her favorites and she had worn them rain or shine. "No. No, you can't be—"

Unlike Jim, the girl seemed alive—the breeze ruffled her hair and she cast a shadow that shifted as she moved. "He's back. Give him what he wants. Let him in, and he'll never seek back again."

"You can't be real." Connie pointed to herself. "You're me and I grew up and I'm here now. *You can't be real.*"

"I'm more real than you." The girl that Connie Petersbury had been stuck out her tongue, then turned and darted through the shrubbery and vanished into the trees, now heavy with leaves in all shades of green.

Connie felt the heat on her skin, the humid weight of summer air. She looked back toward the yard to find Jim gone and the spilled seed vanished and a ceramic birdbath standing where the feeder had been. "Jim broke you." Her voice shook. "He got drunk with Ginny and Lolly and Johnny Hoard, and he tried to sneak in through the back and fell over you and you broke and Daddy made him wear a big piece of you on his head like a hat for a week."

She looked at the house, saw the kitchen curtains flutter through the open window. Yellow gingham, just like the ones her mother had made from the bolt of cloth Emma Cateman had given her just before she disappeared.

Run. But where? She had set her wards like a good witch, but not against her brother. Not against herself. "You bastard." She looked toward the woods, where thirty-seven years before she had seen a man. A man with a lumpy face.

Run. If she could make it out to the road, she would be free. She only had to get past the house—except that now it looked as it had when she was little, chalk white with dark blue trim. And she knew that her Chevy truck would be gone from the driveway, replaced by her father's old green Ford. Knew if she made it to the front yard, she would see her father there, and he would ask her—

"Why didn't you stop him, girl? He was your brother."

"I tried, Mama." Connie walked to the kitchen window, where her late mother stood framed by yellow gingham. Deborah Petersbury looked as she had when she and Emma used to pal around, brown hair gathered in a braid draped over one shoulder, white peasant blouse embroidered in red. "But he stopped listening to me years ago."

"You didn't try hard enough." Deborah Petersbury's face receded into the dark. "But it's all right. He still wants to meet you."

"Well, I don't want to meet him." Connie drew closer to the house, tried to look in the window. "Mama—"

The scream shredded the air, a young girl's cry. Connie took one last look toward the road, toward freedom. Safety. Then she wheeled and ran through the weeds and into the woods toward the sound. Branches slapped her face—she felt their sting, the trickles of blood where they slashed her. She left the path and ran toward the place where she'd played as a girl, the clearing near the river bend where she had first seen the lumpy-faced man.

"I'm coming!" Thorns ripped at Connie's coat and tore her hands as she pushed through a thicket of old rosebushes and into the clearing. Saw the girl she had been standing there, face screwed up and mouth agape, ready to scream again.

"You can stop now."

Young Connie shut her mouth, then looked up at her older self with a sly smile.

"I told you she'd come." A young boy stepped out from behind a rosebush. "They always come when you cry out. You can count on it."

Connie tried to place the boy, but Gideon had few children of any age and he wasn't one of them. She would have remembered. His clothes were simple, a white T-shirt, jeans, and sneakers. But his face was something from a painting or statue, molded bone and skin like ivory touched with rose, framed by a head of glossy black hair. She stared and some deep part of her stirred and she wondered at the man he would become, what the skin and hair would feel like even now to touch. Then she saw the flicker in the boy's eyes, the dark blue of deep water and so much older than the rest of him, and knew that he read her thoughts, and what was worse, understood them.

Oh, let me in. . .

"Come with me." Connie reached out to her younger self. "I have to take you out of here." She waited for the touch of a smaller hand in hers, and when she didn't feel it looked to the place where the girl had been, and found her gone. "What did you do to her?"

"I don't need her anymore. You're here now." The young boy smiled. "You're safe."

"Safe from what? Safe from who?" Connie stopped as voices drifted from the distance. She looked in the direction she had come, and saw Virginia Waycross wandering amid the trees, voice rising and falling and bouncing like echoes in a canyon. She still wore Mike's barn coat, but her other clothes had changed. She had put on her old White Sox cap, a tan shirt, and old brown cords instead of jeans.

Connie started toward her, but as she walked the air grew thicker and thicker. "I'm here, Virginia!" She struggled to breathe, fought for every step. "Virginia!" But her friend kept walking in the opposite direction, and disappeared among the trees.

She can't hear you.

Connie shivered as the voice filled her head. Felt the chill drift of air, smelled crawl-space stink. "Jim? Virginia's wearing different clothes. How long have I been here?"

Time's different here. Jim drew alongside. *You've crossed the border into the wilderness.*

"I can't be in the wilderness. I'm still alive. You can only enter the wilderness after you . . . die." Connie reached out and pressed her hand against air that felt as solid as a wall. "Why? I don't understand."

We sang his song. We let him in. Bloody tears coursed down Jim's face as the summer sun faded and the sky clouded and the breeze grew cold. *Everything that happens from here on is our fault.* Shadows flickered amid the trees, then stepped out into the dimming light. Norma and Junior, Ashley and the girls, their faces grayed and grinning.

"Jim, please." Connie cried as her family crowded around her, tugging at her with their clawed hands, pulling her deeper and deeper into the gloom. *"I didn't do anything wrong."*

We let him in. Jim pushed her from behind, deeper into the gloom. *Now we can't let you out.*

14

Lauren had intended to drive the two thousand miles from Seattle to Gideon nonstop, but even though the weather behaved and roads remained passable, the panicked energy behind that idea petered out after sixteen hours. So she stopped at a hardware store on the outskirts of Rapid City, South Dakota, and bought a bag of garden-stake twist ties. Then, images of *Psycho*-grade motels dancing in her head, she booked a room at the fanciest suites-style hotel she could find, wedged a chair beneath the door handle, then sat on the bed and ate a drive-through dinner as she worked the entire bag of ties into wire circlet eyes. When she finished, she scattered the eyes around the room, then turned on every light and lamp, and fell asleep reading her father's book.

The next day, she gathered up the circlets and stashed them in the empty food sack, then watched for the lurking living and the walking, talking dead as she headed to her car. Her only greeter, however, proved to be a crow, which hopped after her, wings spread for balance, cawing and cackling. She tossed it her leftover dinner, and it stuffed its beak with as many french fries as it could manage before taking wing and settling in a nearby tree.

Lauren watched the bird for a few minutes. No other crows disturbed it, so it took its time setting out the fries across the branch, then chomping them one by one. It looked the same as the crows she had seen in her parents' front yard and outside the coffee shop, but that was only because one large, black bird looked much like another to her. She hadn't looked closely until now and could see no distinguishing marks that would serve to identify it. Were they all the same crow?

The bird of the Lady. Something she had read in the book the previous night. *"And the Lady said, 'You will be my eyes and ears in the mortal world.'"* Crows were her messengers, her watchers. Their presence was a sign of her grace.

"Guess I'm blessed." Lauren loaded her suitcase into the trunk. "Hold that thought." She spotted her father's leather jacket scrunched in one corner, took it out, and put it on. Then she tossed a few of the wire circlets around the interior of the car, shoved the rest under her seat, and resumed her drive.

SNOW SQUALLS DOGGED Lauren across the Plains, but when she crossed into Illinois, the sky cleared. I-88 to state roads to two-lane roads, from the towns large and small to scatters of buildings that wouldn't show up on any map. The GPS rattled off official road numbers in its femme android voice, but the signs themselves displayed different names: HOARD'S FIELD. RED BARN. OLD ORCHARD ROAD.

It was around that time that the satellite radio started to crackle and hiss. Lauren hit the scan button repeatedly, trying to find a clear station, but the sparkly tech may as well have been an antique AM transistor for all the good it did. Finally, when the hiss altered to a high-pitched whine that set her teeth on edge, she turned it off, leaving her with the GPS voice and her own thoughts for company.

As she drew closer to Gideon, her surroundings changed. Open farmland altered to wooded field and forest, stands of apple, oak, and ash mingled with spruce. The road banked and rolled, curving in tandem with the river now visible through the trees. First came the Rock, wide and slow flowing, lined with parks and rest stops. Then,

"About five, ten miles up the road."

Lauren bit back a sharp reply, and took a deep breath. "Is there anyplace closer?"

The man remained silent. Stooped and spindle thin, he shifted a rusty metal toolbox from one hand to the other as his directional gestures demanded. "Lolly's place, two miles that way." He jerked his thumb down the road. He could have been any age from a hard-used sixty to a spry eighty, cheeks reddened from cold and exertion, jacket hanging off coat-hanger shoulders and silver hair poking out from beneath a flap-eared cap.

Lolly. The image in the book, the angry kid with the crew cut. "Thanks." Lauren spread the plastic bag across her seat. "Do you know who put up the sign?"

"I did." The man drew up straight, then stepped out into the middle of the road. "It's the duty of we her children to spread the Lady's word."

As the man drew closer, Lauren could see the stains on his jacket and trousers, a combination of grime and various spills. Silvery stubble dotted his cheeks and chin, accentuating the rash that spread across his face like sunburn. *One of Gideon's witches?* Or just a strange old man who didn't like strangers? "Not very welcoming, is it?" She jerked her head toward the sign, its colors harsh against the dull foliage.

The man stopped, coughed, spit. "Any reason why we should?"

"Why you should what?"

"Welcome you?"

Common decency? Lauren started to get into her car when the squawk of an unseen crow sounded. She scanned the trees for any sign of the bird, but saw no movement amid the bare branches and the odd fringe of evergreen.

"Listen to that." For the first time, a spark of life lightened the old man's face. "But you try to get them to come this far down the road. Just try." He limped toward the sound. "I cut up a possum and spread it along t'fence t'other day. Guts and all, the way they like." He pointed across the road to the fence in question, obscured by overgrowth. "They didn't go anywhere near it. Didn't even call out. Just watched me from way over in the field, all quiet. Wouldn't even fly over to see what was going on."

Lauren squinted through a tangle of branches until she saw the reddish lumps of flesh and strings of intestine hanging from the barbed wire. A tiny head, mouth gaping. She swallowed hard. "You hunt possum?"

"Hunt? Pah! You don't waste good lead on vermin." The man mimed a quick downward thrust. "Shovel blade to the back of the neck. That's how you kill vermin." He searched for the crows for a bit longer, then craned his neck so that he could see Lauren's license plate. "Washington State. You come a ways, Miss—?"

Lauren nodded, eventually. "Yep." Since the man hadn't told her his name, she had no intention of telling him hers. "Why don't the crows come closer?"

"Because they're *smart*." The man hacked and spit again, then pulled a rag from his jacket pocket and wiped his mouth. "You smart as a crow?" He continued to dab his lips with the rag as he watched her.

That's open for debate. Lauren listened for a few moments more, but the crow had either flown off or settled into silence. She got into her car, pulled out into the road, and headed toward Gideon. Checked the rearview to find the old man walking on the spot where she had parked. He kicked at the grass, then bent slowly and picked up something. Then he spit one more time and vanished into the trees.

THE NAMELESS ROAD curved and meandered up and down, back and forth. Lauren passed vacant houses obscured by overgrowth, the burned-out shell of some business or other.

Then, with no warning, she came upon a rise that overlooked Gideon's town square, a bare, brown space ringed by a scatter of businesses. Beyond that, a few large homes showed through the leafless trees, dull brick Federals and a Victorian painted lady, ruby red trim bright as fresh scars.

Lauren pulled over to the side of the road. She had tried to survey Gideon online, but what images she found had been blurry, the buildings hidden by trees. She had planned to stay at a local motel or bed-and-breakfast and get the feel for the place before looking up the people her father had noted in his book. But there was no place to get a feel for, no neighborhoods to wander. Thirty-seven years ago, Gideon had been large enough to support a high school. Now it was a smudge on a map that you passed through on the way to somewhere else.

Lauren watched a single pickup truck drift down the street that circled the square and disappear around a corner. Then her gaze moved to her dashboard and settled on the fuel gauge. She knew that the tank had been well over half full when she stopped to check out the sign, but the needle had moved below that point and now hovered around the one-third mark.

Dubuque. She had filled the tank just outside Dubuque. She did some quick math in her head, swore, and got out of the car and checked underneath for leaks, sniffed for any hint of gasoline stink. Walked down the road and searched the broken asphalt for drips, but found none.

Bad sensor. A problem with the gauge. *How the hell do I know?* Lauren paced back and forth. *Lolly's.* The gas station the old man had told her about—maybe they did repairs as well, or could at least diagnose the problem. Gideon didn't look like a pedestrian-friendly sort of place. From what she had seen so far, it didn't even have sidewalks. She needed a car.

She looked out over the town, the old man's words ringing in her ears. *Any reason why we should welcome you?* As if he had been lurking in the woods awaiting her arrival. As if he knew why she had come.

Don't be an idiot. She got back in her car, fought the urge to floor the accelerator and take off. Instead, she checked her phone, watched the display flicker and fade in and out. No, she couldn't flee. She had to stay put until she knew what had gone wrong with her car. She couldn't risk breaking down on a back road. She didn't want to run into the old man again. Or someone even weirder.

Or someone even worse.

Lauren eased the car down the slope and edged around the square, one eye on the fuel gauge. Gideon appeared deserted but for a battered van and a couple of pickup trucks in the parking lot of a diner. The hardware store next door looked dark, empty. The feed store. She turned down a rutted side street and spotted a pair of gas pumps in front of a whitewashed concrete box, LOLL'S GARAGE painted in black block letters on the side. She pulled into the dirt-and-gravel front yard, got out of the car and knocked on the door, peered through the window. Found no sign that anyone was there.

After a little more pondering, Lauren returned to her car. She swept up the wire circlets that she had scattered about the interior and stuffed them in her pocket, collected her handbag, locked up, then trudged down the road toward the diner, a rickety clapboard sprawl with the name HOARD'S GRILL blinking in red and blue neon in the front window. Heard voices as she drew closer, the crosscut of argument.

"—need to check the river—"

"—ain't going down there no fuckin' way—"

"—call the sheriff—"

Lauren hesitated at the entry, hand hovering over the latch. Then she pushed open the door. An entry bell jangled. Silence fell.

"Are you open?" She blinked until her eyes adjusted to the half-light, swallowed hard as she inhaled the weighty aromas of old coffee and cooking fat. The dining room looked like any other, with a counter along the near wall and a line of booths opposite, Formica-and-chrome tables clustered in the center. Four men sat at the far end of the counter while a young woman stood by one of the tables, a tray of salt and pepper shakers in hand.

"We're not serving." The young woman placed a set of shakers on the table, then moved to the next. "Cook's out." She eyed Lauren up and down, and frowned. "Won't be back until five." She looked about twenty, with streaked light brown hair gathered in a ponytail and a curvy figure packed into black jeans and a white V-neck sweater.

"Thanks—I didn't come here to eat." Lauren pointed in the direction of the garage. "I'm looking for Mr. Loll. My car's acting up, and—"

"What kind is it?" One of the men stood. Bulky and bearded, the crew cut grown into a mess of dirty blond curls, Lolly wore dark blue coveralls topped with a battered black parka. "Your car." He lumbered toward her, eyes straight ahead. "What kind?" He had seemed sullen enough in her father's drawing, but in person he radiated anger, the threat of explosion beneath the surface.

Lauren stepped back as he brushed past, trailing stale cigarette smoke and peppermint. "It's an Outback. Subaru."

"Foreign." Lolly stopped at the end of the counter near the cash register. "Don't work on much foreign around here. Fords. Chevys." He dug into the pocket of his coverall, pulled out a couple of crumpled bills, and tossed them on the counter.

"Jorie Cateman drives that Range Rover," one of the other men offered. He sat against the wall, his face in the shadows.

"Yeah, but she don't bring it to me for service, does she?" Lolly sniffed. "Takes it up to Rockford." He shrugged. "I'll look at it. Later today. No promises. Likely have to have it towed somewhere."

"It runs. It's not leaking. I think it's just the gauge."

"I'll look at it. Later today." Lolly held out his hand. "Keys?"

Lauren hesitated, then handed her keys to him. Yes, she had cleaned up the wire circlets, but she wondered if she had left anything else in the car that might give her away. *The book?* She felt the heft of it in her handbag. Sensed the weight of a stare, and looked into rheumy eyes, pale blue and rimmed in red.

"No promises." Lolly gave her one last searching look, then stuffed her keys in his pocket and started for the door.

"We're meeting at the bend in one hour, Lolly," another of the men called after him.

Lolly stopped. "I said what I think." He didn't turn around, but spoke to the door, his breath leaving a haze of condensation on the window. "It's time for the sheriff. Better to call them before they come around asking—"

"*Lolly.*" The young woman's voice bit.

Lolly glanced sidelong at Lauren. "Yeah." He pushed the door open. "Better keep our mouths shut. 'Cause keeping quiet's worked so good up to now." He let the door slam behind him and headed in the direction of the garage.

Lauren walked to the nearest table and sat. Sensed the men watching her as she unzipped her jacket and opened it without taking it off.

"You want anything?" The young woman had finished setting out the shakers, and now straightened up behind the counter.

"Coffee, please." A sense of dull dread had settled. Numbness, like a weight on the soul. Lauren had felt it as soon as she entered. It reminded her of that hell just three short weeks before, when she sat with her father in the doctor's office and waited for the final damning diagnosis.

"We've got cold stuff. Doughnuts. Cereal."

"No, thanks." Lauren wrapped her hands around the mug the young woman gave her. Held it under her nose to inhale the warm steam, and coughed as the acrid stench of overcooked brew raked her sinuses. "Did something bad happen today?" She set the mug down, pushed it to the edge of the table.

The young woman stared, eyes narrowed. Before she could reply, the shadowed man stood and walked around the end of the counter. "Which way did you drive into town, if you don't mind my asking?"

What light there was touched his face, erased the shadow, and rendered him a man Lauren's age or a little younger, tall and rangy and red-haired. He wore work clothes, weathered jeans and a green-and-black flannel shirt topped with a down vest in an electric shade of orange.

"West." Lauren pointed in the direction she had come. "Only sign I saw was a little billboard. 'Beware the Outsider.'"

"Sounds like ol' Tom's been taking the street signs down and putting up his own," one of the other men muttered. "Again."

"You were on Old Main Road." The redhead perched on the stool closest to Lauren's table. "Did you happen to see anyone on the way in?"

"An old man carrying a toolbox."

"That was old Tom. Tom Barton." The man held out his hand. "I'm Dylan Corey."

Lauren hesitated, then shook Corey's hand. Strong fingers enclosed hers, the palm callused, knuckles scuffed and dotted with scabs. She felt his warmth like the sun through glass, the gentle heat of a banked fire. Then she heard a quiet voice that seemed to emanate from inside her head.

Your hand is so cold—well, you know what they say.

Lauren looked up, met eyes the brown side of hazel, deep-set in a long, serious face, and felt the blush rise. Sensed a different sort of heat from across the room, and glanced at the young waitress to find her glaring back, the dish towel she held twisted into a knot.

"Did you see anyone else?" Corey's voice came soft, as though they were the only two people in the room.

"No." Lauren eased out of his grip. "But I didn't really look. I was worried about my car."

"Did you notice anything strange at all? Anything about the sky or—"

"Dylan." The waitress spoke more gently than she had to Lolly, but her tone held the same warning.

Corey ignored her. "A sense that someone watched you, someone you couldn't see?"

"Is someone missing?" Lauren felt the stares of the other men, the young woman's growing anger. "A child?"

"No." Corey moved from the stool to the chair next to hers. "A friend of ours. We're worried because—"

"*Dylan.*"

"*Dammit, Deena, shut up.*" Corey hung his head, scrubbed a hand over his face. "I'm sorry, but you know Mistress—" He stopped, chewed his lip for a moment. "Miz Waycross told us to do all we could. Leave no stone unturned." He looked at Lauren, his eyes holding the same pain as Lolly's, the same bewildered questioning. "Her name's Connie Petersbury. She's in her midforties. Short gray hair. About five foot nothing. You probably heard about her brother on the news."

The little girl with pigtails. Lauren shook her head, eventually. "I've been driving for two days. I haven't listened to much news."

"Well, he—died. He died, and—"

"He killed Norma and Junior and Ashley and the girls." One of the other men, a skinny blond in cords and battered leather jacket, swung around on his stool to face them. "He killed them, Dylan. Then he killed himself. Lying about it won't make it easier to take."

"I wasn't lying, Phil. I just—" Corey sighed. "You didn't see a woman walking along the road, or wandering through the trees, or anything?"

Lauren struggled to recall any flicker of color amid the dull gray and brown of winter-bare woods. "No. I'm sorry."

"She doesn't know anything. Leave her be." Phil rose and walked to the door. He wore cowboy boots, the taps on the soles clicking like snapping fingers, the sound bouncing off the walls. "We need to get back out there. Only got a few hours of daylight left." He stopped to pay his bill. "You driving, Zeke?"

"Yeah." The fourth man slid off his stool, then paused to crack his back before trudging after his companion. He was older than the rest, white-haired and wrinkled, jeans and barn coat patched and shabby. On his way to the door, he looked at Lauren, and his step slowed. "You used to live around here?"

"No." Lauren fought the urge to look away as Zeke continued to stare. "First time in Illinois."

"I'd ask, 'Are you sure?' but I guess you'd know, wouldn't you?" Zeke gave her a last, probing look, then followed the other man outside.

Lauren waited for the door to close, for the men to disappear from view. Zeke would have been well into middle age at the time Matthew Mullin left Gideon. He had likely known him. *I took after Mom. Everyone said so.* Heart-shaped face. Wavy, dark brown hair. Curves instead of angles. No possibility that anyone would recognize her.

"What are you going to do without your car?" Corey stood. "Do you have any friends you can call?"

"I was just passing through. Headed to New York." Her first outright lie. She had to make sure she remembered. "I don't know anyone local." Corey's scent drifted around her, a blue odor like seawater that made her heart flutter. "Are there any motels nearby?"

"Not for miles. We're sort of off the beaten track here." Corey continued to hover, hands drifting in and out of his vest pockets.

"Cabs? Car rental?"

"Um, no."

"She can't stay here." Deena slammed cupboard doors, then pulled on her coat, swearing as an arm got stuck in a sleeve. "I need to lock up so I can go back out and help with the search."

Lauren dug her wallet out of her handbag. "I still have to pay for the coffee."

"On the house." Deena walked to the door, pushed it open, and stood waiting. Did everything but check her watch and tap her feet.

"*Deena.*" Corey rolled his eyes.

"She can't stay here—Johnny'll kill me." Deena smirked. "It's the insurance. No customers allowed in the place without an employee present."

"Did you just make that up?" Corey glared at the young woman, then waved Lauren ahead of him. "Let's go."

The mist had thickened so it fell like rain, whispering through the air, muffling every sound. Lauren wore a hooded sweatshirt under her father's jacket; she pulled up the hood and zipped the jacket to the neck, but the cold still seeped through. "Is that all you're going to wear?" She pointed to Corey's vest.

"I've got a jacket in my truck." Corey patted the vest as he dug keys out of the pocket. "Hunting season. We all have to wear these this time of year. It's a sign that we're not on the menu."

"Is your friend wearing one?" Lauren caught the flicker in Corey's eyes. "Maybe Mr. Loll is right. You should call the sheriff."

"Wouldn't do any good. She's not officially missing yet. Besides, Miz Waycross says we should keep looking until there's no place else to look."

"You called her 'Mistress' before."

"I work for her. It's just a term of respect. Like ma'am." Corey walked to a dark red pickup with a gold *W* done in block lettering on the driver's-side door. "I don't want you to think—oh, boy—that I'm being forward, or trying to pull something. It's just—" He paused, his hand on the hood. "My house isn't too far from here. You're welcome to wait there until Lolly checks out your car."

"I couldn't." Lauren looked toward Lolly's to find the parking lot empty, which meant he had already pulled her car into the garage and departed. *Reardon, you genius.* Now she was stuck. She should never have given him her keys.

"I don't mean this the way it sounds, but where else are you going to go?" Corey pointed toward the desolate main street. "We're all helping with the search, so all the stores are closed. Lolly's is locked up. No one's here, and we can't have you wandering around by yourself."

"Why not."

"Because it's not safe." Corey unlocked the truck, opened the door, and pulled out his coat. "The woods around here. They're not safe." He removed the vest, donned his coat, then dragged the vest back over it.

"Is that why Tom Barton posts those signs? Because of the danger?"

"Tom Barton posts those signs because he's a crazy old man."

Lauren paced beside Corey's truck, shoes crunching on the gravel, as every "Good Samaritan gone bad" story she had ever read surfaced from the depths of memory. *I can take care of myself if he tries anything.* But she would be in his house. On his turf. At his mercy. "Lolly's got my keys. My suitcase is locked up."

"So it'll be safe until I bring you back here later." Corey walked around to the passenger side of the truck and opened the door.

"I don't want to be a bother."

"You'll be more of a bother if you're out wandering around."

Lauren met Corey's gaze. Hunted for any hint of agitation or anger, but sensed only sadness and concern and an undercurrent of fear. Stepped around the truck until she could see the inside of the door, and checked that the old-fashioned crank handles were all still attached and in the right places.

Corey reached for her as she approached, taking her arm to assist her as she stepped up into the cab. Funny the things that helped you decide. How one touch made you angry and another made you pull away.

Then there were the touches that you didn't mind at all.

"Good." Corey waited until Lauren buckled her seat belt. "One less thing to think about." He flashed his first smile and his eyes lit, allowing a glimpse of the man he would be if the worry released its hold.

Lauren adjusted her heat vent as soon as Corey started the truck, opening it wide and pointing it toward her. The old leather seat crackled as she shifted. Bits of hay lay scattered over the floor mats. A couple of crumpled fast-food sacks.

She pulled down her visor and checked her face in the mirror. Fear had settled in her bones and she needed sleep and wore no makeup and it all showed. The dark smudges beneath her eyes. The dull skin.

Then she caught movement, and spotted Deena in the diner parking lot, watching them leave. She leaned against a beat-up blue Escort, arms folded, lips moving and one hand twitching, signing shapes and symbols in the mist.

15

Dylan Corey's house was located a mile or so outside Gideon, on a dirt-and-gravel path just off the Old Main Road. It stood atop a bluff overlooking a bend in the River Ann, a dark brown L-shaped wood frame that followed the curve of the summit's edge. One wing contained two bedrooms and a bathroom, the other, the kitchen and living room. There was a one-car detached garage, half hidden in the woods, and a ramshackle storage shed next to it.

"It's not much." Corey unlocked the door, then stood aside to let Lauren enter. "The only places worth a damn around here are the big houses in town, and it'll be a bright day in the wilderness when I can afford one of those."

"Is that a local saying?" Lauren walked around the living room, which contained a beaten-up leather couch, a coffee table, a floor lamp, and a line of packing boxes shoved haphazardly against one bare, white wall. "I've never heard it before."

"Gideon nights can be pretty dark, that's all. We're in the middle of nowhere out here." Corey slipped around her and pushed the boxes farther into the corner. "Sorry about the mess. I just moved in last week and I haven't had time to unpack everything." He picked up a T-shirt that lay draped over the arm of the couch. "Mistress Waycross gave me some of her old furniture to tide me over until I can get my own."

Lauren set her handbag on the couch, then walked across the room to a set of glass doors that opened onto a deck overlooking the river. "Nice view." She opened one of the doors, breathed in the chilly damp. Overhead, wet branches shed their drops like a second rain, and the patter of the water hitting the roof combined with the soft roar of the flowing water to compose an all-too-familiar sound track. "It's so much like home, it's almost funny."

"Where is home?" Corey fidgeted with the T-shirt, folding it over his arm and draping it over his shoulder before finally tossing it into one of the boxes.

"Seattle." Lauren closed the door and turned her back on the scenery, pushed thoughts of Katie and Paul and the rest of her friends from her mind. But that left other memories to fill in the gap. Her father's final days. Dilys's broken body. *And now Connie Petersbury, the little girl grown.* Lauren rubbed her eyes, as if that could erase the images. It worked as well as it ever did.

"Washington? You've come just about as far as you possibly can, haven't you?" Corey joined Lauren at the window. "What's in New York?"

"New York?" Lauren stared at Corey until he arched his brow and gave her a questioning half smile. "Oh." She turned back to the view out the window, knocked her forehead against the glass. She always had been a lousy liar. "Nothing in particular." She hugged herself, then rubbed her arms. Her whole body felt itchy, as though she wore wool against her bare skin. "I needed to get away, so I just got in the car and headed east."

"I know that feeling. Just can't do anything about it." Corey stared at nothing. Then his gaze drifted down. "Take a tumble somewhere?"

Lauren felt the muddy swath across the seat of her pants. It had dried stiff and crumbled to her touch, leaving a coating of dirt on her hand. "I fell in a ditch when I got out of the car to see what the sign said."

"Old Tom's signs." Corey shook his head. "I've seen people stop and take pictures."

"He doesn't like strangers?"

"He's an old man. No family. Nothing to do all day but read his book and wallow in his thoughts and prepare for the end times."

"His book? Which book is that?"

Corey didn't answer. Instead, he looked out toward the river, then glanced at his watch. "I need to get going." He started toward the door, then stopped, rocking slightly to and fro as if unsure what to do next.

Lauren walked to the couch and tried perching on the arm, but dried mud flaked off her pants and powdered across the upholstery. "You're worried." She brushed it away, then returned to the window and leaned against the cold glass. "About your friend."

"Of course I am." Corey's voice came harsh, and he raised a hand in apology. "It gets dark so early in the winter. Things happen in the dark." Concern clouded his face, etched lines along the sides of his mouth, dulled his eyes. "Do you believe that a place can be bad? That it can be cursed?"

"I don't know. Maybe." Lauren wanted to say more, but she couldn't let on why she had come to Gideon, that she knew the reason behind the haunted look in Dylan Corey's eyes.

"My grandfather used to say that the wilderness was a dark place, so at night the darkness favored them that came from there." Corey looked past Lauren to the woods beyond. "Even if you stick close, you can't be sure the person you walked in with will be the same one who walks out."

"You make it sound as though the woods are haunted." Before Lauren could say more, she caught movement from the corner of her eye. Out on the deck, a squirrel had leaped onto a weathered bird feeder, sending it rocking. The thing had been fashioned from a length of metal pipe that hung from a wire, and it swung toward her, low and fast, like an arm emerging from shadow. A hand reaching for her throat. "Haunted." Her voice cracked. She looked back at Corey to see if he noticed, but found him rummaging through one of the boxes.

"It's winter days, that's all I meant. The dark comes early. Preys on your mind." Corey straightened, a small nylon pack in hand. "You can make coffee." He pointed toward the kitchen. "And there's stuff in the freezer if you get hungry. Microwave. No TV, but the radio still works."

"Does it?" Lauren turned, pressed her back to the glass. "My satellite radio gave me trouble on the way in. Then the GPS went out."

"Sometimes we have problems out here. One of the joys of being out in the middle of nowhere." Corey shoved the pack in his vest pocket and walked to the door. "Just please, don't leave."

Lauren followed him. "I've worked on search-and-rescue teams before. I could help."

"No."

"Please?"

Corey wheeled. "*No.*" Another apologetic wave. "We appreciate the offer, but this isn't your problem." He gave her one last, long look. "I'm afraid you picked a bad day to come to Gideon." With that, he left, pulling the door closed after him.

Lauren listened to the rattle of keys, the metal slip of the dead bolt. She walked to the front window and watched Corey's truck back out of the driveway and disappear from sight, then unlocked the door and pushed it open, just to make sure he hadn't trapped her. Closed it again and locked it, and sensed the resonances of a strange house. Now the patter of rain on the roof reminded her of the skitter of footsteps, the scrape of branches against wood siding, the scratch of claws.

Lauren swore, pushed open the glass doors, and walked out on the deck. Scanned the roof. Of course, there was nothing to see but shingles glistening in the watery daylight, tree branches shuddering with each sweep of wind.

Then she looked toward the river and the bare woods beyond. Sometimes a finch or a cardinal would flit past, or a squirrel would pop up from behind a log. Normal forest sights and sounds. Nothing out of the ordinary.

Are you out there, Connie Petersbury? Lauren wondered if the woman wore protection from the wet and cold, a waterproof coat, a hat and gloves. Or had she gone wandering in her indoor clothes, wool and cotton and flannel, that held on to moisture like a sponge, trapped the cold and kept it close. One fall in the river would be enough, a slip in a shallow pool. A person could perish from hypothermia in fifty-degree temperatures if enough things went wrong, and things tended to go wrong in the wilderness. Especially if you were distraught. Not paying attention.

Lauren went back inside and started her search for the sorts of things an outdoorsman like Dylan Corey would have on hand. Compasses. Radios. Utility knives. Whistles. Tried not to think about the hiking pack she kept stashed in the trunk of her car, the nylon bag filled with fatwood sticks and matches, small tools and water and high-calorie snacks. Perfect for a search, for warming up and feeding a scared woman as they waited for rescue. All locked away in Loll's garage, where they were of no use to anyone.

No use kicking myself now. From the living room, she moved on to Corey's bedroom. It proved just as bare, the only furniture an old dresser and a full-size bed covered with a homemade quilt. As she hunted through the dresser, she pulled out the drawers and turned them over, on the lookout for her dad's sign. But she found no X-centered circles, only the imprint of a commercial furniture maker. She also kept an eye out for oddities, bits of knotted string or scraps of paper filled with weird doodles. *Are you one of Gideon's witches, Mr. Corey?* If he was, he had left behind no obvious evidence.

Lauren dug a waterproof windshirt and matching pants out of the closet and pulled them on. Added a cherry-red vest, then caught sight of her bulky form in the dresser mirror.

I look ridiculous. She was going to hike through woods outside a small town, not the depths of an Olympic Peninsula rain forest. But even as she argued with herself, she stuffed more warm clothes and extra socks in a backpack freed from the closet shelf. Liberated first-aid supplies from the bathroom. Moved on to the kitchen, and gathered a carving knife, scissors, protein bars. A roll of bright yellow tape, the sort that forest crews used to mark burn zones. Checked her watch again, and calculated the daylight remaining.

Do you believe that a place can be bad? Corey's words echoed in her head as she removed her father's book from her handbag and tucked it into the front pocket of the backpack, then packed everything else. All except the knife, which she tucked into her belt, and the roll of tape, which she shoved over her hand and up her arm like a bracelet.

She left the house through a side door and walked down the sloping front yard to the wheel-rutted excuse for a road. Heard nothing but the crunch of her footsteps and the rush of the river, muffled by distance and damp air. Took out her phone, watched the display flicker and the bars flat-line, felt a physical ache as she shoved it back in her pocket. She never realized how much she could miss the damn thing, how she had come to depend on it.

Now she squinted into the woods past the dead end of the road. Winter-killed leaves and undergrowth meant clear lines of sight—she guessed a quarter-mile visibility or more before fallen limbs and the rise and fall of the land finally blocked her view. *Which way's north?* She scanned the sky, picked out the fuzzy light of the sun smeared behind cloud like a broken egg yolk. Four hours of daylight left, two if she figured in the existing murk.

Do you believe that a place can be bad?

Just before Lauren entered the woods, she thought about digging out one of the wire circlets, just to have it to hold on to. Instead, she yanked a few leaves of dead grass from a clump at her feet and fashioned them into an X-centered circle. A few twists of the wrist and done. She could have made one in her sleep at this point.

She took a step forward, then stopped. A buzzing filled her head like the sounds of insects on a summer's day, and the urge to turn around and walk back to the house grabbed her and held on tight.

Do you believe that a place can be bad?

"Yes." Lauren slipped the knife out of her belt and headed down the slope toward the river.

16

Lauren's nerves steadied as she ventured deeper into the woods, quieted by the wet crunch of undergrowth beneath her boots and the occasional squirrel sighting. Nothing bad would happen if she could still see squirrels. The jumpy little critters would be the first to scatter if anything dangerous showed up.

She followed a path that ran along the river, stopping every so often to mark her trail by twisting a length of the tape around a branch. It felt colder here—she could sense the temperature drop even through the vest and jackets. The air smelled dank, like a crawl space long closed, and though dried leaves fluttered and mist fingered through the treetops, she couldn't feel the breeze that drove them.

Lauren looked back toward Corey's house, and found she had already lost sight of it. Odd. She had been walking only a few minutes, in a straight line heading north—she should still have been able to see the bluff. *Backtrack.* She could still see the last piece of tape she had placed, the neon yellow bright against the dull brown of wood and dead foliage. But even so, she may have veered in the wrong direction or taken a wrong turn.

She checked her watch, and stared. According to the time, she had already been walking for well over an hour. *Time-zone change—I forgot to switch from Mountain to Central when I left Rapid City.* No, that wasn't it—she remembered setting her watch ahead the previous day.

Besides, if she had forgotten to do so, it would read an hour earlier, not later.

She looked in all directions, then back the way she had come. The woods seemed different now. Shifted shadows. Strange trees.

She flinched as a squirrel shot across her path. "You lied to me," she called after it as it vanished into the brush. "Some alarm you turned out to be." She started to turn and continue walking, but stopped when one of the trees drew her eye. A storm-blasted trunk half hidden by surrounding growth, it looked like a figure dressed in a robe or long coat. A lone branch stuck out from one side and angled downward, as though it held a stick or cane in one hand.

Is that you, Mr. Lumpy? Lauren stared at the tree until the mists parted and weak sun washed over it, highlighting the shattered branches, the peeling bark. *Just a dead thing.* Even so, she looked back at it every so often until the downward slope of the land blocked it from view.

Another curve of the trail. Another strip of tape. Below, the river tumbled, the water hazed with mud and debris. Lauren scanned the banks for any sign that someone had been there before her, tracks in the mud or a shoe or piece of clothing. She had no idea how long Connie Petersbury had been missing, whether she had been gone for a few hours or a few days. But now she understood the concerns of Corey and the other men. These weren't the same woods she had seen from Corey's deck. This was not a good place.

She squeezed the grass circlet, and felt it crackle. Opened her hand, and saw the thing had dried up, powdered like ash. She wiped away the mess and kept walking. Even her own protections couldn't help her. She truly was on her own.

As Lauren ventured deeper into the woods, she lost sight of the river. Trees closed in from all sides, limbs crisscrossing overhead and blocking what little sunlight managed to work through the clouds. The trail vanished, leaving her to scramble over fallen branches and wade through undergrowth that reached past her knees. No sound but the crumpled paper crackle of her footsteps. No movement. Even the squirrels had disappeared.

Get out of here now. Lauren turned and tried to walk back the way she had come. But trees blocked her path—as she tried to push through them, branches snagged her clothes, scraped her face.

She stopped, backed up, collided with another tree. Where had they come from—they had been close, yes, but not as close as this. Not close enough to touch.

Lauren forced herself still even as a branch shuddered, then drew across her throat like a knife blade. Something tugged at her hair, and she grabbed it and yanked, swearing at the needling pain as strands gave way at the roots. Looked down at the mess wrapped around her fingers.

Tape. The same yellow tape she had been using to mark her trail. *I brushed against a piece after I hung it, and it stuck to my hair.* She told herself that as she turned and saw the strips hanging from the bare branches, fluttering like strange leaves. The blood-smeared strip that she had hung after cutting her hand on the jagged edge of a stump, and the one she had made by sticking two shorter pieces together. The one she had knotted through needle-thin stalks of shrubbery, so that it twisted like a corkscrew.

Lauren held her breath, listened for the sound of footsteps. Watched for any motion or flicker in the shadows. Someone followed her, some creep who had spotted her in Gideon or seen her leave Corey's house. He guessed the direction she would take, collected the tape strips, and hung them where she would be sure to find them.

"I know you're out there." She slipped the knife from her belt. "You can go to hell." Her voice shook, and she stabbed the blade in the nearest tree trunk again and again, trying to shake out the fear. That she had become lost. That someone hunted her, someone, or something, that she couldn't see, couldn't hear.

Couldn't fight.

"Come out, come out, whoever you are!" Lauren pressed against the trees, using them like a wall to shield her back. "Whatever you are." The sky had gone rose and indigo, coloring the filtered light hazy red.

She tightened her grip on the knife. Waited.

A buzzing in her head—that's what she thought at first. Then the sound deepened, broke into bits that formed into words.

"—spread out—take my—join hands—"

Voices. Normal, human voices. Lauren pushed through the trees, stopped at the edge of a clearing that she would have sworn had not been there a few minutes before. Beyond, the land sloped down to a ravine, a place of waist-high brown grasses shot through with winter-stripped bushes.

People stood there in a circle. Twenty-five, maybe thirty—Lauren recognized the men from the diner, Zeke and Phil and Lolly. Deena, who stood between two other younger women at the far side of the circle.

And at the near edge, deep in conversation with a tall, thin, older woman, stood Dylan Corey.

Lauren tucked the knife back in her belt and trotted down the slope. "I know you told me to stay put, but I thought you could use some more help." She slowed and waited for Corey to look at her, but he continued talking to the woman, his voice low and rushed, his eyes downcast.

Lauren watched the pair confer, their heads bent close. The woman talked now while Corey nodded—the exchange had *boss instructs employee* written all over it. *Mistress Waycross, I presume?* Lauren edged closer. "Hello? I don't mean to interrupt, but—" She waved, tried to catch Corey's eye, but he continued to ignore her.

"*Excuse me.*" Lauren tugged Corey's jacket sleeve—tried to tug Corey's sleeve—but the heavy cloth slipped like silk through her fingers.

She tried again.

Again, the cloth slid from her grasp.

Corey frowned, looked down at his sleeve, pulled at the cuff. Looked up at Lauren, then past her toward the woods.

"What's wrong, Dylan?" Waycross looked in Lauren's direction as well, her sharp blue gaze searching, but never settling. Matt Mullin's Gin, the thin, long face aged, the skin weathered, cheeks reddened from the chill. Steel-gray hair, trimmed into a mess of unruly waves. "What do you see?"

"Nothing. I just—" Corey shook his head. "Nothing."

"I'm standing right in front of you." Lauren waved her hand in front of Corey's face. Caught a glimpse of the shirt collar that poked out from beneath his jacket, saw that the green-and-black flannel had been replaced by brick-red corduroy. Why would he have changed in the short time since she had last seen him? *He wasn't wearing that jacket when he left the house either.* And the orange vest was nowhere to be seen.

"What the hell?" Lauren stood back and watched as Waycross and Corey held hands and joined the rest of the circle, whose members all fell silent and drew up straight, attention locked on Waycross like an orchestra's on their conductor.

"My Lady." Waycross's voice shuddered as though she spoke into a headwind. "Your children have lost their way." She raised her hands above her head, the rest of the circle following suit. "Help us find them."

For a long minute, nothing happened. Then the air above the ring of raised hands hazed and turned golden, like mist in the glow of a streetlight. As time passed, the color deepened, grew opaque. Bubbles formed atop the ring, as though the light boiled.

Then one bubble sent forth a shoot—it grew slowly at first, then picked up speed until it stretched for fifty yards or more. It slashed back and forth in wind-whipped fury, then detached from the ring. Another shoot followed. A third. As the last of them burst forth, the first few darted into the woods—one shot over Lauren's head, and she heard the crackle in the air, felt the hair on the back of her neck stand on end.

They didn't drift, these feelers, but moved with a purpose, fanning out, probing through branches and under debris like dogs tracking a scent. Lauren took off after the closest one. She knew that the woods she had entered back at Corey's house were not the ones she ran through now. But the feelers had come from the place she needed to return to. They might lead her to Connie, guide them both back to safety.

There were no trails in these wooded depths, only trees, leafless and dry. Tumbled stumps, gnarled roots like misshapen limbs. A floor of dead foliage that released the weighty stench of decay as Lauren trod through it—every few strides, she felt her boots sink, and tried not to imagine what she had stepped into. All the while, the light tendril wove out and around, probed and prodded from the tops of trees to the forest floor.

Lauren looked over her shoulder, saw nothing but shadow and gloom. She had expected someone to catch up to her by now, but she saw no one, heard no voices or sounds of running. *Maybe I'm doing it wrong.* Maybe she wasn't supposed to follow the light, but wait for it to find Connie Petersbury and lead her back to the clearing. *Too late now.* The trees had closed in after her, blocking the remaining daylight, and her escape route.

Above, the light continued to dip and dance, filling the air with the ozone reek of an approaching storm. Then, with a sound like a finger skimming the rim of a glass, it swooped low and vanished over a rise.

Lauren ran as best she could as branches battered her and the forest-floor mess sucked at her boots. She swore as she looked over the edge of the rise and found it sloped into yet another ravine, this one tree-filled and as dark as a tomb.

Then she heard, in the distance, an oh-so-familiar sound, fresh and alive. The rush and tumble of running water.

The river. Lauren scrambled over the rise and down, half running and half sliding, backpack banging against her shoulder. At the bottom, she met a wall of bushes, with leaves like razors and thorns as long and thick as fingers, that stretched in either direction as far as she could see. She dragged the backpack around and held it in front of her face, tucked her hands in the canvas folds, wished like hell she had leather gloves instead of the thin knitted things she was wearing, then pushed through.

The bushes proved less of a problem than she feared, the leaves shearing away and most of the thorns snapping on impact. But one of the hard spikes drilled through the back of her glove, pierced deep enough to draw blood. She felt the sting, the warm trickle.

Lauren stuffed a tissue into the glove to cover the wound, adjusted the backpack, and brushed mangled leaves and thorns from her clothes. Then she searched for the light—scanned the treetops, listened for the sing, sniffed the air—but it had vanished, abandoning her to the gathering dark. That left the river as her lifeline. It ran past Corey's house—if it still behaved according to real-world rules, she could follow it back there.

But what if it didn't?

She followed the sound of moving water through the trees and into a clearing. Scattered bricks littered the area. A chimney. The cracked remains of a concrete slab. A house had stood there once, had either burned or been demolished years before. The woods crowded the overgrown yard on three sides. Along the fourth flowed the river, now a ribbon of molasses-dark water that parted silently around rocks and debris and lapped heavily against the banks.

Lauren walked to the water's edge, then followed the current. Every so often she heard rustling in the bushes on the bank opposite, as if something paced her. But when she stopped and tried to see what it was, the noise ceased.

She knew time passed, but even so, she took off her watch and shoved it in her pocket. *Time makes no sense here, so why keep track?* She came to a bend where the river narrowed and became more like a stream—if someone on the other side reached out, they could have joined hands. Again, she heard rustling in the bushes that lined the opposite bank—she quickened her pace, rounded the corner—

—and stopped.

A woman stood in the middle of the river. She was short. A little heavy. Middle-aged, with straight salt-and-pepper hair that grazed her shoulders. She stood bent, hands shoved in the pockets of an old brown barn coat. The water reached her knees, and had soaked the legs of her jeans so that they darkened from blue to black to a point midway up her thighs.

Her gaze held Lauren, even from the distance, piercing eyes set in a broad face, the skin pale, the expression so, so sad.

Lauren took a step forward, but stopped when the woman backed away. "Are you Connie Petersbury?"

The woman cocked her head. "Did I know you?" A soft voice, kind, but tired.

"No, we never—" Lauren hesitated as the word "did" snagged her ear. "We've never met." She pointed to the woman's jeans. "You should get out of the water. It must be cold."

"It's all the same to me." Petersbury tugged at the sodden cloth with a bare hand. "You have to take care where you walk here. This is the borderland. The space between. The worlds blend here, ours and theirs."

"Theirs?" Lauren asked a question for which she already knew the answer. "Who are they?"

"The dead. The corrupted dead." Petersbury's voice cracked. "Some folks call them demons, but they're worse than that. They're us, gone bad." She dipped her cupped hand in the river, brought up some water, then let it drip through her fingers. "There are still places that aren't as awful as others, but you have to be careful. Like when you put the flour and milk and eggs in a bowl and give them that first stir. They're together for good—you won't never be able to separate them. But there are places where it's still all one thing or the other. And those places are right next to one another, so you think you're safe in the flour, and the next thing you know you're in the eggs." She turned back to Lauren. "Am I making sense?"

Lauren nodded, eventually. "A little."

"Because I've tried to figure out ways to explain it, and that's the only thing I can come up with." Petersbury looked toward the bushes that had rustled a few minutes before. "Who are you?"

"My name's Lauren. Reardon." Lauren followed Petersbury's stare. She still saw nothing—the foliage remained still, and quiet. "I was passing through. My car broke down."

Petersbury tsked. "Shouldn't have come here. The stranger passing through town always gets it first—don't you watch the movies?"

"My dad wouldn't let me, when I was little." A memory flashed in Lauren's mind. Her father turning off the television. The anger in his voice. "He said they were a waste of time. I had to watch them at friends' homes."

"I used to like them, back in the day." Petersbury switched her attention from the bushes back to the water swirling around her—she dipped her bare hand up to the wrist, pulled it out, then rubbed her fingers together as though feeling for something. "If you find your way out of here, look for a tall, skinny woman with iron-gray hair, and tell her—" She fell silent, then sniffled and wiped her nose with her sleeve. "Her name's Virginia. She was my best friend. Tell her I'm sorry about the horses. Tell her that Connie said that she was wrong, and she's so sorry."

"Please." Lauren reached out. "Take my hand and—" She spotted something on the ground at her feet, and picked it up. A leather work glove, well worn, and small enough to fit a child. "Is this yours?"

Petersbury looked at the glove, then down at her bare hand. "Keep it. Won't do me no good now."

"There's nothing wrong with it. It just needs to dry out a little—see?" Lauren pointed to a rock in a shallow pool near the river's edge. "I'll set it atop that rock, and you can come and get it—"

"*No.*" Petersbury waved her back. "Don't come any closer. I've come about as close as I can to you. And you've come about as close as you can to me." Her hands fluttered, moving from her hair to the front of her jacket, in and out of her pockets, before finally stilling. "Closer than I thought anyone in your condition could come, I'll give you that."

Lauren brushed dirt off the glove and tucked it in a side pocket of the backpack. "My condition?"

"Being alive and all." Petersbury felt the water again. "I'm trying to stay in the space between, but it keeps shrinking. Shifting. Getting harder and harder to find a safe place." She took a step back, then moved a little to one side. "Water's always running. Never stands still. They can't catch it all at one time, them that live here, so some of it always remains free." She studied Lauren for a moment, then sighed. "You're looking at me like they all do. Did."

"No." Lauren caught movement from the corner of her eye, shadows flickering in the woods on the other side of the river, moving closer to the shore. "I don't understand what you're telling me, but I want to learn."

"How much time you got?" Petersbury looked up toward the sky, which had darkened to charcoal tinged with red. "Not as much as you think." She took another step back, then edged sideways. "Find Virginia and tell her that the space between is getting thinner and there's nothing she can do. Tell her he's back."

"Mr. Lumpy?" Lauren blurted the name.

"How do you know about him?" Petersbury stared. "What did you say your name was?"

Damn. "Lauren Reardon."

"Got family in Gideon?"

"I think I did. Once."

"Who? Odds are I know—knew—them."

Past tense again. Lauren studied the sad, pale face. *I'm talking to a dead woman.* Was it even possible to lie to the dead? Even if you could, was it the right thing to do? "I think Matthew Mullin was my father."

"You think?" Petersbury looked her up and down. "Age is about right. Is your mama's name Emma?"

Lauren hesitated. "No."

"Huh. He come with you? Your daddy?"

"He died about a week and a half ago."

"Well, that explains some. Not a lot, but some." Petersbury nodded. "You need to go to Virginia. You better start walking now." She pointed downriver. "That way. Stay on the side you're on—don't cross for nothing. If you go on that side"—she pointed toward the opposite bank, the bushes and the woods and the gathering shadows—"you'll never get back out."

Lauren took a few steps, then stopped. "I don't want to leave you."

"I appreciate the thought, but there's nothing you can do for me." Petersbury offered the barest smile. "How did you wind up here?"

"I don't know. They're all looking for you, and I went to see if I could help. But they can't see me."

"They can't see me either. Not no more. We're not in the same place as them."

"We're flour, and they're milk." Lauren walked a little farther, stopped again. "They sent a light to find you. I saw it. Why didn't it work?"

"It's light. This ain't the place for it." Petersbury folded her arms, hugged herself. "It's not the place for you either. Go. Now."

"I'm going to tell them I saw you."

"They won't believe you."

"Can't you follow me? I won't try to touch you or anything."

"I wish I could. Now get going."

"All right." Lauren raised her hands in surrender. "Good-bye."

The path ahead looked as inviting as a noir alley, tree limbs overhead interlocked in a gnarled canopy, the fading light hazy. Lauren put a hand to her belt, felt for the knife, wondered if it would make any difference. When she reached a spot where the land sloped down, she looked back, and saw Connie Petersbury watching her.

She waved, waited for some response. When none came, she finally gave up, and resumed walking.

CONNIE WATCHED THE woman until she vanished into the gloom. *She still has the look of life about her.* She shouldn't have been able to survive, not here.

"She's yours all right, Matt." Connie traced a circle and an X on her forehead with her thumb, and asked the Lady to lead Lauren Reardon out safe. "Hope you did better by her than you did by us." But why Reardon? Maybe because there had never been a Reardon in Gideon. "Oh, Matt. Did you really think changing your name would help?"

"Who you talkin' to, Nana?" The thing that had been her great-niece stepped out of the bushes and tottered to the edge of the opposite bank. "Please, Nana. I love you."

"Hello, Baby Bella. They sell mushrooms named after you, you know that? Seen 'em in a store once. Spawn of dark and dirt, just like you." Connie backed away as much as she dared. The river had already changed so much in the short time since she had taken refuge in it. A step in the wrong spot and the water would sweep her into the depths of the wilderness. She had escaped Nicholas Blaine once. He wouldn't let her get away again. "You're not my baby girl. You're a thing. A dead thing."

"So are you, Nana." Bella's voice had altered from that of a toddler into something older, deeper. "Dead as dead can be."

"Maybe. But I'm not like you."

"Not yet."

"Go away. You're trying to wear me down. You're him, for all I know."

"We all are. He is great."

"He's a man."

"Was a man."

"Is. Was. Man is man. He can be had." Connie looked downriver again, toward the last place she had seen Lauren Reardon, just before the woman disappeared from view. "Yes. He can be had."

Not-Bella reached out, tiny claws colored red by the light. "I could touch you, Nana."

"I would like to see you try." Connie felt the water again, the current that sheltered her and kept her safe. It had grown colder, narrower. She would have to find another one soon. "You go back and tell your grampy that it's still milk, eggs, and flour here, and I ain't moving. Tell 'im I loved him once but he's not that person anymore and all bets are off."

"He's your brother."

"*He killed me.*" Connie sniffed. "Mostly, anyway."

"You're going to lose."

"You're trying to distract me. Shut up and go away." Connie watched the little figure toddle off—for all her voice had aged, Bella still walked like a baby. For the time being, at least.

Connie felt the current again, sensed another thread of warmer water, and stepped into it. The darkness pressed closer, and she stuffed her hands in her pockets and huddled against the chill.

Matt's girl is here. Poor woman. Did she have any idea what she had gotten herself into?

17

Lauren followed the path along the river, stopping every so often to check her surroundings. The river had widened, the water lightened to the same silt brown she had seen from Corey's deck. The sky had also grown brighter, the red haze vanished, and the trees had gone back to just being trees.

Almost there. She felt a cold, damp breeze on her face, smelled wood smoke, and almost cried in relief. She broke into a trot, then quickened to a run when she caught sight of the edge of the woods.

Out of the trees and into watercolor light, gold and silver and gray, pale and clear. She stumbled, almost fell, caught herself in time. Staggered to a fresh-cut stump and sat, breathed in the green wood scents that lingered in the air. Buried her head in her hands and tried to slow her racing heart.

Did you enjoy your walk?

Lauren raised her head and opened her eyes.

He stood near the edge of the woods, beneath the shelter of an old oak. Tall and slim, he wore a long, fitted coat, and held something in one hand, a furled umbrella or cane. Shadows obscured his face, muddied the details and colors of his clothes.

But the voice. Something about the voice. Rich and deep and familiar, like the memory of a song heard long ago. *Oh, let me in . . .*

let me in . . . The same dark words she had heard that last day at her condo, filling her head.

"What are you?" Lauren pressed her hands to her ears. "Your voice is in my head. Get the hell out of my head."

I mean you no harm. He pushed away from the tree and paced slowly back and forth. *You do know me. I've been following you for some time.*

Lauren watched him move, felt the tension, the undercurrent of power. "Parking-Lot Man."

I waited for you outside your door, yes. Followed you through the streets. But I sought only to comfort. You must believe that. It proved to be a cane he held, the narrow lines sharpening in the light. *I understand loss. You must feel quite overwhelmed by it all.* His face remained hidden, veiled by darkness and the brim of a tall hat. Old-style clothing. Dickens and Jane Austen and old Victorians.

"I'm fine." Lauren hugged her knees to her chest. She felt the sudden urge to protect herself, followed by the fear that nothing she did would matter.

I think we both know that's not true. He stopped in front of a tumbled pile of branches, and plucked dead leaves like flower petals. *You're confused. Frightened.* Leaf fragments drifted to the ground. *Let me help you.*

Lauren watched him. Not solid, no. Not an actual person. A shade. An image formed from fog and smoke. "I don't need your help."

Even without a face, you could tell he smiled. You could hear the change in his voice, like chocolate melting. *You need my help, and much, much more.* He crumpled one last leaf to dust, brushed off his fingers, then turned to her. *You know why you're here.* It wasn't a question. *You know why you've been called.*

"Just passing through. My car broke down."

Ah. Stubborn, like he was. But strong, too. So, so strong. You passed through my domain unscathed. You should be dead, you realize that?

"Maybe I am."

My dear. He bent at the waist, as though addressing a child. *You have never been more alive.* The shadows that shaped his face swirled and darkened, hinting at features yet not forming them.

Lauren stared into the haze, tarnished silver and ash and cobwebs. "Why can't I see what you look like?" She let go her legs and kicked out, driving him back. Then she stood, slipped off the backpack, and left it atop the stump. "Maybe your face is all wrinkled and decrepit? *Picture of Dorian Gray?*" Took one step forward, then another, until she stood toe-to-toe with him. "I know who you are. You're Pizza Face."

He stilled, whatever he was. Ghost. Demon. The Devil His Own Self. Even the shadows of his face ceased movement. A soft rumble followed, as though he cleared his throat. Then came the voice again, the warmth turned to frost. *And where did you stumble upon that colorful appellation, Lauren, daughter of Matthew?*

"Leave me alone." Lauren struck out, tried to push him back. But her hands met nothing but a chill that enveloped them to the wrists and held them fast.

So angry. So like your father. I knew him well. He leaned close. *And he knew me.*

Lauren felt his cheek brush hers, cold as snow.

You hold something of mine in your hand. I want it back.

"I don't know what you're talking about."

My life in your hands, daughter of Matthew, the man who buried me in this place.

"He killed you?"

As good as. But you can make it right. You can give my life back to me.

"I don't know how."

You can learn. But there are limits to my patience, my tolerance. I suggest you learn quickly.

Lauren felt the pressure around her wrists ease, then vanish. Then light and dark shifted and she found herself alone, hands blue-white and aching from cold, her mind a tumult of fear and anger.

Then came the barest whisper, here and then gone, like breath on glass.

We will meet again.

Silence followed, for a few moments. Then the voices broke through. Women's voices. Not from the woods, but from the direction opposite, coming closer.

Lauren ran toward the woods. Felt something missing, stopped and turned, and saw her backpack atop the stump. *Shit.* She dashed back, was about to grab it and heft it to her shoulder—

—too late.

They bustled into the clearing, five of them, dressed in jeans, jackets, and boots. The glaring orange vests. An older woman, two middle-aged, two younger. Lauren recalled their faces from the circle. One, unfortunately, she already knew too well.

Deena stood hands on hips, and looked Lauren up and down. "What are you doing here?" She had overdressed for a hike—her makeup was obvious even from a distance, and a hefty display of cleavage showed above the open zipper of her jacket.

"I came out to help with the search." Lauren stepped around the stump so that it stood between her and the women. The looks the four strangers gave her ranged from skeptical to hostile, while Deena radiated the sullen anger of a high school bully. "Did you find her?"

"Who? Connie?" One of the middle-aged women stepped forward. Stark black hair poked out from beneath a puffy pink cap, a match for the puffy pink jacket that made an eye-watering contrast with the orange vest. "No, we haven't found her." She gave Lauren the same sour once-over as had Deena. "Is this the one he took home?"

"Yeah. Not even in town five minutes, and he scooped her right up." Deena fluttered her hands. " 'Oh, oh, my car broke down. Help me, help me.' "

"That's not what happened, and you know it." Lauren edged to the other side of the stump, which gave her a clear path past the women. If she left the way they came, she would find the road back to Gideon. "If you'll excuse me, I need to get back to town."

"'If you'll excuse me,'" Deena singsonged. "In a hurry to get back to your new boyfriend?"

"I haven't seen Dylan Corey since he left to join the search for Connie."

"That was three days ago." That from the older woman, who stood away from the others. "We were searching for you, too."

"Maybe we should all just go back to town and let him know I'm okay." Lauren searched the woman's face, looked for some sign that she could be reasoned with. But she seemed content to stand off to the side and watch things unfold, hands in her pockets, face a blank.

"Oh, then we better hurry. I heard Lolly found someone to buy your car." That from the second middle-aged woman, a brunette with blond streaks and a turquoise coat. "Isn't that what you said, Betty Joan?"

"You're exactly right, Ruthie." Betty Joan had moved next to her friend and into Lauren's path, while the second younger woman had crossed to the other side of the clearing and now stood between Lauren and the woods.

They're cutting off my exits. Lauren reached in her belt for the knife, then felt all around her waist. *Gone.* Slipped out during her dash from the woods. She wouldn't have stabbed any of them, no. But maybe the sight of the long blade would have made them back off.

She glanced over her shoulder and scanned for an escape route. Caught motion out of the corner of her eye and tried to make a dash back to the stump. But her legs dragged as though she waded through syrup, and Deena beat her by half a step.

"She's got clothes in here." Deena grabbed the backpack and turned it upside down, dumping the contents on the ground. "What were you doing before you got here, shacking up with someone else?" She kick-sorted the clothes in all directions, then opened the front flap. "Hey, look at this. A diary." She yanked out the book, leafed through the first few pages. "No—it's a Lady's Book. Belongs to Matthew J. Mullin."

"Matthew?" The older woman stirred. "You're his daughter?"

Betty Joan sneered. "Maybe she's his wife."

Ruthie grabbed the book and flipped through the pages. "No. He liked 'em older." She bent back the cover until the spine cracked, then turned the book so all could see one of the Emma drawings. "Remember, Betty Joan?"

Betty Joan laughed. "Oh yeah. Older and richer."

Lauren started to speak, almost choked as her throat closed up. She looked across at the older woman again, and sensed . . . something. Then a fog filled her head, and it was all she could do to form words. "Please put that down—it's fragile."

"'It's fragile.'" Deena took back the book from Ruthie, ripped out one of the pages, crumpled it, and tossed it to the ground.

"What's going on here?"

Laughter ceased. Deena straightened, tucked the book under her arm to hide it.

"Nothing, Tom." The older woman smiled; her voice emerged light, almost girlish. "Just a hen party."

"That you, Amanda?" Tom Barton trudged out of the chest-high grass into the clearing, toolbox in hand. "Hen party? In the middle of the old Hoard farm?" He spotted the clothes in the middle of the clearing, and his eyes widened. "Having a swap meet, too?"

"You just mind your own business." Betty Joan picked up the sweatshirt that had landed at her feet, and folded it over her arm. "Leave us to ours."

"No need to snap, Elizabeth Joan." Tom Barton coughed, then turned his head aside and spit. "I got a right to be here same as any of you." He wiped his mouth with his jacket sleeve, then turned to head back the way he came.

Lauren pushed one foot forward, then dragged the other. Breathed deep and struggled to find the strength to keep moving, to escape. "Mr. Barton? Wait up." She limped toward him. "Are you headed back to town?"

"Nope." Barton shook his head, then pointed in the opposite direction. "Going the other way. Things to do."

"Oh, you don't want to leave yet." Deena turned so that Barton couldn't see what she did. Then she held out the book and mimed tearing off the cover. "We were just getting acquainted."

Lauren stopped. She knew she should try to run, that these women wanted to hurt her. But the book was the only thing she possessed from her father's youth, the only clue to the man he had been, the danger she faced. "It's okay." She forced a smile. "I'll just hang around here a little while longer." She waited until Barton hobbled back into the weeds. Then she turned to Deena. "Why are you doing this? I've never done anything to you."

"You should've just kept driving." Deena tore another page out of the book, crumpled it, and dropped it to the ground. "You'll be sorry you ever came here."

"Wait a minute." Betty Joan beckoned to Ruthie, bauble-covered hands flashing in the weak sunlight. "Take a good look at her."

Ruthie leaned close to Lauren, bringing with her bloodshot eyes and a whiff of liquor. "I see what you mean. Something about the nose and the jaw." She straightened, head bobbing like a balloon on a string. "You were right, Amanda." She nodded toward the older woman. "She's Matthew's girl, all right."

Betty Joan took hold of Lauren's left hand and twisted it so it faced palm up. "Damn right she's a Mullin. They all have the break right here." She ran an acrylic-nailed finger along Lauren's lifeline, then pointed to a gap about halfway along. "Not particularly long-lived, Mullins. The hate takes it out of them." She dropped Lauren's hand like a used tissue. "He's dead, isn't he? That's why you've come in our time of trouble. To finish what he started. To tear this town apart like he did."

Lauren stared into the woman's eyes. She had known dislike before, aversion born of personality clash, competition on the job or in love. But she had never before sensed hatred, cold-eyed animus that would have struck her dead on the spot and stepped over her body without a second thought. She didn't yet know the exact reasons why Matthew Mullin had fled Gideon. But she understood why he did. "This town killed him."

"He *is* dead. See, I told you, Ruthie." Betty Joan nodded, then patted her companion's hand. "Justice." She turned back to Lauren, eyes bright and glittering as the stones on her fingers. "Now, what are we going to do about you?"

"You're going to leave me alone." Lauren stepped up in the woman's face, plumbed her anger, and used it to push forward because it was the only strength she had. "Because you don't know what the fuck you're talking about."

Betty Joan's face reddened. "How dare you throw that word at me." She raised her hand, jewel side out, ready to strike. *"You piece of Mullin trash."*

Lauren dug deep, pushed through the fog that surrounded her, caught the woman's wrist in mid-arc, and held on. Betty Joan struggled in her grip, but twenty fewer years and an athletic past bought Lauren some advantage. She squeezed as hard as she could even as voices sounded in her ear and Deena and Ruthie waded in and tried to pull her away. Felt a pulse beneath her fingers, hammering—

—heard the hard words that poured out of the woman's head, the laughter of a man and the slamming of a door. Tasted the damp, salty heat of tears.

Rudy, please don't—please don't go—

"It really is the money, honey." Words Lauren had never thought to say before, in a voice she had never used, deep and cool and mocking.

The words drove Betty Joan like a whip. She tore loose from Lauren's grasp, then brought her hand around. *"Damn you to hell."*

Lauren tried to dodge the blow. But one of the other women moved in behind her and grabbed her shoulders, held her fast as the back of Betty Joan's hand struck her cheek. Rings raked her skin, leaving razored pain in their wake. Stars filled her vision and blood filled her mouth. Her knees buckled and she crumpled face-first onto the wet turf.

The smell of earth in her nose, damp but sharp, rot and ice and hints of dormant life. Pain in her shoulders as someone grabbed her arms and wrenched them behind her back, bound her wrists.

"You hurt my friends and we hurt you—you see how that works?" Deena's voice in her ear.

Then came the blow to her side, a glancing kick from a booted foot.

Lauren pushed over onto her side. They hadn't bound her legs— she kicked out, felt the tremor along the bone as she hit something hard.

"Shit—she got me in the crotch."

"Grab her goddamn feet."

One of them sat on Lauren and pressed her legs into the ground while another bound her ankles with the same tape she had used to mark her trail.

"We better stand back—what if she works loose and kicks again?"

"So stand back and out of reach. Surely you remember what to do. Old ways are the best, ladies." Amanda's voice, followed by laughter.

Then came a *thunk* as something hit the ground by Lauren's head. She opened one eye, saw the stone. The size of a fist and jagged, dotted with crystals that glittered in the sun.

Another stone. A direct hit to the knee.

Lauren curled as tight as she could, pressed her face to the ground, twisted even as her shoulders screamed. A third stone struck her ribs, a glancing blow, weakened by the heavy jacket.

She tried as best she could to protect her head, but a fourth stone shaved her forehead. A stab of pain. Warmth, flowing.

And another stone in her ribs.

Another.

Another.

They pressed closer. Took turns. Lauren tried to anticipate the blows, but she couldn't move fast enough and there were so many stones.

No more words from the women. Only grunts of effort.

Lauren didn't hear the shouts at first, the sound swamped by the roaring in her ears. Then they grew louder and she heard Deena swear, the thuds of stones hitting the ground and the pound of running feet.

"What the hell are you doing!" Dylan Corey's voice. The sense of his presence and his shadow as he knelt beside her. "Oh, my Lady."

Lauren moved her head, spit blood, tried to twist around until the stab in her ribs stopped her.

"Can you talk?" Corey dug a jackknife out of his jacket pocket and snapped it open. "Old Tom found me." His breathing came ragged as he sawed the tape on Lauren's wrists. "Said something nasty was happening at Hoard's farm, but he didn't say what."

"I'm okay—just hurry up." Lauren sat up, yanked off the tape, and tossed it as far away as she could.

"They ran into the woods." Corey beckoned to two of the men who had accompanied him. "Chase them down and take them to the ranch." He slashed the tape on Lauren's ankles. "Just wait until Mistress Waycross hears about this."

18

The blond man with the round, ruddy face examined Lauren's wrists, then hooked a dollop of greenish ointment from an old baby-food jar and smeared it over the abrasions caused by the tape. He had introduced himself as "Jerome Hoard, physician and son of Gideon," then proceeded to grip her head between his hands and stare into her eyes. After a minute or so, he nodded, smiled, and set about treating her various wounds and bruises.

"How are you feeling?" He wrapped gauze around her wrists, then secured it by slicing the ends lengthwise and tying them like ribbon.

"A little shaky." Lauren felt her forehead, ran a finger along the edges of a bandage. Worked her jaw, and winced as her cheek stung. She sat atop the dresser in Mistress Waycross's spare bedroom, and fought the urge to turn and check her face in the mirror. "How bad is it?"

"Just a graze on your forehead. Deena's aim is as bad as her coffee." Hoard dabbed ointment on Lauren's cheek. "What made these? The stones?"

"Betty Joan's rings."

Hoard winced. "Those would leave marks on a tank." He applied one last dab, then stood back and regarded his handiwork like an artist debating those last few brushstrokes. "This is an herbal medicament. It shouldn't leave much of a scar, if any. Our Miz Petrie is a skilled compounder."

Lauren ran through the short list of Gideon names that she knew, came up empty, and shrugged a question.

"She's Master Cateman's housekeeper." Hoard smeared more ointment, muttered "oh, Lady" under his breath when he dripped some on the cuff of his white shirt. "And I mean a real housekeeper. Manages staff. Keeps the household books." He wiped away the mess, frowned at the resulting greasy smear. "Her family has owned the funeral home just off Main Street for over a hundred years."

That's reassuring. Lauren sniffed her wrist, caught a whiff of spice with an undercurrent of swamp. "What did you say was in this ointment?"

"I didn't." Hoard grinned. "Trade secret." He possessed an actual little black bag, which he paused to rummage through. "When did you last eat?"

"I'm not sure." Lauren took the wax-paper-wrapped square that he held out to her. "What's this?"

"Just some chocolate to tide you over until you get real food. You look pale." He cocked his head. "You are hungry?"

"Yes." Lauren unwrapped the chocolate, which proved to be a small brick of the bittersweet baker's stuff. "They said I was missing for three days." She cracked it in two, wincing as her shoulders and wrists complained.

"By our time, yes." Hoard packed his rolls of bandage, scissors, tape.

"You don't seem very surprised." Lauren inserted a small piece of chocolate into her mouth, taking care to avoid chewing on the injured side.

"Strange things happen in the woods. People have told of walking through them for what felt like a few minutes and emerging to find an entire day had passed." Hoard regarded her sidelong, brow arching. "So, you're Matt's girl. A child of Gideon."

Lauren flinched. *Child—that's what Dilys called me.* "I'm from Seattle."

"Yes, but one doesn't have to come from Gideon to be of Gideon. People have been leaving Gideon for years."

"Why?"

"It's the kind of place you leave. Everything a person needs is someplace else. A job. A life."

"You're still here."

"I live in Geneva. About an hour or so east of here." Hoard paused in his packing. "And a whole world away." He stared at nothing for a moment, then sighed and turned toward the doorway. "Yes, Judith?"

A beat later, an older woman dressed in jeans and a flannel shirt appeared in the entry. "Mistress wants to know how she is."

Hoard nodded to Lauren. "You can ask her yourself."

"I'm okay." Lauren smiled at the woman, then winced and pressed a finger to her bruised lip. "A little sore."

"Mistress says you should stay here tonight." Judith pointed down the hallway. "The bathroom is down the hall, and there are towels in the cabinet next to the sink. Sheets and blankets in the hall closet." She studied Lauren's face, and her brow drew down. "Are you sure she doesn't need to go to the hospital, Jerome?"

"She's fine." Hoard's smile thinned. "I tested her very thoroughly."

"You squeezed my head." Lauren slid off the dresser, slowly worked her shoulders. "You can tell whether or not I'm concussed by squeezing my head?"

"Not squeezing. Contacting." Hoard shut his bag, then picked up a suit coat from the back of a nearby chair and slipped it on. "Not a common practice, but effective, I assure you."

Lauren flexed her wrists, then twisted at the waist one way then the other. Felt some stiffness, but nothing sharp and grinding.

"All those jackets you wore shielded your ribs. You've bruises aplenty, but no breaks." Hoard's light demeanor altered to something more coolly professional. He studied her for a few moments. Then he smiled, sort of. "Welcome to Gideon." He patted her arm, and left.

Lauren listened to his receding footsteps, the squeak of the stairs. Took as deep a breath as she dared, and turned to the mirror.

Well. Not great, but not as bad as she had feared. Her cheek and lip had puffed up on one side, so her face looked crooked. Betty Joan's rings had left tracks like nail scratches, now shiny and pale green with ointment. Hoard had covered the cut on her forehead with a cartoon bandage, a dog with a ball in its mouth.

But her eyes. She could see what had worried Judith. She smiled as widely as she could, tried to think happy thoughts. But none of her efforts showed in her eyes. They shone distant, their light cold. Hard.

Memories. Her father's eyes had looked like that once. After Angela Reardon's funeral, Lauren had found him in his bedroom, staring into the mirror, and asked if he wanted coffee. His gaze had moved to her, stopping her words in her throat. Ice, his eyes had held. Like he had never seen her before. Like he never wanted to see her again.

Then the look passed. John Reardon smiled.

And Matthew Mullin returned to the shadows. Lauren straightened her shirt collar, brushing dried mud from her pants. Anything to avoid her face in the mirror.

The back of her hand itched. She peeled back the bandage that Hoard had applied. Yet another cartoon scene, a mouse being chased by a cat.

The thorn. It had left a neat, round hole that had already scabbed over, and Hoard had covered it with a healthy glob of Miz Petrie's concoction. But the rim of the wound was bright red and warm to the touch, and the color and consistency of the ointment made it look as though pus seeped and spread.

Lauren crept out of the bedroom and down the hall, the old wooden floor creaking underfoot. The bathroom proved to be small and ruthlessly neat—it didn't take her long to find a box of bandages, a tube of antibiotic cream. She removed all of Hoard's bandaging, wiped away the ointment, and re-dressed the wounds. Felt a jolt of energy as she worked. The smell of the ointment had bothered her, reminded her of infection. Removing it made her feel clean.

"No—didn't mean—"

A woman's voice. Corey had brought Lauren in through the back door of the sprawling Waycross homestead, but everyone else had entered through the front and gathered downstairs in the living room. *A convocation,* Corey had called it. A very serious meeting.

Lauren tiptoed out of the bathroom, and followed the voices. The hallway floor creaked no matter how carefully she trod, but given the loudness of the discussion coming from below, she doubted anyone heard. Even so, she slipped off her boots and descended the stairs in her socks.

"—what she did to Betty Joan. It was horrible." Deena, girlish soprano teetering on the edge of panicked squeal.

A low rumble followed, female but not feminine. Calm. Not in a hurry to speak because all would be bound to listen regardless.

Lauren stepped off the bottom stair and sneaked along the wall to the edge. Leaned against rough paneling, felt the ridges through her shirt.

"—still doesn't explain what she did that was so awful." Corey's voice, tight with anger.

"I told you. She said things. Terrible things about—things."

"Nothing she said could justify what you did to—"

Lauren waited for Corey to continue. But the silence lengthened. Then came the calm.

"I know you're there. You may as well come out."

Lauren debated slipping back upstairs, waiting until the convocation got under way again. But something told her that wouldn't work, and that trying to trick the owner of that voice might not be the best strategy.

She smoothed her rumpled shirt. Dragged her boots back on. Wished like hell that she could have changed into clean clothes, even the mismatched things she had stashed in the backpack. Corey had recovered it from the clearing, but had yet to give it back to her.

Too late now. She put one foot in front of the other and rounded the corner.

That sense of being measured. Examined. Like entering a room filled with distant relatives, people you saw once every few years. A connection existed, yes, but did it matter? Or did it make matters worse?

Twenty-five or thirty men and women sat around the wood-paneled living room, on the couch, a love seat, matched chairs from the dining room and mix-and-match from every other room in the house. Faces from the lighting circle, few of them younger than Lauren—Corey, Deena, and her as-yet-unnamed accomplice. Most were middle-aged or elderly, at various stages of wear. Everyone wore work clothes, jeans and flannels or uniforms—waitress smocks, nurse scrubs. Only Jerome Hoard wore anything close to business attire. He sat on one end of the couch, a landline telephone on the cushion beside him.

"On call," he said, by way of greeting.

Dylan Corey sat on a straight-backed chair near the doorway to the kitchen, as far away from the others as he could get and still be in the same room. His face reddened when Lauren looked at him. Then he stared down at his hands while a couple of the men eyed them both and smirked.

Deena stood in the center of the room, her shirt buttoned to the neck, tear-smeared makeup streaking her cheeks. The other women huddled behind. Deena's friend glanced at Lauren, then away, while Betty Joan and Ruthie glared.

The calm woman sat so that the guilty quartet faced her, in a Queen Anne armchair covered in rose paisley.

"I'm Virginia Waycross." She wore jeans, a red cardigan over a pale blue oxford shirt. "This is Gideon business. But as it concerns you, you do have the right to be here."

Lauren nodded toward Deena and the others. "One of them is missing. An older woman. Amanda." She heard a few gasps, then silence. *Could hear a pin drop.* Such a cliché, which didn't begin to describe the quiet, the held breath and sidelong looks.

Waycross sucked her lower lip for a few moments. "What did she look like?"

"You know what Amanda Petrie looks like, Virginia." A gruff voice from the far corner. Lolly, in a dark blue coverall, a plaid shirt collar poking out from beneath. He sat with his chair tipped back against the wall, arms folded, booted feet dangling.

"Thank you for your input, Richard. Appreciated as always." Waycross pointed to an empty chair next to hers, and waited for Lauren to sit. "What did she look like?"

"Short, maybe five two. Not slim. Gray hair pulled back in a pony-tail or bun, I couldn't see which." Lauren shivered at memories too fresh to bear recalling. "I'm not sure if she participated in the attack itself, but she was the one who suggested it. They had just been kicking me up to that point." That drew winces, even from Lolly. "'Old ways are the best, ladies.'" She tugged at a wrist bandage. "That's all I've got."

"That sounds like Amanda. Stand back and let weaker minds do the dirty work." Waycross sighed.

"Dr. Hoard used her ointment." Lauren touched one of the scratches on her face. "I wiped it off."

"I have used that ointment on countless other patients. It is above reproach." Hoard sat up straight, fingers drumming on his thighs. "Amanda would never compromise her craft."

"Your belief in her personal honor is touching as always, Jerome. Let's just say I know her better than you and leave it at that." Waycross massaged the arms of her chair, squeezed so hard her knuckles whitened. "You neglected to mention her, Deena. Care to explain why?"

"She wasn't with us at first. She just—showed up." Deena sniffled, wiped her nose with the wadded remains of a tissue. "Brittany and me met Ruthie and Betty Joan at the woods, and we were cutting through the old Hoard farm, on the way to Betty Joan's. We were go-ing—" She glanced across the room at Corey, and her voice dropped to a whisper. "... going to watch a movie."

"You had volunteered to help search for Miz Reardon." Corey's hands clenched, baritone lowered to a growl. "You came to me and offered to help."

"That's beside the point, Dylan." Waycross held up a hand. "The issue is that Leaf Cateman lets his people run loose to make trouble, and then leaves it to me to deal with the fallout."

Waycross regarded Deena and the others and shook her head. "But the fact that she is powerful and persuasive does not absolve you in the slightest. I don't know what to say to any of you. With all we've lost, all we're going through. To attack a stranger, with no provocation—"

"She's his daughter. She has a copy of the Book with his name in it. He defaced it with his drawings. Pictures of Emma." Betty Joan jabbed the air, rings glittering in the lamplight. "I keep telling you and you don't listen. Ruthie sensed it. I saw it in her hand."

"Ruthie's senses—straight up or on the rocks." Lolly's shoulders jerked in silent laughter.

"I've had about all I'm going to take of your wise-ass comments, Richard." Waycross worked her neck. "Whether she is or isn't Matthew's daughter is immaterial, Betty Joan."

"Jim and his family. Connie. She done it, or had it done. She is *involved*." Betty Joan shook off Ruthie's restraining hand. "Blood tells, and Mullin blood is tainted."

Silence settled, different from before. Lauren felt probing stares, curious and questioning and not altogether kind, and wondered if Matthew Mullin had ever undergone the same ordeal. Of not being the one on trial, yet being tried just the same.

Waycross turned to her. "Where were you six days ago?"

Lauren debated answering, even as she knew she had no choice. If she wanted to find out what in hell was going on, she needed information, cooperation. She would get neither if she stonewalled. "Crossing Idaho into Montana."

"And you can prove this with credit-card receipts and such?"

"Those can be faked," Betty Joan piped. "My Rudy could tell you stories—"

"I'm sure he could."

"I can prove my whereabouts." Lauren met Betty Joan's glower until the woman sneered and looked away.

Waycross worried her jewelry, first tugging at her watch, then twisting her wedding ring. "Well, Miss Reardon. As Mistress of Gideon, I must beg your forgiveness for the actions of these women. They committed a grievous wrong against you and threatened your safety, if not your life."

Deena's head came up. "I never would have—"

"I have known you since birth, girl—I know what you are." Waycross's lip curled. "I know what you get up to when you think no one's watching." She held her hand to her mouth, then let it fall. "You brought this upon yourselves."

"No, Mistress!" For the first time, fear showed on Betty Joan's face. She knelt before Waycross, her eyes brimming. "Please, not the binding. Not now. I have—" She shot a look at Lauren, and for a bare moment hatred overwhelmed dread. "I have things that need doing. Such important things—I need my powers, Mistress."

"You should've thought of that before you listened to Amanda Petrie." Waycross lowered her head and squeezed the arms of her chair while the other three women knelt next to Betty Joan, clasped hands, and wept. Mutters rose from the far corners of the room and folks shifted in their seats. A few looked at Lauren, their expressions varying degrees of grim. As if they blamed her.

What the hell did the Mullins do to you people? Lauren had a feeling that after tonight, the residents of Gideon would stand in line to inform her.

Leaden anticipation settled. Waiting room dread.

"Ruth Tuckwell. Elizabeth Barnes. Deena Trace. Brittany Watt. By your own deeds, be you judged. By your own actions, be you sentenced." Waycross's voice emerged a rough whisper, almost drowned out by sobs. "Hands be bound. Hearts be bound. Minds be bound." She closed her eyes. "Blind you were, so blind you will remain. Until the Lady deems you fair. Until your debt is paid." As she spoke, Deena and Brittany crumpled to the floor and Betty Joan covered her head with her arms as though warding off blows.

Lauren's breath caught. She felt it, whatever it was, radiating from Waycross to the women. A deadening. Suffocation. A power that would suck the life out of her if she drew too close.

"Virginia." Ruthie looked up, eyes glistening. "You doin' this to us now, leaving us defenseless, it's like murder."

"Ruth." Waycross met the woman's pleading gaze. "You know what they say about turnabout and fair play." She bowed her head, fingers flexing and lips moving in silent speech. Then she struck the arm of her chair as though she pounded a gavel. "By the Lady."

"In her name." A gabble of voices, some soft, some hesitant.

A few moments of quiet followed as it sank in that the hearing, trial, whatever the hell it was, had finished. The four women struggled to their feet. Brittany broke down and was led away by Deena, who shot Lauren a chill look as they passed. Betty Joan and Ruthie followed, looking the other way as they passed Lauren's chair and bowing their heads as they passed Waycross's. The four of them collected their coats and purses from a table by the front door, and left together without speaking.

Lauren waited. No one else had moved, and the thought occurred that they were waiting for her to leave. "If you need me to go—" She started to rise.

"We're not done here." Waycross waved for Lauren to sit down, then reached over the side of the chair and hefted a backpack onto her lap. "I have a few questions for you, Miss Reardon."

Lauren looked over at Dylan Corey, who appeared to be in deep conversation with the man sitting next to him—he glanced at the backpack, then away, again taking care to avoid her eye. "You had no right to search my things."

"Given that you stole this backpack from my foreman, I don't believe you're in any position to object." Waycross rummaged through the main compartment, laid out items on the floor at her feet. The sweatshirt. The socks. "Is there anything else of his in here?"

"A roll of tape. Some first-aid gear." Lauren watched the woman pick through every compartment, open every zipper. "I wanted to help search for Ms. Petersbury, but Mr. Corey declined my assistance, so—"

"So you went out anyway." Waycross tugged a stubborn zipper. "Another listener. Great."

Lauren braced, waited for Waycross to find the newspaper clipping with her father's picture. *Then there's Connie's glove.* Waycross was bound to find it, bound to ask why there was only one, and what happened to the other. *I should tell the truth.* Of course she should. Because telling the truth had worked so well for her in the clearing.

But Waycross missed the clipping and the glove. She did find the book, however—she pulled it out of the front pocket of the backpack, along with the pages that Deena Trace had torn out. Examined the cover, front and back, then opened it. "This is Matt's." Her voice came soft. "This is Matthew Mullin's."

Lauren nodded, eventually. "Yes."

"So how did you come by it?"

"It came into my possession after his death. He was my father."

"Matt's . . . gone?" Waycross blinked rapidly, then set the book on the arm of her chair and rested her hand on it.

"Looks like Betty Joan was right." Lolly again, not quite under his breath.

"I never denied it." Lauren looked down at her palm, ran a finger along the broken lifeline.

"Could've said something earlier." That from Zeke, the old man from the diner.

Lauren sensed the hurt in the man's tone. "You knew him?"

"We all did." Zeke fiddled with a brimmed cap, unsnapping the size adjustment tab, then closing it. "Said I thought you looked familiar, didn't I?"

"Everyone says I look like my mother."

"There's more to resemblance than physical features." Waycross had taken up the book again, stroking the cover before leafing through the pages. "Reardon. Married name?"

"My father's name. He called himself John Reardon."

Waycross nodded. "And why did you come to Gideon, Lauren Reardon?"

Lauren started to speak. Stopped. Where the hell should she start? With the story of a deteriorating desk, and a shadowy figure in her condo parking lot? With those who died, and her fears for those still alive? With the knowledge of what her father had been, and what she feared it might mean?

How much time have we got? She couldn't shake the sense that it was less than any of them thought. But how could she convince them, these people who had driven her father away, who looked at her now as an unwelcome reminder of a troubled past?

Memories. Of a woman standing in the river, testing the water again and again. Milk and eggs and flour and the thinning of the space between. And the reason for it all. The only words that mattered. The only ones that needed to be said.

"He's back."

19

Things settled down eventually. Waycross dispatched Corey and a few others to the kitchen; they returned with glasses, bottles of whiskey and tequila and cans of soda, which they distributed and dispensed according to preference. The soda didn't find many takers.

Lauren was one of the few—she sipped ginger ale, hoped it would settle the stomachache brought on by the overall tension and the uproar when she said those two simple words.

He's back. She didn't even have to tell them who she was talking about.

"Poor ol' Jimbo was right all along." Phil stared into his glass. "He tried to warn us, and we all laughed at him."

"Oh, we believed him." Zeke, his cap hanging off one knee, glass of whiskey cradled close to his chest. "We just weren't ready to talk about it out loud." He paused to drink, then wiped his mouth with the back of his hand. "It's not really real until you talk about it out loud."

Lauren felt the pressure of a steady stare, and looked up to find Lolly watching her over the top of his glass.

"The 'it' we don't want to talk about? His name's Nicholas Blaine. You could say him and Gideon go way back." Lolly's smartass edge had dulled. He sat leaning forward, shoulders rounded, a bear on alert. "You've seen him, haven't you?"

205

Lauren nodded. "Back in Seattle, after Dad died. And here, in Gideon. In the clearing, after I found my way out of the woods. Right before Deena and the others showed up."

Waycross raised her glass to her lips, then brought it down without drinking anything. "Did he say anything?"

"He asked me if I enjoyed my walk." Lauren shuddered at the memory of the voice, the promise it held if she complied, the veiled threat if she didn't. "I heard bits of a song. *'Let me in.'* It sounded old—"

"*'For I'm the laird o' Windywa's, and I've come here withoot a cause.'* " Lolly rocked back and forth as he sang, his bass a mournful lowing. "*'But I've got mair that thirty fa's, comin' oot owre the plains. O let me in this ae nicht, this ae ae ae nicht. O let me in this ae nicht, and I'll never seek back again.'* " He raised his glass in a toast to himself, then emptied it. "It's a rude little tune about a man . . . visiting a lady not his wife. We've all heard it, at one time or another."

Lauren nodded. Yes, that sort of song fit with the man—ghost—whatever it was that accosted her. The sexual undercurrent when he spoke, like words whispered in the dark. "What does he want?"

"From us? Or from you?"

Waycross's eyes narrowed. "Judith, this is a formal convocation."

"Yes, Mistress. But we are still allowed to speak at these things last I heard, unless you changed the rules without us knowing." Judith rose from her chair, and stood with her hands clasped waist-high, like a singer in a recital.

Lauren watched as Waycross sat up straight, jaw working, one hand clenched. The Mistress of Gideon wanted to tell the woman to sit back down—that was obvious. But all eyes had fixed on her and no one so much as breathed.

She's damned either way. Either she silences the opposition and looks weak, or she gives them a chance to poison the well. Lauren's stomach twinged in commiseration. She sipped some more ginger ale, set the glass on the floor, and looked up to find Judith looking at her.

"Leaf has said that—that there's a curse on this town because of—

because of our history. Things we did, because Mullins told us they were the right things to do. Only later, we found out they weren't. The right things." She gestured around the room. "And things like this, like what happened to Jim and his family and what likely happened to Connie, are going to keep happening until we, well, Leaf says 'effect reparations,' but that's just how Leaf talks." Her composure faltered—she dropped her gaze, tugged at her fingers. "Until we make things right."

"Who cursed you? Blaine—?" Before Lauren could finish, Waycross waved her quiet.

"Judith." Waycross pointed to Lauren, voice hushed with dismay. "Amanda Petrie tried to kill her."

"Yes, Virginia." Judith raised her head and once more met Lauren's eye, gentle Judith who had asked whether she should go to the hospital. "I'm saying that maybe she had good reason." With that, she gathered up her purse and coat, walked to the door, and left. Others followed, well over half the room, bowing their heads to Waycross as they passed. All ignored Lauren, except for Jerome Hoard.

"There was nothing to fear from the ointment. Amanda has her pride." He frowned at her fresh bandaging, then fell in behind the others.

"You're making a mistake." Corey followed them to the door. "Leaf Cateman is the liar. He has his own reasons for every damn thing he does, and if you think they include what's best for Gideon, you're crazy." He stood in the open doorway, hands braced on the sides of the jamb, and shouted into the dark. "Is this it? You've picked your side?"

"They're gone, Dylan." Lolly stood and walked to the coffee table by the couch, where the liquor bottles had wound up. "Leaf tells them things they want to hear. Anything that happens is someone else's fault. If we throw the right body over the side, all will be forgiven and the crows will return. The Lady's grace will shine upon us once again, and a new age will dawn in Gideon." He grabbed the whiskey and splashed a healthy shot into his glass. "Might even get a casino."

"Lolly." Waycross shook her head.

"Virginia." Lolly downed his drink, then wiped his mouth on his sleeve. "You think if you talk reason to these people, they'll listen? You think if you lay out the facts, they'll suddenly wake up and realize that just because ol' Matt was a rotten bastard didn't mean he was wrong?"

Zeke nodded toward Lauren. "Dammit, Lolly, the man's daughter is sitting right there."

"Yes, she is, and if she came here to get the facts instead of a fairy tale, that's what she should get. Given what happened to her today, I'd say the time for facts is here." Lolly sauntered over to Lauren. "Ask Leaf if you can see his wall. Everything you need to know is there. Hell, your daddy helped build the damn thing."

Waycross's measured alto filled the room. "I think now would be a good time to step back and take a deep breath."

"I agree." Lolly held out his hand. "I'm sorry about your daddy. Not about Matt, but about whatever it was in him that allowed him to make a family."

Lauren's hand vanished in the man's winter-rough paw. His coverall exuded garage smells, cleaning solvent and gasoline, his breath a hint of peppermint that the liquor failed to vanquish. "You were his friend once. I found your picture in his book."

"'Friend' is pushing it." The light in the man's eyes flickered. "Sometimes you gotta work with the tools at hand, even if they aren't the best." He smiled, displaying a ragged row of tobacco-stained teeth, then released her and trudged over to Waycross, planting himself in front of the woman's chair and staring down at her until she met his eye. "And then there were two," he muttered. Then he ambled to the door, handing Corey his empty glass along the way.

The few remaining Gideonites rose, collected their coats and scarves and handbags, then formed a line in front of Waycross, bowing low enough for her to place her hand on their heads. Phil and Zeke, Dylan Corey, eight or nine others.

"Leaf should be here." An older man in jeans and a sweatshirt took his place in front of Waycross. "Master and Mistress together, as it should be."

"I asked him like I always do, Seth. And like he always does, he declined. Had Jorie write the note this time, which is a first." Waycross stood. "Dylan has organized a search team to check the river," she called out over their heads. "Seven o'clock tomorrow morning. We meet again in the evening to plan next steps, depending on what we find."

"Any plans to call the sheriff?" asked a heavyset man holding a lunch pail, the name RUSTY sewn across his shirt pocket.

"Think it would do any good?" Phil shook his head. "If the light didn't find her, she ain't around to be found."

Lauren stood and watched them leave, the unlikeliest coven she could have imagined. Closed her eyes for a moment, then opened them to find Corey standing in front of her.

"That could have gone better." He scanned her face, and reddened. "I'm so sorry about what happened to you."

Lauren cataloged his cuts and bruises, his haggard appearance. It had been a rough day in the woods, in more ways than one. "It's not your fault."

"Yes, it is. I should have brought you here instead of taking you to my place. But I was in a hurry." Corey stepped closer. "You feeling okay?"

Lauren caught fresh scents, sea and soap and clean clothes, calming and quiet. "What did Judith mean? About Mullins and a curse on Gideon?"

"You should talk to the Mistress about that." Corey took her hands, wincing when he caught sight of the bandaged wrists. "But you've been through a lot. If you ask me, you need to take it easy for a few days."

"Judith told me I was staying here." Lauren fought the urge to pull away as Corey's tangled emotions zipped along her skin like tiny shocks. Confusion. Fear. Anger. *Will this happen every time I touch someone?* Whatever this new talent of hers was, she didn't like it. "All my stuff is in my car."

Corey released her with a smile and started toward the front door. "I'm going to follow Lolly to the garage, pick up what you need. One suitcase?"

"And a couple of shopping bags." Lauren fell in beside him, rubbing her arms to erase the residual tingling. "I left Seattle in a hurry. Had to buy things along the way."

"I'll just bring everything, let you sort it out." Corey opened the door partway, then closed it. "I think I know why Deena—I flirted with her once in a while. Only at the diner, never anywhere else. I mean, she's a kid—I've known her since she was—" He held his hand to his waist, let it fall. "You might need to bug Lolly about your car. Otherwise, the week'll go by and he won't have touched it. He'll complain if you ask about it, but he's just one of life's complainers."

Lauren nodded. "I will."

"I'll mention something to him, too." Corey opened the door again, and edged outside. Shuffled his feet. "Well. Good night."

"Good night." Lauren watched him get into his truck and drive away. Closed the door and started back to the living room, and found Waycross standing in her path, Connie's glove in her hand.

"I gave Connie these for her birthday, seven years ago. Special order from a place in Chicago. Her hands were so small that she could never find the really good work gloves in a store. Always wound up with ones made for children, flimsy cloth things with bears or flowers all over them." She inserted her hand halfway, as far as it would go, then pulled it out and pressed the glove between her palms. "Anytime you're ready."

Lauren imagined Connie standing beside them, hands in her pockets, worry etched in her face. That tiny woman, surrounded by the darkness and decay. "She's the one who told me he'd come back. She said to tell you that she's sorry about the horses. And the space between is getting thinner and there's nothing she can do."

20

Lauren set a cup of coffee on the kitchen table next to Waycross's elbow, then added a healthy shot of the whiskey. "I'm sorry. I shouldn't have blurted it out like that."

Waycross wrapped her hands around the cup, held it to her nose, and breathed deep. "Why didn't you say something earlier?" She studied Lauren through the steam. "Forget that. No one would have believed you."

Lauren sat across from her. "Why not?"

"Because you apparently met Connie on the other side, and you brought something back." Waycross placed a hand on Connie's glove, which rested on the table between them. "You don't bring things back. It's like raising the dead. You're trying to bring back something that isn't part of this world anymore." She sipped the spiked coffee, grimacing as she swallowed.

"You believe me?" Lauren bit into her toast, which was Waycross's prescription for her jitters and pounding head. "After what happened today, I didn't think anyone would."

Waycross regarded her, eyes not quite soft with sympathy. Still chips of ice floating in the mix. "That last morning, she was helping me here. I asked her questions she didn't want to answer, and she tried to distract me by setting my horses to fighting. No one knew about that except her and me." She nodded toward the glove. "It feels wrong to me. Like it has grease or dirt ground in, and no matter how many times I wash it, it will never come clean. She's not in a good place, poor thing. How did she look?"

"Tired. Worried." Lauren thought back to the strange dark waters and the rustling in the bushes. "Determined. Like she was going to win no matter what."

"That's my Connie." Waycross smiled. "She's in the borderland, the boundary where this world and the next meet. She told you about the milk, flour, and eggs? I've heard that from her before. She used to call it 'the scientific explanation.'" She drank a little more coffee, then set the cup aside.

"She was having a hard time finding a safe spot." Lauren mimed Connie's finger-rubbing examination. "She kept dipping her bare hand in the water, feeling it. Then she'd move one way or the other. I think she was watching for something on the opposite bank. I heard rustling in the bushes."

Waycross picked up the glove. For all she claimed it felt wrong to her, it was her friend's, and she couldn't leave it alone. "Why did you bring this back? Did she ask you to?"

"No. I tried to give it back to her, but she told me to take it. She said she didn't need it anymore. I think she needs to keep one hand bare to test the water." Lauren finished eating, then poured herself coffee, waving off Waycross's offer of the whiskey bottle. "She must have dropped it on her way to the river. I found it on the bank, near the remains of an old house."

"A house?" Waycross's brow drew down. "What kind of remains?"

"A foundation slab. A chimney. Some scattered bricks."

"Almost sounds like the old Mullin place. What's left of it." Waycross got up and walked to the sink with her cup. "But it's nowhere near the river. They lived west of the square. There's a no-name street with a couple of small houses." She dumped her spiked coffee down the drain, then started rinsing cups and plates and putting them in the dishwasher.

"My dad's house?" Lauren rose and carried her dishes to the sink. "What happened to it?" She tried boosting herself up onto the counter, but her ribs complained, and she settled for leaning.

"It burned. A week or so after Matt left." Waycross switched on the dishwasher, then returned to the table. "Place was vacant. Mark and Becky, Matt's parents, your grandparents, they died a few years before in a car accident, and there were no more Mullins around to claim the place." She sat heavily, closed her eyes for a moment before continuing. "Fire chief blamed squatters."

"You don't sound convinced." Lauren waited for Waycross to say more, but the woman toyed with Connie's glove instead. "Wasn't my dad too young to live by himself?"

"Fifteen going on forty." Another smile, that faded quickly. "It wasn't easy for him here. Leaf Cateman took it upon himself to look after him. Gave him odd jobs, made sure he stayed in school."

"That was good of him. That doesn't jibe with what I heard out there."

"Leaf Cateman never does anything without a reason. If he isn't trying to pull something, he's laying groundwork. He'd had an eye on your father for a long time."

"Why?"

"Power." Waycross played with her wedding ring, pulling it off, putting it back on. "Main reason Mullins get blamed for all the bad that happens here is because of the power. It's in your blood." She glanced at Lauren, then away. "Matt always said the hatred built the anger, and the anger built the power. I used to think it was just his own anger talking. Lady knows, he was filled with it." She paused. "I've no experience with children—the Lady didn't choose to bless me in that way. But I'm a good listener. If you need to talk to someone, I'm here."

Lauren watched the woman fidget. *You loved him.* She didn't need supernatural power to figure that out. "I'll be okay."

"I'm not just asking to be nice." Waycross flipped from kind to stern in a blink. "My home is threatened. The children of the Lady who look to me for guidance and protection."

Lauren followed Waycross back to the table, and sat. Food had cleared her head, and questions tumbled like numbers on a wheel. *Which one to ask first?* "Who is he? Blaine? I call him Parking-Lot Man because that's the first place I saw him, the lot outside my condo. I sensed him tracking me through the streets. At the time, he looked like he wore modern clothes." She thought back to that first sighting. It seemed like months ago instead of days. "But he's old. His clothes are old. Whatever happened, it happened a long time ago."

Waycross toyed with the plastic butter dish, popping off the lid and snapping it on. "We burned Nicholas Blaine at the stake almost two hundred years ago for a crime he didn't commit. It was the word of a Mullin that condemned him." She set the lid one last time, then pushed the dish aside. "Since then, things haven't gone so well here."

"No crows." Lauren saw them in her mind's eye, the feathered escorts that turned up at every stop. *Until they didn't anymore.* "Tom Barton tries to lure them back with possum parts, but it doesn't work." She looked across the table at Waycross, who regarded her with head-cocked puzzlement. "The Lady's birds—"

Waycross snorted softly. "I know what they are."

"I didn't mean—I read it in Dad's Book of Endor."

"I know what it's called." Waycross picked up the glove and draped it over her hand.

Lauren quieted. *Slow down.* She couldn't afford to alienate Waycross. The woman didn't have to put her up. She would have been perfectly within her rights to send Lauren to a hospital and then on her way. "Blaine told me that I held his life in my hands." She watched Waycross for any signs of irritation. "He said my father killed him."

"Your father made sure he stayed buried."

"Did Emma have anything to do with it?"

Waycross's lips thinned. "You have been busy."

"Everyone knows who she is. There are pictures of her all over

Dad's book." Lauren retrieved the book from the living room, tucking in torn pages along the way. "Connie asked if she was my mother." She held out the book to Waycross, but instead of the Emma portraits, the woman fixed on the sketch of a rose.

"What happened to him?" Waycross took the book from Lauren, lingered on the rose for a few moments, then turned pages as though she were looking through a photo album.

"Lung cancer." Lauren struggled for some detail to soften those hard, hated words. "It was fast."

"Like an avalanche, you mean. No time to get your feet under you." Waycross swallowed hard. "And your . . . mother?"

"She died last April. Heart attack."

"Did she practice?"

"You mean, was she a witch? No." Lauren took her phone from her pocket. "Everyone says I take after her." She hunted through stored photos until she found her favorite. Her mother, dressed in summery yellow, standing in the middle of her garden holding an armful of freshly cut hydrangeas. "Angela Olivetti Reardon."

Waycross stared at the phone, then set the glove aside and took it. Her eyes widened when first she saw Angela's image. Eventually, she nodded. "Long, dark hair. That was his type." She handed back the phone. "So you have family, back in Seattle."

"Not really." Lauren took a last look at her mother's smiling face, then closed the photo app, tucked the phone away. "They never had much to do with us. My grandfather didn't like Dad."

"Fathers usually didn't." A corner of Waycross's mouth twitched. Then she sombered. "He changed his name. Changed his life." She closed the book, placed her hand on the cover as though taking an oath. "And he never told you anything about any of this. Never trained you. Never tested you to see what you were capable of."

"I think he always knew." Lauren sat back, massaged sore knees, an aching shoulder. "During the drive here, I had a lot of time to think. I used to have nightmares." She told it all, slowly, haltingly, the doctors and the investigation and her mother's tears. That final talk with the social worker, when Lauren held her hand and told her what she wanted to hear. "I think that scared Dad. I think that when he stroked my hair, he did something. Cast a spell? Whatever he did, it stopped the nightmares. But it stopped the feelings, too. They started coming back after he died."

Waycross remained silent for a time, eyes on her hands, still settled atop Matt Mullin's book. "Nasty talent to have, that feeling sense. I can see why it worried him." She opened the book, slipped out the torn pages, fit them back where they belonged. "Same thing happened with Betty Joan, didn't it? Whatever Deena didn't want to tell me about what passed between you."

Lauren nodded. "If her husband's name is Rudy, I don't think he's going to be her husband much longer."

Waycross's brow arched. "You need to learn to control that before someone takes a shot at you." She sighed. "Still, it was no excuse to leave you in the dark."

Lauren stood, stretched her sore back, then paced the small kitchen. "Dad fled Gideon for a reason. He changed his name for a reason. Maybe he hid me for the same reason, and now that he's gone, and his wards have weakened—"

"You know about wards?"

"I picked up a few things over the last week or so."

"Over the last week or so." Waycross put a hand to her mouth and shook her head.

"I realize that doesn't make me an expert."

"I'm glad you realize that."

Lauren stopped, stared at the floor, forced herself calm. "The woman who died back in Seattle, the one who tried to help me, she was a witch. I think she had an idea about what was happening, at least from my end, and that was why she died. She came to see me afterward—"

"After she died."

"*Yes.*" Lauren returned to the table. "She told me not to come here. She said that was what he wanted. She was talking about Blaine. He wants something from me. He will cause pain in order to get it. I need to find out what it is."

"I don't think you should get involved in this." Waycross sat up straighter, tugged at the sleeves of her sweater, rubbed the back of her neck. "I don't doubt that you mean well, and I can tell that you're a quick learner. But your lack of experience could get someone killed—"

"It looks to me like people are dying regardless." Lauren backed away from the table as Waycross's glare drilled deep. "I wasn't questioning—"

"We can talk more tomorrow." Waycross massaged her temples, pressing so hard that her fingertips whitened. "You've had a helluva day. Better get some sleep."

Lauren pushed in her chair. "So should you."

"I'm going to stay up awhile longer." Waycross picked up the glove again. "Dylan should be stopping back with your things. I'll tell him not to get his hopes up about the search for Connie. If he asks why, I'll just say that I have a feeling. He's used to my feelings." She sniffled, removed a handkerchief from her sleeve, and wiped her nose, her eyes. "Want me to call you when he shows up?"

"Not tonight. I'm too tired to be lucid." Lauren paused in the doorway. "Thank you. For taking me in."

Waycross nodded, eventually. Closed the book, and handed it to Lauren. "Phil repairs bindings and such. He should be able to take care of this for you."

"Thanks. I'll talk to him."

"The hot-water tap sticks. I need to fix it but I haven't had the time. There's a set of channel locks on the toilet tank."

"Thanks." Lauren walked down the short hallway to the back staircase, then paused at the foot of the stairs. Then she buttoned her shirt to the neck, zipped her vest, and headed for the back door.

The damp night chill startled her awake, like a splash of cold water in her face. She sat on the step, looked up at the dark country sky, picked out stars twinkling between the clouds.

Tensed when she heard the dead grass crunch of footsteps.

"Hello? Hello?" Tom Barton tottered into view. "Thought it might be Mistress catching a few drags. She does that once in a while." He had stuck strips of reflective tape to his gloves, jacket sleeves, and both pant legs, so that when he moved, he looked like a glow-in-the-dark stick man.

"Dylan Corey said you're the one who told him I needed help." Lauren held out her hand. "Thank you."

Barton stared at her. Then he lunged forward, arm stuck straight out, and gave her hand the briefest of taps. "Welcome." He backed up, twitching back and forth like a fencer looking for an opening. "I found this by where your car was. Out by the sign, just before you come into town." More uncertain rocking. Then he stilled and reached out again, this time more slowly. "Thought you better have it back."

Lauren braced for a messy surprise, a corroded penny or broken bit of jewelry caked with mud. Instead, Barton dropped one of her wire circlets onto her open palm. "It must have fallen out when I got out of the car. Thanks. Again."

Barton nodded with his entire upper body, jerky as a puppet. "Change comin'."

"Yes. I think you're right." Lauren tucked the circlet in her vest pocket. When she looked up, Barton had gone.

21

Jerome Hoard turned onto Old Main Road, hands tight on the wheel. He had always hated Ginny's convocations, but this one decided him. Liquor. Binding curses. Women's tears. No more. Son of Gideon he may well be, but there were limits.

She shouldn't have come here. Mullin's daughter. He had sensed it immediately, the tumult, the chaos, emanating from her like the stink of cheap perfume. She knew better than he did how to treat injuries, oh yes. Amanda Petrie's ointment wasn't good enough.

Hoard hit a wave of mist thick as fog, switched his headlights to the low-beam setting, and slowed down. Damned depressing weather—he needed to get away. Far away, this time for good. San Diego. Miami. Someplace with beaches, clear sky, sunshine. Someplace where he would no longer feel the tug at his soul, the eternal call to never-ending duty.

Dammit, he hated this place.

The car hit a series of ruts, shuddered and shook like it would fall apart at any moment, and Hoard slowed to a crawl. Funny. He should have reached the turnoff to the state road by now. *Damned Tom Barton probably took down the sign again.* Easy to miss the turnoff without the sign, no matter how many times one traveled the route. Gideon had no money to pay for road maintenance, and at least five years had passed since the county had sent a crew to trim trees, resurface the road. Every year that passed, conditions grew worse and worse, Gideon more and more isolated.

"Dammit." Hoard pulled to the side of the road, and rolled to a stop. Checked the time on the dashboard clock. Just as he thought—he should have been halfway to Geneva by now. *Damn you, Tom Barton.*

As if on cue, the mist changed to rain, a monsoon pounding of water that Hoard knew sure as hell was falling on his car and nowhere else. That's how it went every time he came home. Every moment spent in Gideon served to remind him why he had left in the first place.

"Calm yourself, Doctor." Hoard pulled in one deep breath, then exhaled through his mouth. *Whoosh.* Concentrated on expanding his chest muscles, felt the tension as they resisted. Wound up tight, yes he was, but he would be home soon. Just needed to wait for the rain to let up a little.

He unclasped the black bag that sat nestled in the passenger seat, and rummaged until he found the jar of ointment. He unscrewed the cap, checked the underside for any sign of mold. "Perfectly clean." He expected nothing less. Amanda's compounding methods had always been meticulous.

Old ways are the best.

"Yes, they are—" Hoard flinched. He had heard the voice as clear as if the speaker sat in the car. *Gideon nerves.* That hypersensitivity that alerted one to any hint of an incursion by those who inhabited the wilderness. A blessing as well as a curse . . . no, it was a curse no matter how you looked at it. Betty Joan and the others didn't realize how lucky they would be to have it stripped away, if only for a little while. What a relief it would be, not to feel that eternal tingling, like hooks under his skin. The inability to work spells and set wards would be a small price to pay in exchange for that feeling of peace.

Hoard glanced in the rearview mirror at the backseat, then checked over his shoulder. Of course it was empty. Of course no one sat there, mumbling witch words in his ear. *I need a vacation.* As soon as he got home, he'd go online, book something. A weekend in Las Vegas. Anything.

He took another long, slow breath as he stared at the ointment. It didn't appear different from any other batch. The same baby-shit-green color. The same herbal stink.

He turned on the interior light, held up the jar to the weak glow. Sniffed the ointment again, then took a dab between his fingers and rubbed it. Set his conscious self aside and let his senses wander . . .

. . . *dammit*. Yes, there was something. So, so subtle—the work of a skilled talent, and no mistake—

The interior light flickered. Then the bulb blew with a soft *pop*.

"*Shit.*" Hoard resealed the jar and tossed it back in his bag, then tapped the light cover with his knuckle even though he knew it was a lost cause. Brand-new car, too. What was the point in spending thousands extra for European luxury when things broke after only a week?

At least the rain had let up. Hoard shifted into first, pulled out onto the road—

—then hit the brake, but forgot to downshift. The car shuddered, then stalled, headlights illuminating the middle of the road, and the body that lay there.

Hoard stared at the still form. It hadn't been there before—he would have seen it, even in the rain and the dark. Light-colored gown, light blue or white, sodden cloth stuck to curves like second skin. Bare feet and dark, waist-length hair soaked into strands of twisted rope.

Hoard checked his phone. Still too close to Gideon to get a good signal, which meant he couldn't summon an ambulance if needed. Oh well, he had blankets in the trunk, plastic bags to protect the leather upholstery from the wet. He knew what had happened, had seen it too many times before. *Someone's been chasing fairy lights.* Gone out in the night to commune with the spirits. Bottle up teenage girls during long winter nights, add Gideon nerves, and you'll learn of all the ways witches could kill themselves, accidentally or otherwise. He had to give the Mullin woman credit—at least she had dressed properly for the woods. Synthetics. Layers.

Hoard flipped up the hood of his rain jacket and struggled out of the car. The girl hadn't moved yet, which wasn't a good sign. "Hello?" He trudged through puddles, over shards of shattered asphalt. "Are you hurt?" He felt a surge of relief when the girl flexed her arm and turned over. It would have been a struggle for him to move a limp body of that size. Nothing but deadweight—

"No, Dr. Hoard." Ashley Petersbury smiled. "I'm just fine." She sat up, flipped back her lank hair. Her gown rode up her thighs as she moved, revealing mottled skin, a thatch of pubic hair. "See something you like?" She peeled back the neck of the gown, flashed a flat, white breast, the nipple blue from cold.

Blue from dead. Hoard backed away. *It's blue because she's dead.* "You can't be here. You can't."

Dead Ashley stood and started toward him. "It's nice to see you again, Doctor."

Hoard stumbled, caught himself before he fell, scrambled on all fours before righting himself. Ashley's laughter jangled his ears, like fingernails across slate. He fell against the car, grabbed for the handle. Pulled. Pulled.

I didn't lock the doors. He rooted through pockets, looked inside the car, saw the keys on the driver's seat.

"Could you give me a ride into town?"

Hoard ducked just out of reach of Ashley's blackened fingertips. Avoid the touch. *Avoid the demon touch and ye shall survive.* Words of the Lady. *Lady help me.* He spun away from the girl—corpse—corpse-girl—bounced off the car, and careened down the road.

Jerome, son of Frederick.

Hoard steadied. Ran. Toward Gideon.

You don't care about Gideon anymore, Jerome. Why should it care about you?

"I care! I care!" Pain in Hoard's knee, a god-awful wrench like the stab of a knife. "Lady, help me. *Lady help me!*" Through the haze of rain and pain and panic, he saw a figure walking toward him, a man in a long coat.

Someplace warm, Jerome—isn't that where you want to go?

Hoard staggered as the pain ripped through his chest and burst through his hands, flames in orange and gold, swirling around him. *"My Lady!"* He crumpled to the road, watched his hands blister, blacken, rupture.

Someplace bright and warm. . .

22

Stiff. That was Lauren's first thought when she opened her eyes. Her ribs, thighs, every place the stones had struck, fought her each time she tried to move, tensing to the edge of cramp. She peeled back the bandage covering the thorn wound. At least that looked better—the itching had ceased, the redness paled to pink. Chalk one up for her distrust of Amanda Petrie's ointments.

She sat up slowly, worked her shoulders. The mattress on which she had slept felt hard as a board, the feather pillows flattened by use and age. The bedroom, a narrow space with just enough room for a twin bed and dresser, smelled musty, and she knew she was the first person to sleep there in years. A lonely room, in a lonely house.

Dreams. Only one, that replayed over and over. The man in the long coat, leaning close, his face a smoky blank and his breath like the gust from an opened freezer. Only the voice held warmth, like a caress. A promise in the dark. *Let me in . . . let me in. . .*

Lauren edged out of bed, and stood in stages. Moving around helped, and removal of tapes and bandages revealed that her wounds had begun to heal. Her face still looked a little lopsided and her jaw felt stiff, but she could talk without too much difficulty.

By the time she had dressed and gone down to the kitchen, Waycross had already breakfasted and departed, leaving a carafe of coffee on the stove and a Crock-Pot of oatmeal on the counter, a scrawled note tucked beneath. *In the barn—yell if needed.*

Lauren ate, cleaned up, then wandered the front rooms, coffee in hand, and pondered her options. *Stay put.* She greatly reduced the chance of being attacked if she did so, but then it would be highly unlikely she would uncover any useful information. *Go into town.* She liked that choice better.

She hesitated in the doorway of Waycross's small office, which was located just off the kitchen. The door had been removed from the hinges, which implied it wasn't a private space. But Waycross lived alone, and she was Mistress of Gideon. For her, doors and locks may not have been necessary.

Lauren stepped over the threshold. Felt a mild tingling in her hands, chalked it up to nerves and residual soreness, and looked around, on the alert for sounds of approaching Mistresses.

The office was tiny, windowless, with three walls lined with shelves. The small table that served as the desk held nothing but an ancient black dial phone, phone books, a soup-can pencil holder. Lauren picked up one of the phone books and searched for the number for Lolly's garage. Took out her phone, turned it on. No bars. No signal.

Lauren shut off the phone and tucked it away. Dialed the number on the landline, listened to the rings. Mr. Loll apparently had no use for voice mail.

She hung up, then walked to the front window to check the weather. Dylan Corey had indeed delivered her things the previous night as promised, allowing her to finally switch out her filthy clothes for flannel-lined jeans and a red crew-neck sweater. She now had thicker gloves, and a heavier coat to take the place of her father's leather jacket.

"All geared up with no place to go." Well, in truth, she did have a place to go. She just needed to get there without Virginia Waycross finding out and trying to stop her.

Lauren donned her coat, then gathered her wallet and her father's book and tucked them into the inside pockets. One of the pens from Waycross's office. Nothing to carry, drop, leave behind. Hands-free, just in case any friends of Deena or Betty Joan decided to express their irritation with her in person.

She found the front door unlocked, which surprised her at first, until it struck her that if there was one person in Gideon who never needed to worry about a break-in, it was its Mistress. *Different world.* Different dangers.

Lauren walked out onto the front porch, closed the door after her. Down the steps, the long gravel driveway, keeping to the edge in case she needed to dart into the nearby trees to avoid being seen.

The road that ran past the Waycross place had been paved once, but the asphalt had cracked and rubbled over the years, tufts of brown grass pushing up through the gaps. This morning, it looked like the sort of place you saw in dreams. Shreds of nighttime fog still remained, heavy enough to mist your face and whiten the air like drops of milk in water. Trees were visible only as looming grayed shapes that closed in from both sides.

Lauren could see only a short distance in any direction. Vehicle tracks had the glassy look of water that had melted and then frozen again, as though hours had passed since anyone had driven past. For all she knew, she had already reentered Connie Petersbury's world—it all felt the same to her, close and dark and wet and cold, the worlds of the living and the dead combined.

She looked up into the soft white sky, saw the faint shadow of a hawk as it glided overhead. "I would love to know how anyone gets to where they're going in this damn town." She looked back toward the house. There were no vehicles in the driveway—they were all parked in the back near the barn. No way would she be able to sneak one out without Waycross knowing.

Dammit. She started the long trudge back up to the house when she heard the crunch and whine of a truck changing gears, and squinted in the direction of the noise.

A shadow in the fog. Then an ancient International pickup rumbled out of the murk, a barn-red tank with an unbent wire coat hanger sticking up where the antenna used to be.

Lauren caught sight of the driver, and stepped out into the road and waved him down. "Hi." She waited until the truck eased to a grumbling stop, then walked up to the driver's-side window. "You're Zeke, right?"

"Ezekiel Pyne, Miz Reardon. Spelled with a *y*." He looked like the quintessential old farmer from a commercial, weathered benignity topped with an iron-gray crew cut. "Waiting for someone?"

"Well, thing is, I need to get into town. Could you give me a lift?" Lauren smiled her brightest. "I wanted to check and see how Lolly's doing with my car."

Zeke glanced past her toward the house, and frowned. "Couldn't you just phone?"

"I tried. No answer."

"In a hurry for your car, are you? Thinking of leaving?"

Lauren took a deep breath. Wasn't it true that if you kept smiling no matter how irritated you felt, it came through in your voice and calmed you down? "No, but I would feel better if it were here in the driveway instead of in a repair shop. I just thought if you were headed that way . . . ?"

"I am, but . . ." Zeke again looked toward the house. "Situation seemed a bit tense last night. Mistress might not like you going off on your own."

"You know, she said nothing to me this morning about staying put." She hadn't said anything at all because she hadn't been in the house to say it, but, well, details. "I'm guessing that means things are safe enough."

"Maybe. But then . . ." Zeke's voice trailed. Then he reached across the bench seat to the passenger side and cranked the door handle. "Oh hell—get in. I've already lived a long, full life."

The seat felt hard as wood and the shocks had seen better days—

Lauren jostled and bounced as frigid air found its way to her from the holes rusted through the floor.

"She's an old rattletrap." Zeke rummaged a pack of gum from his pocket and pulled out a stick, then passed the pack to her. "But I can still fix 'er myself. She'll probably outlive me."

Lauren took out a stick of the gum. It proved to be cinnamon, one of those odd old brands you found on the bottom rack in a store checkout line, with flavor harsh enough to bring tears. "Is her name Betsy?"

"Lois." Zeke made a swooping motion with his hand. "Because she just glides down the lane." He chuckled, quieted for a few moments, then cleared his throat. "I'd like to tell you that last night was just a bad night. Because we've been through a rough stretch here and folks are upset." He kept his eyes on the road. "But that wouldn't be true. Things have been bad here for a long time."

Lauren picked her words with care—she didn't want to risk offending one of the few people who had made any effort to be kind. "I wasn't sure what to expect when I came here. I knew Dad must have left for a reason, but I had no idea he was so disliked."

Zeke nodded, eventually. "He wasn't a bad kid. Good-looking. A little wild—beer and driving too fast and such. Helluva ballplayer. Different town, he woulda ruled the roost." He gnawed his gum for a bit. "Hard on him getting pulled outta his old school in the middle of the year, too. Big change comin' from a Chicago school to little ol' Gideon."

"Chicago?" A jet of cold air whistled up Lauren's jeans leg, and she placed her booted foot on one floorboard hole, then another, until she blocked the right one. "He wasn't born here?"

"Nah. Hadn't been a Mullin in Gideon for years. And I mean *years*. Since the fire, all the way back to 1871." Zeke popped another stick of gum in his mouth. "Then one day back in '74—1974, you know. I ain't that old—Leaf goes to Chicago on business. Few days later, Mark and Becky-please Mullin—she didn't like folks callin' her Rebecca, thank you—they show up, your daddy in tow. Future daddy. Making amends, Leaf said. Mark was outta work—there was the recession back then, you know. The oil embargo. Businesses cratering left and right. 'Doin' a man with a family a favor,' he said."

Lauren looked out the window at the winter-brown landscape. "Think he went looking for him in order to make amends?"

Zeke arched a shaggy eyebrow. "Possible, I guess. If anyone had the money to hire detectives, it was Leaf." He wrinkled his nose. "Not usually his way, though. Leaf never spends a nickel unless he knows he'll get a dollar back, you know what I mean?"

"I know what you mean." Lauren sat quiet, mind wheels turning. *Cateman needed a Mullin for something.* But what? After a few moments, she dug the book out of her pocket and opened it to a blank page, scrabbled for the pen. Wrote the name "Leaf," drew a rough sketch of a maple leaf next to it. Looked over at Zeke, and found him eyeing her sidelong.

"You takin' notes on me?"

"No." Lauren drew a line of X-centered circles. "Sometimes I think better when I doodle."

"Yeah, your daddy was like that. Always had something in his hand. Pen, pencil, piece of chalk. Can you draw like him?"

"No." Lauren paged to one of the Emma sketches. "He was amazing."

"Yeah. He drew me a picture of one of my dogs, just before he left. I'd just lost ol' Tillie, but didn't have nothing to remember her by, and Matt drew me a picture of her, from memory. Still got it, hanging in my living room." Zeke sighed. "He could be kind, when you least expected. But he had a tough row to hoe, being a Mullin in Gideon. Didn't help that the recession overstayed its welcome and most all the decent jobs went away."

Lauren squinted, caught a glimpse of a battered sign through the fog: WELCOME TO GIDEON. "Folks blamed him for that?"

"Well, he didn't help matters by goin' wild. Losin' his folks hit him

hard. Left him without a pa at a time when a boy really needs one."
Zeke clucked his tongue. "No reason for that accident. No reason for
Mark and Becky to have gone out that night. We would've helped
them. We would've figured something out." He banged a hand on
the steering wheel. "Stubborn. The whole damn bunch of you." A
silent stammer. Then he shrugged an apology. "Sorry."

The truck hit a deep rut, and Lauren winced as the jostling aggravated aching muscles. "We do seem to bring it out in people."

"Roads were icy and the sheriff told folks to stay home. But Becky
had a stomach thing that wasn't getting no better, and they headed
out to the hospital. Never made it."

"Couldn't Amanda Petrie have helped with one of her concoctions?" Lauren saw the stern face from the clearing, the cold, steady
gaze. "Let me guess—they asked her for help, and she refused."

Zeke grumbled in the affirmative. "Folks figure that's why Leaf
reached out to your daddy. Guilt. I say it's better to not do the bad
thing in the first place, but what do I know? I just live here."

They rode the rest of the way in silence. Zeke pulled into the garage parking lot just as Lolly emerged from the diner, paper sack in
hand. "There he is. Good luck."

"Thanks for the lift." Lauren bested the balky door handle and
disembarked. "Do you think you'll be coming back this way soon?"

"Sorry. Headed out to Sterling to see a man about a chain saw."
Zeke grappled with the stick shift, coaxed the truck into reverse.
"Good day to you. Give my best to the Mistress." The clash of gears
sounded again, and Lois rumbled forward, onto the road, into the
fog.

Lauren trotted across the parking lot, intercepting Lolly just as he
reached the front office door.

"Not leaking anywhere." He switched the sack from one hand to
the other as he rooted through his coverall pockets. "Level sensor,
probably. Had to order it. Be here day after tomorrow." He pulled out
a set of keys. Apparently not everyone in Gideon felt secure enough

to leave their doors unlocked. "Could've told you that over the phone. Saved you the trip."

"I called earlier, but you must have been at the diner." Lauren followed him into the front office, an unheated wood-panel-and-linoleum space that reeked of cigarette smoke and old coffee. "I was starting to go a little stir-crazy, anyway. I needed to get out." Her breath puffed with each word, and she kept her coat on and zipped it to the neck for good measure.

"After one day?" Lolly set the sack on the desk, pulled out a cup of coffee and a disposable takeout container. "Figure you'd want to keep your head down, given how well things went last night."

Lauren walked to a small bulletin board that hung next to the entry to the garage proper. "Why didn't you like him?" The wall calendar still showed the previous month—she took it down, paged forward, tacked it back in place.

Lolly sat, opened the top of the food container, waved away the rising steam. "Ain't it a little early in the day for true confessions?"

"You seem to get off on shocking people. I didn't think you'd mind." Lauren dragged a rickety chair from against the wall and set it on the opposite side of the desk. "From all I've heard so far, Mullins were responsible for everything from the Civil War to the Black Death. I just wondered if anyone could give me a reason why the townfolk believe this to be the case." She sat down, tucked her hands inside her sleeves to warm them.

Lolly smashed biscuits into sausage gravy, then shoveled a forkful of the mess into his mouth. "I would think you had other things to worry about." He sprayed crumbs across the desk, swept them off with his sleeve.

Lauren unzipped her coat just far enough to dig out the book. "Blaine found Dad in Seattle. The more I think about it, the more I'm wondering whether the stress of hiding from Blaine was what sickened him. I know Blaine is responsible for the death of a woman who tried to help me. Now he's latched on to me."

Lolly continued to eat, swigging coffee in between bites. "Blaine and the Mullins go way back. But I'm guessing Miz Waycross filled you in about that."

Lauren leafed through the book until she came to the sketch of the gnarled visage. "That woman last night. Judith. She talked about reparations, because of things my family did to Blaine. He was a victim. He was wronged." She turned the book around so that Lolly could see her father's sketch. "The thing is, the figure I've encountered, he's not begging. He's ordering me to help him."

"Someone who's been hurt bad enough might get tired of waiting."

"He wants more than an apology."

Lolly glanced at the drawing. "What does he want you to do?"

"He thinks I know. But I don't." Lauren stood and walked to the office window. On the other side, the fog had cleared, and a weak sun shone. "Last night, you mentioned the wall my dad built. The Catemans' wall. You said everything I needed to know was there. What kind of wall is it? Is it in a place where I can go now and look at it?"

Lolly licked the fork clean and tossed it in the trash can next to the desk, then followed with the food container. "He never told you shit, did he? Just let it slide and left you to figure it out for yourself. Looks like he never changed." He opened the top drawer of the desk, took out a pack of cigarettes and an old-fashioned lighter, lit up, snapped the lighter closed. Took a deep drag, then watched her through a haze of smoke. "You look a little shook up, and I'm sorry, but just because you don't know your past doesn't mean you don't pay the price for it."

Lauren opened the book to the page of young faces. "He drew you." She held it out to Lolly.

"He drew everybody." Lolly glanced at the sketches, and for a moment his permanent glower softened. Then he caught himself, snorted, and looked away. "He'd draw a pile of manure if it was an interesting shade of brown."

"You know what hits me when I look at these faces?"

"No idea."

"Just you and Mistress are left. And it matters. I heard what you said to her last night as you were leaving. 'And then there were two.'"

Lolly sucked his teeth, stared past Lauren at the wall opposite his desk.

"What did you do? With my father? Thirty-seven years ago—what happened?" Lauren waited, then turned to one of the Emma drawings. "Folks have been making comments about this woman and my dad. Betty Joan and Ruthie and—" She bit back Connie's name just in time. "Who is she?" She held the book out again so Lolly could see.

Lolly glanced, then sniffed. "Just like the drawing says. It's Emma."

"Could you be more specific?"

Another puff, another cloud. Then Lolly balanced his cigarette on the edge of the desk, and took hold of the book. "Emma was Leaf Cateman's first wife." He wore a high school ring on his wedding finger—he exhaled on it, smacked the page as if impressing a seal, and gave the book back to Lauren.

Lauren looked down at the drawing, felt once again the sensuality, the desire. "Oh."

"Yeah." Lolly picked up the cigarette and stuck it back in his mouth. Then he opened another drawer and pulled out an old black landline telephone. "Doin' his Master's wife, the same Master who took him in after his folks died. What a guy."

"You a friend of Leaf Cateman's?"

"I don't run in those exalted circles."

"Then why do you care?" Lauren took one last look at the cameo face, then closed the book. "Cateman's married to Jorie now. What happened to Emma?"

"Make yourself a list. Stick that question on top." Lolly pulled some index cards out of his coverall pocket and lined them up across the desktop. "She disappeared around the same time Matt did." He reached back in the drawer, pulled out a calculator, and held it out to her. "Two plus two—you need this?"

Heat flooded Lauren's face. "She wasn't my mother."

"No? Well, then that opens up a whole new set of questions, doesn't it?"

"He wouldn't have saved these drawings if he had hurt her."

"How do you know?"

"Because he wouldn't have stopped with her. And he never purposely hurt my mother, with words or deeds." Lauren fielded Lolly's eye-rolling skepticism. "You know the man who left. I knew the one who reared me, and worked hard, and—"

"—died and left you to twist in the wind."

"You said yourself that you admired him for making a family."

"That was the whiskey talking." Lolly sniffed. "I'm not that sentimental as a rule." He snorted, then shook his head. He had yet to shave, and still wore the same clothes he had worn the previous night. "Look, I'm sorry, but I don't have time to hold your hand. You want counseling, see a shrink." He lined up the index cards, and picked up the phone. "Now, if you'll excuse me, I have parts to order."

Lauren sat frozen until the *clackety-clack* of an old rotary dial jarred her. Lolly's gruff voice.

"Yeah, Bill—I need the exhaust for a '92 F-150—"

She stood, forced one foot in front of the other, into the cold, the sun that was too weak to fight it. *They think you killed Emma Cateman, Dad. I know you didn't.* Across the parking lot, and onto the road. She had come here for answers, and left with more questions. But the answers to those? Did she really want to know?

23

Richard Loll stared at the card in his hand. Wondered at the buzzing in his head, realized it was the dial tone, and put down the phone. Poor kid—the look on her face as the truth about her father sank in. He knew how it felt, to believe in someone that much, then to have that faith chipped away until nothing remained.

Matt, you bastard. You never told her. Never instructed her. Worse than worthless, someone like that. Dangerous, even. For good or ill, folks in Gideon expected a Mullin to know things; some would even assume she had returned to fix what her daddy broke. And here she was, about as useful as tits on a boar.

I could help her. Almost duty bound to, wasn't he? So was Ginny. After all, they were the last of the five—him and Ginny, Matt and Jimbo, and poor little Connie, so powerful but not old enough to understand. They had practiced together, learned together. Closer than family, they had been, until Matt betrayed them all.

I could help her. Maybe she was worth it. *Or maybe she would just make things worse.* Loll shuffled the order cards, then stuck them back in his pocket. He needed to think. He couldn't talk on the phone at a time like this. He had to work.

He pulled a jacket on over his coverall, stubbed out his cigarette, and entered the garage. Stood in the doorway for a few moments and tried to remember the last time there had been a vehicle at every station. Two pickups. A van. Reardon's Subaru. Looked like he would be able to pay the utilities this month, maybe even salt away a little cash.

"Assuming we all live that long." Loll flipped on the lights, walked past Phil's Chevy to the workbench. He had parked the damn thing too close, and had to wedge between the tailgate and the cabinets to get to his tools. Well, he would just have to move it later. He didn't trust himself to get behind a wheel at the moment. He felt so jittery, no telling what he could do.

Shouldn't have drank last night. He could still taste the smoky burn of good whiskey, feel the warmth as it flowed into his gut. From that dark place in his head came the whisper that one more drink would calm him right down, help him think, and he wanted to believe even though he knew it had never been true.

Then he hated himself, because he had been so good for months and months.

Cleaning tools—that would settle him, help him forget about Lauren Reardon and son-of-a-bitch Matt Mullin. Poor Jim, and Connie. *Just the two of us now, Gin.* Not enough strength between them, for all that Gin was Gideon's Mistress. Not enough power.

That means we're dead. Loll rummaged through the tool bench, pulled out a small can of gasoline, a couple of shop rags. *Maybe I should go ahead and have that drink.* After all, what difference did it make? He paused, then shook his head. He swore he would die sober, not pants-pissing drunk like his old man. Sometimes the most important promises were the ones you kept when it didn't matter.

He picked up one of his socket wrenches, took comfort in the cold heft of steel. He relished the harsh stink of the fuel as it rattled his sinuses, the oily feel as it soaked into the shop cloth and dripped down his hands to the concrete floor. Real smells. Simple things. He needed simple right now.

Time passed. Maybe he had heard the door open, and it just hadn't registered. But he sensed it now, the way he always did. Someone, in the office.

"Who's out there?" Loll tossed the rag aside, but held on to the wrench. "Phil, is that you? Next week, I said, okay? It's a special or-der." He waited for Phil, or whoever it was, to answer. Waited.

Then he felt a chill, like snow melting on his skin.

Phillip is not here, Richard, son of Lucas.

Loll gripped the edge of the bench. The voice buzzed in his ear, along his jaw. Like when the dentist stuck the needle in the gum, and hit the nerve. "Who the hell are you?"

I think you know.

"You don't play games with me in my place—you answer the Lady's damn question."

The figure stepped into the office doorway. Tall and dark, but not solid—Loll could see the bare outline of the doorjamb through the black.

Hello, Richard. It has been a while.

"Blaine?" Loll backed against the tool chest.

If memory serves, Pizza Face was your preferred name for me. I believe I have you to thank for hanging that around my neck.

Loll forced a laugh. "At least you learned to hide that puss of yours from sight."

Only for a little while longer. It seems that help has finally arrived.

"You think so?" Loll threw the wrench aside, picked up a hammer. Wait—a gun, yes, he had one. His old man's .45, on the bottom shelf of the chest. He ducked down, reached for it.

Gone.

Do you truly believe it would help? I can return it to you, if you wish, and we can see what happens when you try to use it.

Loll straightened. His breakfast bubbled to the back of his throat, and he swallowed again and again to keep from vomiting.

It is so changed here. Nicholas Blaine shifted, then leaned against the doorway like a customer stopped by to chew the fat. *So many familiar faces gone.*

"You wouldn't know anything about that, would you?" Loll set down the hammer but held on to the rag, kneaded it, tied knots, then undid them. He had locked the big door to the garage, the one for the vehicles that led to the outside, and left the key in the office—no getting out that way.

No getting out, period.

You didn't tell her. Blaine held a shadow walking stick, which he used to point at Lauren Reardon's Outback. *Matthew's daughter. You could have told her all about me. You could have told her all the things you did, you and Matthew and Constance. James and Virginia. All the little tricks you pulled to try and stop me.*

"We did stop you." Loll reached into his coverall pocket. It was still there, the wire circlet, the charm that Matt had taught them to make. The others had stopped using them after Matt left, said that they didn't do any good. But he had always kept one with him. The Lady's all-seeing eye. A poor substitute for the crows that had abandoned them, the good part of the world that had cast them aside. But now it was all he had. "We did stop you."

Only until Matthew Mullin deserted you, and you realized how small was your power without him. I simply allowed myself a chance to heal, and bided my time.

Loll pulled out the circlet, which he had fashioned from a piece of coated wire. It had looked brand-new when he put it in his pocket a few hours before. But now the red plastic sheath had faded, cracked away in places. "At least I'm alive." He let the thing drop to the floor, hoped the fear that twisted his stomach didn't reveal itself in his voice. "Alive, like you want to be and can't ever be."

For now.

"She can't save you—she doesn't know anything. Matt never taught her."

She is intelligent, and she has power. She can learn.

"Who's going to teach her?" Loll surveyed the garage. He had turned off half the overhead lights to save money, and he sensed movement in darkened corners, heard the skitter of running feet.

Tiny feet, light as feathers, quick as rats. "It'll take years. You don't have the patience."

I've waited almost two hundred years. What's a few more? Blaine pushed away from the doorjamb, his coat flowing around him as though he moved underwater. *But I do need to begin, and you know what that means, don't you, Richard?*

Loll took up the hammer again, kept it below the level of Phil's truck to hide it from sight. "No, I don't—why don't you tell me."

It's too late, Richard—put down the hammer. The smile in that voice, as hard as a fist. *You should have told her everything when you had the chance, but you let your hatred of her father stop you. So predictable. I could set my watch by you, if I needed one.*

Loll started to edge around the back of the truck. Stopped. The footsteps had slowed—he could hear them, soft on the cement floor but growing louder, from whisper to murmur, as though someone crept toward him.

Someone. Or something.

Are you thirsty, Richard? A flicker of black, and Blaine stood in the center of the garage. *Perhaps you would like a drink before we continue.*

Loll caught movement out of the corner of his eye, and turned just as a small figure emerged from the shadow of the second pickup. Little Bella Petersbury, long brown hair in ringlets, the lacy hem of her white dress dragging on the floor. "Unca! Unca!" She tottered toward him, cradling a bottle of whiskey like a doll.

Loll backed away. He thought Bella a ghost at first. But then he saw the shadow trailing after her. "She's dead. She's at Petrie's, on a table. Connie picked out the coffin. White lined with pink. She came here after and told me all about it and she cried and cried." He wadded the rag and threw it, hitting the child in the face. *"Get away from me."*

Bella stopped. Blue lips quivered, and tears spilled down her sunken cheeks. "Unca?" She held out the bottle. "I haffa gif' for you."

Loll stared at the honey-brown liquid, his mouth watering even as anger gripped him. He raised the hammer, but stopped when Bella cringed.

Go ahead, Richard. Hit her. Blaine leaned against Reardon's Subaru, cane swinging back and forth like a metronome. *She still has form and substance. You could hurt her if you tried. Just pretend you're Lucas. Pretend she's you.*

Loll stepped back as Bella once again drew closer. Her eyes shone too dark and cold, and her hands looked more adult than child, the fingers longer and thinner, the nails red and tapered. "What the hell did you do to her?"

Nothing she did not wish done.

"What the hell can she wish for? She's a baby."

If it comforts you to believe that, then by all means do so. Blaine pointed his stick toward Bella. *Look at her. Look at that* baby. *The light in her eyes—it's positively feral.* He laughed, the deep, rich toll of a funeral bell. *Give me a child until she is seven, and I will give you such cruelty as you have never seen. But I don't believe it will take that long with this one— she possesses a certain predisposition.*

"Takes after her mama, you mean," Loll muttered. A slinky little bitch, Ashley Petersbury. One of Jorie Cateman's pack. *Like mama, like daughter.* He looked at the hammer in his hand, felt the pain of long-healed wounds. *Like father, like son.*

Now you understand. Blaine cocked his head, shadows swirling like an oil slick on water. *I don't change people, Richard. I simply encourage what's already there. Like a gardener, coaxing tiny shoots until they flourish and bloom.* A shift of light, and he stood within arm's length.

Loll tried to back away, but his feet felt stuck in place. His breathing quickened as he fought whatever held him. It had gotten colder— his hands ached from it. It had grown darker as well. Blackness filled each corner and crevice of the garage and streamed across the ceiling, the floor, like shadows cast by things unseen.

I so wanted it to be James Petersbury to tempt you. Blaine stood shoulder to shoulder with Loll now. *He had been your friend for so long. He knew your struggles well. It would have amused us so, to watch him lead you back down the tangled path. You're the least of them, Richard. Son of a brutish drunkard, a brutish drunkard yourself. What resistance can you muster? What wondrous feats could you possibly perform?* A hint of a face became visible in the murk, the gnarled features of a damned thing. *Give up. Give in. Accept your fate.*

Loll stood still as the words battered him. He looked down at the thing that had been Bella—she smiled up at him, baby teeth black and dull as old oil, and held out the bottle.

"Uncle." Her voice came clearer now, darker and deeper. A woman's voice.

Loll took the bottle—the glass felt greasy, gritty, as though it had sat collecting dust on some shelf for years. He tried to read the label, but the lettering shuddered and smeared into a blurred mess. But the cap twisted off like any other, and the whiskey smelled like every lost day he had ever forgotten until that moment.

He raised the bottle, tipped his head back. One swallow. Another. Then he filled his mouth with as much as it would hold, spat it in Blaine's face, hurled the bottle at Bella. *"Go to hell,"* he shouted over the child's wail as he ran past them, through the garage to the office and out the door.

Night. No stars or moon, no lights from the diner, the hardware store. Icy rain stung Loll's face, ran into his eyes, down his neck, and inside his coverall. He slowed to a trot and tried to close his jacket, but his fingers had gone numb and he couldn't feel the zipper to close it.

Run. He let the jacket flap open and picked up speed. Down the road, past darkened houses. How could it be night already? Where had the time gone? *Blaine.* Matt had tried to explain to them how he could play with time, wind it and unwind it like string on a reel.

Loll pressed a hand to his side, the stitch that knifed him with every stride. He sucked in air, great frigid mouthfuls, but his lungs still burned. His leg muscles. *Run, you old drunk.* Down Main Street, toward Old Main Road. If he could get out of Gideon, he'd be all right. If he could get out—

Shortcut. Through the woods. It would trim a half mile, maybe more, and he needed all the help he could get. Fat, that's what he was. Lungs full of cigarette smoke. *Shoulda drove.* Stolen Phil's truck. *Too late now.*

Too late.

"Didn't tell her nothin'." Loll huffed, every word a gasp. "What good—would it do?" He splashed along the river for a good fifty yards, hunting for a narrow spot where he could cross. Found one and waded in, felt the current tug at his ankles like claws.

One step. Another. Then rocks shifted under his weight and he stumbled, fell, howled as something sharp cut into his knee. Scrambled to his feet and limped to the opposite bank, arms outstretched for balance.

Warmth flowed down Loll's leg. Blood. He had hurt himself bad, but he had to keep running. Otherwise, *he* would catch him, and that would be worse than bad.

So hot. Night had turned to day again. No more rain. Only sun, the heat of summer. Loll pushed himself despite the pain, the ragged ache in his chest. Branches whipped his face and snagged his T-shirt, caught on the pockets of his shorts. He looked down, caught a glimpse of chubby knees scabby with mosquito bites, the fresh gash bright against his pasty skin.

Then he heard, coming up fast from behind. The crash of branches and the grunting. The curses.

"The woods won't hide you, you little bastard."

Faster. If he could reach Old Main Road, he'd be okay. If he could—if he could—

"Come back here and take your punishment like a man!"

The crack of leather sounded. That meant the belt. A snake of brown cowhide, a silver buckle like a snap trap.

"I am going to air you out. Do you hear me, boy?"

Keep running—that was the trick. If he stopped, his father would catch him. If he stopped.

Don't stop—never stop—keep running through the trees and over the fence. He jumped across the ditch and out onto the road and into the light—

—bright, bright light, bright as the sun—

—and heard a horn like the howl of an animal, headlights bearing down like two glowing eyes—

CONNIE WATCHED LOLLY cross the river. He changed as he passed over the water, from his grown-up self on one side to a young boy on the other. That was Blaine's doing, of course. He controlled the woods now. Soon he would control Gideon itself, and that would be that. The end of everything.

She called out to Lolly even though she knew he couldn't hear. Asked the Lady to take care of him, even though she knew it made no difference. Moments later, she heard the screech of air brakes, felt the shudder of impact as though her own body had been struck. Felt wetness course down her cheek, touched it, tasted it. Tears. *Still human enough to cry.* Some comfort there, at least. She hadn't become one of *them* yet.

"Gone like his daddy."

Connie looked toward the riverbank, the shade that flickered like dark flame. "How would you know? Lucas Loll died before you were born."

The thing that had been Ashley Petersbury stepped into what passed for the light. "I know everything now. All your secrets. Everything you and ol' Jimbo used to hide from me because you thought I was too stupid to understand." She looked like something from the covers of the vampire books she had once devoured, too-thin and lank-haired, her skin white as bleached bone. "I even know more than Jorie now. I should visit her some night, surprise her."

"She might turn out to be more than you bargained for, missy." Connie edged away from the riverbank even though the current streamed colder than any she had felt so far. Ashley had been obnoxious enough when alive. That she had gotten even worse after death just didn't seem possible. "Jorie Cateman's a spiteful little thing, but Leaf wouldn't have married her if she didn't have talent."

"He promised that I would be more powerful than her. That was my gift for helping to bring him ol' Jimbo, because I'm his favorite."

"If you're his favorite, why ain't you with him? Why'd he take little Bella instead of you?"

Ashley's chin tilted up and she folded her arms, like a stubborn child refusing to eat her peas. "He's saving me for something special."

"He's saving you, all right." Connie felt the water, which had turned thick as syrup in places. Red as blood. Just ol' Lumpy, she figured, letting her know that he knew what she was up to.

"You bet he's saving me, and I will be there for him when he calls. Change comin'." Ashley clapped her hands, the sound muffled by the heavy, still air. "Won't be no stopping it." She twirled in place, the folds of her gown barely fluttering. "Be nice to get out of these woods. Back into the world again. It's warm there. And there's bleeding and pain and despair, and I will feed on all of it."

Aren't you the cheery one. Connie started to tell Ashley to go away, but before she could open her mouth, the thing had already vanished into the trees.

She scanned the bank, saw no one else, wondered if they were all off planning something or if they had finally gotten bored with taunting her. Well, all but Jim. He had taken to hiding from everyone, though whether out of shame or guilt, she had no idea. Angry as she was at him, she wished he would visit. There still had to be some part of him that she could reach. They were the last real Petersburys, weren't they? Norma didn't count, or Junior, or idiot Ashley and the babies. Just her and Jim, working with Ginny and Lolly and Matt. Now there were four of them on the dead side, and she wished like a wishing thing that she knew where Matt was. If he was here in the wilderness, why couldn't she sense him?

She paused. For a split second, the current in which she stood felt warmer, the water as quick and bubbly as it would have been on the living side. Then the moment passed and the cold returned, the thick tumble of whatever in hell it was that flowed in this dead river. But she knew what she had felt. For that thinnest slice of time, she had not felt the monster's power.

She needed help, someone on the living side to tell her what was going on. *Lauren. Where are you, girl?* If only she could reach her without Blaine or any of her idiot family finding out. If only . . .

24

After she left the garage, Lauren wandered with intent toward the town square. She stuck close to shelter—trees, doorways, the odd trash bin—in case she needed to slip out of sight. Kept a lookout for vehicles, faces in windows, anyone else who happened to be out for a stroll on this foggy, drizzly morning. Judging from her reception the previous night, half of Gideon wanted to kill her, and most of the other half wouldn't have lifted a finger to stop them. Strange feeling, to be the focus of such hatred. Hard for her to comprehend that her father had grown up with these people, and that they had nursed their animus for so long.

So here I am, walking around with a target on my back. Lauren ducked into the doorway of a shuttered beauty shop, and scanned the nearby buildings. The diner appeared quiet, with only a handful of cars in the parking lot. A couple of pickups stood parked on the street in front of the hardware store. No people, though. Lolly had been the only person she had seen since her arrival.

She stepped out of the doorway and crossed the street to the square proper, a desolate oval of browned lawn. In the center stood an ancient wooden gazebo surrounded by shrubs. Someone had taken the trouble to prep the shrubs for winter by covering them with mulch and plastic cones, but this only emphasized the bareness of the rest of the space, the state of neglect.

The steps leading up to the gazebo creaked and sagged under Lauren's weight. The interior had all the charm of a bus shelter; food wrappers littered the floor, and a six-pack's worth of empty beer bottles stood lined up against the far wall.

A crack like a gunshot sounded and Lauren stilled, heart pounding, then scuttled to the gazebo entry and looked toward the diner. In the parking lot, a man stood behind an old Corolla, looking down at the tailpipe.

Lauren waited for the man to drive away. Then she leaned against the gazebo wall, and brushed off the flakes of chalky white paint that broke loose and fluttered over her clothes. The wood beneath had gone silvery and cracked with age, and she scraped off a large chip—as she did so, she pressed her fingers to the bare wood, and felt—

—furnace heat that blistered her skin—pain like razors slicing deep—smoke black as pitch that roiled around her, filled her lungs, suffocated her, and saw—

—a woman standing in an upper window, framed by fire, screaming a name—screaming for help—until the flames cycloned around her and she vanished—

Lauren looked around the gazebo. She sat pressed against cold wood, opposite the spot where she had been. The paint she had peeled away lay crushed and powdered on the floor, while the wood she had touched showed smooth and bare, a wound with the scab torn away.

She checked her fingertips. They looked pale and undamaged, but they tingled, as though she had touched something hot enough to burn.

She sat still for a time, cradling her hand. It had all seemed so real, the pain and the heat, the strangling stench of the smoke. *The woman.* She had been young, a teenager. Blond, her hair gathered at the nape in a large bun, her dress or blouse dark steel blue, face smeared with soot and tears, eyes round with fear.

Lauren thought back to the moment when Dilys had asked her to hold her father's book. The gentle scent of cut wood, there and then gone as though carried on a breeze. But this emotional hammering had been as brutal as a physical assault, had ended in a death that had seemed as real as if she witnessed it in person.

She breathed deep, chill damp to drive out the memory of fire. Checked her watch. Two hours had passed since she left the Waycross place, assuming time still behaved and whatever inhabited the woods had not yet taken over Gideon itself. *I need to get back.* Waycross would be furious with her, but she would accept whatever the woman threw at her just to have a roof over her head and four sane walls surrounding her. Shelter. Refuge.

She pondered her options. *Back to Lolly's.* She would have better luck there than at the diner. She would ask to use the phone, wait outside for whomever Waycross dispatched to collect her. She rose, waited for her knees to steady. Walked to the gazebo entry and found Tom Barton looking up at her from the foot of the stairs.

"Mornin'." Barton looked as ancient and rickety as the gazebo. He still wore the same battered clothing he had the previous day, this time topped with a red rain jacket that looked as though it had spent some time as a painter's drop cloth.

"Hello." Lauren remained in the gazebo, her foot hovering above the top step. She would never have called Barton "kind," even though he had been helpful and had quite possibly saved her life. But on a Seattle street, she would have hurried past someone like him. She might even have crossed to the other side to avoid an encounter depending on how hard he pinged her weirdo radar. *He's just a grumpy old man.* A small-town fixture. *And I'm just a little on edge.*

"Not safe up there." Barton cocked his head, revealing a nasty razor scrape along his jaw. "Floor weren't made right. Not enough joists." He kicked the bottom step. "Every winter, they say they'll fix it in the spring. Then comes spring, everybody forgets." He squinted at her. "You all right? You look a mite peaky."

"I'm fine." Lauren leaned against the railing, but pulled back when the wood creaked and wobbled.

"Not too smart, you being out on your own, is it? Considering?"

"You're not the first person to ask me that this morning." Lauren felt a tingle between her shoulder blades as she looked around. *It's just nerves.* "Seems pretty safe." She scanned every doorway and window. "No one's about."

"Some folks out lookin' for Miz Petersbury. Others? Work, I guess." Barton made a show of looking everywhere else but at Lauren. "What are you doin' here, if you don't mind my asking?"

"I just wanted—" Lauren stopped. Simple enough question. If Corey or Waycross had asked, she would have told the truth. *Probably.* "I just wanted to check things out. First chance I've had to look around."

Barton stared at her for one beat, two, squinting as though the sun blazed. Then he shook his head. "Not much to see. Not anymore." He jerked his chin toward the empty square. "Used to be something. Lots of rosebushes. Market during the summer and everybody bringing in the stuff they growed, all the vegetables and fruits and flowers. Lambs and calves and pigs." His voice lightened, the memories shaving away years. "And there was a harvest dance in the fall, lanterns hanging in all the trees and the ladies in their best dresses and their men all done up in Sabbath black. Fiddle playing and tables piled with cakes and roasts and frosty bowls of rum punch—" He stopped, wiped his sleeve across his mouth. Licked his lips. "Those were the days."

"Must have been fun." Lauren waited for Barton to say more, but he remained silent, staring into some middle distance, a boyhood long past. She left him to his memories, eased down the steps past him, and walked around the gazebo. She flattened clumps of mulch underfoot, straightened the plastic cones. A soggy shred of newspaper lay plastered over one board—she peeled it away to find it had hidden a small copper plaque gone green with age.

This poor remnant of the home of Micah and Ruth Corey we display in memory of the Great Fire that consumed the town of Gideon on the Eighth and Ninth days of October in the year Eighteen and Seventy-one. Rest with the Lady, dear Ruth.

"This was from their house." Lauren brushed the wood with her fingertips. No heat this time, just the cold roughness of chipped paint and old wood. "That was Ruth Corey who I saw in the window." She looked toward the steps, but Barton had gone. Then she heard a hacking cough and sounds of spitting, and caught sight of the old man shambling toward the large houses that lined a short street just off the square.

Lauren heard Corey's soft voice in her head, his glum assessment. *The good part of town.* Where else would the Master of Gideon live? She waited until Barton had crossed the road that encircled the square, then started after him. She walked slowly at first, off at an angle, so that he wouldn't suspect that she followed him if he happened to turn around. But he continued his straight-line trudge toward the houses, arms bent and elbows jutting, like a puppet controlled by a skilled master.

Lauren tried to pick out which house best suited the Leaf Cateman she had heard the others speak of, the secluded Master who rejected Virginia Waycross's invitations. Was it one of the glum Federals with stone sills and black awnings? The white colonial, one green shutter knocked cockeyed by weather or neglect? Or the red-brick Georgian, solid as a prison?

Barton passed by all those places, walking until he came to the rambling rose-and-gray Victorian that had caught Lauren's eye when she first entered Gideon. He paused in front of it for a few moments, surveying like a buyer sizing up a potential purchase. Then he walked up the sloping driveway and disappeared around the back.

Lauren broke into a trot, keeping an eye on windows and doorways, on the lookout for any flicker of shadow or movement of curtain, any sign that she had been spotted. Off the square and into the cul-de-sac. Off the pavement and onto the cracked, buckled sidewalk. A tall yew hedge bordered the Victorian's lot, and she slipped behind it, bent low, scuttled like a sneak thief.

As she moved deeper into the yard, her skin tingled, tiny static jolts. Any other place, any other time, she would have blamed adrenaline and fear, but now she thought of spells and curses and whether something watched her that she couldn't see.

Then the voice found her, that peevish old man's singsong.

"—time to waste—haven't got all day—"

Through gaps in the hedge, Lauren watched Barton pace around the Victorian's rear yard, then stop when the back door of the house opened.

"Sorry it's late, Tom." Amanda Petrie walked out onto the rear landing. She had thrown a coat over a severe black pant suit, and held it closed at the neck with one hand as she balanced a covered dish on the other. "Groceries only arrived an hour ago."

"Jus' leave it there." Barton pointed to the lowest step. "I don't want you coming near me."

"Why, Tom—"

"Stoning. Be whipping us through the streets like dogs next. Just like dogs."

Petrie had been smiling, almost jovial. But a shadow fell across her face as Barton railed. "You don't know what you're saying, Thomas Barton."

"I know what I seed and I know what I heard."

"Then you don't know anything." Petrie clumped down the steps, the dish close against her chest, free hand gripping the iron railing. "And a wise man keeps his mouth shut about things he doesn't know."

Barton stilled. "Are you threatening me, Amanda Petrie?" His voice roughened from wheedle to grumble. "Been a long time since someone threatened me."

"I never threaten." Petrie set the dish on the second-lowest step, muttering under her breath as she struggled to bend, pressing her hands to her lower back as she straightened. "I merely advise."

"Save your advice for someone that wants it." Barton sidled up to the step and grabbed the dish like a jackal grabbing a bone from a sleeping lion. "I worked for this. Earned it. Fixed that gap in the fence this morning. West side of the orchard. You tell the Master. Won't be no one getting through there to steal his fine applewood." A wet chuckle. "Nope. Not a soul." He lifted the edge of the cover off the dish, sniffed, then set it back in place. "You tell him."

"When I can." Petrie's edges softened, a little. She kneaded her hands, lowered her head. "Master's feeling poorly. It's the damp. It always affects him like this, Lady bless him."

"Tell him no one will be stealing his applewood this winter. That'll cheer him up." Barton tucked the dish beneath his coat, then turned and limped toward the line of trees that bordered the yard.

"Just hurry up and eat that before it gets cold," Petrie called after him. "I don't want to hear your complaints about soggy piecrust on top of everything else that's going on." She mounted the steps, then paused and looked back over her shoulder. As she scanned the yard, one corner of her mouth turned up, a bare hint of a smile. Then she reentered the house and closed the door.

Lauren crouched in the shadow of the hedge, shifting as sore muscles cramped and bruises stung. *Good morning, Amanda Petrie.* Dressed in black, the coat draped over her shoulders like a cape, the woman had looked more like a witch than anyone else in Gideon. *Old ways are the best, ladies.* The quiet triumph in her voice as the other women attacked, as though she had won a long-desired prize.

Lauren touched the wound on her forehead, felt a slimy remnant of Petrie's ointment that had somehow survived all her scrubbing and washing, rubbed it away so hard she broke the scab. Warm blood trickled down her face and dripped to the ground, bright red against the dull brown—she tried to stanch the flow with one hand as she scrabbled through her pockets with the other for a tissue.

The gash stung as cold air brushed over it. Then came pain, like the slice of a knife. She pulled her hand away, found a red smear thick as paint coating her palm.

Lauren pulled tissues from her pocket. A wadded mess, but all she had. Pressed them to the wound. *Lady, if you can hear me, if you're even there, help.* She choked down acid that rose in her throat as black spots formed before her eyes, started small and then spread, like inky rain striking the ground.

"I don't know—the right words." Lauren rocked back and forth, then put out a hand to keep from toppling over into the dirt. "Just—get out, whatever the hell you are." The same words she yelled at the desk. *It didn't work that time.* This had to work. "Get out—out—out. Go back—where you came from." Muttered the words over and over and over and—

—her vision cleared. Pain ceased. Bleeding . . . stopped.

Lauren kept the tissues pressed to her forehead, then used them to wipe her face as the aches, the pain, the nausea and weakness continued to subside.

Like magic. Her shoulders shook, her laughter silent, until it hit her what someone looking out their window would see, a rumpled, bloodstained woman crouched in the shadows, grinning. She sobered, finished cleaning her face, then studied the stained tissues as though she could figure out what had just happened if she stared at them long enough. Something she did had countered the effect of Amanda Petrie's ointment.

I just wished real hard. Lauren stood. *Maybe I'm getting better at this.* Or maybe the magic in Amanda Petrie's ointment wasn't as strong as whatever destroyed her father's desk. Oh well—she had to start somewhere.

Baby steps. She set one foot in front of the other, one hand grazing the hedge for support. Touched the gash, and found a new scab had already formed.

She searched the ground, picked up everything on which her blood had dripped, the dried grass and dead leaves, even clods of dirt. Then she folded the mess inside the stained tissues and stuffed the bundle in her pocket as scenes replayed in her head from the television shows and movies she watched at friends' homes. The books she read behind her father's back. How a strand of hair, a piece of clothing, could destroy—an enemy could work all sorts of evil if they got hold of them. One could only imagine what havoc Petrie could wreak with a person's blood.

Lauren peered through the hedge at the Cateman house, the place her father had worked and, according to Lolly, where he had betrayed the man who had helped him. *Ask Leaf if you can see his wall. It's all there.*

Lauren paced and pondered. *I could walk up and knock.* She tried to visualize Amanda Petrie's face when she opened the door to find the woman she'd tried to kill standing on her back step. *Element of surprise.* It might even work. *For a minute or two.* Petrie did not strike her as a woman who could be caught off guard for long.

She pushed through a gap in the hedge and walked toward the house, head held high, as if she belonged there. The backyard of the place stretched for a good two hundred feet, filled by a sweeping brick driveway and a couple of large outbuildings. A four-car garage. A decrepit old shed.

As she approached a rear window, she slowed, ducked low, then peeked over the sill. A storeroom, judging from the details she could pick out through the hazy glass, the walls lined with shelves filled with glass bottles of various sizes. Wooden boxes.

Lauren wiped the window with her jacket cuff, but the clearer view didn't help much. The storeroom had a single entry that opened onto a dim corridor; through the doorway opposite, she could see the corner of a table, a wall of cabinets. The kitchen, most likely. Not the room where she would expect to see the wall that Matthew Mullin built.

"—too much going on—"

Lauren's breath caught. She darted around to the side of the house just as two men rounded the far corner and entered the backyard. They wore jeans and barn coats; one carried a heavy canvas tool bag while the other hefted a shovel.

"I told her that we'd get to it after we fixed Jorie's shower." Tool

Bag hefted the canvas sack atop the steps. "And Jorie's sink. And her porcelain throne." He freed a pouch of chewing tobacco from his pocket, hooked a large wad, and crammed it inside his cheek.

"Ol' Petrie better not hear you call her by her first name." Shovel spit, then wiped his mouth with the back of his hand.

"Like she carth." Tool Bag lisped around a mouthful of chaw.

"Well, better get to it if we want to get home before midnight." Shovel jammed the tool into the ground, then started up the steps. "Never thought I'd miss crazy ol' Jim."

Tool Bag followed. "Don't thpeak ill of the dead."

"Better than the dead speaking ill of you." Shovel entered the house, then held the door for Tool Bag, who trudged in after him.

Lauren listened as the men's voices faded, only to be replaced by sounds of a high-pitched argument. Two young women bickering about whose turn it was to wind the clocks in the east wing. *This isn't a house, it's a household.* Never empty. Never still. Not the sort of place where one slipped inside and wandered. There would be someone around every corner, in every room. *I need a better plan.*

She edged along the side of the house until she met shadow, which she used as cover as she pushed through a thin spot in the hedge and into the front yard of the house next door. Hands in pockets, she strode across the lawn and onto the sidewalk, a woman out for a walk. Nothing to see here—just moving along.

25

Leaf Cateman stood at the front window of his bedroom and watched the young woman creep along the hedge that bordered the side yard then vanish into the leaves quick as you please. *Lauren.* Not a traditional Gideon name, but he supposed that was to be expected these days. *A sneak, just like your father.* Funny how blood always told.

He tensed as a noise sounded from the hallway, just outside his door. The squeak of floorboards. "Amanda?"

The door opened a crack. "Master? Are you decent?"

"Of course."

Amanda Petrie stepped inside, then shut the door. "I just gave Tom his pie." She carried a tray bearing some folded cloths, rolls of gauze, a jar of ointment. "The old crank—he didn't want to take it from me. Made me put it down on the step, then back away."

"What did you expect?" Leaf walked to the sitting area at the far end of the room, rolling up the sleeves of his pajamas along the way. Tried not to look at the gauze that swaddled his arms from wrist to elbow, the areas of pink-tinged seepage. "I had to field a few interesting phone calls this morning from various concerned parties. Never thought I would ever need to concoct inventive lies on your behalf. Rehearsing a play about the Salem trials. Just an accident." He tried to smile, but his cheeks felt strange, stiff, as though a tooth infection had come to call. "Quick thinking, even if I do say so myself."

"I only tried to do what needed doing." Amanda set the tray on a side table next to the chair. She had already donned a pair of latex gloves, which fit so tightly her fingers resembled pale sausages. "It will turn out as it did with her father, just you see. Sooner trust a rabid dog not to bite than a Mullin to do what's right." She paused to watch him as he moved, and frowned. "You should take some time for yourself, Master. Go to Chicago. See your doctor."

"I can't leave now." Leaf sat down, shifting as the nubs of rough brocade upholstery poked through thin flannel. He eased off one slipper, then the other, peeled off the white cotton socks to expose his pink, flaking feet. "Too much going on. Too much to do." He glanced up to find Amanda looking at him, lips pulled in between her teeth like she wanted to say something but didn't dare. So, time to change the subject. "Where is my wife?"

"Downstairs, whining to Maureen." Amanda opened the jar of ointment, dug into it with her gloved fingers, and spread the muck on strips of gauze. "She fell in the kitchen a bit ago. Slipped on Lady-knows-what, whacked herself good on the edge of the counter."

"I trust the wound isn't severe?"

"Maureen is seeing to her. She's going to have a nasty shiner, but she'll recover."

"Perhaps it knocked some sense into her." Leaf wrinkled his nose as the smells hit him. The marshy rankness of the ointment. The strange odor of his skin, like the stink of old fireplace ashes. He sat back as Amanda removed the old bandages and applied fresh, took what comfort he could in the cool numbness as the treated herbs did their work. "You shouldn't have done it, you know."

Amanda kept her eyes on her task. "Don't know what you're talking about, Master."

"It's just the two of us here. Not really a time to play dumb." Leaf shifted again as the upholstery abraded and stung. "Grandfather learned the hard way that only a Mullin could break the curse, a curse that shackles Gideon as strongly as any chain. Father wasted his life trying to prove him wrong—"

"Your father, Lady rest his soul, knew Mullins for what they were. We can work out another way."

"She showed up, out of nowhere. Unbidden. Unexpected. It's a sign."

"I thought you didn't believe in signs."

"I believe in taking advantage when it presents itself." Leaf shrugged, then caught himself as the stinging burn spread across his upper back. "If we play her properly, she will realize we offer the more attractive option."

Amanda wadded the old bandages and stuffed them in a paper sack for later incinerating. "Virginia already has her."

"Virginia won't be able to see her straight. Memories of Matthew, all the things that might have been. The girl will sense the resentment. It will drive her away." Leaf stretched his legs as far as comfort allowed. "From what I have heard, last night's little get-together didn't go at all well. Over half the attendees walked out. Theo Fuller's applied for a job at the orchard and Judith Merton has signed up to help with the winter service, and there will be more where they came from." He imagined the scene in that poky living room. The accusations. The denials. "Soon we'll have them all, and Virginia Waycross will be left alone with only her horses to preside over."

Amanda remained quiet as she folded a towel into a tight roll, then used it to cushion her knees as she knelt to examine Leaf's legs. "She never stood a chance with Matt. Virginia." She applied ointment to a fresh lesion on Leaf's knee. "It was sad, really. The way she used to follow him around. I always wondered what made Mike Waycross think he would ever be able to compare. Fireplug with legs and bald before he was twenty." She pointed to an older wound, a raised red-brown smear that covered the inner side of Leaf's calf. "This looks better."

"Looks the same to me." Leaf flexed his toes, winced as the pins-and-needles sensation radiated up his legs. "Feels worse." He lifted his arm as high as he could and pointed behind him. "The one on my back has spread." He felt the heat rise up his neck. Damn, but he was too old to blush. "Downward."

Amanda straightened, stripped off her soiled gloves, snapped on a fresh pair. "Take off your shirt and lower your bottoms. Go to the bed and lie on your stomach." She eyed him with motherly irritation. "Don't you give me the fisheye, Leaf Cateman. Won't see nothing I ain't seen a thousand times at the funeral home."

"Such a comfort, Amanda. Thank you."

"You know what I mean." Amanda sighed, then turned away so he could ready himself. "She was here, you know. I could smell her, like meat gone bad."

"I saw her, just before you came." Leaf removed his pajama shirt, winced as the cool air raked across the sores on his back. "From what I understand, Matthew told her little and taught her less. She's probably heard all sorts of things from Virginia and the others. She's curious." He rolled the bottoms down past his hips, held on to them as he lay down to keep them from slipping farther. "That provides me an opportunity to make an impression. I don't intend to waste it." He waited, heard nothing but the grind of scissors cutting gauze, and Amanda's breathing as she slathered ointment. "You don't approve."

"Not for me to approve or disapprove. You'll do what you want. Like always."

"And you will be there to assist. Like always." Leaf boosted on his elbows to relieve the pressure on his stomach. The skin there was clean, dammit. No reason for it to hurt. "I need her, Amanda. Gideon needs her." He gave up the struggle with his pajama bottoms, and twisted until he sat on the edge of the bed.

"*She* won't like it." Amanda jerked her chin toward the door.

"When what my mistress wife likes or dislikes enters into the equation, I will let you know." Leaf licked his lips. At least his discomforts had not yet interfered with his appetite. "Been some time since we had a dinner party in this house, don't you agree?" He nodded without waiting for an answer. "See to it."

"Don't I always?" Amanda took up the tray. "Get some rest. I'll come by later to see how you are." One last long look. Then she departed, the door closing with a soft click.

Leaf listened to the muffled clump of Amanda's heavy shoes on the thick carpet, so different from Jorie's light step. He sometimes wondered whether there were other reasons for her steadfastness besides the loyalty of a longtime retainer. Her condemnations of poor Virginia's hopeless affections, so much like the pot commenting on the shade of the kettle.

Reverie claimed him. What might have been. Life would no doubt have been simpler if he had married a woman like Amanda, a plain, no-nonsense hedge witch, content to remain in his shadow. So different from the women who shaped him, his grandmother Barbara and his mother, Alice.

Youth. Power. Beauty. Cateman men craved them, claimed for themselves anyone who possessed them. Emma, the dancer and artist. Matthew, the athlete.

And then there's Jorie. Well, she possessed a base sort of attractiveness, glossy and brittle as her hair. Pickings had, unfortunately, become rather slim in Gideon over the years. Beggars couldn't be choosers.

Leaf adjusted his pillow to avoid pressing against the bandages. Dear, dull Amanda—she was right, as usual. He needed to see his doctor.

"Later." After he had acquired Lauren Mullin, brought her into the fold, assessed her. Instructed and guided her. Only then he would see to himself. Until that time, he would just have to bear whatever test the Lady imposed upon him.

Binding punishments. Sometimes Virginia Waycross's lack of imagination astonished him. *Be the rack and thumbscrew next.*

Poor, foolish Amanda. Loyal though she was, he really could not allow her to interfere. The dream of his father and grandfather was now so close to becoming reality. Wealth and glory. The power to bend time, forestall death, and transform Gideon into the shining city it was always meant to be.

"So close." He could sense it in the air, like the soft static before a storm.

26

As Lauren reached the entry to the cul-de-sac, she heard the crunch and grind of an old transmission. *Zeke?* She broke into a trot, crossed her fingers that the old man had been successful in all matters chain saw and would be more than happy to cart her back to the Waycross place.

But as she rounded the corner onto Main Street, she caught sight of a chrome bumper, a dull black body streaked with orange flames. She ducked behind an overgrown yew as the truck rounded the corner and she recognized the driver and passenger as two of the men who had walked out of the previous evening's debacle.

The truck slowed to the curb. The men got out, slammed the doors, walked around the vehicle, and kicked tires.

"Jake wants three for it."

"I wouldn't give him no more than two. Needs a new transmission."

"Brakes felt mushy, too."

Lauren hunched and backed into the shrubbery. Maybe the men would have left her alone. But they hadn't liked Matt Mullin, and thought stoning an appropriate welcome for her. She didn't want to take the chance.

She pushed farther into the yew, felt a shower of twigs tumble down her neck, the inside of her sweater. The hedge looked solid and green on the outside, but the inside had browned and rotted—dried needles scratched like claws and weakened branches flexed under her weight.

Then one of the thicker branches snapped and she tumbled backward onto the broken end. It drove into her side, and she cried out before she could stop herself.

"Who's there?"

Lauren righted herself and looked out through the tangle in time to see the driver reach into the bed and pull out a shotgun.

"Who the fuck's out there?" He headed toward the hedge.

The other man leaned on the hood, chin in his hands. "Jeez, it's probably just a cat."

"Fuckin' big cat." The driver held the shotgun against his chest, barrel pointed up. "Shit's been goin' down round here lately, ain't no time to fuck around."

Lauren edged farther into the tangle. The collapse of the branch had opened up a gap behind her. If she made it through, she could run along the hedge to the stand of trees that hemmed the backyards. She edged toward it as dirt and needles tumbled into her hair, her face and clothes and the stink of rotting vegetation and other decaying things wafted around her with each movement.

The man walked along the hedge, poking the shotgun barrel into it every few feet. "Here kitty, kitty. Gonna blow your brains all over the fucking yard, kitty, kitty."

Lauren held out one hand behind and felt her way, gripped branches with the other to keep her balance as she crab-walked backward. She wedged into the gap, positioned herself to bolt, then hesitated because she knew she would make noise and draw fire. Counted backward. *Three . . . two . . . one*—shot through the gap and bent low, running along the hedge as shouts sounded from behind.

Then came the blast.

Lauren stumbled. Righted herself, then ran. No pain. No blood. *Missed me!* She darted into the trees, felt the silence close around her like a shield.

Then she stopped, looked around at the overhanging branches that dripped mist. Felt the weight of the dark as it pressed from all sides. Looked behind her, and saw the man with the shotgun shimmer in and out of focus, the houses fade into faint shapes seen through fog.

"I did it again." Lauren brushed droplets from her hair, then wiped her hand on her jacket again and again. The water felt slick, greasy. Only the threat of death by dehydration would have induced her to taste it.

She stayed still, even as every nerve and sense urged her to run. Out beyond the trees, the image of the men grew faint, then vanished. No more sound. No more movement. It was as though someone had pulled a plug.

Lauren held out her hands, felt for . . . what? Drafts? Changes in temperature? She sniffed, caught whiffs of damp and burning leaves. But here and there she found a cleaner scent, like nothing at all with a trace of spice. Cinnamon. Clove. It came and went like distant memory, lost, then found again.

Milk, flour, eggs. Connie Petersbury's words. *The scientific explanation.* The interface where her world and Lauren's world met.

Lauren stepped forward, then back, moved side to side, then paused and smelled the air again. Eventually, her fingers felt what her nose smelled, gritty dryness like grains of sand, a sere path through the stinking wet. She followed the trail with toddler steps, slow and unsure, as she grappled with the new knowledge that there actually were rules to this game and the woods, at least for the moment, followed them.

One step forward. Another. Lauren felt weightless, head like a balloon and stomach quivery and ready to flip at any moment. *So this is magic.* Lost in the dark and wanting to vomit. The stuff of song and legend.

Minutes may have passed. Hours. A lifetime. She felt that she had taken no more than a dozen steps at most, but when she looked back over her shoulder, she saw nothing but dark. No more house shadows. No more milky sky.

She kept walking forward. The spice scent grew stronger, warmer, as though she stood before an oven and smelled what baked within. Glimpses of light followed. A thinning of tree and branch.

Then, before she realized she had crossed a threshold, she stood in an open space. Saw the same scatter of bricks she had seen before encountering Connie, the same bare foundation and remains of a chimney. The old Mullin place. Her father's house.

"Hello, Dad." Lauren stepped onto the brown lawn, imagined a small boy running after a ball, the young man in the newspaper article pulling into the driveway at the wheel of his first car. Happy thoughts. She had already had her fill of the other kind.

She walked around, kicked at the ground, looked under bushes and the odd brick, on the lookout for . . . what? The street remained empty. It was a weekday, so most folks were at work, or out searching for Connie.

Connie is teacher. Do what teacher does. Lauren studied the street more closely. She had thought at first that she had stepped back into the real world, her real world, when she walked out of the trees. Now, she wasn't so sure.

She held out her hand, then fought the urge to plunge it into her pocket. She couldn't define what she felt, but she knew she didn't want it on her skin. Dirty oil. Slick mold from the wall of a cave. The best descriptions she could think of, and they didn't even come close.

She stilled again, and listened. Heard movement, on the other side of the street. Rustles in the bushes.

"You can't come here. Because I'm here, and this is my place." Lauren took out the crumpled leaves and tissues from her pocket, streaked with her dried blood. Walked to the edge of the lot that bordered the street, dug a shallow hole in the ground with her boot heel, and stuffed one of the bloody leaves into it. "My home." She pushed dirt over the mess, trod on it until the ground lay flat and packed. "You touch it, and it will burn you."

She walked the perimeter of the lot, stopping every few strides to dig a hole and plant a bloody shred of tissue, a few blades of grass, a leaf. A piece of herself.

By the time she finished, the sky had lightened and the sense of dread had lessened from scream to murmur to a light chitter in her ear. A rustling sound, like a nest of rodents.

I'm back. Back in the human world, the living world. *For now.* But the other world, Blaine's world, was seeping through more and more. Gideon was running out of time.

Lauren walked around the lot until she stood beside the remains of the chimney. She sat on the brick ledge, felt the chill through her clothes. Wedged partway into the firebox to hide from passersby. Leaned back, looked through the shattered chimney top to the yellow sky.

After a minute or so, her eyes adjusted sufficiently that she could see details, the gaping hole where the damper had been, the patches of creosote, the missing bricks. The chimney itself had grown crooked through age and damage or because it had always been that way. One area just above her head bubbled out, black and shiny, and she scooted deeper into the firebox and stretched until she could feel it.

The creosote cracked as soon as she touched it, rained on her in shards that clung to her clothes and smeared her skin.

Then she spotted something else in the mess. Flecks of metal, dull silver and brittle, crumbling when touched. Foil.

Lauren maneuvered until she knelt in the firebox. Pulled her hood over her head and held it in place with one hand as she tore at the creosote bubble with the other. More garbage showered down, ash and oxidized foil and bits of woven fabric that looked an awful lot like duct tape.

Then her hand closed around something flat, hard. She lifted it free from its hiding place and pushed out of the firebox. Brushed ash from her face and clothes, then turned her attention to the packet.

It had been carefully wrapped in layer after layer of foil, duct tape, stiff fabric coated with wax, careful preparations that fell away in pieces or crumbled to dust when she touched them. What remained looked familiar, the black leather cover worn to gray by years of use, the gold embossing erased.

Lauren tilted the book one way, then the other, until the light hit the cover just right and she could pick out the faint indentations. *Another Book of Endor.* She sniffed it, smelled nothing but age and ash. Opened it, and read the inscription.

> *To my dearest Barbara*
> *On this anniversary day*
> *Your loving husband*
> *Hiram*
> *July 10, 1868*

The binding crackled each time she turned one of the deckled pages, themselves yellowed and brittle from age and exposure to the chimney heat. *Who the hell would hide something made of paper in a chimney?* Unless the fireplace was never used. Or the book wasn't supposed to remain there for long.

The sound of a vehicle accelerating claimed Lauren's attention. She looked toward the street just as a pickup truck veered to the edge of the road, and just had time to pick out the faded *W* on the door when the driver slammed on the brakes.

"Where the hell have you been?" Dylan Corey jumped out of the cab and hit the ground running. "We have been hunting for you all morning." He stopped in midstride, looked her up and down. "What the hell have you been doing?"

Lauren tugged at the leg of her jeans, sending a cloud of soot puffing into the air. "I came to talk to Lolly about my car."

"Did anybody see you?"

"Zeke gave me a ride into town."

Corey made a show of looking around. "Was he going to wait for you? Because I don't see him anywhere."

"He had to see a man in Sterling about a chain saw." Lauren tucked her new find into her coat pocket. "Did something happen?"

Corey beckoned for her to follow him. He hurried ahead to his truck, grabbed a blanket from the back, and threw it over the passenger seat, then waited for her to get inside before getting in himself. "Lolly's missing." He dug a shop rag out of the pile on the floor of the cab and handed it to her, eyes fixed on her face, a hard stare that didn't like what it saw.

27

They drove in silence until the Waycross place came into view. Then Corey spoke, his voice ragged, as though it hurt to talk.

"Phil came by the place right before I left to look for you." He pulled into the driveway, made the long, slow swing around to the back of the house. "He had stopped by the garage to bug Lolly about his truck. He found the door to the office wide open. Couldn't find Lolly anywhere. Said the place felt wrong, like something bad had happened." He pulled in next to a tractor mower, shut off the engine, and sat still, hands on his thighs, and watched the horses meandering about the corral.

"He always locks his place." Lauren fielded another hard look, surprise sharpened by anger. "I saw him unlock the door. After Zeke dropped me off."

"Did anyone else see you?"

"Tom Barton."

"Great."

"Barton never struck me as a gossip."

"He turns up everywhere and yammers at everybody, and he can say the wrong thing at the damnedest times." Corey thumped the steering wheel. "Well, let's get this over with." He opened his door. "I'll tell you right now, I have never seen the Mistress this pissed and I've known her my whole life."

Lauren waited for him to round the truck and open her door, not for the sake of etiquette but because she didn't want to face Virginia Waycross. *I didn't do anything wrong.* She had a right to know about her father, to search for answers.

All those arguments faded when she looked in the passenger-side mirror and saw the tall, slim figure standing on the backdoor step.

Corey opened her door, then held out his arm for her as she stepped out of the truck. "Maybe if you limp a little, it might help." He put his hand over hers, and squeezed it.

Waycross watched them approach, back straight, arms at her sides. Like Corey, she looked Lauren up and down, brow arching ever so slightly in question. Unlike Corey, she kept those questions to herself.

Interviewing 101. Lauren stopped at the foot of the steps. *She wants me to jump in and fill the silence.* The angle was such that she had to lean back and look up to meet Waycross's eye, and she wondered if the older woman had staged the scene that way on purpose. *Of course she did.* Leading the witches of Gideon appeared about as simple as cat herding. One had to take advantage where one found it.

So. Lauren clasped her hands in front of her and waited, while behind her, Corey shuffled his feet.

Waycross understood. Her eyes glinted, and a flush began the long, slow journey up her neck. "Did I say you could leave?"

Lauren shrugged. "You didn't say I couldn't."

"I thought you had more damn sense." Waycross leaned forward, hands taking a white-knuckled grip on the railing. "There are people in Gideon who would string you up as soon as look at you, and you just waltzed in like—"

"Zeke drove her," Corey piped.

"Did he, now?" Waycross glared until Corey muttered an apology and started pacing.

"He said he'd lived a long, full life." Lauren smiled at the memory, forced herself serious when Waycross fixed back on her.

"Has he?" Waycross closed her eyes, hung her head. When she

looked at Lauren again, her face had gone slack, her eyes, dull. Years older, in the span of a few heartbeats. "What happened to you?"

Corey stepped forward. "She ran into ol' Tom—"

"Are you her interpreter, Dylan?"

"No, Mistress." Corey held up his hands in surrender.

"I found the lot. What was left of the house." Lauren reached into her coat pocket. "Dad's house." She pulled out her find, held it on her open palms like an offering. "I found this—"

Waycross leaned over the railing. "Where did you get that?"

"—up in the chimney." Lauren took a step back, driven by the expression on Waycross's face. Anger, yes. Disgust. Rage. All those, she would have expected, understood. But horror, no.

And fear. Never fear.

"That's not possible." Waycross shook her head, eyes wide. "We searched. So hard, we looked. Even while the house burned, Jimbo and Lolly—Jimbo almost got caught when the roof collapsed, and Lolly had to drag him out." She pounded the railing with her fist. "Because Matt had already vanished. He ran, but we hoped that maybe he had left us something we could use to keep us safe." She folded her arms across her chest, and backed away. "What's wrong with it?"

"It's old." Lauren brushed a smear of ash off the cover. "It's dirty. It's been stuck up in a chimney for almost forty years."

"And I'm telling you that we looked. Over and over again, we searched that chimney. Lolly ripped out the damper. He tore out the throat and the smoke shelf and smashed the bricks to dust." Waycross stilled, the edge returning. "How did you find it?" Cold eye, and a voice that knew your worst secret. "You crossed over again, didn't you?"

"She did what?" Corey held out a pleading hand as he looked from Lauren to Waycross. "Crossed over—what does that mean?"

Waycross twitched her head in the direction of the barn. "Dylan, go and check on the hay delivery."

"Mistress—"

"I said, go." Waycross waited until Corey turned on his heel and muttered his way to the barn. Then she looked to Lauren, and sighed. "You should clean up."

Lauren nodded and started toward the house, then stopped when Waycross met her at the foot of the steps.

"In there." Waycross pointed to a rickety wood-frame building about twenty yards distant. "It was a storage shed, so it's a little sparse. But it has power, and I had a shower and toilet put in for Dylan and the workmen. I don't want any of what's on you in my house. It's nothing personal, but we're past manners at this stage." She sighed. "Dylan told you about Lolly."

"Yes." Lauren held the book close. It felt normal. Wouldn't she have sensed if it were tainted? "But he's only been gone a few hours. He probably just went to an auto-supply house. Or he could have been working, and didn't hear Phil come in."

"If you knew him like we do, you would know—" Waycross's mouth moved soundlessly. Then she pointed again to the shed. "Don't come in the house. I'll bring your things to you."

LAUREN WRAPPED A towel around herself and stepped out of the tiny half bath to find Waycross walking around the outer edge of the room that served as the workmen's break area. The woman held a small wooden bowl in one hand, a wire whisk in the other; every few feet, she dipped the whisk into the bowl and flicked her wrist, spraying liquid across the walls. Clear and thin, whatever it was, with a sharp, herbal scent.

Lauren waited until Waycross finished. "I did that today. First time. Around the lot. Dad's house. I heard things in the trees across the street, and I wanted to keep them away." She described the scene by the hedge, the way the wound on her forehead bled, how she cleaned herself, and what she did after. "They didn't like it, whoever they were. Whatever they were. I think it'll keep them away."

"That was warding." Waycross studied her. "We don't use our

own blood, though. We wouldn't have any left." She nodded toward the rivulets streaming down the near wall. "It's a protective formula. Keeps the bad things at bay."

Then why spread it inside? Lauren felt her forehead, had to search for a bit until she found the tiny remains of a scab. So fast, the healing. *Like magic.* "But others have used blood before? It works?"

Waycross wrinkled her nose. "It's old school, from back when Gideon was first settled. Before they realized how much more important thinking and influence were. How the will of the many could work to strengthen the barriers, hold back the demon hordes." She held up the dripping whisk, then lowered it back into the liquid and slowly stirred. "Coupled with smells they don't particularly care for." She glanced at Lauren sidelong. "But blood magic? That's for the television shows. Yours is the first use I've heard about in years."

"I think it worked." Lauren adjusted the towel, fought the sense of being naked in more ways than one. "Did Dad—?"

"Matt wasn't the sort for spells. He was an arranger. I figured that out years later. He built and maneuvered and put something of himself in everything he did. Everything he touched. A constant witch, we call his type. Always adjusting. Manipulating. Influencing." Waycross smiled, a thin, distant curve of lip. "I remember the first time ever I saw him. Mrs. Ellison's ninth-grade algebra class. Principal Hoard brought him in and introduced him and all the girls sorta went 'huh.'" Her stirring slowed, then ceased. "He didn't like us much at first. He was a big-city boy. Gideon was quite the comedown for him."

Lauren walked to the center of the room, where Waycross had set her suitcase, the shopping bag filled with toothpaste, shampoo, underwear, other things bought along the way. She opened the suitcase and rummaged for jeans, the shirt with the fewest wrinkles.

Felt the silence, and looked up to find Waycross sitting cross-legged on the floor, back to the wall, bowl cradled in her lap.

"I worry about you." Waycross hugged the bowl like a young child would a stuffed animal. "Connie was born here and lived here her whole life, and this place ate her alive. She had tried to build up, what could you call them, calluses? Armor? What good did they do her?" She paused to wipe her eyes with her sleeve. "You're sensitive, like she was. I can tell. You have abilities. Unschooled, but still . . . I can't imagine what it's like to be in your head right now. I worry about you breaking, and what that could mean."

Lauren grabbed the shopping bag, hunted for a bra, socks. "I just came here to find out about my father. I'm outside of all this. Why should you care about me?"

"Because you could serve as a conduit and not even realize it. Something could get inside your head, tell you things you want to hear."

"It can't offer me anything I want."

"Not even truth about your family?" Waycross nodded. "That's what it offered Matt. He wouldn't admit it, but I knew. That's what it does. It offers something good. Something kind. It offers peace to one in exchange for torment to the rest."

"You put Mullins through hell, then wonder why they look out for themselves?" Lauren glanced out the small window by the door, saw no one meandering about, dropped the towel and dragged on her clothes. "You don't understand as much as you think."

"What do I not understand? That you crossed over into the borderland again, easy as crossing a street, and brought back a book that couldn't possibly exist?" Waycross had set the bowl aside and worked into a crouch, an old cat set and ready to spring. "And before you could get hold of it, you had to ward the land to keep things away, things you didn't want near you. But that meant they were able to walk that land before you got there. For all you know, they put that book there for you to find."

"I came back to this world, this side of the divide, before I found the book." Lauren pulled on socks, then grabbed her boots. But the leather was coated with soot, and she took another sock from the bag and tried to wipe it away. "It's another Book of Endor, a couple years older than Dad's. From Hiram to his dear wife, Barbara."

Waycross stared at her for a long moment, then stood and took up the bowl. "Hiram Cateman was Leaf's grandfather." She circled Lauren, and sprinkled the floor around her with the potion.

"Dad worked at the Cateman house. He could've swiped it, I guess." Lauren brushed off the drops that splashed her. From across the room, the smell tickled her nose; up close, it stung like burning leaves. "Unless Emma gave it to him."

Waycross paused in midspray. "You were busy today, weren't you?"

"However Dad got hold of it, he hid it for a reason." Lauren rose and returned to the bathroom, where she had left both books. "Maybe there was something in there that he wanted you to see. Something that would help you."

"Did you not hear what I said earlier? That book cannot exist. Whatever you have there is tainted." Waycross set the bowl on the floor, then stood and looked to the door just as a knock sounded. "What is it, Dylan?"

The door opened slowly. Then Corey stuck his head in the gap, sniffed the air, looked from Waycross to Lauren, then back to his Mistress. "Ed from the diner just called. Sheriff found Jerome's car out on Old Main."

Waycross muttered something under her breath. A curse? A prayer? "Was it an accident?"

"Car was locked. His keys and bag were inside. That's all they know. They're going to send someone to talk to you. What time he arrived yesterday. What time he left. The usual." Corey edged farther inside. "Couldn't you meet with Leaf?"

"You think I haven't tried? After they found Jimbo, I went to him—you know what he said to me?" Waycross roughened her voice. " 'You know how the Petersburys were, Virginia. Too sensitive. Unfit for the rigors of the world.' After I had sat up all night with Connie, held her as she wept like a baby." She picked up the bowl, gave the contents another slow stir. "I'm going to spread the rest of this outside." She glanced back at Lauren. "We'll be having dinner in an hour. I'll leave yours on the back step."

"If I'm being exiled, I'll need something to sleep on." Lauren followed the woman outside, ignored Corey's warning headshake.

Waycross waved the whisk in the direction of the barn. "There's an air mattress in the tack room. I keep it there for when one of the horses gets colicky." She circled behind the shed, leaving a trail of biting scent in her wake.

Lauren headed for the barn. Heard the pound of footsteps behind.

"Don't be an idiot. Apologize. Say anything you have to. You can't stay out here." Corey drew alongside. "If Jerome Hoard showed up at my door, bleeding and begging for help, I wouldn't let him in because I couldn't be sure whether it was still him or not."

"You live by yourself."

"I'm going to move back here. I don't like the Mistress being here alone."

"She's not alone. I'm here." Lauren threw her hands in the air. "Oh, wait, I forgot. I'm a danger to all concerned, which is quite a feat considering that I don't know anything." She quickened her pace and left Corey behind, kicking the dirt and calling her name.

DINNER CAME AND went. Lauren sat on a bench near the corral and ate as she watched the low clouds scud across the sky and listened to the air move through the trees. Every so often, Corey's face would appear in the backdoor window, but she had begun to find his anxious solicitude as wearing as Waycross's stern judgment, and she ignored his tight smile and occasional wave.

Afterward, she walked around the yard as gloomy dusk fell, winter's early night. The horses had been stabled, the workmen departed for home, leaving the place a desolation of empty corral and parking area, the barn a looming shadow and the shed in which she would spend the night a tiny outpost, dim light shining through the single window, casting a fan of pale yellow across the packed dirt.

As she approached the shed, she spotted patches of darkness at the edge of the light, and her dinner turned to lead in her stomach. "Blaine."

So nice to be called by my real name. Nicholas Blaine edged farther into the light, his coat a swirl of black and tarnished silver. *Instead of those insulting epithets.*

Lauren tried to pick out his features amid the gloom, hunted for detail through the ebb and flow that defined it. He could have shown her what he looked like, of that she had no doubt. *But he's sensitive about his face, the scarring from the flames.* "I've been told that my family wronged you, and you want an apology. Reparations. But something about you tells me that's not enough."

The deeds of your family bound me to this place. I need you to release me.

"Why didn't you tell me this before?"

Better that you saw for yourself what injustice and hate can do to a place, a people. Better that they told you themselves what brought them so low. Blaine took one step toward her. Another.

Lauren backed away until she collided with the fence. "Just stay away."

Blaine raised a hand to the brim of his hat and bowed his head. *As you wish.* He leaned against a fence post. *I watched you walk through my woods today. Again, you emerged unscathed. You did so on your own, with no one to guide you.*

"You saw me?"

I see everyone. Every thing. Your wards are as nothing to me now—this place is mine. Blaine turned and leaned on the top fence post and rested one foot on the lowest, like a ranch hand bellied up to a bar. *There are those here who are willing to teach you. If you went to them now, they would take you in, feed and shelter you, see to your every need.*

"There are people here who know you?"

More than you realize.

"Fools."

Pragmatists.

Lauren looked toward the house, the lights burning in the windows. The kitchen. The rooms upstairs. *Waycross can't sense him—if she could, she'd be out here. He's broken through her wards, and she can't tell.* "What happened to Lolly and Jerome Hoard?"

Blaine waved a hand. *They aren't important. Your mother and father, however—they are pearls of great price. I can give them back to you. Just imagine them, happy and healthy and together once more. Your life as it used to be.* He looked at her. *You want that time back. You crave it like a drug.* His voice like a balm, all kindness and concern.

Lauren started to speak, but her throat clenched and tears sprang to her eyes, and even though she had known deep down that this would be his temptation for her, it still hurt. "What did you offer my father?"

His good name.

"He turned you down."

He was young. Foolish. You're older. Wiser. You know what loss truly means.

Lauren stood quiet, as reality warred with wishes and fear trumped them all. "Why did you kill Dilys Martin?"

What makes you believe she wished to help you? What makes you so sure that she had your best interests at heart?

"I knew it. I felt it."

She sought to keep you from me—that could not be allowed. Blaine waved a dismissive hand. *You refuse to think beyond your self-imposed limitations. You're too caught up in the little lives of little people. You don't need them. I could make you great. Or I could destroy everything you hold dear.*

"You already did that."

Oh, Lauren, daughter of Matthew. You really have no idea. He pushed away from the post, shadows eddying like tumbling storm cloud. *I am tied to this place. Earth, air, water, and flame work to hold me here. A Mullin set these bindings long ago, and only a Mullin can sever them.*

"Whoever chained you must have had reasons."

Jealousy. Anger. Injured pride.

"Not because you killed someone they loved? That seems to be your specialty."

Blaine stilled. *Long ago, I knew one who reminds me of you. You look nothing like her. I would know you anywhere.*

A buzzing filled Lauren's head.

Don't make me do to you what I did to her.

Out in the darkness, Lauren could sense things milling, listening, waiting for her reply. "You're trying to back me into a corner."

You're in the corner, Lauren Mullin. I'm offering you the way out.

"No." Lauren shook her head, stopped as the world seemed to tilt. "It's not what a Mullin did, it's what you've done. It's not what my family was, it's what you are. You're the danger. They don't realize it. Mistress Waycross is the only one left who knew you for what you are, and she—"

Hates you because you're the walking embodiment of the life she never had with the only man she ever loved.

"You know everything, don't you? Everyone's secrets. Their weaknesses. It hasn't done you a damn bit of good, has it?" The buzzing in Lauren's head ramped up to a throbbing wail as the sky darkened and the air thickened. "I won't help you. Go back to Hell."

No—let me bring it to you.

Invisible hands grabbed Lauren's shoulders and rammed her against the fence. A force closed in around her, a wall of black that funneled and roared as though she stood in the midst of a tornado.

The faces formed in the darkness, gray and grinning, bodies rank and decayed. They reached for her, the grasping hands of her nightmares, brushed her face, left acid burn in their wake.

Then something took hold of her—she felt herself lifted off the ground, feet and arms dangling, a puppet on a cursed string, as bony hands tugged at her and wailed her name.

I have tried to be kind, little witch, but it isn't my nature. Now see what else I can be. Another smile in the shadows, colder and more cruel. *I tell you for the last time, I can give so much. Or I can take away what little you have and more besides. I've waited long enough. The fate of Gideon rests with you.*

With that, the darkness vanished and the figures with it. The roaring ceased. Whatever held Lauren dropped her and she fell hard, slammed against the fence on the way down, banged her head on the railing. Lay in the dirt, gasping and shaking, face burning. Swallowed, and tasted blood. Looked up at the sky as clouds blocked the stars.

28

Lauren banged on the back door of the Waycross house for five minutes before someone answered. First she heard a heavy footfall. Then came the rustle of the shade and Corey's worried face in the window, the clatter of chains and dead bolts.

"You can't come in. I know I sound like a sniveling coward, and maybe I am. But I'm under orders and she will bind me if I disobey." Corey glanced over his shoulder, then joined Lauren on the back step and carefully shut the door. Bent close to her, and winced. "What the hell happened to you?"

"He was here." Lauren brushed dirt from her clothes, then pointed toward the shed. "Blaine."

Corey shook his head. "Mistress set wards—"

"They're not working." Lauren leaned on the stair railing, shivering as the damp chill seeped through her shirt. "What is she planning?"

"I can't tell you."

"Dylan. Please."

"She—" Corey gnawed his lower lip. He had aged ten years since the morning, his face pale and grooved with fatigue, his eyes dull. Gideon's price, paid in installments over a rapidly dwindling life-span. "She's digging through old books. Papers she keeps locked away. She won't tell me, but I think it has something to do with your dad."

"I'd say that's a given." Lauren slid down the railing and sat on the step, hugged her knees to her chest. "Blaine said I held it all in my hands. There's a curse or spell or something that binds him to Gideon. A Mullin cast it, and a Mullin needs to break it."

Corey sat down next to her, then scooted closer to the house until he hid in the shadow. "So what do you think?" He kept one eye on the upper windows, pressing against the house when one light went out or another went on. "Is that something you can do?"

"*No.* I don't want to release him. Releasing him would be the end."

"How do you know?"

"Because he just gave me a taste." Lauren folded a bloody tissue until she found a clean spot, and held it to her nose. "How can you ask me that—is that something I can do? People have died."

"I didn't mean—" Corey buried his face in his hands, then lowered them and turned to her. "Do you have any idea what you look like right now? You've got cuts all over your face, your nose is bleeding—"

"I'm aware of that, thanks."

"—and your eyes are—" Corey swallowed hard. "I can tell what you saw from the look in your eyes."

Lauren rubbed her ears, which itched as though infected. She could still hear it, so loud in the quiet dark. The never-ending chitter. "Blaine has followers. The unclean dead. If he's freed, they're coming along for the ride. They'll overrun us." She waited for Corey to answer, turned to find him studying her, his expression pained.

"Mistress calls you a conduit." He looked toward the barn. "Look, I'm sorry. But she remembers what happened back then, and she knows the part your dad played, and there are reasons she wants you bottled up." He stood. "I need to get back inside before she wonders where I am."

Lauren struggled to her feet as battered muscles cramped and complained. "You're just a nicer version of Judith and the rest of them."

"That's because you're not listening. I'm worried about you."

"Yeah, sure you are." Lauren limped down the steps. "Mistress Waycross is the last one left of the group that fought Blaine thirty-seven years ago. All the others are missing or dead. I want to help. Tell her that. She knows where I am if she wants to talk to me." She stuffed her hands in her pockets, trudged across the yard to her new home.

"Lauren."

Lauren kept walking, even as the footsteps grew louder and the hand gripped her shoulder, then let go as though she burned to the touch. A few strides farther. Then she stopped. "What?"

"I just think—" Corey maneuvered until he stood in front of her. "You didn't know anything about any of this for so long and now you're here and—" He extracted one of her hands from her pocket, then the other, held them, rubbed warmth back into them. "I— admire you, that's all. Because some folks would have tried to ignore it and others would have gone crazy. And you walked right into the lion's den." He hesitated. Then he leaned close and kissed her lightly on the lips, brought with him hints of coffee and simple human warmth. "I wish things were different." He kissed her hands, held them as he walked away, only let go when he had no choice. "I'll tell her what you said, but I don't think it'll do any good." He walked backward toward the house. "See you in the morning."

"Yeah." Lauren clasped her hands to save the warmth, the sensation of Corey's touch.

"I wish you were inside with us."

"I have work to do anyway."

"You sound like the Mistress." Corey flashed a smile, and for that moment things seemed normal. He stuffed his hands in his pockets, turned, and trotted back to the house, through the bars of illumination from the windows, light to dark to light.

LAUREN TRIED TO secure the shed. But the flimsy bolt lock rattled out of its slide if she so much as bumped the door, and after the third try, she gave up. Not like it would keep anything out, anyway. At least, not anything that mattered.

She had pushed the air mattress in the corner farthest from the door. She had also draped a towel over the window, liberated an ancient coffeemaker from the back of the cabinet and cleaned it, then scrubbed the sink and single-burner hot plate. Nervous energy. Returning a little order to a disordered world.

Finally, she dug the bag of wire circlets out of the suitcase. The room still reeked of Waycross's ward, which Lauren suspected was meant to counteract whatever evil had piggybacked onto what she had come to think of as the "ghost book" even though it felt as real as every other book she had ever held.

They just didn't look hard enough—I don't care what Waycross said. Lauren scattered the circlets over the floor, in the half bath, on the tiny windowsill, and across the mattress. *Three terrified teenagers and a little girl—how thorough could they have been?* She paused to sniff the air, felt a slight jolt when she realized the herbal reek had lessened, become barely detectable. *Odor fatigue.* She couldn't smell it anymore because it had overwhelmed her nose.

Then Waycross's words came back to her. That calming voice. *Thinking and influence.* That's what gave a spell its power. *The singer, not the song.*

"It's not the words, it's the will," Lauren chanted, steam puffing from her mouth in time. Damn, but the shed was cold. Waycross had offered the use of a space heater, but the fear of falling asleep and being awakened by flames had concerned Lauren enough that she refused. She took a shower, the water as hot as she could stand, then dressed in layers. Flannel pajamas over long underwear. Thick socks. A wool cap.

Lauren got into her improvised bed, burrowed beneath blankets that still had stalks of hay clinging to them, told herself she had slept in worse places. Hell, memories of some of her camping excursions still gave her the shakes. At least here she had walls, a roof. Running water and electric power. The only difference between this shed and a five-star hotel was the absence of an ice machine and the little chocolates on her pillow.

And maybe the soundproofing. Lauren rested her head against the rough-hewn wall. She sensed the presence of something on the other side, perhaps several somethings, heard the light patter of feet, a higher-pitched version of the never-ending buzzing that filled her head.

Then she flinched as something sounded closer to her ear. Light scratching, like claws brushing against the wood.

Animals. They were out in the middle of the woods, after all. Of course critters would wander in at night to pillage and scavenge. Raccoon. Possum. Coyote. Feral cat.

But this seemed different. Lauren couldn't put her finger on how, but . . . *It knows I'm here.* She pulled the blankets more tightly around herself. *It came here for me.*

"I know you're—there." Her voice cracked, and she swallowed, waited, tried again. "Are you part of this?" The scraping sounds continued, and she eyed the spot where the walls met the floor and wondered how well joined they were, whether something could force itself in between. "Did you help kill good people?" The scraping slowed. "Do you want to kill me?"

Silence, like the split second after a thunderclap, the minutes before an earthquake.

"No, you don't. You know your boss wouldn't like it." Lauren picked up the ghost book, opened it, reread the inscription written by a man almost a hundred and fifty years ago. "He wants me alive to the end, so I can watch. So he can hang everything that happens around my neck. 'Not my fault—you made me—if you had just given me what I wanted from the first, none of this would have happened.' Except that it would have happened anyway because he hates Gideon more than anyone or anything, living or dead. He'll toy with it like a cat until he gets bored, and then—"

—and then he would make a world of Gideons, filled with deaths and disappearances, stonings in quiet fields and rustlings in bushes and the midnight scrape of claws across a windowpane. A world where nothing was as it seemed, where the living fought the angry dead, while those stuck between worlds, all those Connie Petersburys who refused to give in, struggled to keep from being sucked into the abyss. A world without peace. Without rest. A world in which there was nowhere to hide, where even death provided no escape.

She turned to the ghost book's title page, a few lines of block text—

The Book of the Lady of Endor

Howell Printers
Gideon, Illinois
1852

Howell. Waycross's maiden name. *Old families, old books.* But how did this one survive a fire, followed by almost forty years exposure to heat and cold and damp?

Lauren paged carefully. The interior leaves were all made from the same tissuelike paper and split into columns filled with single-spaced text, the font so tiny that she had to drag the lamp close and tilt the shade so she could reread the story of the Lady. She kept her father's book alongside as she read, every so often checking it, noting the differences. A few of the words. A more archaic tone.

As the silence from outside continued, sounds from inside filtered through to take their place. Lauren had laundered her filthy clothes by wearing them in the shower, then hung them over the curtain rod, and the *patpat* of water dripping onto the floor of the stall now filled the shed. The soft *tick* of the alarm clock that Corey had scrounged for her from the main house. The slide of paper as she turned pages, and read the 1852 version of the journeys of the Lady of Endor.

Then she turned the page, and stared.

Instructions for the binding of demons and those forced to do their bidding.

She had seen nothing like this in her father's book. She would have remembered. Page upon page of instructions on how to control demons, and the humans they enslaved.

Binding. There was that word again. The removal of power. Neutralization, like the spell that Waycross cast on Deena and the other women.

To bind the outsider, gather friends in an elder-spread place—

To bind a sister-in-law or other female relation by marriage, twist a lock of her hair through a ring woven of straw as you say her name—

To bind a dead son, add three drops of sweat to the strip of cloth cut from the shroud—

To bind a husband, living or dead—

—a wife

—a stillborn infant

—a friend. . .

Lauren paged through the lists, as matter-of-fact as a computer manual, yet weirder than anything she had ever read.

To bind a demon is to bind all who serve it; to bind one that serves weakens the demon, but not until all who serve it are bound is the demon itself bound.

Lauren checked the title page of her father's book, found no notation that it had been edited or abridged. *A Cateman translated it.* Somehow that didn't surprise her. *You, Leaf Cateman. It's something to do with you.*

Lauren stopped, rubbed her eyes. Her head felt heavy, sinuses aching from the chill and her body aching from Blaine's battering. She checked the clock: *3:17 A.M.* Closed the ghost book and set it near her pillow next to her father's. Turned off the lamp and tunneled under the blankets.

She heard once more the faint chitter and scratch of whatever lurked outside. Imagined setting a match to it and watching it burn to a cinder. Not the most pleasant thought she ever had, but the idea of striking back against the dark settled her enough that she could close her eyes, and sleep.

29

Pounding. Louder than the chitter and the footsteps. It shook the walls, vibrated along the floor.

"Are you awake?"

The banging shook loose the lock—Lauren could hear the metal clatter, the sound of the door opening.

"It's Virginia Waycross—are you awake?"

"I am now." Lauren opened her eyes, then pulled the blanket over her head as the full force of morning light hit her in the face. "What time is it?"

"Eight fifteen." Waycross sniffed. "Is this the time you usually wake up back in Seattle?" She wore jeans and a yellow sweater topped with a tan vest, boots, and the superior air of the lifetime early riser.

"When I fall asleep after four, yes." Lauren ratcheted into a sitting position, hampered by the mushiness of the mattress and bruised ribs that grabbed if she moved too quickly. She worked her twisted pajamas back into place, dragged the cap off her head. "Did something happen?"

Waycross surveyed Lauren's scraped-up face. "I could ask you the same question." She walked to the counter, taking care to avoid the scattered circlets, and made quick work of setting up the coffeemaker.

"I had a visitor last night, remember? After dinner."

Waycross wheeled. "Blaine was here? On my land?"

"I told Dylan last night. I told him to tell you."

"I ordered him not to disturb me." Waycross traced the Lady's eye on her forehead.

"You threatened him with binding. He listened." Lauren worked her aching shoulders, and sighed. She liked Corey, and could like him even more without much effort. But his unquestioning obedience had begun to irritate. "He could've told you this morning."

"He left before I got up. Went to get his things, I imagine." Waycross took a seat at the small table set in the corner nearest the door. "What did he want? Blaine."

"He's cursed. He wants me to lift it."

"Do you have any idea how?"

"No. He did say that he was bound here by earth, air, water, and flame. Does that help?"

"Maybe." Waycross passed her hand over her face, then jerked her chin toward Lauren. "From the look of things, he threatened you."

"Me. My friends. And Gideon." Lauren watched Waycross, face so drawn. "You're planning something, I can tell. What are you going to do?"

Waycross didn't answer. Instead, she rose and walked to the bed. "This came for you." She pulled an envelope out of her vest pocket, heavy cream paper edged in black.

"Mail? This early?" The envelope crackled in Lauren's hand, thick as cardboard but satin-smooth. She turned it over, but found no stamps or address. Just her name, in flowing black script. *Miss Lauren Mullin.*

"Personal delivery. One of Leaf Cateman's men. He's waiting for an answer."

"Outside?"

"In the driveway. Leaf doesn't attend my convocations, his messenger boys can sit in my damn driveway."

Lauren opened the envelope, pulled out a card bordered in gold and filled with line after line of ornate calligraphy. "It's an invitation."

"I gathered that."

"To dinner. Six o'clock tonight." Lauren looked over at her suitcase. "I didn't bring anything to wear to a dinner." She worked her neck, inhaled the rousing aroma of brewing coffee. "Tell me about the Great Fire."

"I'm sorry?" Waycross waited for the coffeemaker to finish its chorus. Then she rose and returned to the kitchen area. "How do you take yours?"

"That powder creamer. Sugar." Lauren set the invitation aside, worked to her knees, then stood slowly.

"What has the fire got to do with Leaf's invitation?"

"Just humor me, please."

"Very well." Waycross walked to Lauren and handed her a mug, then returned to the table with her own. "We didn't all believe it. That a Mullin started it. Eliza Mullin—she was the only Mullin still living in Gideon then. The one that stories say started it all. She lived alone, in a big house on the edge of town. She . . . experimented, I guess you could call it. Communicated with her demon masters, most thought. Whether by accident or design, she brought down the fires of wrath. Gideon burned, along with Chicago and a few other places, in October, eighteen and seventy-one."

"So the Gideon fire burned all that." Lauren walked to the window, feet dragging as her socks snagged on the unfinished hardwood. "Must have been one hell of a long match."

Waycross studied her for a beat, then shook her head. "They say now that it was the hot summer, drought, the winds. But people know what they know, and you can't tell them different." She took a healthy slug of coffee, then stared into her cup.

"The gazebo on the square. All that remained of the Corey house." Lauren stood at the window, twitched the towel aside, and looked out at the low clouds. "Ruth Corey—she died in that house."

"Yes?"

"Dylan's a descendant."

"Of Micah's, yes. Micah and Ruth had only been married a few weeks when the fire occurred, so they had no children."

"You know a lot of the detail."

"Gideon's a small town. We all know its history."

"Where do you keep the records?"

"We all keep our own."

"Didn't they burn, though?" Lauren turned, leaned against the wall. "In the fire. Weren't they lost?"

"Some. What we lost, we reconstructed. I have family documents dating back to that time." Waycross sat elbows on the table, coffee mug held close, as though she needed the warmth. "Other things were just known. We heard about—"

"Heard about? From whom?" Lauren shook her head. "I'm not try-ing to start an argument."

Waycross sniffed. "You could've fooled me."

"I'm just saying that a fire destroys Gideon in 1871. Later that year, Hiram Cateman distributes brand-new copies of the Book of Endor to one and all." Lauren pushed away from the wall and walked to the bed. Reached beneath the pillow, and removed the ghost Book of Endor. "It was similar to this older version in most respects, but the 1871 version didn't contain instructions on how to bind demons and the humans that they co-opt." She walked to the table and held out the book so Waycross could see it.

The woman's eyes rounded. She reached for it. Hesitated, fingers flexing. Then the need to know got the better of her—she plucked the book from Lauren's hands and paged through it, frowning when she came to the list of demons. "I never saw any of this before." She read, every so often clucked her tongue. "It's possible that—"

"That a demon rewrote the book and added spells that we would think would defeat them but that would actually call them forth. A trickster book, stuck in the chimney of my father's house to trick me or anyone else who found it." Lauren massaged her forehead to erase the growing ache. Thoughts had churned the night long even as she slept, the realization that however much everyone talked about what happened in Gideon, there seemed to be so little that they actually knew. "There's a simpler explanation." She finished her coffee, then set about straightening the bed. "That Hiram Cateman removed those passages because he didn't want others to have that knowledge." She turned to Waycross. "Out of character?"

Waycross looked up from the ghost book. "I didn't know him." She snorted softly. "I'm not that old."

"But you know Leaf. You knew Leaf's father."

Waycross set the book on the table and sat back, arms folded. "Your mind works just like Matt's did. Corkscrew."

"The arranger. The manipulator and influencer. That's what you called him." Lauren pounded her pillow into shape, tossed it onto the bed. "Maybe he learned it from someone else."

Waycross's voice grew harsh. "You're saying he fell in with Leaf. You're his daughter, and you're saying that?"

"He did to some extent. He and Emma had an affair. Lolly told me about it, but you only have to take a look at these drawings to know what happened." Lauren retrieved her father's book, opened it to one of the Emma sketches, and held it out to Waycross, waited as the woman stared, blinked, then looked away. "Leaf wanted my dad because of the power. You said that yourself. Not because he could fix what was wrong with Gideon—you didn't say that. You said 'power.'" She shifted until she met Waycross's eye, saw the glisten, hated herself for hurting the woman even as she wondered what choice she had.

Waycross set the ghost Book of Endor aside, stood, and walked to the window. Swept aside the towel curtain and stared out in silence as the ticking of Corey's purloined alarm clock filled the space. "You push hard, don't you." She paused. Shook her head. "Matt did, too. Guess it's in your blood." She leaned on the narrow sill. "Leaf wants to call forth demons? Why?"

"Why would anyone want them?" Lauren set the books on the table, then gathered her clothes. Jeans. A blue flannel shirt with patched elbows. "As servants. As sources of knowledge and power."

"You realize what you're saying?"

"It fits, doesn't it?"

"He is sworn to protect—"

"He thinks he can control them. He wouldn't be the first man to make that mistake." Lauren ducked into the corner farthest from the window, and dressed. "You really won't consider this?"

"But to take it that far, it's just—'insane' is the only word that I can think of." Waycross turned from the window and paced to the far end of the shed, hands pressed together and fingers steepled, a jeans-clad nun at prayer.

Lauren sat on the edge of the mattress to drag on socks and boots. "Dad learned that Blaine wasn't the injured party that everyone claimed?"

"That's what he told us, yes. He said that Blaine was a witch gone bad, halfway to being a demon himself by the time he arrived in Gideon." Waycross slowed, stilled. "And we all believed him, me and Jimbo and Lolly and little Connie, who wasn't old enough to cast a spell but oh, how she adored Matt. All of us, together, were supposed to destroy Blaine for good."

"Why didn't you?"

"We tried. We arranged to meet in the woods near the Petersbury place because it was far enough out of town that no one would run into us. Matt was supposed to tell us what to do, but he never showed." Waycross turned to her, the fears of thirty-seven years past etched anew in her face. "Why did he run? If he was right and Leaf Cateman was wrong, then why did he run away?" She wiped a sleeve across her eyes as tears spilled. "I thought he ran off with Emma. For years, I believed that. Leaf had her declared dead, but that was just him saving face. And now you're here and you're not Emma's daughter and that means he just ran." Her voice fell to a whisper. "And everyone's gone now except for me." She struggled to settle herself, smoothing her curls, straightening her sweater. "Why did he leave?"

"I think he was scared, so scared that he didn't think anything he did would do any good." Lauren stood, then made a project out of folding her pajamas and stashing them under her pillow because seeing Waycross so shaken rattled her. "I'm not saying what he did was right. But something happened that drove him to run, and the answer is in Leaf Cateman's house."

"I wish you wouldn't go." Waycross went to the sink, splashed water on her face, dried off with a paper towel. "Yes, Leaf's been a thorn in my side since before I was chosen as Mistress. He had wanted the position for Emma, but Amanda Petrie's aunt was serving then, and then Emma disappeared and he didn't remarry until the child bride came along." She shook out the towel, then crumpled it again. "That may seem unimportant to you. Stupid witch politics. But if you're seen going to his house, at his invitation, it won't just make me look weak. You would be walking into a trap, just like Matt did. It would be lined with promises, but it would be a trap all the same."

Lauren nodded. Her only experiences with power struggles had been in the corporate world, but none of those had involved death, the bone dread of seeing the world turned inside out. So much more at stake now—nothing could change her mind. "Trust me. I'm immune."

"Are you?" Waycross's steadiness had returned, her quiet voice and clear eye. "If they offered you all you had lost, all you ever dreamed of having, would you still say no?"

I already did. Lauren nodded. "Would you?"

"If it meant the world? Or even just Gideon. I would refuse, of course. It's my duty as a child of the Lady. But you're not me."

"It killed my father—I know he died trying to prevent it from getting to me. It killed a woman who tried to help me. It may have even killed my mother. Do you really believe I want to see it win? That I would want to help it?" Lauren waited for Waycross to answer, but the woman had started to pace, with the long, slow stride of the career worrier. "Lolly said there was a wall—"

"Leaf's office, yes."

"He said it was all there. He said I should go and ask Leaf if I could see it. I have to go."

Waycross stopped, sighed. Then she walked to the sink and dug into the storage box underneath, pulled out a whisk broom and a dustpan. "Better pick up these eyes before something happens to them. Stepping on them just isn't right."

Lauren dug the paper sack out of her suitcase and followed Waycross around the room as she swept up the circlets. "I'm going."

"Yes, you said that." Waycross kept focused on her task. "You also said that you have nothing suitable to wear."

"That's what I'll tell them. I'll plead lack of packing skills."

"Leaf will wear black jeans and a white shirt because that's what he's worn since five minutes past birth. Jorie will wear something that cost more than my first car, and there's nothing to be done about that." Waycross straightened, eyed Lauren up and down. "A couple of my friends are about your size. Between them, we can find you a nice top and a dressy skirt. Some shoes." She concentrated on dumping the circlets into the bag. "And after you return those things, they will be burned, because they won't want anything that touched a Mullin in their house."

"Then they should make sure that they don't give me anything too expensive." Lauren crumpled the bag closed and set it on the bed. She would wait until Waycross left, then spread the circlets again. She trusted them, as much as she trusted anything in this restless place. "I would be happy to reimburse them, but I'm guessing that they wouldn't want my money either."

"I daresay you're correct." Waycross sighed. "Stubborn, aren't you?"

"I just want answers." Lauren checked her face in the half bath's shoe-box-size mirror. "I wouldn't have expected your help, after yesterday." She turned to Waycross, who had started for the door. "Thank you."

Waycross paused, her hand working the knob. Open—closed—open. "Whatever else you are, you're a guest in my house." She tried to grin, but only succeeded in looking sad. "My shed." The expression faded. "And you're Matt's girl. I know what you've heard, about how I felt—don't bother to deny it. People are going to think me a fool anyway. May as well give them a reason." She cracked open the door, and the light that leaked in fell across her face, deepened the lines and shadows. "You're going to need to be on your toes with Leaf. Pardon my saying this, but you don't look up to it."

Lauren joined her in the open doorway, smelled the cold damp, the harsh stink of diesel fuel. Real smells, from this real world. "I don't have a choice."

Waycross bent and picked up a small clod of dirt, rubbed it between her hands, smeared it over her fingers. Started to speak, then brushed the dirt off and walked across the yard to the house, step slow, head bowed, her thoughts her own.

BY THE TIME Lauren arrived at the house, Waycross had put aside her grim mood and set about playing hostess. With her were two of the women who had stuck out the convocation to the end. Penny, one of the nurses, and Beth, who kept the books for most of the Gideon businesses. They had each brought clothes for Lauren to try on, dressy evening wear in bright jewel colors that gave her the jitters.

She pointed to the two most somber items, a long black skirt and high-necked maroon blouse, and they slipped them off the hangers and handed them to her, silent, smiles frozen, children sharing because Mother told them to. When Lauren asked questions about fit or comfort, they simply nodded, and when she reached toward the table behind them for a lint roll to brush some cat hair off the skirt, they both backed away.

She took the clothes into Waycross's office and put them on, face burning and eyes stinging, even as she told herself that it was a small price to pay to get into the Cateman house.

She emerged to murmured assurances that she had made just the right choices. The two women bundled the rest of the clothes into garment bags and muttered hurried good-byes. After seeing them out, Waycross stood silent by the front door. Then she returned to the living room, her face a study in determination.

"You can't wear those things." She pointed to Lauren's hiking boots. "Wait here." She trotted up the stairs; then came thumping sounds, the opening and slamming of doors.

After a few minutes, Waycross descended, holding a pair of well-worn black boots. They were a cross between cowboy and English, knee-high and low-heeled, leather shafts adorned with scrollwork, buffed to a satin sheen.

"Had them since forever." Waycross handed them to Lauren. "I gave riding lessons for a few summers, years back. Treated myself."

Lauren held the boots as though they were made of cobweb. "Are you sure?"

"Yes." Waycross blinked, then turned away. "And I apologize."

"I don't think they meant—"

"Yes, they did, and I'm not apologizing for them."

Lauren stood still for a time. Then she perched on the arm of the couch and pulled the boots on. Stood up, clomped around the room, then presented herself for inspection. "They're a little snug in the calves, but they fit."

Waycross cocked her head, chin in hand, and smiled. "I don't think Jorie's going to like you. Not that you'd expect her to." Her expression held an edge. "I just think you've pretty much guaranteed it." The smile wavered. "I want you to sleep in the house tonight."

"I'm not leaving the books out there."

"Bring them. Bring everything inside."

"Are you sure?"

"Yes."

"All right. Thanks." Before Lauren could make a move toward the back door, a knock sounded. Then the door opened, and Dylan Corey entered carrying a suitcase. He was dressed for the woods in worn jeans and scuffed hiking boots, a heavy pine-colored sweater topped with the usual orange vest.

Waycross held her hand to her mouth, and spoke through her fingers. "Any news?"

Corey shook his head. "Phil and Zeke did their own search around the garage. They didn't find anything you could take to the sheriff's, but Phil said he doesn't want that truck back. He's going to sell it as is to someone from outside Gideon." He trudged into the living room, set down the case, fell back into one of the easy chairs. "I think we know what happened."

"My car's still there." Lauren lowered to the chair next to his. "Can't drive it because it's missing a fuel sensor." She shook her head. "The man's gone, and I'm worried about my car." After a few moments, she grew conscious of the silence, turned to Corey to find him staring at her. "What's wrong?"

"Nothing." Corey looked away, then back again. "You look . . . nice."

Waycross took a seat on the couch opposite them. "Lauren has received an invitation to dinner at Leaf's this evening. It shows all the signs of turning into a battle for dominance, and I didn't want her to start out at a disadvantage. Hence the clothes." She nodded to Corey. "I want you to go with her."

Corey and Lauren piped up as one.

"Mistress, I—"

"I don't think the invitation mentioned a guest."

"I don't care if you had plans or not, Dylan, and if you think for one minute that I am letting you go to that house by yourself, Miss Lauren Reardon Mullin, you don't know me for beans." Waycross rose. "And I expect a full report when you come back. No matter what orders I gave before. No more surprises—do you understand?"

Corey reddened. "Yes, Mistress." He remained still and silent until Waycross left the room. Then he turned to Lauren. "What did you say to her?"

Lauren looked to see if Waycross could hear, lowered her voice just in case. "I had to tell her about Blaine. Why didn't you?"

"How do you tell the Mistress of Gideon that her wards aren't worth shit?" Corey slumped back. "I took a walk after you went back to the shed. After we . . . talked."

Lauren clasped her hands, felt the memory of Corey's touch, the press of his lips. "And?"

"What is it that ol' Tom always says? Change comin'?" Corey yawned. There were pits beneath his eyes the same dull green as his sweater, and he sported a day's growth of beard. "I think he missed it. The change is already here." He laid back his head, sagged deep into the chair, and closed his eyes.

Lauren tried not to stare at the way Corey's lashes brushed the peaks of his cheekbones, the way his hands rested on his thighs. After a few minutes, the sounds of his light snoring drifted through the room, and she left to change her clothes and gather her things from the shed.

30

Lauren spent the hours prior to dinner quartered in Waycross's tiny office, comparing the old and new versions of the Book of Endor. In addition to excluding instructions on controlling demons and their human puppets, Master Hiram Cateman had also edited out recipes for salves and ointments and other medicinal preparations. Household spells that one was supposed to say while mending a pot or sewing a garment. All those little things that would have helped make a difficult time easier, allow an onerous task to go more quickly.

She wondered how long Hiram Cateman had waited after the fire to hire the best herbalist in Gideon to be his housekeeper, then to commence cornering the market on useful spells and potions. "Bet you were a wily one." And daring, too. One would think that the witches of Gideon had read the passages so many times that they would have noticed their absence, or already have memorized the recipes.

Maybe they hadn't bothered. Maybe they had already begun to shed old practices, their Master simply providing that little extra push.

"Or maybe he spelled them so they forgot." Lauren didn't even know if such a thing was possible—could a single man spell the population of an entire town, however shocked, stressed, or afraid they were? She thought back to the convocation, the stream of people who abandoned Waycross to cast their lot with Hiram Cateman's grandson.

I don't think he had to spell them. Lauren closed the books and pushed them away, then laid her head on the desk. *Fear is a marvelous aid to discipline.* And of course, her presence hadn't helped. *I was the icing on the cake.* That extra push that Leaf Cateman needed to cement his authority.

Lauren closed her eyes. Her night's sleep on the air mattress had been fitful at best, and the sounds of Corey's snoring emanating from the living room lulled her. *Just a few minutes.* A short nap. A little blessed quiet. *Just a few—*

She opened her eyes to find herself walking along the river, the same murky path she had followed days before. The water bubbled thick as tar now, complete with the eye-watering stink of molten asphalt. No one could drink that water and live.

That's because nothing living is meant to drink it.

Lauren looked to the side. The diminutive figure walking beside her should have rattled her, but nothing Connie Petersbury did could surprise her anymore. "You got out. Of the river."

That's because I'm dreaming, too. Petersbury looked up, offered a crooked grin. *Didn't think I could sleep anymore. Guess there's enough left of me alive to need it.* She gave Lauren's arm a gentle punch. *How ya doing?*

"How do you think?" Lauren looked to the bank opposite, where bushes and low tree limbs rustled as whatever followed them kept pace. "A few of the women tried to kill me after I got out of the woods."

Which ones?

"Deena. Brittany. Ruthie. Betty Joan. Amanda Petrie provided encouragement."

Heh. Doesn't surprise me.

"Nicholas Blaine has visited me a few times. I've told him I won't help him, but I don't think he'll take no for an answer." Lauren coughed as the tarry stink of the river burned her throat. Conditions had worsened since she had last walked here, and it worried her. *It's getting closer.* Whatever it was. "And tonight I'm going to dinner at Leaf Cateman's."

Oh, that should be fun. Petersbury screwed up her face in a sour lemon frown. *Once Jorie took over the kitchen, things went downhill. Lotta salads, from what I heard. Raw vegetables.*

"It's not the menu that concerns me."

No. Petersbury paused to pick up a stone. *You found another Book, I see. An old one.* She tossed the stone across the river into one of the bushes, then smiled as branches shuddered and something yelped.

Lauren watched the rustling path as whatever Petersbury hit scuttled away from the riverbank and out of range. "You saw me?"

Word gets around.

They walked in silence for a time.

"Can I ask you something?" Lauren waited until the woman looked up at her, took note of the pale face, lips tinged with blue. "Virginia Waycross is your—was—your best friend. Do you ever visit her?"

Does she talk about me?

"Quite a bit."

Petersbury nodded. *I miss her, too. But there's not enough of me left that I can afford to spread it too thin, and she's not the most important piece of this puzzle.* The woman hung her head. *She's not the person for this. It's your baby, I'm afraid.*

"Because I'm a Mullin."

Yup. Petersbury tugged her jacket more tightly around her. Her brow furrowed. Her step slowed. *He's getting impatient. More than you realize. He's waited a long time, and now you're here and he wants out.* She stopped, and without warning took hold of Lauren's hand. *It's getting harder to find the good parts of the river. They're getting thinner and weaker. Feel like I have to keep moving most all the time now. I'm afraid of what's going to happen if I don't move fast enough, or close my eyes at the wrong moment.* She swallowed hard. *You don't have much time, is what I'm trying to say.* Petersbury gave Lauren's hand a squeeze, then released her. *You know what to do.*

"No, I don't. I don't know anything."

If you didn't know anything, you'd be dead. Really dead. Dead dead. Petersbury started walking again, shaking her head when Lauren tried to follow. *Keep reading. It's all here.* She held up her hands, bare and gloved, and waggled her fingers. *You know when things are right. It's not something that can be taught.* Gloom swallowed her, until only her voice remained. *I'll do what I can from this end. But I'm not the one with the touch.*

"Neither am I." Lauren stood, alone in the gathering dark; the chittering from across the river resumed, then grew louder and nearer.

Then she heard footsteps coming up from behind and turned—

Lauren opened her eyes, and looked up to find Corey standing over her.

"It's almost four thirty. We should probably start getting ready." He reached into his pocket. "I'm surprised Mistress let me sleep so long." He pulled out a quarter, then held it out so Lauren could see both sides. "Heads or tails?" He flipped the coin in the air, then caught it and slapped it on the desk, keeping it covered with his hand.

"How can it be that late?" Lauren pushed back from the desk and stood. The stench of the river still filled her nose, so real that she wondered how it was possible for Corey not to smell it. "What are we tossing for?"

"Bathroom. Second person to shower's going to find conditions a little chilly." Corey shrugged apology.

Lauren checked her watch, then looked toward the living room windows to find the first hints of fading light as Connie Petersbury's words replayed in her head. *You don't have much time.*

"Lauren?"

"Yeah." She shook her head. "Right. Shower." The room tilted, and she grabbed the edge of the desk. "Tails."

Corey pulled away his hand, then stood back so Lauren could see George Washington's shiny profile. "Sorry. I'll keep it short—don't worry."

"I'm not." Lauren fell back into the old wooden office chair, which squealed in protest. "I'm fine." She massaged the back of her neck as the never-ending buzz in her head escalated to a humming.

"You sure?" Corey crouched at her feet. "You look like you're coming down with something."

"Just a little woozy." Lauren took a deep breath. Another.

One knee crackled as Corey stood. "We're both in good shape." He bent down and kissed her. "Just be a couple minutes."

"Thanks." Lauren listened to the wood creak as he climbed the stairs, caught a whiff of his scent, stale sweat and the faded remains of deodorant. Human, at least. Normal. She sat unmoving until he called down that he had finished. Then she stood and headed upstairs, Connie Petersbury's warning still sounding in her ears.

"WHERE'S MISTRESS WAYCROSS?" Lauren pulled on her coat, then checked in her handbag for her wallet and phone. *Force of habit*. She had turned off her phone the previous day because *what was the point,* but now she turned it back on. Petersbury had essentially told her to trust her instincts, and however vague, it was all the direction she had.

"Been out in the barn all day." Corey stood before the entryway mirror and fingered the collar of his white shirt. "Kermit's been off his feed, so she's been sitting with him. Personally, I think he's fine. It's just when things get anxious, Mistress would rather be with horses than people." He tugged at the red-and-black-striped tie that Waycross had found among her late husband's things. "Do I look as stupid as I feel?"

Lauren took a step back and looked him over. He had returned to his house to collect a pair of dark gray dress slacks, but had drawn the line at his Mistress's offer of one of her late husband's suit coats. Instead, he opted for a battered leather jacket he excavated from behind the seat of his truck. "You look fine. Better than fine." She pointed to his tie, then to her own outfit. "We match."

"That was the plan." Corey ran a hand through his hair, then dug his truck keys out of his pocket. "Call Jorie 'Mistress' even though she isn't Mistress of Gideon. Otherwise, she'll crab at you all night. Leaf interrupts her constantly. Calls her 'young, silly.' She sticks her tongue out at him when he turns his back. It can get uncomfortable. Food's decent as long as she isn't on one of her fad diet kicks."

"That's what I—" Lauren swallowed the word "heard" just in time. "That's what I wanted to ask." She followed Corey out of the house, once again fought the urge to lock the door. "Is Amanda Petrie the cook?" She suppressed an image of what could happen if Petrie prepared food the same way she prepared her ointment.

"No. She's the housekeeper, so she doesn't actually get her hands dirty." Corey helped Lauren into the truck, then waited as she tucked her skirt out of range of the door. "That's according to Millie Chatham, who is the actual cook."

"Good to know." Lauren hugged her handbag as she waited for Corey, patted it when it struck her that it seemed lighter than usual. *The books.* She had left them in Waycross's office. *No reason to take them.* Besides, she wouldn't want Leaf Cateman touching them, seeing the drawings that Matthew Mullin had made of Emma. *No, that would not be good.* They were better where they were. Safer.

A light drizzle started to fall as they pulled out of the driveway, and Corey flipped on the wipers and lights. "Just another crappy night in Gideon." An oncoming truck flickered its headlights, and he switched to low beams.

As the truck passed them, Lauren caught sight of rusty red through the gloom. An iron-gray crew cut. "That's Zeke." She turned around and watched as the man pulled into the Waycross driveway.

Corey slowed until Zeke disappeared around the back of the house. "He stops by sometimes, when Mistress has tools or whatnot that she wants to get rid of."

"I'm sorry I missed him." Lauren faced front. "He's nice."

"Yeah, he's a good ol' guy." Corey veered closer to the edge of the road as another set of headlights became visible. "Rush hour."

"That looks like Phil in the passenger seat." Lauren craned her neck to try to see who was driving. "He's with Beth—I'm wearing her skirt." She turned, and watched the car until she saw it turn into the Waycross driveway. "Did Mistress Waycross call a convocation?"

"If she did, we wouldn't be headed out to dinner at Leaf's." Corey shifted in his seat. "Sometimes the elders meet informally, just to talk." He tapped the gas pedal for emphasis. "Isn't like they don't have a lot to talk about, with all that's been going on."

Lauren focused on the view out the window, which resembled every other view of Gideon she had seen since her arrival. Mist obscuring bare trees. A crumbling road, with no other vehicles in sight.

"This is Old Main," Corey said after a time. "They found Dr. Hoard's car here." He pointed out the passenger window to the muddy roadside.

Lauren picked out the deep ruts left by the tow truck, the tamped-down grass. "Can you stop?"

"Are you kidding?"

"No."

Corey grumbled under his breath as he brought the truck to a stop, then slowly reversed until he drew even with the spot where Hoard's car had been parked. "I want you to stay within arm's reach at all times."

If you insist. Lauren got out of the truck, then waited for Corey to join her. "It was raining that night."

"Yes." Corey stuffed his hands in his jacket pockets and hunched his shoulders as a light gust shook droplets from the trees and sent them spattering down.

Lauren looked over the place where the car had been parked, but nothing about it touched her in any way. "It's just weird that he would stop and get out of the car in the rain, yet leave behind his coat and umbrella."

"What are you saying?"

"Something lured him out." Lauren walked out to the middle of the road, and felt—

—evil for the impure joy of it. A sick shudder of fear. "It got him out of his car, and fixed it so he couldn't get back in." She crouched and touched the road, ran her fingers over cracked asphalt. "Then whatever happened, happened."

Corey stayed by her side, every so often checking the road in one direction or the other. "So he isn't just . . . missing. You think he's dead."

"Or as good as." Lauren straightened. "Or worse." She brushed dirt from her hands. "You live near here?"

"Not really." Corey jerked his thumb in the direction opposite. "Two miles, that way."

"Not far enough." Lauren took a few steps toward the other side of the road, stopped when she heard Corey's warning grouse. She could just detect it, the rustling in the bushes. The flicker of leaves, and movement of shadows. "It's no good out here."

"That's why I moved back to the Mistress's." Corey nudged her elbow. "Now could we please get back in the nice, warm truck so we can go eat rabbit food?"

Lauren walked back to the truck, Waycross's boots clicking on the asphalt. Got in, locked the door, buckled herself in. Yanked down the visor and watched in the mirror as the place where Jerome Hoard had met his fate receded until it was swallowed by the dark.

After a few silent minutes, Corey touched her arm.

"You okay?"

"Yeah." Lauren pressed a hand to the back of her neck, felt a tingle sharp as an electric shock. Something had watched her as she examined the last known location of Dr. Jerome Hoard, physician and son of Gideon. Something that would kill for the sheer joy of it, slash you with its claws and laugh while you bled.

"You don't look okay." Corey held out his arm. "Come here."

Lauren unbuckled her safety belt and scooted across the bench seat, pressed close to Corey as he wrapped his arm around her shoulders. Reached up and took hold of his hand—the chill startled her. "Cold hands—you know what they say?"

Corey stiffened. "What?"

"When you introduced yourself in the diner, you shook my hand. I read your thoughts, I guess. Sensed them. Cold hands, warm heart. That's what you were thinking."

"Right." Corey frowned. "I'm not sure I like that."

"Mistress Waycross said it was a nasty talent. It's not something I'd have chosen."

"But you didn't have a choice." Corey shook his head. "There are times when I hate this place. It would be different if we had a choice. Maybe. I don't know. Like the army, or something."

"It is like an army." Lauren looked out the window as they entered Gideon, drove past Lolly's darkened garage, the blinking neon of Hoard's Diner. "We're fighting a war."

"But we should have a choice whether to fight or not. How long." Corey rounded the town square, past the memorial to his dead ancestor. "If we could just put in a few years and then out. If you wanted to spend your entire life here, fine, but if not—" He jerked his head in the direction of the desolate square. "I mean, look at this place. There's nothing here."

"Jerome Hoard said pretty much the same thing to me. But he came when his Mistress asked him."

"And look what it got him." Corey turned into the cul-de-sac and stopped at the edge of the street, across from the Catemans' Victorian sprawl. "Well, here we are." He shut off the truck, killed the lights. "Kiss for luck?"

"Yes, please." Lauren's heart stuttered as their lips met. Corey tasted like coffee and spice and mint. His hair felt soft and his body warm through his clothes, and she unzipped his jacket and snaked her arms around him and pulled him close. They broke apart eventually and she said, "We better get going." But he continued to hold her and she buried her head in the crook of his neck and closed her eyes and wished that if time had to stop, it could stop at that moment.

And yet . . .

"You buzz like a wasp nest when I touch you." Lauren wiggled her fingers until the prickling subsided.

"Thanks."

"Are you nervous?"

"Aren't you?"

"Yeah."

Corey kissed Lauren's forehead, stroked her hair. "I wish things were different."

"I know." Lauren nodded, felt the cotton shirt collar rough against her cheek. Through the drizzle that webbed across the windshield, she saw the Catemans' porch light shine, the brightness in the windows. "It's showtime." She gave Corey one last squeeze, then let him go.

31

"Have you been here before?" Lauren held on to Corey's arm as they mounted the steps to the sweeping columned porch.

"A few times. Diplomatic courier service behind enemy lines." Corey wiped away his smile when a middle-aged woman in a maid's black dress and white apron opened the front door. "Good evening, Sharon."

"Mr. Corey." Sharon's smile wavered when she turned to Lauren. "Ma'am." She ushered them inside, took their coats. "Mistress is in the green parlor with the other guests."

"Other guests." Lauren whispered as she and Corey negotiated one overstuffed room after the other. "I don't know if that's good or bad."

"Guess it depends if they're all here because of you." Corey stroked the silky sleeve of Lauren's blouse. "I wish I had taken up Mistress's offer of that suit coat."

"You look fine."

"I look like a waiter."

"Leaf Cateman wears black jeans to dinner."

"It's his house." Corey stopped in the doorway of a high-ceilinged salon decorated in eye-watering shades of green: sea-silk walls, viridian curtains, carpets in emerald and forest. Not one but two crystal chandeliers. A half-dozen people turned as they entered, the three men in dinner jackets, the three women in varying degrees of evening dress.

Lauren felt a stab of irritation. "The invitation didn't specify dress code."

"Well, it's too late now." Corey bowed toward a diminutive blonde encased in gold brocade. "Mistress Cateman."

"Hello, Dylan." Jorie Cateman tottered toward them on nosebleed heels covered in the same blinding cloth as her dress. "It's been too long." From a distance, she looked well into her thirties, her hair upswept and makeup heavy. But the years fell away as she drew near; up close, she looked more like a teenager turned loose in her mother's closet.

After a fistfight. Lauren tried not to stare at the bruising and puffiness under one eye that the heavy makeup failed to hide. *Did Leaf do that?* Surely she would have heard about it from someone—even the richest man in town wouldn't have been able to hide spouse abuse.

"You must be Lauren *Reardon,* is it?" Jorie extended a hand as small as Connie Petersbury's, the nails shiny scarlet. Her eyes widened when she sensed Lauren's examination. Then she stood back and looked her up and down. "What a . . . fascinating outfit. The blouse is an unfortunate shade, though. Highlights all those things on your face."

Looks like we have something in common. Lauren held back the comment, and touched one of her many cuts. "I wasn't expecting to be invited to dinner anywhere. Mistress Waycross and a few of her friends were kind enough to help me out."

"I thought I'd seen these things before." Jorie sniffed. "Quite a few times." She turned to Corey and waggled her finger. "You should know better."

"I was swept into this at the last minute." Corey glanced at Lauren, and twitched the barest of winks. "I don't see the Master."

Jorie's smile could have opened a can. "Master Cateman won't be joining us this evening. He's indisposed." She nodded to someone who had entered the room, and a beat later Corey found himself being helped into a gray suit coat by Sharon.

"Apologies, Mistress." His words came barely audible, his face reddening.

"One can't help what strangers do, but you should know the rules by now." Jorie tapped his chest with one carmine-tipped finger. "We always dress for dinner." She turned and walked back into the room, her gait unsteady as her heels sank into the layers of carpet.

Lauren paused to straighten Corey's tie. "I hope whoever wound her up lost the key." He barked out a laugh, covered it with a cough, then offered her his arm.

Lauren leaned close. "Would Leaf ever hit her?"

"Are you kidding? If anything, it would be the other way around."

"She's covering up a shiner." Lauren watched the woman totter. "Maybe she fell off her shoes."

"I doubt you've met anyone here, Miss Reardon—it is Miss, isn't it?" Jorie turned her back on Lauren's affirmative, and gestured to the trio of men, interchangeable upper-management types with clipped gray hair, dark suits, and indoor complexions. "May I introduce Thaddeus Trace, Emlyn Howell, and Jeremiah Coates." She then nodded toward the two women on the other side of the room, both older, both dressed less richly in somber brown and navy blue, like good ladies-in-waiting. "Susannah Trace and Eva Coates." Then she pointed to the short couches arranged in a U-shape in the middle of the room. "Why don't we all sit down?"

Lauren lowered to the edge of one of the end couches, sat silent while the others arranged themselves. The women opted for the top of the U, Coates and Trace bracketing Jorie Cateman, while the three men sat in a row on the couch opposite hers. She moved to let Corey pass, and he gave her a warning arch of the eyebrows before taking a seat next to her.

And so it begins. Lauren knew the attempted humiliations, the gamesmanship, were ploys to unsettle her. But she also knew she needed to keep calm, that anger could lead to mistakes, and she wondered whether she possessed the skill to outmaneuver what was obviously a well-planned assault. "A meeting of elders." She took note of the surprised looks, arched brows, and a few frowns. "I assume that's what this is?"

Thaddeus Trace leaned forward, tumbler of whiskey in hand. A double, from the looks of it. No ice or water. "A little smaller than Mistress Waycross's gathering, I assume. But yes, one could call this a convocation."

"Not without Leaf, surely." That from Susannah Trace, her tone scolding for all its softness.

"Leaf's not here in person, true, but we all share the same concerns." Thaddeus Trace paused to drink, then regarded Lauren over the top of his glass. "I believe you know what we want to speak with you about?"

"Right down to business, and you haven't fed me yet. Hell, you haven't even offered me a drink." Lauren sat back, arms folded. "You must be scared."

Jorie sat primly, hands folded in her lap, her gin and tonic untouched on the table in front of her. "You presume a great deal for someone who has only been here a few days."

Lauren nodded. "Perhaps, but during that time, three people have disappeared. I went into the woods for a few hours to help look for one of them and emerged three days later, at which point some of you, including your housekeeper, Mistress Cateman, tried to kill me. My time here, while short, has been eventful and instructive."

After a beat of silence, Emlyn Howell stood and walked across the room to the sideboard that served as the bar. "What will you have, Miz Reardon?"

"Club soda with a twist, please."

Howell smiled. Fixed Lauren's drink, then poured scotch into a tumbler and added ice. "I'm sorry that your first exposure to our way of handling things was the meeting at Mistress Waycross's." He set everything on a tray, along with napkins and a dish of mixed nuts, and returned to the couch. "I'm afraid she has fallen on hard times in more ways than one." He served Corey first, then stood before Lauren, glass in hand.

"Mistress Waycross's maiden name was Howell." Lauren looked into eyes the same shade of blue, sensed the same sharp assessment. "You're related to her?"

"Cousins." Howell sniffed. "Distant cousins." He tried to hand Lauren her drink, gave a little snort of surprise when she hesitated taking it. "I wouldn't dare try to spell you. In my Master's house?"

Lauren shook her head. "I think you would."

"Not yet." Howell set the glass on the table in front of her. "Now is the time for negotiation." He returned to his seat and regarded her with head-cocked bemusement, as though he doubted her abilities in that regard.

Jeremiah Coates nodded agreement. "We have an idea what you learned from your father about the history of the Mullins in Gideon, the part that your forebear, Eliza Mullin, played in the damning of Nicholas Blaine. We can guess what you learned from Virginia Waycross. You've been deceived."

Lauren shrugged. "If you haven't noticed, my name is Reardon, not Mullin. My father left the ways of the Lady behind when he left Gideon. He didn't want me exposed. He didn't teach me anything."

"Then there will be that much less for you to unlearn." A hard smile from Jeremiah Coates.

"Oh, quiet, Jeremiah." Jorie picked at one perfect nail, then clenched her hands and shoved them beneath her thighs. "Of course he taught you things. He couldn't help himself. He's a Mullin."

"Was." Lauren studied her examiners in turn. "He passed away two weeks ago. I assumed you knew. I guess your sources weren't as thorough as you thought."

"Actual experience isn't as important as the fact that you are Matt's daughter. Blood tells." Thaddeus Trace held out his hands, palms up, a generous offer of his good opinion. "And word has gotten around of your woodland adventures."

"I wandered. I got lost."

"You emerged from bewitched woods twice, alive." Trace raised his glass to her. "That required some skill, whether you admit to it or not."

"So I'm both pariah and saving grace." Lauren's throat ached, forcing her to relent and sip the drink Howell made for her. "You are desperate."

"And you're as arrogant as your father was." Susannah Trace sighed in disgust. "He's not remembered kindly here. Are you sure you want to repeat his mistakes?"

"Let's back up." Emlyn Howell held up his hands. "This is a bargaining session, after all. Don't give me that look, Jorie. We knew this going in. As it stands, Miz Reardon has no reason to trust us, and little reason to give us the time of day." He offered Lauren another smile, blue eyes twinkling. "Our goal is to attempt to change her mind."

You're the good cop. Lauren smoothed her skirt, plucked a few errant cat hairs that the roller had missed. *When they all threaten, you'll offer explanation, comfort.* She watched the man, looking away each time he glanced in her direction. *Did they think that I would trust you? Sense Virginia Waycross in your eyes?* "I wish you would just get on with it and tell me what you want from me."

"You've heard of the curse that binds Blaine to Gideon. The weight of false accusation. We know you discussed it at Waycross's gathering. Our sources were quite informative in that regard." Jeremiah Coates's voice boomed. He seemed to relish his role as designated blunt instrument. "We want you to lift the curse. It couldn't be simpler."

"Yes, it could. I don't know what the curse is, much less how to lift it."

"We can teach you that," Howell said. "Leaf has all the source documents here."

"Were they written before or after the fire?" Lauren caught a few confused looks. But Thaddeus Trace studied her for a time, drummed his fingers on the couch, then raised his hand to speak.

"You work in the business world—we checked. You have an M.B.A. You understand about value, investment, the good that people derive from owning something worthwhile." His brow drew down. "Gideon has been a cipher for far too long. We would be able to make it a center of commerce, of industry. People would come from miles around to live, to work, to buy all we have to sell."

Lauren thought of a small figure standing in the middle of the weird river, and her never-ending search for a safe place to stand. "People have died, and you're talking about shopping malls."

"People die every day." Trace waved off his wife's mouthed warning to hush. "Gideon must live. Moreover, it must thrive. Thousands once called it home. Look at it now. It isn't even a town anymore. It is an unworthy vessel. We must remake it into a place of influence, in this world and the next. Power. And yes, wealth, because in this world they are one and the same. Such a place as that will keep back the dark for decades to come." He drained his glass, set it on the table with a clatter. "That's enough for now, I believe. As Miz Reardon says, we haven't even fed her yet."

Jorie shook her head. "No, it can't be enough. We haven't decided anything."

"I'm sure that over the course of Millie's excellent dinner, we can impress upon Miz Reardon the urgency of the situation." Thaddeus Trace smiled. Reptile warmth. "After all, she has skin in this game, too. Something to lose. Perhaps more than most."

Lauren had to smile. Deep down, she had expected this. *Lift the curse or else.* "Threat?"

"Fact." Trace shrugged. "I work for the coroner's office. Jeremiah is an attorney of some repute in this part of the state, and Emlyn, well, he knows people who know people." Another snake grin. "As you yourself said, three people have disappeared during your time here. How involved would you like to become in the investigations?"

"I wasn't aware of any investigations."

"Give us time. And motivation."

After a long, silent minute, the doors to the salon opened. Jorie Cateman stood. "Dinner is served." She beckoned for everyone to get up. "Miss Reardon, I thought that instead of Dylan, Emlyn might do well as your dinner partner, given your business backgrounds. You may find a great deal to discuss." She cemented the arrangement by taking hold of Corey's arm and steering him toward the door.

Howell started toward Lauren, but she dodged him with a hurried apology, even as she imagined his conversation. That Thad Trace was just a hothead who didn't mean what he said. That it could work out to everyone's advantage if they all just behaved like grown-ups.

She scooted past the others and into the hall. She had passed the main staircase when she and Corey had first entered, and she headed for it now. If she encountered any staff, she would say she had been looking for a bathroom, taken a wrong turn, lost her way.

She heard the muffled pound of footsteps from behind, softened by the carpets. "Where are you going?"

Lauren stopped, waited for Corey to catch her up, then pulled him into an alcove. "I have to find Leaf's office."

"It's on the third floor, I think." Corey pulled her close. "You can't go up there now."

"I didn't come here to be threatened. Not that I didn't expect it, but damn." Lauren felt too agitated to be held and Corey's persistent unease made it worse—she pushed away from him and paced the small space. "This entire evening has been designed to put us on the defensive."

"It's working." Corey slumped against the wall, his borrowed jacket bunching around his shoulders.

"We can't let it." Lauren stuck her head out of the alcove, on the lookout for irritated hostesses or threatening witches. "I may be gone awhile. Cover for me."

"How?"

"Tell Jorie I've been stricken with some embarrassing GI ailment—she'll like that."

"They're going to make sure you wind up in prison if you don't help them."

"Prison would be cake compared to what will happen if we turned Blaine loose." Lauren started toward the stairs, but stopped when Corey grabbed her arm. He pulled her close again, this time kissing her. Then he spoke in whispers, his breath in her hair.

"I've heard stories about those men my entire life. Howell, Trace, and Coates. Leaf paid for their college, then helped them get jobs where they'd do him the most good. They get their hands dirty so he doesn't have to."

Lauren unwound Corey's arms, touched his face, tried not to see the fear in his eyes.

"I have to go." She dodged him when he reached for her, and bolted up the stairs.

32

auren bounded up the stairs, past the second floor, to the third. No sense in sneaking. If caught, she was screwed no matter what she said. Jorie and the other elders would know where she was headed.

Darkness grew as she ascended, ornate sconces throwing thin light that cast weird shadows on the paintings that lined the curving wall. The air grew still, chilly, and damp. *Like being in a tomb.* An over-decorated mausoleum, gilt-edged and velvet-draped.

And smelly. Lauren paused at the third-floor landing. The odor had been faint at first, medicinal, with an ammonia sharpness that re-minded her of her father's dried elder leaves.

But now the rankness intensified, changed to something more . . . organic. *Meat gone bad.* That first hint of rancidity, of rot. She hesi-tated as scenes from reality-TV shows played through her head. Old newspapers and boxes stacked to the ceiling. Fifty cats in a room, and Grandma's blanket-wrapped corpse stuffed in a closet.

Turn back. And then what? *Ask permission.* Good luck with that.

It's all there. Lolly's words. *And now Lolly's gone, too.* Gone to the same place as Connie Petersbury, murdered—or something worse—by Nicholas Blaine. *I have to stay.* For herself, and for them. She had to put one foot in front of the other, and keep walking. Right to the very edge of the abyss.

No illumination touched the hall but for the faint glow that traveled up the stairway—the doors were all closed, the sconces dark. Lauren listened for any sounds—music, voices—that indicated the presence of someone on the floor, but heard only the occasional muffled creak of her footsteps as she crept along the wall.

How would she find the office? Even if there were a sign or a nameplate, it would be impossible to read in the dark. *Open every door.* She stopped in front of the first one she came to, started to turn the handle—

—then froze when she heard the wet rattle of a labored breath. It came from the far end of the hall, a shadowed dead end, black as the opening to a cave.

Lauren backed away from the door, and waited. Concentrated.

Then she felt it. A malign presence, like a weight on her soul.

"The first time I saw your father—" An old man's voice, like a creaking hinge. Another wheeze. "—he stood where you are now." The prolonged footfall of an uneven step, as though the speaker fought to maintain his balance. "Fourteen, he was. Completely unaware of his talents." The shadow emerged from the cave, took shape. A tall figure. Huge head. Broad shoulders. "He had come with his father, your grandfather, who I had just hired to manage some of my orchards." The head bobbed, the slightest of bows. "I am Leaf Cateman, Master of Gideon."

Lauren fought the urge to flee. The stench emanated from Cateman, grew stronger the closer he came. *Indisposed.* Bullshit. *Dying.* Even that slow deterioration didn't smell like this. *Dead.* Yes, that was it. All over but the burial.

"I see nothing of Matthew in you." Cateman stopped where the hallway shadow met the dim light from the stairway. "He was tall, lithe, a panther cub of a boy." He cocked his head, and whatever he wore—a scarf or turtleneck—bunched and shifted so that he looked bull-necked. "You seem quite ordinary."

"Sorry to disappoint."

"Don't be flippant." Cateman sighed. "An unfortunate quality.

One he possessed, as well." He lowered his head, and the half-light touched his hair.

What there is of it. Lauren swallowed hard at the sight of Cateman's scalp, a blistered, oozing mess dotted with a few cottony clumps of fuzz. *Chemo?* She tried to remember if she had seen or smelled anything like this during her hospital visits. She focused on the carpet at her feet, steeled herself, then looked up at Cateman to find him regarding her in turn.

His was a ravaged face, cheeks sunken and scabbed, beard patchy, eyes red-rimmed and fever-bright. What Lauren had thought was a scarf turned out to be a thick swaddle of gauze, safety-pinned in place, the ends tucked inside Cateman's bathrobe like an ascot. More gauze poked out from his sleeves and the legs of his pajama pants, mittened his hands.

He's wrapped in it. Lauren tried not to stare at Cateman as he grimaced, then shifted from one slippered foot to the other. *Like a mummy.*

"You must pardon my—appearance." Cateman hid his hands behind his back. "I suffer an affliction of the skin that tends to flare in times of stress. I assure you—that it is not contagious." He tried to smile, but winced instead. Swallowed with a gulping sound, as though the action pained him.

No, you didn't give Jorie that shiner. The man barely had the strength to stand. "Shouldn't you be in a hospital?" Lauren wondered at Jorie, downstairs, entertaining guests. Didn't she realize the condition her husband was in? Hell, couldn't she smell it?

"I cannot leave Gideon in a time of crisis." Cateman trudged to the wall opposite and rested against it, then took a handkerchief from the pocket of his robe and dabbed his forehead. "Something your father, unfortunately, never understood." He glanced at the cloth and frowned, then wadded it and stuffed it back in his pocket. "I watched you from my window yesterday morning as you crossed the square. Brave of you, considering."

"Considering most folks here want to see me dead, you mean?"

Lauren watched Cateman stand up straighter, smooth his hand over the front of his robe. *I am not as sick as I appear.* Who was he trying to convince?

"Amanda regrets her lack of action on your behalf." Cateman cocked one bushy eyebrow. "But she did feel that Betty Joan was due some satisfaction, given what you did to her." His look took on a different flavor, appraising rather than judging. "You got the sense of her. A valuable talent, as long as the object doesn't realize your intention. There are ways to mask it, of course, but not many know them." A beat of silence. "Three days you walked the wilderness. Quite a feat for someone unschooled."

Lauren hid a smile. *And the trap is baited.* The promise of knowledge, of training. How long after his parents' death had Matthew Mullin been so tempted? Were they even cold in the ground? "It didn't seem that long."

"No. Time passes differently there." Cateman turned so that he could lean with his back to the wall. "I know why you've forsaken the pleasures of my table to visit me here."

Lauren looked toward the stairwell, listened to the silence. Maybe they had expected her to seek out Cateman. Maybe their Master had ordered them not to interfere. *Maybe they're one step ahead of me.* In that case, she needed to pick up her pace. "My father built you a wall. I would very much like to see it."

"How did you learn of it?"

"Mr. Loll."

"Mr. Loll." Cateman's lip twitched. "That is a first." He eased upright. "It is a pity that you will miss dinner. Millie is a fine cook, and Emlyn an estimable conversationalist." He turned back toward the darkness at the hallway's end, one hand resting on the wall to steady himself.

"I don't mind." Lauren fell in behind him, alternating between holding her breath and inhaling in quick little bursts. "Just means I'll miss the second round of threats."

"Threats?" Cateman stalled in midshuffle. "From Thad, I assume? How common of him." He resumed walking, slippers *shushing* over the thick carpet. "They are anxious, of course. All of Gideon is on edge. Still, you are a guest in my home. I will speak with him." He glanced over his shoulder, shadow obscuring the sores and hair loss so that he looked normal, healthy. Only his voice betrayed his actual condition, that asthmatic rasp. "But you must realize that the situation in which we find ourselves might drive some of us to—acts of desperation." He stopped before a double-paneled doorway. "Your father truly told you nothing of any of this before he passed?"

Lauren shook her head until she realized that Cateman couldn't see her. "No, he didn't."

Cateman sucked his teeth. "Negligent." He cranked the handle and pushed open the door.

Lauren followed Cateman inside. The flash as he turned on the lights took them both by surprise—she covered her eyes with her hands, heard Cateman gasp and mutter under his breath.

Then she lowered her hands, gave her eyes time to adjust.

Stared.

Not quite round, the office. More an octagon, the angles gentle, one side flowing into the next. In contrast to the rest of the house, the space was bright, sparsely furnished. A massive desk near the center of the room. A file cabinet. Bookcases and a visitor's chair. Oak-plank floors visible beneath a scattering of Persian rugs, the wall paneling stained soft cream, the ceiling a smooth white dome topped with a round glass window divided into quarters by trim work.

The Eye of the Lady. Lauren traced an X-centered circle on her skirt as she walked to the middle of the office and looked up through the window to the night sky beyond. Sensed Cateman at her back, close enough that his stink surrounded her like a wall and she could hear the breath rale in his lungs.

"*'And the Lady gave to her followers a round blue stone, and said to*

them: "*Take this gift which I present to thee, this Eye with which I see all.*" ' "
Cateman circled Lauren, pointed toward the window. Ill though he
was, the wonder in his voice showed in his face, so that he resembled
an old prophet caught up in some divine ecstasy. " '*With it thou shalt
control all those who live in the wilderness, and with their help thou shalt
build up a shining city.*' "

And no one knows this except you and your followers. The passage had
been missing from her father's Book of Endor, but Lauren had found
it in the ghost book. *Your grandfather didn't want just anyone to know.*
That with the help of the right words, the right magic, the Lady's
power could be acquired by anyone. *No, we couldn't let that happen.*
She browsed one of the bookshelves, filled with volumes as old as
her ghost book, if not older. So much knowledge, bottled up by one
family.

"It had been my grandfather's dream, then my father's, to make
Gideon great again." Cateman sighed, his shoulders slumped, the sick
old man returned. "Now the task has fallen to me." He looked down
at Lauren, and anything in his gaze that might have been called kind
had vanished. "You know why you were called here?" He circled her
once, then walked to the wall, and placed his hand upon the panel.
"Come here, and look upon the injustice that has damned this place
for generations."

Lauren approached the wall at an angle so that she could stay as
far away from Cateman as possible and still see the painted scene. It
had been composed in a flat, primitive style, and lacked the rich detail, the coloring, of the drawings in her father's book.

But the sequence of events showed clear enough. A scene from a
trial, a woman standing in the witness box and pointing to a black-
haired man seated in the middle of the room. The same man being
led down a street toward a platform, then tied to a stake. The lighting
of the fire and the burning, the man holding up a pleading hand to
the crowd, which laughed and jeered.

Then came the tumble of storm clouds, which left the dead scattered through the streets.

"Eliza Mullin bore false witness against a poor traveler named Nicholas Blaine." Catemen pointed to the woman in the witness box, a dark-haired beauty rendered in haughty profile. "She was Eliza Blaylock then. The Freeze left her a widow, free to entrap another poor soul."

"And that's Blaine." Lauren pointed to the man at the stake. "What did she accuse him of?"

"Embezzlement. Theft." Cateman sighed, a sound made worse by the rattle in his chest. "Murder."

"And he was innocent."

"Without a doubt."

"Why did she do it?"

"She had gone over to the darkness, and required innocent blood to seal her unholy bargain."

Lauren kept her face turned toward the wall so that Cateman couldn't see her expression. *Innocent blood.* Nicholas Blaine. *As if.*

Then she looked closer. The stain let the grain of the wood show through, the dark knots and variations in color. But some of the boards looked as though they hadn't been cleaned, leaving large patches of gray and streaks of black visible through the milklike coating.

She touched one of the dark smears, flinched her hand away. The same sensations she had felt in the gazebo, the fear and the pain and the heat of the flame. She glanced at Cateman to see if he had noticed, but he seemed lost in reverie.

"I will never forget the day that Matthew told me that he had found old boards stacked in the shed. Blackened in places, he said. As though they'd been burned. 'Salvaged from the Great Fire,' I told him. 'If they're in decent shape, use them anywhere.' So he paneled my office. 'Gideon history, Master,' he said to me. 'I know how much you enjoy it.'" He pressed his hand to the wood, this time more gently. "Such a good boy, in the beginning."

Until he slept with your wife. Lauren touched one of the Gideon dead, a dark-haired man sprawled next to a horse trough. Again, the sense of pain, of loss. "Who drew the figures?"

"I don't recall." Cateman rapped a board with his knuckle. "Matthew composed a few. He possessed a distinct talent."

Even now, you won't say Emma's name. Lauren tugged at her blouse. The office felt hotter than the rest of the house, and the combination of the heat and the stink made her stomach roil.

"You were called. To make things right." Cateman took a step, then stopped. Shook his head as though dazed. His face had paled, the sores bright as paint against his skin. "You will move into this house, and receive instruction by those who know the true ways of the Lady."

Lauren stopped in front of a panel that showed the crows departing Gideon after the burning of Nicholas Blaine. "You don't want Blaine here."

Cateman's lips curved, more rictus than smile. "And what has led you to this conclusion?"

"I've met him."

Cateman's friendliness, such as it was, vanished. "That is not possible." His voice, low and measured, like a knell.

"In Seattle. Those were silent visits. We didn't exchange words. I've spoken with him here twice. The second time, he roughed me up a bit." Lauren touched one of her facial cuts, then turned to find Cateman regarding her with curled lip.

"Why do you lie?" He shook his head, then raised his hand to his throat. It all showed in the bright office light, the stained bandages, the yellowed whites of his eyes and deathbed pallor. "Why do Mullins always lie, and betray, and wallow in the dark?"

"And yet you keep calling us back." Lauren turned and braced herself against the wall, struggled to ignore the heat that seeped through her clothes. "You offer us what you think we want most and you threaten us when we refuse." She fought to keep her voice down. "What did you offer my father? What bait? A home? A job?"

Cateman drew himself up as straight as he could, an effort that made him appear even more enfeebled. "I offered him all I had to give."

Lauren stared into rheumy eyes, caught the flicker of that last remaining bit of flint. *You bastard—you handed him Emma on a plate.* No magic needed to figure that out. Only the realization of how desperate Cateman was, and had been for a very long time. "What went wrong?"

Cateman started to speak. Stopped. Then he staggered to a chair set against the wall, and sank into it.

Lauren looked toward the desk, then the door, for any sign of an intercom or house phone. Cateman appeared on the point of collapse. Two hundred pounds of deadweight, at least. Impossible for her to handle by herself.

"Ingratitude—betrayed—" Cateman's voice cracked and he coughed, a ragged hack that grew louder and more intense until he stood doubled over, his hands on his knees.

First came the spatters of saliva. Phlegm.

Then came the blood.

Lauren ran to the office door and flung it open. *"I need some help here."* She stood in the doorway, waited until she heard voices, the pound of footsteps on the stairs. Then she hurried to Cateman, grabbed his arm to keep him from toppling off the chair, and felt the wet slide of gauze, the dampness through his sleeve.

"Get away from him."

Lauren turned just as Amanda Petrie elbowed her aside. "He needs to be in a hospital."

Petrie ignored her, beckoning to two men in work clothes and directing them as they took hold of Cateman's arms and legs and hoisted him in a sitting position. "Take him to his room, yes, and get him into bed—I'll be there directly." She herded them to the door, a bustling haystack in a shapeless yellow bathrobe, her hair still wet from the shower.

Lauren followed close behind. "Did you hear what I said?"

Petrie turned on her. "Get out of this office."

"He's coughing up blood."

"I said, get out and stay out." Petrie grabbed Lauren's arm and dragged her into the hallway. "Or you will wish you had died in the woods." She closed the office door, then hurried down the hallway after the men and their stricken burden.

"Are you going to use more of your miracle ointment?" Lauren rubbed her arm where Petrie had squeezed. "I'd think twice about that if I were you."

Petrie's step slowed. "You're all alike. He offers you everything, and you spit in his face." Then she quickened her pace and vanished into the dark, leaving Lauren alone.

33

Lauren expected to find an irate wife and a phalanx of faithful companions waiting for her at the foot of the stairs, all ready to berate her for her mistreatment of Leaf Cateman. But the entryway proved dark and empty, the only sound the occasional clatter of dishes coming from the rear of the house.

Lauren circled around the staircase and followed a narrow hallway that led past a walk-in pantry, a storeroom scented with dried herbs, a large kitchen in which a quartet of older women wrestled with large pots and arranged plates on trays. It looked as though the dinner had been going on without her.

At the end of the hall, Lauren came to a door. She opened it, and found herself outside, overlooking the same backyard she had reconnoitered the previous day.

She pulled in the damp, cold night air, one lungful after the other. Tugged at her blouse, gathered the folds of her skirt, and shook, scrubbed her hands through her hair. Smelled her sleeve, caught a whiff of rotten meat, and wondered if she would ever be rid of the stench of Cateman's illness.

She sat down on the top step, pulled her knees to her chest, tucked her skirt around her legs. Low clouds hid the moon and stars, leaving the yard as dark as a cellar, shadows twitching each time a light breeze drifted through the trees.

Then one of the shadows took the shape of a man, who crept along the rear fence, then close to the shed.

Lauren watched the shoulder-hunched shambling, now all too familiar. "You again."

"Me again?" Barton limped to the center of the yard. "Who were you expecting—somebody else?" Different clothes this time, stained khakis and a dark shirt topped with an ancient barn coat. A battered baseball cap, the insignia long since lost.

"I wasn't expecting anyone." Lauren rubbed her arms to warm them, taking care to avoid the sore spot where Petrie had grabbed her. "Were you born here?"

Barton shrugged. "What's it to you?"

"Just asking. No need to get riled." Lauren stopped, took a deep breath. The man's peevishness rubbed off. The way he spoke. "I wondered if you knew my father. Matthew Mullin. He left Gideon almost forty years ago. He would have been about eighteen, nineteen. Tall, thin, curly hair."

Barton kicked the ground. "I knowed him," he said, nodding. "We used to talk sometimes, about the crows. That we hadn't seed any in years and that meant that the Lady didn't favor us no more. He used to ask a lot of questions about the crows." His expression brightened. He even smiled. "Then one day I goes home, and I finds this picture shoved in under the door. It was a crow, all colored like a photograph, and underneath it said 'To tide you over until the real ones come back.' He drew it. Signed it and all, like a real artist."

Lauren thought back to the lovely crows in her father's book, how much it might have meant to someone like Barton to receive such a drawing as a gift. "I'd love to see it."

Barton shook his head. "Ain't got it no more. I used to carry it with me"—he patted the breast pocket of his jacket—"and I would fold it and unfold it to look at it and it got old, and one day 'bout three years, four years ago I was out working in Master Cateman's orchard and got caught in the rain. It got all wet and fell apart." He made a straightening motion with his hands. "I tried to put it back together, but the tape wouldn't hold. It wouldn't hold." He sniffled, wiped his nose on his sleeve. "So I buried it, like it was a real crow."

"I'm sorry." Lauren glanced down, brushed away yet another cat hair from her skirt. "I have some other drawings of his—maybe you'd like—" She looked up, and stared at the spot where Barton had stood. Checked the yard, standing so she could see past stacks of firewood. "Where the hell did you go?" Here, and then vanished. Like a ghost.

Lauren leaned on the railing, then straightened. Paced. Tried to gird herself to go inside and face Jorie Cateman and the others. Checked her watch. Ten minutes had passed since she had left Leaf Cateman in the care of Amanda Petrie, at least a half hour since she had left to search for Cateman's office. Either Corey had made up one hell of a good excuse, or Jorie and her little helpers had moved on to Plan B.

Which would be what? Kidnapping? Some sort of mind-control spell? *Maybe it's already started.* She held out her hands and concentrated, tried to sense if she felt any different, but felt nothing but the light breeze through her fingers.

The batter of raised voices reached her through an open window. The kitchen women, arguing about the timing for a soufflé. A normal argument about a normal, everyday thing. Lauren let the sounds wash over her, cleanse her mind the way the night air cleansed her clothes. Let her thoughts drift.

After a time, her gaze settled on the shed, the single small window boarded, paint peeling, the eaves pocked with rot. So unkempt compared to the rest of the property, a blemish on perfect skin.

Lauren descended the steps, walking on her toes to avoid the hard click of boot heels on cement. Trotted across the lawn to the shed, searched until she found the door.

Look at that padlock. It caught what light there was and flashed it in her face like a dare. The door proved to be steel, but it had been set in the old jamb, which was cracked and worn. But even so, she would need a hammer and crowbar to pry off the hasp, and there was no way that could be done without the entire household hearing, assuming she had the tools to begin with.

Lauren looked around the corner toward the garage, which was also closed, the only lighting a safety lamp that illuminated the driveway. Then she walked around to the rear of the shed. Let her eyes readjust to the dark. Nothing but a mess to be seen, long-forgotten firewood strewn amid waist-high weeds that had dried to spiky stems with leaves like razors.

Lauren hiked her skirt above her knees, and let Waycross's boots take the brunt of the punishment. Kicked through the dead vegetation to the shed wall, then walked along, tapping the frame with her toe.

She found the loose boards at the halfway point. The bottom board shook when she nudged it, then slid into the weeds, taking two other sections of the frame with it and leaving a gap big enough for her to wedge through.

Lauren crouched and maneuvered through the gap between the wall studs, pushed through into the shed. The interior proved to be a large open space, about the size of a two-car garage, one corner set up as a kitchen with a sink and a refrigerator, the opposite corner a walled-off compartment with a plastic curtain hanging in the doorway, a shower or toilet.

A bare low-watt bulb above the sink provided the only light, casting Lauren's shadow across the length of the floor and along the walls as she explored, kicked up dust, breathed in the musty air.

Emotions. She sensed them in the air, faint but distinctive, like the perfume of a long-departed wearer. *Fear. Happiness. Lust. Love.* At some point in the past, her father had entered this place. More than likely, he had made love to Emma Cateman here. *Did you know you had been set up, Dad? Did you care?* She leaned against the wall and looked around, tried to visualize the room as it had been almost four decades before, the refuge for the fine-boned woman and her angry colt of a young man. *Did you report to Leaf about your progress, Emma? Did you laugh at my father behind his back?*

Lauren pushed away from the wall and walked the perimeter of the room, brushed her fingers along the bare plank wall. One circuit. Another. Then she stopped, studied the floor, and spotted the shadows on the boards nearest the kitchen. She thought it a trick of the dim light at first. Then she drew closer, and picked out the hinges. The handle.

Don't go down there. Every idiot move by every horror-movie screamer replayed in her head. *But I'm in the movie now*. And according to this script, she needed to face whatever was in the cellar, because the odds were good that her father had faced it, too.

Lauren lifted the door. Faint light shone from bulbs strung along the packed-dirt wall, revealing narrow wooden stairs. She heard her mother's voice in her head, a saying that Angela Reardon fell back on whenever she pushed a point so hard it snapped. *In for a penny, in for a pound.*

The first step. The next. No railing to grip, but the walls were close enough that she could press her hands against them to steady herself. Wooden steps changed to dirt at some point. The walls pressed closer and the air grew thick and damp as she descended lower, lower.

Funnel me down to hell. Lauren paused, then looked back over her shoulder. No light visible at the top—the stairway had twisted and skewed that much. Someone could close the door and lock it and she wouldn't know until it was too late.

She took the next step down. The next. Most of the bulbs had gone dark, leaving her to feel her way. She didn't realize she had reached the bottom until she felt with her foot for the next step and found nothing but a stretch of flat dirt floor.

She edged forward. Caught a flash of light and heard the sizzle of a failing bulb. Rounded a corner and found herself looking down a long, narrow passage, dirt walls shored up with wooden posts and beams, bulbs stuttering so that light pulsed with a flickering beat that hurt her eyes.

A room at the end. A chamber.

I know where this is going. But she went anyway, because she was a witch of Gideon now, however inexperienced, and this was what they did. The walls closed in, brushed her shoulders, and she told herself that she had never suffered claustrophobia before and now was not the time to give it a try.

She saw a platform in the chamber, an altar or bier. Stepped inside, then reached up and twisted one of the remaining bulbs so that it shone upon the mound resting on top.

A drape of some sort, stained and stiff with age. She peeled it back, and looked upon a face. What remained of a face, after rot and damp and time's passage had taken their toll.

"Who are you?" Lauren looked down at the blackened form, the arms curled and tucked like wings.

She didn't catch the tremor at first, then thought it a trick of the light.

Then the body's arms twitched. Straightened. A growl rose in what remained of its throat.

Lauren let go of the bulb. It swung back and forth, casting warped shadows across the ceiling, the walls, as the body sat up, dragged its legs over the side of the bier.

Raised its head, and started at her with eyeless sockets.

Lauren backed up, hands pressed to the wall. "Who are you?"

The body stared, all stillness.

Then it groaned and pushed off the bier. Held on until it steadied, then staggered forward. Clicking noises sounded as teeth and bone clattered. Desiccated skin flaked like dark snow.

Lauren stopped. Was her Gideon sense worth a damn—well, she would find out now because she sensed nothing from this creature but fear and confusion and need.

"Help." It shuffled toward her. "Me. Help." Half-spoken words, half howls, sounds uttered in dread.

"Do they know you're here?" Lauren took hold of wrists thin

and brittle, crackly as broiled fat. "Who are you?" She tried not to squeeze, knew its arms would shatter like spun glass if she squeezed too hard. And still it came, until its face pressed close to hers and she could smell ash and rot and see through its cracked eye socket to the back of its skull.

"Help."

Lauren stepped back, and let it go. It remained in place. tottering like an infant finding its footing for the first time. "I'll get someone. I'll go get someone."

"Help."

"I'll be back. I promise." She backed up until she found the steps, then took them two at a time, the thing's crumbling voice chasing her like an echo.

She stumbled once. Twice. Barked her knee on the wooden edge of the top step. Shot through the trapdoor into the still, dark shed, then through the gap in the boards into the night.

"A BODY?" JORIE Cateman sat at the head of the dining room table. "In a shed that hasn't been used in decades and will be demolished in the spring?" She tapped the handle of a serving spoon against the rim of her plate, kept up the clatter until Emlyn Howell reached over and plucked the utensil from her hand.

"I told you. There's a trapdoor in the floor. Steps leading down. A narrow corridor. Body's in a small chamber at the end. There are bulbs and everything—someone knows what's down there." Lauren stood off to the side, flanked by the pair of kitchen workers who had served as escort. All the men had stood when she entered. Then came the flurry of questions. A resigned shake of the head from Corey. An order from Jorie to *get a rug for our guest to stand on so she doesn't dirty the carpet.*

The silence when she told them what she had seen.

"And you discovered this how?" Jorie looked Lauren up and down, and grimaced. "Just happened to wander outside after harassing my husband to the point of collapse."

336

"He belongs in the hospital."

"I'd tell you to mind your own business, but I'm not sure you know the meaning of the expression." Jorie pulled her napkin off her lap and tossed it onto her plate, then pointed to one of the women. "Olivia, bring me the house keys, a coat and boots, and whatever else I'll need. Emlyn? Dylan? You come with us." She brushed past Lauren, cheeks mottled pink, eyes fixed straight ahead.

"What the hell have you been doing?" Corey prodded Lauren in the back, steered her toward the door. "What happened with Leaf?"

"He's sicker than they want to admit." Lauren lowered her voice when she spotted Howell within eavesdropping distance. "I saw the office, though."

Corey chuffed. "I hope it was worth it."

"How was dinner?"

"I've had pleasanter root canals."

They suited up in coats and gloves and bustled to the rear door, where Amanda Petrie awaited them. She had dressed since the altercation with Lauren, in a drab brown housedress, errant curls sticking out every which way from a messy chignon.

"Mistress?" The emotion that Petrie managed to pack into that single word. Disdain. Irritation. Injured pride.

"We need to examine the shed." Jorie brushed past her. "My house keys." She snapped her fingers at Olivia, who held them out to her in her cupped hands, like an offering. "We have bodies, apparently."

"The Master doesn't like anyone to go in there—"

"The Master is indisposed." Jorie smiled and met Petrie's eye. One beat. Two.

Petrie tried to rally. "But you don't have—"

Jorie held up her key ring and shook out a shiny silver padlock key. "Yes?"

Petrie paled, and sagged against the wall.

"Let's go." Jorie barged past her, then turned, hands on hips, and waited for the rest of them to follow.

THEY CROWDED DOWN the stairs and into the narrow corridor, the four of them, Howell remarking about the history of the place and Corey muttering about the quality of the supports.

Then they fell silent and looked down at the floor, then into the empty chamber.

Lauren's stomach clenched.

"So, where is he?" Jorie grimaced and waved off a spiderweb that had dropped down from the wood support. "The fiend. The zombie."

"It wasn't evil." Lauren pointed to the place where the body had collapsed. "I left him—it—here in the corridor." The dirt appeared disturbed, but then she had walked on it, hadn't she? They all had. "It asked me for help. I asked who it was, but it didn't tell me."

"Nicholas Blaine was burned to a cinder in 1836." Howell, the fountain of historical information. "Then there were the folks killed in the Great Fire. Leaf must have uncovered something."

Jorie sighed heavily. "All right. It was supposed to be a secret. He read about these cellars in one of his old books. They used to hold rites down here. Baptisms and whatnot. It was one of Leaf's dreams to reopen them for all of Gideon to use once more. It was meant to be a surprise, but now—"

"So that explains the excavation, but not the body." Howell smiled, a thin curve of lip that rivaled Thad Trace in the amount of reptile contained therein. "Perhaps our visitor had a vision. It wouldn't be out of line to suppose that Blaine's troubled spirit might appear to her. She did say it asked her for help." He looked over the top of Jorie's head to Lauren. "And you know what the answer to that is, don't you, Miz Reardon?"

Lauren gave herself a mental kick. *I should have kept my mouth shut.* "It wasn't Blaine."

"How do you know?"

Because it was gentle, and so, so scared. "Ask Leaf Cateman."

"That's *Master* Cateman to you." Jorie pushed past Howell toward the exit, brushing her hands over her coat sleeves in a futile effort to clean off the dirt. "My sick husband, who you browbeat until he collapsed. Don't think I won't remember that, *Miss* Reardon." She started up the stairs. "This is a waste of time."

"Agreed." Howell shot Lauren a look of disgust, then turned and followed Jorie.

Corey tugged on Lauren's arm. "What the hell?"

"Later."

"I told them you had stomach flu—I'd kinda like to know what I got myself into."

"I don't think you're the one who needs to worry."

Jorie had already departed by the time they made it upstairs, leaving Howell to deal with them. He said nothing as he walked them to Corey's truck. Recovered the loaned suit coat from Corey, then followed Lauren around to the passenger side, and held on to her arm when she tried to get in.

"I don't know what you thought you would accomplish with this little charade, but between this and the episode with Leaf—"

Lauren tried to extract herself from his grip. "I didn't—"

Howell shook his head. "Amanda told me what happened. Not a smart move to mistreat a sick old man who offered you a kindness." He released her, then held the door for her, closed it after she got in. "And who has most of Gideon on his side." He remained in the window, ignored Corey's warning glare. "The offer still stands, for the time being. You would be wise to take it. The alternative would be extremely unpleasant." He waved as they backed out, the designated host bidding them good evening, and watched them until they turned off onto the square.

"That could've gone better." Corey pulled a roll of antacid tablets out of the glove compartment, tossed a couple into his mouth.

"How?" Lauren waved off his offer of the rest of the roll. "I shouldn't have told them about the body."

"That's the least of your worries."

"I saw it, okay?"

"I'm not saying you didn't." Corey dug into the glove compartment again, this time pulling out a CD. "I just wish you hadn't made them angry. They can get back at you in ways you never imagined. I had a feeling it would be bad, but I didn't think they'd pull out the heavy artillery so fast." He shoved the disc into the slot in the dash, then fiddled with the volume. Soft jazz filled the cabin, a quiet, settling sound.

Lauren looked out at the passing scenery. Nothing had changed, yet everything seemed different. "They just let me go."

"You're complaining about that?"

"They threaten me with a murder charge, and then Jorie leaves and lets the second team read me the riot act."

"I don't think that means you're off the hook."

"They didn't ask why I went in the shed in the first place either."

"Why did you?"

Lauren thought for a moment, then shrugged.

"Nosy pain in the ass. That's what I thought." Corey flashed a weak smile that faded as quickly as it appeared. "That's what they thought, too." A fine mist fell, and he clicked on the wipers. "I'm not saying that you didn't see what you said you saw. I'm not saying that you were dumb to go upstairs and hunt for the office. What I am saying is that they want something from you, and if you don't give it to them, they will take it, somehow. And they will make sure it hurts." He took her hand. "And I don't want it to happen."

Corey's touch felt quiet for a change. Lauren rested her head on his shoulder. Enjoyed the peace, for however long it might last.

"You want to stop and get a drink somewhere?"

"Where?" Lauren shook her head. "Not the diner."

"My place?"

"I thought you wanted to stay away from there?"

"Well, yeah." Corey glanced at the dashboard clock. "Night's still young. We could drive around, find a bar."

Lauren sat up straight. Thought back to all the cars and trucks pulling into the Waycross driveway, and let go of Corey's hand. "What's going on?"

Corey turned down the music. "What do you mean?"

"Dinner didn't last as long as you thought it would, did it? You still need to kill some time."

"What are you talking about?"

"There's something going on tonight, isn't there? Mistress Waycross is planning something."

"I don't know what you're—"

Lauren pushed away from Corey to the far end of the bench seat. "Back to the ranch. Now."

34

Corey and Lauren arrived at the Waycross place to find a dozen cars and trucks parked behind the house, the horses milling and fidgeting in the corral. Lauren jumped out as soon as Corey came to a stop, ran up the back steps and into the house to find it dark.

The barn. She collided with Corey on her way out the door, ignored his shouts for her to stop. Her right foot cramped in the stiff boot, and she staggered, caught herself, limped the rest of the way.

The barn was lit bright as day by lamps and lanterns arranged in the ring in the middle of the floor. Inside the ring sat Waycross, Zeke Pyne, Phil, Beth and Penny, and fifteen or twenty others—faces Lauren recognized from the convocation. They all turned when she entered, their expressions stopping her in her tracks. Only Zeke offered anything close to a smile. Even Waycross eyed her with suspicion.

"What are you doing?" Lauren squinted, stared into the light. It formed a dome over Waycross and the others, a force field from a science-fiction film, and she knew that if she touched it, physical pain would be the least of her problems.

"This isn't your concern." Waycross rose from her place at the top of the circle. "Go back to the house."

Lauren sniffed, caught a now-familiar whiff of cat piss, looked up to find the beams hung with wreaths and branches of elder. In the corners of the barn sat clusters of pots and bowls, all steaming, exuding the same stink. Protection. By the bucketload. "I can help."

"No, you can't." Waycross's words came stern and hard, a voice with no patience left. "Dylan, take her back to the house." She lowered herself to the floor. "And keep her there until we're through."

Lauren turned to find Corey behind her—he tried to grab her wrist, but she twisted beyond his reach and ran outside. Looked up at the sky.

Country night. No light to mar the view of the stars when skies were clear. No light to cut through the murk when they weren't. And the skies weren't clear now—in the time that had passed since Lauren had sat on the Catemans' back step, the clouds had thickened and lowered. *Reach up and touch.* Yes, she could if she tried, except the thought of that swirling dark brushing over her skin twisted her gut and made her mouth go dry.

In their enclosure, the horses whinnied, pawed the dirt.

"Come inside, Lauren." Corey stood at her elbow. "Mistress's orders. Please."

"Afraid she'll bind you if you don't keep me quiet."

"That's not fair." Corey leaned close, soft words in her ear. "She has a job to do. We need to let her do it."

"That was always the plan, wasn't it? Get me out of the house, keep me out until they did whatever?" Lauren looked into eyes gone as chilly as the rest. "What are they trying to do?"

"The—the space between is thinning. They're going to close it, or make it thicker, or something."

"And trap Blaine on this side with us?"

"Mistress only has your word that you saw him." Corey made another move to take Lauren's arm, stopped when she flinched away. "Please—we'll just go inside and wait it out."

"It's not right!" Lauren looked overhead at the roiling sky.

One of the horses screamed. So human a sound, like a cry from Hell.

LEAF CATEMAN MANEUVERED out of bed, probed for his slippers with toes numbed by gauze and another of Amanda's concoctions. Pain reliever, this one—it soaked through his skin and clouded his mind like drink.

He stood. Held his arms out to the sides for balance, like a baby taking its first steps. Tottered to the door, turned the handle, and pulled. Pulled again.

"Lock me in, will you?" Cateman pressed his hand to the brass escutcheon, willed the mechanism behind it to move. Felt the clicks, even through the gauze. Turned the handle again, opened the door, stepped out into the hall.

Closed his eyes, and for the first time in his life struggled to get a sense of his own house.

For a while, nothing but confusion. Millie and the others, their squabbles and petty jealousies. Amanda, stolid and dull, her power as graceless as her form.

Then he felt it, like a comet trail in the sky, clean and bright and sharp and cold and so unlike anything he had ever known. The feeling drove him to the stairs, sent him pounding down with a burst of young man's strength. He pushed past a shocked Millie, sent one of the other women into a screaming fit when she saw him.

Swept open the door of the green parlor, and found Jorie, Thad Trace, and the others seated in a circle in the middle of the floor. They held hands, their heads bowed, a golden haze shimmering above them.

"I said, no interruptions." Jorie looked toward the door. "Oh, fucking hell."

"You dare?" Cateman staggered into the room as weakness reclaimed him. "In my house?" He gripped the arm of the couch and fell to his knees, his bandaged hands sliding across the smooth up-holstery.

"It's my house, too, Leaf." Jorie turned back to the others, and closed her eyes. "My house, my land, my money, my name." The golden haze grew more luminous. "My Gideon."

Cateman dragged in one long breath, then another, his rattled wheezing filling his ears. It felt stronger in here, this new power. But it felt wrong, as well, a rogue horse under the rein of an inexperienced rider. "What have you done?"

"What you never would. I freed Blaine. Pulled out the plug. Let the dark light in." Jorie smiled. "Now Virginia is trying to put the plug back, and I am going to stop her."

"Now's not the time. You must wait—"

"Wait for what? Reardon doesn't know anything. He never taught her. Dear Matthew. Your precious Emma's jailbait boyfriend." Jorie glanced at him, and tsked. "Oh, the look on your face. What's left of it. As if you didn't plan that all along. As if you didn't dangle her in front of him like a prize. It's your way, dear. I know I'm not the first snack package you threw at any man you thought could help you."

Cateman fell silent. His mind had clouded anew, and he struggled to track his thoughts. He looked to the faces of the other men he had raised from boyhood, felt the heart sear of yet another betrayal. "Thad? Emlyn? Jeremiah?"

"A man gets tired of waiting, Leaf." Thad Trace kept his eyes closed, declined to grace his Master with even the barest of acknowledgments. "My father waited for your father, and then he waited for you until the day he died. 'It's our forty years in the desert,' he told me on his deathbed. But it's been a hell of a lot longer than forty years, hasn't it?" He shook his head. "We've waited long enough. It's time."

"You can't." Cateman pushed to his feet, arm muscles cramping from the strain. "Blaine is still bound to Gideon. As the demon is bound here, so will all his be bound here. Entrapped here with him—you can't—" He crumpled again to his knees as pain gripped him.

Heard Jorie swear and call for aid, looked into her face, and saw the brittle beauty of a china doll, painted and hard. So unlike the other one. Yet in the end they both betrayed him.

Emma. Her name in his mind, for the first time since the last time. Her face, her form. His gift to the one he thought would free Blaine, free Gideon, release them all from the bondage of that first dreadful curse. Until the betrayal that broke his heart.

You weren't supposed to fall in love with him. He saw her now, standing in the middle of the room, hair an ebony tumble, clad in the dress she wore that last horrible night. Vermilion, brilliant as flame. *Emma. You were supposed to bring him to me.*

Then Cateman felt arms surround him, iron holds around his arms, his legs. He tried to fight, even as his strength failed and the blackness closed in. "All is betrayal."

"That's life, darling." Jorie's voice, bright and cheap as tinfoil. The last thing he saw.

Then the darkness claimed him.

LAUREN DARTED AROUND Corey and ran back toward the barn. The golden glow had intensified so that she had to squint to look at it, saw Waycross and the others seated within, hands joined, heads bowed.

Eventually, Waycross's voice emerged, tinny as a radio announcer's, filtered and warped by the power that enveloped them all. "Thin as water, be now ice. Pale as daylight, be now night." The glow swirled and shimmered, reflected rainbows, like some opalescent concoction. "Until the final time to come, when this world and the next are one. Disjoin, divide, disjoin, divide—"

"Disjoin, divide." The others took up the chant, repeated the words over and over, some rocking to and fro, others nodding their heads in time. For a time, their voices grew louder and louder.

Then the gold haze deepened to something that looked solid to the touch, and the voices faded to whispers on the edge of hearing. One minute passed. Another.

Then the haze lightened, and the voices sounded like a chant of re-bellion, loud enough to drive nesting birds from the barn rafters and drive the horses to gallop in circles in their corral. Waycross shushed them, and the volume lowered until they fell silent and the gold had faded to nothing.

Then they let go of one another's hands. Zeke lumbered to his feet and cracked his back, then dug into the pocket of his barn coat. Removed a pouch of tobacco, hooked a chaw with his finger, and crammed it in his mouth. Phil pulled his knees to his chest and rocked back and forth, then stretched his legs in front of him. Way-cross buried her face in her hands. One of the women sobbed while her neighbor held her.

Lauren looked overhead. The cloud cover had lifted, the sky light-ened to run-of-the-mill darkness. Was she disappointed—no, she wasn't that selfish and stupid. But she truly had not expected the spell to work. She still felt the restlessness, the tingle in her hands. "That's it?"

"You've no idea." For the first time, Corey eyed her with annoy-ance bordering on disgust. "The—strength they needed to put into that spell. If any of them are sick, weak?" He folded his arms, hands clenched into fists. "They all sacrificed life, some of them a year or more. They sacrifice every time they work a protection spell. Mis-tress Waycross is only in her fifties, and she looks what, seventy?"

Lauren thought back to a few short weeks before, and the emaci-ated figure in the hospice bed. "Like my dad."

"Yeah." Corey pulled the roll of antacid tablets from his jacket pocket, tossed a few more into his mouth. "Twenty years or more he gave up, to keep you out of it. For all the good it did him, or you." He turned and headed back toward the house.

Lauren met Waycross's eye. The woman gave her nothing but a level stare, the old dog showing the young pup how it was done.

Zeke waved everyone quiet. "I say it's time to give a cheer for our good mistress." As Waycross shook her head and everyone else applauded, he motioned like an orchestra conductor. "And a one—and a two—"

A rumble like summer thunder sounded, rattled the barn and everyone inside. Silence descended, an uncertain quiet that said that this was not something they expected.

"Snowstorm headed this way? Thunder snow?" Penny kneaded her hands, flexed her fingers. "I feel something in the air—"

The wind blew in out of nowhere, a chill gale sharp as a slap to the face. It funneled through the open barn door, the windows, blew caps off heads, and kicked dust and hay into the air.

Lauren looked up.

The sky boiled, black cloud tumbling counterclockwise as the wind picked up speed and pushed it along, faster and faster, a hurricane in miniature that blew with a manic howl, first high-pitched, then low, an orchestra gone mad. A few birds erupted in squawking scatter, vanishing into the trees. Then there was no sound but the panicked whinnying of Waycross's horses, and the wind.

"Get inside the house! Now!" Waycross herded the others out of the barn. "Go right down to the cellar and stay there."

The protests rang out. "My Bill is home—my Kate—the kids—" A few people obeyed Waycross and headed toward the house, but most ran to their vehicles, scrabbling in pockets and purses for keys.

Then, over the course of a hammering heartbeat, the wind quieted. The sky stilled.

People stopped in their tracks and looked up.

A whine like jet engines, first distant, then growing louder and louder, closer and closer. And with it came snow, from zero to blizzard in a blink, and cold like the blast from a deep freeze. People ran, slid on the snow, on wet ground changed to ice in moments, stumbled, fell. Most made it to their vehicles, started them, and peeled out of the driveway, in reverse or forward, tires spinning, snow and gravel flying.

Then came a crash as two pickups collided, the loser sliding across the driveway onto the grass. The driver tumbled out and scrambled onto the winner's flatbed, and they vanished into the storm.

Lauren helped one of the fallen, an older woman, mount the steps into the house. Started back down to look for more stragglers, and met Phil halfway.

"Don't need you freezing on top of everything." He pushed and prodded her into an ancient barn coat. "Damn stupid getup for all hell breaking loose."

"I was out to dinner."

"That's nice. You look great." Phil tugged a wool cap down over Lauren's ears. "Dressed to die—just please don't."

"I love the smell of panic in the middle of the Ladysdamn night." Zeke hobbled to the corral, where Waycross tried to hook a lead to one of the horses' bridles as it tossed its head and pulled away. "Just open the gate and let 'em go, Mistress."

"Don't ask me to do that, Zeke." Waycross pointed toward the house. "Just get your butt inside."

"You're more to us than those critters and I ain't having you risk your life for them." Zeke loosed Waycross's hands from their grip on the bridle. Then he shooed the horses toward the open gate. "Go on—get on with ya!"

"*Zeke—no.*" Waycross ran to close the gate, but Zeke grabbed her around the waist and held her back.

"They're Gideon horses, Virginia. They either know their way around or they never will." He waved to Lauren. "Get her inside."

Lauren grabbed Waycross's hand and pulled her toward the house. The woman's fingers had gone white and frigid, her nose and cheeks bright red. Lauren's own hands ached, and she could no longer feel her face, her toes.

They stumbled up the steps, the leather soles of their boots like skate blades on the ice. Penny met them at the door with a blanket, wrapped them together, and pulled them inside.

"I don't understand—I don't—" Waycross shook out of the blanket and returned to the doorway. *"Ezekiel Pyne, get your ass in here now."* She stepped aside as the old man stumbled in, coated in snow.

"That's my Ginny." A wave of shivering overtook him, and he let Corey and Phil bundle him into a blanket while Penny checked him for frostbite.

"I need to get the furnace going." Waycross opened one of the kitchen drawers and pulled out a box of matches. "Been saving it for a cold snap. Don't think it could get much snappier." She stood by the back window, looked out every so often.

Lauren walked to the back door, saw only blowing snow, swirling cloud. No horses. No signs of life of any kind. "It looks like it might be letting up a little."

"We can't stay here, Mistress." Zeke took a steaming cup of tea from Penny, and hugged it close. "You're out in the middle of nowhere, and if anything happened, no one could get out here to help."

Waycross still stood by the window. "I'm not leaving my home."

"Don't make me carry you. And I will do it. I've known you longer than anybody here and I've got the right." Zeke stood, dragged off the blanket, and handed it to Penny. "This is the lull. Do you really want to wait for the storm?"

Waycross looked around her kitchen as if to memorize it. As if to say good-bye. "Into Gideon?"

"My house, yes, Mistress. Right on the circle there where you don't like to go. Across the street from Leaf's." Zeke shook out one leg, then the other. Bent his knees. "We need a better truck than mine. I don't think ol' Lois would make it through that mess that's piling up out there now."

"Nothing we've got will make it through there if we don't get going," a younger man with a heavy beard piped up. "The way it's coming down, we've got a half hour tops or we ain't getting out of here."

"Think you can fit all of us in that tank of yours, Rocky?" Waycross returned to the back door and looked out through the window at the storm.

The young man nodded. "If you all pack light."

"I think we should go to the Master's." Penny shrugged off Waycross's look of surprise. "Not to insult you, Mistress, but two heads might be better than one in this instance, no matter how much they've butted in the past."

"It's ground zero. The Cateman house." Lauren hesitated as all turned to her. She told them about the body she encountered, the threats from Trace and Howell. Her encounter with Leaf Cateman, and his illness. "He talked about making Gideon a 'shining city.' He quoted something from his version of the Book of Endor, about the Lady giving the King the power to control demons."

Penny stared into her cup. "Easy to tell us what he said when he's not here to say yea or nay."

Lauren shook her head. She couldn't summon the energy for anger, not anymore. All she felt was numbness, with no clue as to how to proceed. "I honestly don't give a damn whether you believe me or not."

Penny rolled her eyes while the rest of them stared at their hands, the floor. Then Corey spoke up.

"They did threaten her. Thad Trace. Emlyn Howell." He boosted himself onto the kitchen counter. His tie had vanished at some point, his trousers ripped at the knees. "If she didn't break the curse, they were going to frame her for the murders of Lolly and the others. But Jorie seemed impatient, like she didn't want to wait."

"What could Jorie have done?" Waycross paused as the wind gusted and rattled the windows. "She's no weakling, but she isn't strong enough to do this."

Lauren met the older woman's eyes again. This time, Waycross looked away. "Blaine is bound to Gideon because of the curse. Everyone thought he was quiet, some poor captive soul awaiting release. He wasn't. He's always been here, and he wants out."

"He helped Jorie." Waycross pressed a hand to her mouth, closed her eyes. "He shared his power with her."

"We need to move." Zeke dragged on gloves, buckled his flap-eared cap.

CONNIE PETERSBURY WEDGED herself between two rocks and held on as the wind roared. She didn't feel the bite of the ice and snow—she was past that. But she sensed what drove the storm, what it would soon sweep into Gideon.

Let go. Part of her wanted to do just that, let herself be carried back into the living world with the rest of the half dead, the all-dead. Even though she no longer belonged. Even though she would wind up hurting those she loved, doing to them accidentally what Ashley and Norma and the others wanted to do on purpose.

Ease the pain. She could see it in their faces, even Ashley's, the slow, steady torture of the fate they had chosen. Like the scrape of fingernails across a blackboard, except that the blackboard was your soul and the fingernails were claws that tore right into it and shredded it like tissue paper. And then they learned that sharing that pain with the living eased their own, if only for a short time. He made sure the relief didn't last long. He made sure that they would always need to keep hurting.

Blaine. How could something that had once been human have fallen so far?

No. She would stay behind. However lonely the river, it was her home.

LEAF CATEMAN LAY in bed and listened to the wind batter the windows, the clatter of old glass panes shaking in their frames. From downstairs had come sounds of argument, a scream cut off by either a faint or a slap.

If he concentrated, he could hear noises in the distance, car horns and shouts, the wind howling above it all.

Time passed. A footfall, in the hallway. Then came another sound, quieter, closer. The door, opening.

"Aman-da?" Cateman coughed, tasted blood.

"Yes, Master. It's me."

"What is happen—?"

"Just the wind, Master." A sniffling sound. "You rest." The door closed and the pad of Amanda's footsteps faded. And then there was only the wind.

And the Master of Gideon listened. And the Master of Gideon wept.

35

Lauren followed Waycross upstairs while the others packed whatever cold-weather clothing they could find. First-aid items. Batteries, matches, lighters.

"Should we bother with these?" Waycross rooted through a drawer in the bathroom vanity, and pulled out an old box of tampons. "They're years old. Do they go bad?"

"I don't think so." Lauren took the box and stuffed it into a knapsack. "I think they make good bandage material."

"I can see us trying to use one of those on Zeke. He'd howl that next we'd be putting a dress on him." Waycross smiled for the first time since the rite in the barn. But it faded, and she picked through a holder full of toothbrushes as though she had never seen them before.

"I'm sorry about your horses." Lauren opened the medicine chest, poked through the expired prescriptions and half-empty tubes and bottles.

Waycross stared at nothing for a few moments. Then she nodded. "Zeke was right, though. They should be able to find someplace safe." She took a flower-shaped bar of soap from the dish by the sink, sniffed it, then put it back. "I don't know if you noticed, but there aren't many animals in Gideon."

"I know that the crows left."

"They left because they're the Lady's birds, and we displeased her when we burned Nicholas Blaine." Waycross arched a brow, as though the thought had occurred that the Lady had gotten that one wrong. "But pets brought in from outside run off. Cats. Dogs. Birds pull their feathers out and need to be let go. Even snakes tie themselves in knots. It's the nearness to the thin places. Gideon nerves. Poor things are sensitive anyway, and living here is just torture for them."

Lauren rubbed her ears—their incessant ringing had already become a feature, not a bug. The tingling in her hands. "I don't know much about horses, but I always thought they were pretty skittish."

"They are, but my boys were born and raised here." Waycross shrugged. "They just . . . adapted." She plucked a tissue from the box on the toilet tank, and wiped her eyes.

Lauren squeezed Waycross's shoulder, as much of a hug as she felt the woman would ever accept. "They'll come back."

"I know they will," Waycross said under her breath, her voice uncertain, as though she knew no such thing.

BY THE TIME they had gone through the house and gathered essentials, the snow and wind had let up enough to allow Rocky to pull his SUV close to the backdoor steps. The rest of them formed a relay line in the kitchen, handing bags and boxes down to Corey and Phil, who packed with silent dispatch.

Lauren recovered her father's books from Waycross's office. Then she switched out her battered skirt and blouse for jeans and a sweater. Donned her comfortable old hiking shoes.

Then they crowded into the vehicle, Waycross in the front with Rocky. Zeke, Penny, and Phil in the second-row seat. The rest of them pressed close in the third row, while Lauren opted to straddle the gear in the luggage compartment.

"By the Lady," Rocky intoned as he pulled out of the driveway.

"In her name," replied the rest of them.

"I see people." Penny pressed her face to the window. "In the woods. So many of them."

"Don't look at them." Zeke tried to pull the woman away. "They'll take your mind if you stare too long."

"Who are they?"

"They're his, Penny." Waycross signed herself. "Whatever they look like, they're his."

The ranch was only a couple of miles outside Gideon. But there were no lights except the SUV headlights, and the snow had blown and drifted. Rocky managed no more than five miles per hour, and stayed in the middle of the road to avoid sliding off on either side.

They came upon the first ditched vehicle within minutes. A newer Ford pickup, the headlights still blazing.

"That's Rusty's." Penny crawled over Phil and Zeke to the other side of the cabin and crouched next to the door. "We have to stop."

"I'm not stopping, Penny." Rocky gripped the wheel hard with both hands. "I do, I may never get it going again."

"I can see him—he's still in there."

"I'm not stopping."

"How can you say that?" Penny flipped the door lock—the door flew open and she tumbled out onto the road. Phil and Corey grabbed Zeke to keep him from falling after her, and together they managed to pull the door closed.

"Can you slow down, Rocky?" Waycross's voice cracked.

"Don't want to, Mistress."

"Can you back up?"

"Don't want to do that either." But he did, slowly, until he drew even with the ditched truck.

Lauren watched out the back window. Saw Penny open the driver's-side door, then lean close to Rusty. Saw his head nod, then rock back and forth. Saw him reach out and touch her.

Then she felt it. The same strange sensations as in the woods, the place where they had found Jerome Hoard's car. The currents of air, warm and cold, flowing and stagnant.

She watched Penny slowly back away from the truck, Rusty slide out after her. "I think we should go."

Zeke craned his neck to see past her. "They're headed this way. We gotta make room for 'em."

Lauren grabbed the inside handle of the rear door and held on. "Lock the doors."

"But they're coming—"

"Lock the goddamn doors." Lauren held on to the handle as Penny pressed close to the door and tried to open it. She smiled at Lauren as she pulled on the latch, eyes too bright and face grayed and snow caking her hair.

"I'm gonna get you, Mullin." A weird voice, harmonics that razored the nerves.

"Lock the doors, Rock." Corey held on to the handle as Rusty banged on the window.

"I did." Rocky switched gears, started the SUV rolling forward. *"Wait—oh shit—I hit the damn thing again—"*

Corey held on to the door as Rusty tried to pull it open. Then Penny joined him, shoving her hand through the gap, fingers raking the front of Corey's shirt.

Rocky hit the gas, jerked the steering wheel—the SUV skidded, knocking Rusty and Penny free. Corey and Phil pulled the door closed, and Rocky hit the panic button that locked everything.

"We're not stopping for anyone. I don't care who it is." He tapped the gas, sped up as much as he dared. "Fuckin' zombie apocalypse."

"At least you can kill zombies." Lauren watched as a few more undead—*nearly dead? demon dead?*—emerged from the woods and joined Penny and Rusty on the road.

"What happened to them?" Phil watched, wide-eyed.

"Blaine." Waycross faced front, her hand resting on Rocky's shoulder.

They came upon more vehicles, some abandoned, others not. As they passed the occupied vehicles, those inside emerged, and joined the others who walked the road into Gideon.

"They're following us." Zeke drummed his fingers on the back of Waycross's headrest. "It's like they're following us."

"Zeke, please don't do whatever you're doing to my seat."

"But they're following us." Zeke clapped his hands, then shoved them under his thighs.

The minutes ticked by as they continued their crawl, the wind battering them and snow caking the mirrors, coating the windows.

"This isn't normal snow." Rocky ran the wipers, activated the windshield defroster, swore. "It doesn't want to melt, and it smears like a son of a bitch."

"I haven't seen one other car on the road actually moving." Corey had reached back and taken hold of Lauren's hand, squeezed it every so often.

"Maybe they're all home." Phil nodded. "They're all home safe, waiting out the storm."

"Okay, this is going to be interesting." Rocky slowed as they came to the spot where the road sloped down past Gideon's business district and through the town square. "Because I'm not sure what's going to happen once we start down the hill."

Lauren looked out the back window, saw their followers through the blowing snow. "They're getting close."

"We can't get out and go on foot." Corey looked across the square toward the houses, a few scattered lights shining through the storm. "We'd never make it."

"Give it your best shot, Rocky." Waycross squeezed his shoulder, then braced her hands on the dash.

Rocky looked back at Lauren. "You might want to buckle up back there in case we flip."

"She can take Penny's spot." Phil held out his hand to Lauren, and he and Corey helped her slide between them, then buckled her in.

"Are we ready?" Rocky tapped the gas, and they started forward. "Here goes nothing."

All went well until about halfway down the hill, when they hit a bump or a pothole hidden by the snow. The SUV swerved one way, then the other. Then it spun—once, twice, thrice. As it spun a fourth time, it slammed into a parked car and slid to a stop on the edge of the square.

The engine shuddered, then died. Rocky tried to turn it over, pressed his hands to the ignition, muttered under his breath. "A little help would be nice."

They joined hands. Waycross started to speak, hesitated, sighed. "My Lady, please just start the damn thing."

Lauren looked back, and saw the followers gathered at the top of the slope. One heartbeat. Another.

On the third, the followers started down.

"They're coming." Lauren unbuckled her seat belt. "We need to run for it. Now."

Waycross unbuckled, edged forward in her seat. "Can you make it, Zeke?"

"I'll outrun the whole damn lotta you." Zeke unsnapped his belt, pumped his arms.

Lauren checked once again. "They're halfway down the slope." She squinted. "Some of them have rocks. Hammers."

"Let's go." Rocky hit the panic button and unlocked the doors.

The cold took Lauren's breath away, needled through her coat, her gloves and boots. But the square was an open stretch exposed to the wind, which meant the snow had blown away, leaving wide stretches with little or no coverage. They bunched together, walked as quickly as they could.

Looked back, and found their followers gaining.

"Let's pick up the pace, shall we?" Phil broke into a trot, moved to the front of the pack.

As they approached the Great Fire Memorial, Lauren heard scratching sounding from beneath. A muffled voice.

"Don't stop." Zeke quickened his pace until he drew even with Phil. The men spread out, taking the front, the flanks. Corey tried to move to the rear, and motioned for Lauren to move to the middle of the pack.

But Lauren and Waycross looked at each other, and fell back.

"You boys keep the way clear up there." Waycross stooped, gathered a handful of snow, tossed it into the air. "We'll handle the rear."

"What are you doing?" Lauren gathered her own handful of snow. It felt gritty, sandy, even through her gloves.

"No idea." Waycross looked back at the followers, Blaine's demon horde. "Oh, my Lady, I see—" She swallowed hard. "I see Ruthie and Betty Joan and—"

"Help! Help!"

As they passed the gazebo, a figure wriggled out from beneath and hurtled after them. *"Please."* Brittany, filthy, wearing a coat pulled over a nightgown, snow boots on her feet. *"Please wait!"*

"I think she's all right." Lauren lagged back, waved Corey ahead when he tried to join her. In the distance, the followers dogged them, a wall of quiet menace.

"Thinking's not enough at the moment." Rocky picked up a long stick, swung it like an ax.

"She's all right." Lauren slowed, held out her hand, staggered as Brittany barreled into her.

"M-mommy," the girl stammered, wide-eyed and pale. "We hid in the diner, and they came in, and they got Mommy and Joesy and Johnny—"

"She's okay." Lauren held the girl close. "Blaine's followers don't cry." She caught Waycross wiping her eyes, read her thoughts as if they were her own. That Waycross had bound the girl, taken away whatever power she had, left her defenseless.

And then the monsters came.

"We can't get down to Zeke's place this way." Rocky pointed to the entry to the cul-de-sac. "Must be a ten-foot drift blocking the road."

"We can go around, back behind Leaf's place." Zeke pointed to the next street over—

—the unnamed street—the scattered remains of a house—

"I don't think they'll hurt me, no matter what they say." Lauren pushed Brittany into Waycross's arms, then fell back. "But they'll hurt you to get to me."

Waycross put her arms around Brittany, who still whimpered like an injured animal. "So what does that mean?"

"It means go where I tell you to go, and stay there until I say move." Lauren looked back at the horde, Blaine's foot soldiers, his cannon fodder, pitied them even as she feared what they would do to avoid their Master's wrath. "They're spreading out. They're going to try to surround us and cut us off."

"Why now?" Waycross picked up the pace, taking Brittany's hand and dragging her like a balky toddler.

"Because they know where we're going." Lauren broke into a run, slowed by knee-deep drifts. "There's a vacant lot on the right, with a chimney—"

"I know which one." Corey picked up the pace. *"Come on."*

They ran, as behind them, Blaine's horde howled and yipped like coyotes on the hunt. Lauren heard laughter amid the din. Threats.

"Gonna get you, all of you—get you—get you—"

They turned onto the street. Zeke fell behind, and Phil and Rocky grabbed him under the arms and pulled him along.

Lauren ran, the buzzing in her head ramping up to a clatter that drowned out her every thought. She felt the pounding of running feet coming up from behind, knew then that the half dead of Gideon could move more easily in the snow than the living, that they had been toying with them up to now. *Fuck you.* She dug deep, forced searing thigh muscles to pump faster, crossed the line onto the old Mullin property just as claws raked the back of her coat.

They ran to the fallen chimney. Zeke sagged to the edge of the old hearth, stared at nothing, mouth agape and sweat dripping despite the cold. Rocky, Corey, Phil, all stood doubled over, inhaling in great gulps. Waycross slumped against the cold brick, while Brittany stared at Lauren wide-eyed.

Lauren turned to look out at the street at the followers who surrounded them on three sides, and drew up straight. "Wands out, Harry."

"What?" Waycross and the others looked around, shook their heads. All but Brittany, who crouched down and picked up a short stick, then brandished it in front of her.

"Why don't they come closer?" Zeke stood slowly. "They're stopping at the edge of the lot—what's holding them back?"

Lauren touched her forehead, the wound that was no longer there. "It's the blood."

"What you buried, you mean?" Waycross nodded. "So now what?"

"Yeah, really." Rocky huddled. "Because we sure as hell can't stand around here much longer."

"Does anyone have a knife?" Lauren waited, then looked at each of the men in turn. "Are you telling me that not one of you is carrying a knife?"

"I've got one." Brittany dug into the pocket of her coat. "Will this work?" She handed Lauren a folded jackknife, the metal case brushed silver engraved with roses.

"Pretty." Lauren pried open the knife. "Hands bleed a lot, right?" Before anyone answered, she drew the blade across her palm, then raised her hand. "Do you see this?" She felt the warm blood well, flow inside her sleeve. Then she pressed the wound to Brittany's forehead. Waycross's. The others. "They're mine, as this place is mine. You can't touch them, or harm them in any way, or your Master will destroy you." She felt a tap on her shoulder, and turned.

"Just making sure you know." Zeke pointed to the woods. "The house is just through here and across the street."

"We have to go through the woods?" Lauren wiped the knife blade on the leg of her jeans, then folded it and handed it back to Brittany.

Zeke shrugged, one eye on the followers. "It's only a short stretch."

"Not anymore." Lauren reached out to Zeke. "Join hands. I'll lead the way. Don't let go, no matter what you see or hear or sense, because we can't come back for you." She waited until they all lined up. "Let's go."

"I don't want to be at the end." Brittany looked back at the followers, made a sign of the Lady over her heart.

"Curl in next to me and Dylan, girl." Waycross smiled. "Like a question mark." Once the girl had nestled in, Waycross looked past the others to Lauren, and nodded.

Lauren took one step toward the woods. Another. She could see the shadows moving along the border where the trees met the lot, and as she drew closer, they grew still and took form.

"They're not moving out of the way." Zeke's voice shook.

"They have to let us pass. It doesn't mean they have to make it pleasant." Lauren squeezed the man's hand, felt him flinch.

"It's the arthritis, you know." He squeezed back, more lightly. "Hang on, just not so hard." He paused. "Please don't let go."

They entered the woods. Lauren felt things brush her face, her hands, snake around her legs. Heard Zeke's voice in her ear. "I changed my mind. You can squeeze as hard as you think you have to."

But for this one time, and likely for the last time, the woods of Gideon played fair. The group emerged after a few short strides, intact, together.

"Let's get inside before they figure out where the hell we are." Zeke led them across the street to an immense brick Georgian with barred windows, his house key at the ready. Unlocked the door and led them inside. Smelled the air, stamped a clockwise path three times in the entry, and pronounced the place clean.

Lauren sagged against the wall and slid down to the floor as black spots waxed and waned before her eyes.

36

We need bandages—we need—" Waycross took hold of Lauren's bleeding hand. "Up above your head—hold it up—" She touched Lauren's cheek. "That's it. I don't think you've lost all that much blood. Just the sight of it and the stress of the moment, I expect." She pried open Lauren's palm, and winced. "That should be sewn up."

"Just—wrap it and tie it tight." Lauren held her hand to her chest, refused to let Waycross touch it until the woman held up her hands in surrender. "I don't think I could handle stitches right now."

Brittany hustled back with an armful of first-aid supplies. Waycross applied a heavy layer of antibiotic ointment to the gash, then wrapped the palm in gauze and tied it snugly. "So why didn't our binding spell work?"

"It did. But Blaine was already here, nailed in place by the Mullin curse." Lauren flexed her injured hand, felt the sting of slashed skin beneath the heavy bandage. "The spell dragged all his creatures here after him."

"So I made matters worse." Waycross rocked back on her heels and sat cross-legged on the floor. "I read the Book of Endor that you brought back. I followed the spell to bind an outsider to the letter. It should have at least slowed him down."

Lauren shrugged. "Blaine's not really an outsider, though, is he? I mean, I've seen him. Connie. Lolly and Jerome Hoard probably encountered him as well. He's known to us."

"We could unbind him."

"He'd still be on this side of the divide, with all his followers."

They both fell quiet, captive to their own thoughts until the sound of approaching footsteps brought them back to the present.

"Mistress. Miz Reardon." Zeke bobbed his head, thumbs hooked through cherry-red suspenders. "Brittany's started calling folks, telling them to stay put, check their wards. She's keeping track of places that don't answer." He straightened the hallway runner with the toe of his boot. "When she called Bill and Lottie's place, the call cut out in the middle. Could be that those things out there are smart enough to cut phone lines."

"Power lines will be next." Waycross closed her eyes. "Propane tanks."

"Yup. They'll either freeze us to death, burn us out, or blow us up." Zeke stood in head-cocked silence for a moment, then turned and headed toward the back of the house. "Gonna disconnect the gas, fill up the spare rooms with as much firewood as we can haul in before those things figure out how to climb the back fence."

"Strengthen your wards, Zeke," Waycross called after him.

"Done that, Mistress. Gonna do it again right now."

Lauren gauged her weakness as she sat up straight. *So far, so good.* "We have to act fast."

"And do what, exactly?" Waycross brushed snowmelt from her coat sleeve. "This doesn't even feel like water. It's oily—" She held her fingers to her nose and grimaced. "—and it stinks."

"I'd like to know what's going on at the Cateman place." Lauren's breath puffed as she spoke, and she hugged herself as the house chill crept through her coat. "Jorie let us go too easily. I expect she tried something after we left that probably didn't help matters."

She dug through her bag for her books. "It wouldn't surprise me if she did something to the ointment Leaf was being treated with. It made me sick when Doc Hoard used it."

"Without Leaf holding Jorie back, Lady only knows what she'll get up to." Waycross stood, then jerked her chin toward the books Lauren held. "What are you going to do?"

Lauren braced against the wall and pushed herself to her feet. "Try to find something to weaken Blaine." She paced the hall, looking in doorways until she found a sitting room with a desk. "I'll need your help."

"Let me see how the others are getting on. Then I'll be along." Waycross turned and headed down the hall, head bowed, step heavy.

Lauren watched her from the doorway. "Leaf pointed Emma at my dad. It was a team effort—she was bait to lure him in."

Waycross stopped. "Then the Judas goat did her job." She looked back over her shoulder at Lauren. "So what happened to her?"

"I don't know." Lauren waited until Waycross left, then walked into the sitting room. Lace curtains trimmed the windows—she could see the snow drift and swirl, heard it beat against the glass with the *tick-tick* of tiny claws.

She crept to the window and looked outside, saw the followers milling in the street, pacing the sidewalks. Wards kept them out of the houses for now. *But Blaine will figure something out.* Then the power would go out. Homes would fill with gas.

"I dreamed all this." Lauren spoke to the glass, watched her breath fog and fade. "Hands reaching for me from out of the dark. Snow. We've seen those. But we haven't seen the fire yet." She traced the Lady's sign in the air. "Fire's next." She pulled the curtains closed, then took off her coat and covered the window so that no one on the outside could see in. Sat at the desk, turned on the small lamp, and set to work.

WAYCROSS DROPPED BY at intervals, in between warding the property and helping prep the house for a siege. Lauren took breaks from reading to inventory canned goods, the contents of the Pyne deep freezer.

But Zeke spent most of his time on the family farm outside Gideon, so supplies at this main house proved sparser than they hoped.

Lauren sat back, closed her eyes. Drifted, sought a few moments of peace for her troubled mind.

Then she heard the creak of footsteps, and looked up to find Corey standing over her. He had avoided her to that point, leaving rooms as soon as she entered, not meeting her eye when they met in the hall. Now he regarded her with something akin to pity. Then he walked to the window, peeled away her coat, and looked outside.

"They're all running around like we stand a chance." He drummed his fingers against the glass. "We're all hands on deck, but we're taking on water and there's an iceberg dead ahead."

"So what are we supposed to do?"

"I don't know." Corey shook his head. "I don't know anything anymore."

Lauren watched him, tried to uncover the tender ally from the previous night, and gave up. "What's the matter with you?"

"Where've you been for the last few hours?" He turned, leaned against the wall. He looked as wrung out as they all did, dark smudges beneath his eyes, a day's growth of beard. "We're dead—you know that, right?"

Lauren opened her mouth to speak, then closed it.

"So you know I'm right." Corey looked down at his hands, then at Lauren. Then he walked to the desk and knelt at her feet. "If we went there—"

"Where?"

"To Jorie's." Corey leaned close. "They would welcome you with open arms."

Lauren stared into soft, sad eyes. Relived the previous evening in a heartbeat. Every word. Every touch. "He knew what you drank. Thad Trace. He brought you scotch, and he never even asked."

"I'd been there before—I told you."

"You were supposed to know the rules for dinner because you'd eaten there before."

"Diplomatic missions for the Mistress. I told you that." Corey took hold of her injured hand. "Hey, remember me? I saved your life when they tried to stone you."

Lauren pulled away as the same tingling jolts that she always felt when they touched radiated along her arm, raked her injured hand as though she'd slashed it anew. "Tom Barton saved my life." She thought of him now. Had he found shelter from Blaine's storm, or had it already claimed him?

Corey stared, eyes pleading, hands hovering close to her but not touching, as though he knew what would happen if he did.

Lauren held her injured hand close as the last few days replayed. Like the picture of the goblet that turned into two profiles, it was amazing how much sense the most innocent details made when you looked at them differently. "When you introduced yourself in the diner, you took my hand, and I heard a voice in my head.'*Your hand is so cold. Well, you know what they say.*' I thought it was you. I thought that I had read your mind and it was you, but when I mentioned it later, you had no idea what I was talking about."

"I don't—"

"It was him. You carried him with you. He saw everything you did, felt everything you felt." Lauren shuddered, thinking of the shadowy figure with the unseeable face sharing every kiss, every caress.

Corey boosted to his feet. "Not everything. And I didn't volunteer for that. Blaine—" He paced, then sat on the edge of a low table. "He considered that part of our deal. A way to feel until he could experience things himself."

"Did you help him reach me in Seattle, too? Did you help him kill Dilys?"

"Who the hell is Dilys?"

"What did he promise you? Sentence commuted to time served? An honorable discharge from Gideon's army?" Lauren wanted to feel hatred, but couldn't. Anger, yes. And pity, for anyone who could listen to that oily voice and find truth in it. "You think that just because he says you can go that you're free? Bill paid in full? Blaine will do to the rest of the world what he's done to Gideon, and when he finds you again, he'll mow you down with all the others."

"What the hell do you know?" Corey's face reddened. He put his hands in his pockets, pulled them out. "You should come with me." For a bare moment, he looked as he did during those few times when they had been alone. Kind. Gentle. "We liked each other, when we had the chance. We would have that chance again." When Lauren didn't answer, he snorted a laugh. "He's going to get you sooner or later. Why not make it easier on yourself."

"Get out." Lauren stood. "Tell him that you tried but I turned you down. I'm sure he'll be very understanding."

Corey flinched. Then he pointed toward the back of the house, where the others still labored. "He could give you everything. Everything you ever wanted, in exchange for the lives of a bunch of relics who are too stupid to get out of their own way." He lowered his voice. "He wants you. He'll have you. Give yourself a break. Go to him."

"What part of 'get out' do you not understand?" Lauren heard a soft throat-clearing, turned to find Waycross standing in the doorway.

"Well, well." Waycross ran a hand over the woodwork, never once looking at Corey. "You had better go, Dylan."

"Fine. Yeah." Corey stared at the floor. His former boss's presence seemed to shake him more than Lauren's anger. "I need my stuff. It's upstairs."

"Stay right there, where we can see you." Waycross called down the hallway. "Phil? Go upstairs and get Dylan's things."

"Yes, Mistress." Phil looked into the room and stared down Corey before going upstairs. If looks could have killed, Dylan Corey would have been struck down in an instant.

Then Brittany stepped out of the hallway shadows. "Dylan?" She clutched a dish towel like a rag doll. "You helped them do this to us? You helped that bitch Jorie do this to us?" She pointed toward the kitchen. "Zeke and Rocky helped dig out Mistress's truck when you went off the road last winter and hit that sign, and Lolly fixed it and no one said anything when the sheriff came around asking, and all that time you were working with her?" She twisted the towel harder and harder, then worked it into a knot and held it out in front of her.

Waycross remained fixed on the doorway woodwork. "Brittany Watt, you mind yourself."

"Ain't I allowed to be mad, Mistress?"

"I didn't give you back your powers so you could waste them on the likes of him, girl." Waycross gave the jamb a final pat. "We need your strength here." She stood back as Phil descended the stairs and tossed Corey's backpack on the hall floor. "Go on, Dylan."

Corey looked over at Lauren and started to speak, then stopped. Shook his head and walked out of the sitting room, retrieved his backpack and headed for the door.

Lauren followed. She sheltered in the doorway next to Waycross, leaned against the jamb for support.

"May you find something waiting for you, Dylan Corey." Waycross's voice, soft as a prayer. "Something cold that knows your name."

Corey stilled, his hand on the door handle. Then he jerked the door open, stepped outside, pulled it closed after him.

Lauren walked to the window next to the door, twitched the curtain aside. Saw Corey, poised on the step, looking out at the followers that milled in the street and crowded the front gate. "Think he'll make it?"

"Think I care?" Waycross rubbed her eyes, pinched the bridge of her nose. Looked up at the ceiling for respite that would never come.

Phil stood, rocking from one foot to the other, hands bunched into fists. "What could he have done? Could he have weakened anything? Destroyed anything?"

Waycross shook her head. "We will redo all the wards here. And check the propane tanks. Look it all over, in case Mr. Corey took it into his damn-fool head to add sabotage to his list of accomplishments." She hesitated, then walked over to Lauren, touched her hand. "He fooled me, too."

Lauren nodded. Let the curtain fall back into place. Stood by the window until she heard Corey's footsteps recede. Until she heard nothing.

DYLAN COREY STOOD on the sidewalk and watched the demons, ghosts—whatever the hell they were—mill about. Mindless, from the look of them. Like a clip from every bad zombie movie he had ever seen.

Then one of them spotted him, and a beat later, the rest stopped and turned as one toward him. Still, alert, like predators catching the scent of prey in the air.

"Hello, Dylan." Deena Trace weaved through the crowd, stopped when she came to the front gate. "Come out to play?" A scoop-neck sweater and jeans that once strained at the seams hung on her bony frame. Smooth, pink skin that had begged any and every touch had faded to blue-mottled hide. "Toby's here. And Brian. We could have a party, just like the old days." A stink drifted around her, thick and eye-watering, like a sewer on a summer day.

Dylan scrabbled through his pockets until he found the charm that Jorie had made for him when he first agreed to spy on the Mistress for her. An Eye of the Lady, fashioned from herb-infused putty and baked hard as stone. "I have safe passage." He held it up so that they all could see it. "If any of you so much as lay a finger on me, you know what will happen." He took his time walking down the sidewalk, held his head high. Tried to hide his fear of the shadows of those he once called friends.

He held the charm above his head as he trotted across the street to the Cateman house. Through the gate and up the walk. He knocked on the door, waited, knocked again as the minutes passed and Deena shouted that she had learned some new and interesting ways to pass the time if Jorie proved too busy.

He felt his face redden, wondered if Lauren heard. He had liked her. If things had been different, they might have had some fun. But he had a goal, a plan. He had to be free.

New York first. Then London. Paris. Cities only. No small towns, ever, ever again.

He knocked one last time. Wondered where in hell Amanda and the other women had gone. The events of the night shouldn't have touched them. Jorie had told him they were safe.

He finally gave up, trudged through the snow to the back of the house. Jorie didn't like him entering that way—the women all saw him, and they did like to talk. But he didn't care. The night had been hell, and the time for secrets had long passed.

Something cold that knows your name.

Corey shivered as Mistress Waycross's words rattled through his head. Mounted the steps to the back door, and knocked.

May you find something waiting for you. . .

Corey heard noise from behind. The open and close of a door. *Jorie.* She had been pissed as hell when Lauren stumbled over the body in the cellar below the shed. No one but Leaf was supposed to see it.

Corey trotted down the steps. "Hey, Jor—" But the woman was nowhere to be seen. "Jorie?" He walked out to the middle of the yard, through the weird, stinking snow.

Heard a noise behind him, the whisper of air. Dropped to his knees when something hit him, hard. Felt warmth run down his face. Tasted blood.

Slumped to the ground. Saw the battered boots, so close to his head. Looked up, and saw the glint of the shovel blade as it came down—

37

Master Cateman?

Leaf opened his eyes, blinked away the haze that had grown heavier with each passing hour. They had visited him more than once—he remembered Thad Trace's irritated mutterings, his dear wife's false wishes for his recovery. Amanda's prayers and silent weeping. Her salty tears, falling on what remained of his skin.

Occasionally, sounds filtered in from outside. Screams. Gunshots. Then silence, which somehow seemed worse.

And now this. He had finally realized it, after the disaster of Jorie's spell casting. Feared it, as he lay in the dark and felt his life ebb. Hoped he had made a mistake, even as the understanding settled that the time for hope had long since passed. "Blaine."

Ah, he opens his eyes. Nicholas Blaine sat in the chair beside his bed. Dark-suited, face a swirl of shadow, hands resting on the head of a walking stick. *I thought perhaps I was too late.*

"She saw you. She told me." Leaf forced words through lips gone raw, tasted the blood as it flowed down the back of his throat. "I didn't believe her."

Who? Blaine cocked his head. *Ah, the excellent Mistress Mullin. Of course you didn't believe her—that wouldn't have suited your purpose.*

"I only wanted—what was best—"

That's what Catemans always say. Blaine sat back, rested his stick

373

across his lap. *I have been to this dance before, you know. Since a Cateman first took charge of Gideon, I followed the trail. Planted seeds, waited until they bore fruit.* He paused. *You're all the same. Ambitious, vain, venal. Only your women change.*

Cateman tried to speak, but the ability had left him. Too weak. End of his days at hand, and no son to take the reins, see things to completion.

Well, there had been a son of sorts, once, but he had proved a cruel disappointment.

Your Mistress wife has taken to her bed, there to dream of her ascension to Queen of the Universe. I have just taken leave of her. Shadows shifted, formed a smile. *So accommodating. You Catemans always trained your women well.* Blaine stood. *Ambition—my favorite weakness. I always enjoy the expressions on your faces, the utter surprise as the trap closes.* He walked to the door, coattails fluttering in the nonexistent breeze. *Farewell, Master Cateman. Many thanks for your excellent service.*

38

Amorning of sorts arrived, eventually, after a night spent taking turns standing watch. Brittany took over coffeemaking duties, and proved so adept that Rocky teased her about taking Deena's job at the diner, and didn't catch himself until she ran from the kitchen in tears.

Lauren returned to the sitting room. Hesitated before walking to the window, reluctant to view what the new day had brought even though she knew that she needed to see it. The morning light shone dull, heavy gray clouds hanging low enough to skim the roof of the Cateman house. The weird snow had been trampled flat on the streets and walkways where Blaine's horde had gathered, and lay piled on the lawns like cold ashes.

Zeke's house rested on a slight elevation, which allowed Lauren a clear view of the town square, now filled with a hundred or more of the restless dead. During the night, they had torn down the Fire Memorial and stacked the wood in a conical pile, maneuvered a post so it stuck up in the middle.

"What do you think they're planning?" Waycross drew alongside, coffee mug in hand.

"I think it's pretty obvious, don't you?" Lauren backed away from the sight and returned to her desk. "Just a question of when, and who."

"They try tying me to that thing, I'll make them wish they'd stayed all the way dead." Waycross pulled a chair next to Lauren's and sat, elbows on the desk. She still had on the same jeans and heavy sweater that she had worn during their escape, and her sleep-mashed curls lay flat against her head. "Rocky and Phil found a couple of old snowmobiles in the garage out back. They think they can get them running."

"So we make a break for it?" Lauren turned the pages of an old notebook that Zeke had scrounged for her, which she had spent the night filling with notes about spells, symbols, the odd curse word. "That doesn't solve the primary problem."

"It would give us a chance to regroup. And if he's trapped here with his minions, well, much as it pains me, maybe we just let this place die. Let it fade from memory."

"You really think that's what would happen? Blaine found me in Seattle. He killed a woman there and drained my father dry. He'll never die, and he'll always find someone to help him." Lauren reached for her own mug, the dregs long since grown cold. "What about the ones we'd leave behind?"

Waycross hung her head. "Brittany got answers from less than half the homes. And that was yesterday. Who knows how many lived—" Her voice cracked, and she paused. Took a swallow of coffee. "Who knows how many lasted the night?" She took a tissue that she had tucked up her sleeve and wiped her eyes.

"Maybe they were too scared to answer the phone. Maybe their lines had already been cut." Lauren took out her phone, turned it on, knew what she would see before the status bar flashed: *No Service*.

"Or maybe they're out there on the square, planning our burning." Waycross jerked her chin toward the notes. "Are we any closer to anything?"

Lauren shook her head. "The elemental spells are so specific—you have to know your relationship to whoever you spell, and you usually need some part of them, an item of clothing or hair or sweat."

She paged through the ghost book, pointed to one of the spell diagrams. "And according to what I read, it's only possible to affect one element at a time, but Blaine said he was bound by all four—earth, air, fire, wat—" A roar of an engine interrupted—it blasted for a few seconds, then stuttered into silence.

"Sounds enough like a chain saw, maybe." Waycross shrugged. "I think we're past trying to sneak at this point. We'll have to meet them head-on and bull our way—" She quieted, and looked toward the window. Then she slammed her mug on the desk and bolted out of the room.

Lauren listened, heard a hard clattering sound. *Hoofbeats?* She ran out of the room and almost collided with Zeke, who had dashed out from the rear of the house.

"My boys." Waycross pulled at the door handle, worked the dead bolt with a shaking hand. "If they've come back—Zeke—is there any way we can—" She threw open the door, and stopped.

Lauren pushed past her and walked out onto the front step.

Good morning, Miss Mullin. Mistress Waycross. I trust I find you well. Blaine sat astride one of the Waycross horses, his followers crowded around him like revelers welcoming a triumphant general home from the wars. *I wanted to thank you personally for the use of this fine mount, Mistress Waycross. I expect he will serve me quite well in the days to come.*

"Kermit." Waycross raised her hand to her mouth. "Kermit, my boy. My poor, poor—"

Lauren slumped against one of the entry columns. She could see the blood that flowed down the horse's flanks, feel the pain as Blaine struck it with his stick, gouged its side with the spurs that glistened on his boots, yanked on the reins, and drove the bit into its mouth. Flesh gashed, wounds laid open, as though it had been beaten over and over.

I just wanted to pay my respects, and let you know that you can expect more where this came from. Have you seen what my chosen have built in

the square? *Such wonderful festivals we used to have in Gideon, with danc-*
ing and bonfires. We will have those times again, starting today, unless
Miss Mullin sees her way clear to do me one small service. With that, he
touched his hand to the brim of his tall hat, wheeled Kermit around,
dug in his spurs, and galloped through the snow down the street,
vanishing into the murk.

"Oh, dear Lady." Zeke took hold of Waycross's arm, steered her
back into the house. "Mistress, come inside now, come in and sit.
Come in—" He ushered her back down the hall into the kitchen and
to the large worktable. "Sit right down here." He held out a chair
for her, tapped her on the shoulder to get her to sit down, pushed
the chair in. "Whiskey, I think." He rummaged through cupboards.
"Something strong."

Lauren sat across from the woman, took hold of her hands, and
held them until the wide, dazed eyes met hers. A look she understood
all too well, the continuous replay, a loop in the brain. The same hell,
over and over and over.

"My boy. My poor silly—" Waycross finally closed her eyes. The
tears fell.

"Blame me, Mistress." Zeke set down a tray with a bottle and
glasses, and poured. "I told you to leave them. I told you there wasn't
time to see to them."

Waycross shook her head. "No, Zeke, they were my boys, my
charges."

"That's how he works." Lauren rubbed one of the woman's hands,
then the other. Both so cold. "He finds what you love and tears it
apart." She released Waycross when Zeke sat next to her. "He enjoys
it." She stood, let one old friend minister to the other as the rest stood
by in stunned silence.

Lauren walked down the hall, grabbing her coat off the hook
along the way. Returned to the sitting room, gathered the books and
her notes, and started to stuff them in her handbag. Stopped, and set
them back on the desk.

"What are you doing?"

Waycross stepped inside the room, folded her arms and tucked her hands, and leaned against the jamb.

Lauren walked to the window and looked out. The snow was falling again, greasy flakes smearing the glass. She sensed eyes watching from the murk, saw a stocky figure standing at the gate like a suitor awaiting his beloved. *Lolly.*

"I asked you a question." Waycross drew up beside her. Caught sight of Lolly, and drew in a shuddery breath.

Lauren stepped away from the window, pressed her back to the wall. "He said it himself. I'm the one he wants, and he will never stop until he has me. He'll kill the rest of you off, one by one, until I'm the only one left. And if he doesn't get what he wants out of me, then he'll think of other things to try, and I'm not sure I want to know what those are." She started to pace, but her knees felt weak and something like static worked like hooks beneath her skin because she knew what she had to do. Knew that she had no choice.

Waycross remained at the window, her eyes on Lolly. "You have a plan?"

"I have shit." Lauren stopped, leaned against the desk. "In the kitchen, I heard Rocky tell Phil that he felt the snowmobiles were in pretty good shape. It's your decision whether or not to leave, but you'll have a better chance to make it if I'm not with you."

Waycross's head snapped around. "No."

"Hear me out."

"I said, no."

"It's not your decision." Lauren pulled on her coat. "I think I know why Dad ran. He realized the choice he had to make. I don't know why he didn't follow through. Fear? Or maybe he needed Emma to help him, and she wasn't there." She shrugged. "I think he thought that if he left, things here would stay the same. They might not get better, but at least they wouldn't get worse. I don't think he understood what he was up against until it was too late."

"But if you don't have a plan, how can you fight him?" Waycross walked to her side, took her hand.

"Maybe I can figure out how to fight on the other side. Guerrilla witch in the borderland. Maybe Blaine can't hurt me if I'm dead." Lauren eased her hand from Waycross's grasp. The contact, the kindness, hurt too much, reminded her of what she would leave behind. "When I go out the front, you go out the back. Pack as little as possible. I doubt supplies would do any good, anyway. I'm not sure you'd be able to survive for long out there."

Waycross nodded, eventually. "When?"

"Now? This moment is the best it will ever be." Lauren heard a cough, and turned to find the others in the doorway. She could tell from their expressions that they heard, that they knew. "I'm sorry it's come to this."

"Not your fault." Zeke sniffed. "Blame the Catemans for sheltering him all these years. Hell, may as well blame the Lady, come to that, for letting something like Blaine get back to this world in the first place."

"Can you give us an hour?" Rocky grabbed a coat from the wall hook, dragged on gloves. "That'll give us a chance to move the snowmobiles into position, load a few things we might need."

"Sure." Lauren started to follow him to the back door. "I'd like to help." She wanted to keep busy. Best not to think too much at times like these.

But then came the tug on her elbow, the staying hand. "Be there in a minute." She stilled. Waited.

"I just want to say—"

"Please don't."

"—that you are as much of this place as any I have ever known." Waycross paused to breathe, one slow inhalation. A sigh. "I am bound to call you witch, and I hope I can call you friend."

Lauren nodded. Stood in place until Waycross released her, then headed out back to help the others prepare.

LAUREN WAITED UNTIL she heard the back door close, the rev of the snowmobiles. Then she opened the front door, and walked out into the gloom.

They sensed her, Blaine's horde, and crowded around the gate like revelers at a homecoming. Lauren spotted Deena, smiling widely, anticipating the destruction to come. Betty Joan and Ruthie, clinging together in half death as they had in life, their hatred just as strong.

But it was Lolly whom she met first. He held the gate open for her, then fell in beside her as she crossed the street to the Cateman house, his step heavy and his face a mass of bruises and scabs and scar tissue.

"He knows—you're coming." Lolly's voice sounded with the same gutter fierceness it had possessed in life, tempered by gasps of pain as his overlord sought to silence him. "He's—preparing."

"You'll get into trouble if you keep talking," Lauren said under her breath.

"You mean it'll get worse?" The rough laugh sounded. "Not for me. Can't get much worse for me." He pushed with her through the gate even as the others remained behind, walked with her as far as the Catemans' front porch, stopped at the first step. "You, on the other hand . . . ?" He shook his head, neck cracking with every movement. "Good ol' Matt, leavin' his little girl to twist in the wind."

"It wasn't his fault." Lauren turned to look into eyes gone milk-filmed and dull.

"Whose is it, then?" Lolly's swollen lips twitched as he spoke, a line of blood streaming from the corner of his mouth.

Lauren turned her back on him, mounted the steps to the porch, and reached for the doorbell. But before she could ring it, the door opened, and Amanda Petrie stepped out.

"Master hoped you'd come. He's been waiting for you." Circles ringed Petrie's eyes. She had discarded the jacket of her black pant suit, revealing a white shell stained with sweat and other, darker effluvia. "We should go inside." She looked past Lauren to the silent throng that crowded the sidewalk outside the gate, then down at Lolly, who still stood at the foot of the steps. "Begone, you foul thing."

Lolly grinned, then turned and limped back the way he had come. "I'll save you a seat, Mandy." He pushed through the gate, jostling others out of the way. "We're all waiting for you. All your old, dear friends."

Petrie hurried Lauren inside, then ducked in after her. Slammed the door and locked it, then dragged a chair from alongside the entry wall and jammed it beneath the handle. "That'll keep the damned things out." Then she dug into her trouser pocket. "Put some of this under your nose. It will help." She removed a tin of ointment, slid off the lid, and held it out to Lauren.

"You're kidding, right?" Lauren shook her head. "Not if my life depended on it."

"It's just chest rub. Stuff you get in the store." Petrie hooked a glob with her index finger and slathered it beneath her nose. "I'm not trying to spell you. Master's wish, and I am bound to obey."

Lauren looked toward the staircase, twisting upward into the darkness. "Which Master are we talking about?"

"I serve the Catemans and only the Catemans." Petrie's voice came tight. "The true Catemans, not the tramps they fall prey to, those stupid, stupid men." Red splotches bloomed on her cheeks, her neck. "That bitch polluted my ointment. She—" Tears poised on the brink, ready to spill. "I made it with my own hands. I never let her near it."

"Where is Jorie?" Lauren scraped a small dollop of the ointment and smeared it above her upper lip. "I didn't see her face in the crowd outside."

"She's still here, the useless bitch." Petrie pocketed the ointment tin and headed for the stairs. "Waiting for the rising. The final unveiling." She plodded upward, crepe-sole shoes whispering against the runner. "Thinks her reward is imminent for the foul way she treated my Master."

Lauren ascended behind the woman, past the second floor and

onto the third. They walked past Leaf Cateman's office to a set of double doors that capped the end of the hallway, knocked, then entered. "Master? She's here." A pause. Then she beckoned to Lauren. "He'll see you."

Lauren entered. The bedroom was huge and high-ceilinged, the walls covered in imperial-purple silk, the armoire, dresser, and bedstead hulking walnut monuments to another time. The battery-powered lanterns that Petrie had placed in each corner filled the space with weak yellow light, allowing one to see just enough, and leaving imagination to fill in the rest.

The stench intensified with each step toward the bed—by the time Lauren reached the foot, not even the menthol in the chest rub could make a dent. She stared at the form that lay prone beneath an ornate blanket until a cough from Petrie let her know that she had stood silent for too long. "You wanted to see me."

A hand swaddled in stained gauze twitched in the direction of a bedside chair, and Lauren sidestepped around the bed and sat.

Leaf Cateman lay propped up on pillows. He wore no pajama shirt, and his exposed skin had been wrapped in gauze from forehead to chest, including arms and hands. Only the top of his head lay exposed, a crusted, festering wound of a scalp from which a few remaining strands of lank white hair sprouted. Petrie had cut a slit in the gauze to allow him to see, and his eyes glittered like black marbles amid the bloodstained white.

Despite Lauren's contempt for the man, the extent of his decline, the speed at which it had occurred, stunned her. Only the day before, ill though he had been, he had still radiated some sense of presence, some power. Gone now, all that, replaced by a gasping, twitching form like something out of a tale by Poe.

"It's all the fault of the Mullins—that's all I've heard since I've been in Gideon. The Freeze. The Great Fire. The curse on this town because Eliza Mullin bore false witness against Nicholas Blaine."

Lauren paused. "I've even heard that my dad was responsible for Emma's disappearance." She stopped, tried to gather thoughts scattered by fears of what lay ahead, then struggled on. "Did you know that after the fire, your grandfather Hiram had Books of Endor reprinted for the entire town. Did you know he left things out? Spells for binding demons, among other things. It would have been nice if everyone in Gideon knew those, given what's been happening, don't you think?"

The light in Cateman's eyes sparked, his hands twitched and flexed as though they had taken on a life of their own.

"I wouldn't have let you in here if I'd known you were going to abuse him." Petrie sat on the edge of the bed opposite Lauren's chair, patting Cateman's hands until they stilled, adjusting the bandages.

Lauren caught a glimpse of Cateman's chest through a gap in the gauze. Raw red. A bit of yellow. Exposed muscle and bone. Did the man feel pain? Or had his nerve endings deteriorated along with the rest of him? "I just want to ask him a few questions. Whether he answers, that's up to him." She watched Cateman's eyes as she spoke.

After a few moments, a weird sound emerged from Cateman, a dust-dry croak that replayed over and over. The remains of laughter. The effort drained him—he faded into the pillows even more, and his eyes rolled back, revealing crescents of yellowed sclera.

He has no eyelids left. Lauren swallowed hard. *Can he even see me?* She leaned forward, elbows on knees. Nose fatigue had taken up residence—she could barely detect the rot emanating from the bed. "You took in my father after the deaths of his parents. Convenient, their dying. Left you a clear shot at the key you needed to free Nicholas Blaine. But you needed to make sure that you had him, so you set Emma before him like a dinner before a starving man, and let nature take its course."

Petrie leaped to her feet. "Stop it! I let you in—"

"You let me in because he wanted to see me. And you'll do what he tells you, right to the end." Lauren shrugged. "I have no proof of anything. I just think it odd that everything bad one hears about Mullins seemed to have originated from Catemans, yet Catemans seem to need us so much."

Cateman took a deep, rattling breath, then released it in gasps. "Your father—was no—saint."

"He was young, and alone, and when he didn't give you what you wanted, you tried to destroy him." Lauren looked across the bed at Petrie, who stood as still as her Master. "Can he be moved?"

Petrie hesitated, then she shook her head. "There's nothing left to him. He'd fall apart if we tried."

Lauren stood and walked to the window, pushed aside the heavy drape. Black outside, but not night, swirling shadow that chattered and runneled and scraped the panes. She wondered whether Waycross and the others had managed to get away, or if Blaine's horde had chased them down.

"You know what he wants?" Petrie still stood in the same place, tears coursing down her cheeks. "He wants you to take him out of here. He doesn't want to be caught by them. You can pass through the thin places, so you can take him where he needs to go."

Lauren watched the snow. "And why would I do that?"

"Because it's right."

"What do I get in return?"

Petrie drew up straight. "I am to answer one question—one—" She stammered as Cateman raised a shaky hand, then let it fall once, then again. "Two. I am to answer two questions."

Lauren returned to the bed, lowered to the edge. "What do I do?"

Petrie waved toward the bed, then turned away. "Just guide him."

As if on cue, Cateman lifted his bandaged hand.

Lauren grasped it, felt the slide of rotting tissue beneath the damp gauze. Closed her eyes and with her free hand felt the flow of the room, the currents and eddies of all the realities that led across the borderland to the wilderness beyond. Blaine's darkness polluted most every stream, but here and there she found a clean thread and followed it. The flour amid the eggs and milk. Her cloud. Her source. Her beacon amid the despoiling, encroaching dark.

After a time, the thread thickened to a line, a path, a trail, that opened into an expanse of treeless rolling land, hills so blank and smoothly curved that they could have been cut from paper. The first cleansing stretches of the wilderness.

Lauren felt a tug on her hand, and turned to find Cateman walking behind her, struggling to keep up. Petrie had wrapped him in gauze from face to feet, and as he stumbled, it unwound, streaming behind him in the undetectable breeze, revealing skin halfway to healed, scabbed and crusted, angry red lightened to pink. His lips moved, the sound emerging muffled, a voice under glass.

Then his eyes widened. He stopped, and when Lauren tried to pull him along, he refused to move.

Lauren followed his gaze, and saw, at first in the distance, then closer and closer still. The woman was young, with a cameo face framed with waist-length black hair parted in the middle, the ends wafting in the almost-breeze. She wore a dress the color of flame, bound at the waist with a gold cord, but as Lauren drew closer, the cord vanished for a beat, then appeared again around the woman's neck. Her face was now bruised, her nose bloodied. One of her pierced earrings had been torn away, leaving the slashed earlobe, drops of blood bright as ruby against her skin. She glanced at Lauren only once, then looked down at Cateman.

Eventually, she smiled.

Cateman struggled in Lauren's grasp, but she held tight until she reached the black-haired woman in the flame-colored dress. Then she stopped, studied the face of the first woman her father had loved, and after a time, Emma Cateman studied her in turn.

Then Lauren shook loose Leaf Cateman's grip and backed away, leaving him with his late wife. His skin had healed completely now, and he stood naked, pink and pleading, his voice barely above a whisper. Then he sank to his knees, one arm stretched out, grasping for the hem of the flame-colored dress.

As Lauren turned to go, she saw Emma unloose the cord from around her neck. A few strides later, she heard the muffled scream.

The wilderness, she realized then, could be many things, but one thing it always was, was wild.

39

Lauren opened her eyes. She still stood beside Cateman's bed, still held his hand. His cries for mercy still rang in her ears.

She heard a woman's voice at mumbled prayer, and turned to find Amanda Petrie kneeling on the floor at the foot of the bed, hands over her face, begging the Lady for mercy.

"You need to leave." Lauren lowered Cateman's hand to his side. "Go across to the Pyne house. No one is there, but the wards should still be working."

"Where did they go? Virginia and the others?" Petrie struggled to her feet. "I thought they were there with you?" When Lauren didn't answer, she shook her head. "They won't escape this."

"Neither may you." Lauren departed the bedroom, Petrie at her heels. "But you'll be as safe as possible until it ends, one way or the other." She descended the stairs two at a time, down to the first floor, then waited for Petrie at the foot. "First question. What happened to Emma?" She watched Petrie's mouth work soundlessly, and knew the woman wanted to keep her secrets to the end, to protect her late Master even if by doing so she broke her pledge to him.

"She—she gave your father one of Master's Books. One with the spells." Petrie glared at Lauren, eyes bright with anger almost forty years old. "She betrayed the Master after he raised her up from nothing." She swallowed, looked away. "Of course he killed her. Executed her. It was his right." She dug a tissue from her pocket, blew her nose. "Then we—years ago, we had our own cremation unit at the funeral home." She sighed. "Now we contract all those out. Changing times."

Lauren just nodded, and bit back the other questions that begged answers. Had Emma loved her father? Or had she felt guilty about using him, and sought to make amends?

But there was one question that superseded all those. Lauren felt she knew the answer, but she wanted to hear it out loud. "The Catemans have served Blaine for a very long time, haven't they? Since the beginning?" She waited, as Petrie grabbed the banister in a white-knuckled grip, mouth opening and closing like a fish out of water, until finally she twitched her head in the smallest of nods.

"So, we're done." Petrie shook herself, a beast of burden freed from the yoke. She reached into her pocket again, but instead of a tissue, she removed a folded handkerchief. "The Master said I should give this to you. It's been in my family since—since the fire." She held it out.

Lauren took the bundle, felt something hard beneath the cloth. She unfolded the handkerchief, and uncovered a small silver locket.

"It got passed down." Petrie wiped her hands on her pants legs. "Great-uncle Joseph—he fought in the Civil War and lived through the fire—he had it in his things."

Lauren looked down at the round case, the etched letters *EB* in the center, framed by tiny flowers. Opened it, and found a short lock of black hair nestled within, bound with a faded thread of blue ribbon. She closed it and tucked it inside her pants pocket, then turned and walked to the door. Opened it, then stood aside to let Petrie pass.

"We should have killed you when we had the chance. Master would have lived out his life chasing his dreams, not hurting anyone. Instead, he died in nightmare." Petrie raised her eyes to meet Lauren's, eyes bright with hate that would survive until the end of days.

Lauren simply nodded. "You need to go now."

Petrie looked out over the cul-de-sac, the milling throng that filled the sidewalk and the shadows that filled the sky. "I won't make it."

Lauren dug her thumbnail into the back of her wrist, sawing back and forth until the blood welled and ran. But before she could swipe her wrist across Petrie's forehead, the woman shied away.

"Keep your filth to yourself. Keep it." Petrie stumbled as she hurried down the steps, hesitated as the horde crowded near the gate and jeered. Then, head high, she strode down the walkway. She slowed when she reached the gate and found Lolly waiting for her. "I am Mistress Amanda Petrie, and I order you back." When Lolly failed to budge, she brushed past him and out into the street—

—at which point Gideon's demons closed in around her like wolves around a calf. Petrie screamed once, then vanished, as howls of laughter rent the air.

Lauren waited until the melee subsided. She held her breath, closed her eyes, and strained for any sound of a snowmobile engine, wondered if the silence she heard instead meant good news or bad.

Then she went back inside and closed the door. Heard no sound but the ones she made, sensed no life but her own.

She felt it then, the gentle tug. Heard the brown voice in her head.

I've let you in. . .

Lauren started toward the back of the house, on her way to meet Nicholas Blaine.

CONNIE PETERSBURY LOOKED up at the sky, or rather, what the sky had become. Low, black, and thick. Alive. She could hear whatever lived in the mists that tumbled overhead, yammering about the freedom to come, the terror and the joy and the meat. Fresh meat.

Connie shifted back and forth. The threads of warmth had diminished, the growing cold pushing her closer and closer to the riverbank. Ashley waited there now, sitting cross-legged on a rock, filing her nails to a point. Getting ready for the fun.

"Almost time, Aunt Connie." She smiled her black-toothed smile.

"You just came back here to torture me, didn't you? You look like something from one of those TV shows you used to watch. Walking death." Connie tested the water again, and again. "Don't get excited, my girl. You ain't got me yet."

"Only a matter of time."

"Time ain't the boss of me." Connie swirled currents with her fingers, tried to tease out whatever traces of life she could find. "Not anymore."

In the distance, she heard noise, getting closer and closer. Engines, running rough, straining for all they were worth. Caught glimpses of the snowmobiles as they shot past. The flash of a familiar barn coat, and a White Sox cap.

"You go, Virginia. You go, girl!" Connie pumped her gloved fist in the air. Savored the excitement of a friend's escape attempt. *You go, girl.* She ignored Ashley's mocking laughter, tried not to think of the bad end she knew would likely come.

She tested the water. Tested the water.

Then she felt it. A warm golden thread. Thin, though, and getting thinner.

She sank her hand up to the wrist into that warm line of hope, and prayed.

40

Lauren walked out into the Cateman backyard. The strange snow that had fallen the night before still lay in piles on the brown lawn, lending a metallic tang to the air.

She didn't see the body at first. She saw the shovel handle sticking out of the ground, and thought that someone had tried to dig their way out, or clear a path to the firewood stacked by the back fence.

Then she saw the flash of red hair. Walked slowly until she could see it all, the splayed limbs, the blood-splashed snow, the way the shovel blade to the back of the neck had neatly severed Dylan Corey's head from his body.

Acid rose in Lauren's throat. Her knees buckled and she sagged to the snow, then rocked back and forth, the distant gibber of Blaine's horde counterpoint to her pounding heart. After a time, she brushed the snow from Corey's cheek, felt the skin cold and stiff. Sensed some remnant of him, the barest fragment scrabbling for purchase, still trying to hold on to life. Then it vanished, the final wisp of an extinguished flame.

Lauren rose. Then a surge of anger struck, driving away the shock, the fear. She grabbed the shovel by the handle, yanked it clear, tossed it aside. Pulled off her coat and spread it over Corey so that it covered his head.

Varmints—that's how you deal with varmints—

Lauren stared at the shovel as Waycross's words flooded back—

I followed the spell to bind an outsider. . .

—then her own.

Blaine's not really an outsider. He's known to us. She walked to the shovel, picked it up, thought of a man she had just come to know. A man who kept turning up wherever she happened to be.

The man who had met her as she entered Gideon.

The man who saved her life.

Lauren walked to the shed. Raised her hand to knock on the door—

"Please. Come in." The chocolate voice, warm as a flame.

Lauren undid the latch, and stepped inside.

The man who once called himself Tom Barton sat at a table in the center of the room, eating a slice of pie. After he ferried the last bite into his mouth, he scraped the plate with his fork, the metal grating against the china with a sound like fingernails across glass.

"I must beg your pardon," he said, in a voice with no trace of wheedle or peeve. "I don't mean to be rude." He licked the fork clean, then set it down and sat back, crossed his legs, clasped his hands around his knee. "But good Mistress Cateman discovered that if she rewrapped foodstuffs in the places outside Gideon at which they were purchased, it allowed me several minutes to enjoy their flavor before the air of Gideon settled and rendered them dust." He jerked his head toward the cot in the far corner of the room. "You and the good Mistress have met, I believe."

Lauren looked toward the cot just as what she took to be a bundled blanket shifted. A face appeared amid the pile, eyes glaring daggers.

"What the hell is she doing here?" Jorie sat up and the blanket fell away to reveal her naked torso, breasts and stomach dotted with bite marks.

"The good Mistress came to me for comfort. It seems her good Master has taken a turn." Nicholas Blaine smiled. "You just came from his sickbed, I believe. How is he?"

"Dead." Lauren leaned on the shovel because she needed to sit down and knew she didn't dare. She needed to be able to move, and quickly.

"Really?" Blaine's voice held a trace of doubt. "You stayed with him until the end?"

"I helped him pass into the wilderness. Then I left him with Emma."

"Did you?" Blaine's brow arched. "That was . . . poetic." He tapped the tabletop with his open hand. "My compliments. Brava." He stilled, gaze settling on the shovel. "I see you found the superfluous Mr. Corey." His eyes narrowed. "Put that down."

Lauren shook her head. "I don't think—" Her words stopped as something grabbed her by the scruff of the neck and lifted her, whipped her back and forth, then slammed her against the wall. The shovel flew from her grasp and whatever held her dropped her—she slid down the wall and sagged to the floor, gasping for breath.

"I said to put it down." Blaine stood, and walked around the table toward Lauren. As he moved, he straightened his bowed back, his hunched shoulders, grew taller with every step. Rheumy eyes cleared, revealing the blue of twilit skies. His hair had grayed over the years, and fine lines crazed the smooth skin, the ridges and thicknesses of the few burn scars that remained. Thirty-seven years it had taken for Nicholas Blaine to heal, but heal he had.

"Now, I have been extremely patient with you, but that time is past." He crouched in front of Lauren, gripped her chin between his thumb and index finger, and twisted her head until she faced him. "You have work to do."

"She can't do it—she told us." Jorie tucked the sheets about her waist. "He didn't teach her anything."

"And yet, here she is. She who walks through my woods unscathed." Blaine released Lauren, then stood and looked down at her, head tilted, as though he were studying a particularly interesting ant.

"Earth, air, fire, and water, Miss Mullin. Tell them what they need to hear to let me go." He turned and walked back to the table.

Lauren worked herself into a sitting position, stopping every so often as battered muscles seized. "I don't believe I'm in the proper frame of mind."

"Try harder." Blaine perched on the edge of the table, one leg swinging, a pendulum marking off her time.

"She hurt me, you know." Jorie pointed to her eye, the bruising like shadow in the harsh light of the shed. "She did something while she was hiding in our yard like a sneak and it made me fall and hit my head on the counter." She cupped her hand over her eye. "You should make her pay for that."

Blaine's leg stilled. "What did you do, Miss Mullin?"

Lauren tried to sort through all that had happened over the last few days. *So much.* "The ointment. I had tried to wipe it away, but there was still some left and it made me sick and I started to go under and I told it just to *stop.*"

"You deflected the curse. That . . . is not easy to do." Blaine's look sharpened. "I should have sought you out from the start. I would have saved so much time."

"Hey, wait a minute." Jorie slid off the bed and stood. "I killed my husband for you."

Blaine laughed. "Don't use me as an excuse. Leaf was husband to you in name only, and you had wanted to kill him for quite some time. I just gave you a little push."

"You're cutting me loose?" Jorie flicked a finger toward Lauren. "For that?"

"For the most raw power I have ever encountered on this side of the divide." Blaine turned to Lauren. "With a single exception, you understand."

Lauren nodded. "Eliza Mullin."

"Eliza." Blaine's eyes clouded for a moment. Then his gaze returned to Lauren, and cleared. "But you will do. You will do quite well, for some time to come."

"You. Bastard." Jorie hurtled toward Blaine, hands extended, fingers bent like claws.

When the woman came within arm's reach, Blaine stood, grabbed her jaw with one hand and the back of her head with the other, and twisted. The gravel grind of snapping bone sounded, and Jorie collapsed in a heap, a puppet with the strings cut.

"Always so noisy. Why can't caged birds ever learn to stop singing?" Blaine stepped over Jorie's body. "It's just the two of us now, as it always seems to be. I've enjoyed our talks. I always meant to tell you. Mullins have always provided the most entertaining challenge."

Lauren stared at Jorie Cateman's body. Gone so fast. So many, gone so fast. "You killed a woman in Seattle to get my attention."

"I needed to get you to leave." Blaine shrugged. "It worked, didn't it?"

"Yes, it did." Lauren nodded. Sensed the man's impatience, the chafing of his bonds. "Wards fade after the one who sets them dies. Spells. I'm the last Mullin. Why don't you just kill me and wait it out?"

Blaine frowned. "Such a question." He gestured around the room with the studied ease of an experienced actor. "Sweet Eliza sacrificed her life to bind me to this place. The power of voluntary sacrifice lasts so long. It's the ultimate gift after all. To give up your life for piles of dirt—"

"Gideon is more than land. It's people—"

"I was talking about the people." Blaine sighed, then looked around the room as though he wondered how he had come to be there and when he could leave. "I don't need to make a deal because you're here, alone, with no means of escape. But I am nothing if not generous." He walked toward her. "Tell me what you want."

Lauren tried to scoot along the wall as he approached. The shovel had flown across the room, but it had struck the wall at an angle and rebounded toward her. *Just a few feet away.* She edged closer. *Just a few—*

"You're afraid, I can tell. You want to take me on, but you're nowhere close to ready." Blaine crouched, rested his chin on his fist, *The Thinker* in worn flannel and denim, with eyes as dead as a shark's for all their beauty. "But I think Matthew did me a favor, leaving you unformed. I can shape you in my image, make you useful to me." He snapped his fingers. "In exchange, I will give you the world. Quid pro quo."

Lauren slid a bit closer to the shovel, then stopped as buzzing sounded in her ears. She wanted to stop fighting. She wanted to say yes.

"I can teach you all the things your father couldn't, or wouldn't." Blaine edged closer, grazed her hand with his fingers. Pulled back, then closed in again. "I already know what you feel like, thanks to the accommodating Mr. Corey. What you taste like. The sort of touches you crave. After you release me, I will tumble you on the floor like a dollar whore. And you will beg me never to stop."

Lauren felt Blaine's breath on her cheek, smelled the faint hints of cinnamon and caramel from the pie, flavors that he couldn't taste. She put a hand to his face and felt the roughness of beard and beneath that the ridges of his scars. "I have to touch you."

"Do with me as you will. Mistress." Blaine embraced her and pulled her to her feet and they moved in a lazy circle, a slow dance, as she stroked his hair and pressed her hands to his chest and felt for memory that survived in each cell. Memories of death and life in the wilderness. Pleasure and pain.

And in the nucleus of each, like the cores of infinitesimal stars, the memory of fire.

Lauren felt it, sparks that stung her fingers and radiated along her arms like shocks. It must have shown in her face, this discovery, because Blaine's arms tightened about her and his eyes widened and their dance slowed, then stopped.

"You know how?" His voice, rough as a whisper in the night. "I can tell. You know how."

"I need—I need—" Lauren broke out of his grasp and pushed him away, then—

—dove for the shovel and swung it. The edge of the blade caught Blaine as he leaped forward, slashing his shirt and the skin beneath. Blood sprayed and he staggered, caught himself on the edge of the table.

"*You bitch.*" He stumbled toward her, slipped on his own blood, righted himself.

Lauren staggered back as Blaine shoved her. She struck the wall, and slid along it as he came for her. She reached for the door, but he caught her as she put her hand on the latch. As he grabbed her shoulder and spun her around, she shoved her knee into his groin and he had enough flesh and nerve about him that he felt it.

"Kill you." Blaine howled as he staggered after her, stumbled to one knee. "Every second of pain you bring me, I will return a thousandfold."

Lauren flung open the door just as he reached her, shook off his fumbling grasp. Sprinted across the yard, past Corey's body, through the weird snow. Prayed that Blaine would be hampered by age and injury and pain.

But he righted himself and ran for her, low to the ground at first and scuttling as no human had run since the dawn of time. "*Storm.*" More shriek than voice, a howl under moonlight.

Lauren felt the first gusts, then the blast like a gale as wind wrapped around her and held her like chains, sent snow in tornadoes about the yard, ripped away shutters and tore branches off trees and sent them all swirling to form an infernal cage.

But a gap remained in the tornado wall. Just large enough. Lauren pushed through it and ran up the back steps of the Cateman house.

Memories of fire. Like the gazebo. There was wood in the house that remembered.

She knew where she had to go.

Just as she opened the back door, the howling winds ceased. Blaine's voice sounded.

"Stumble, stagger, and still."

Lauren shot through the back door into the house just as the spell struck. Her legs went to lead and she fell to her knees, fought the ice that webbed through her limbs, regained her footing just as Blaine grabbed her by the collar and spun her, pushed her into the wall opposite.

"I will pull—your words out of you—with tongs gone white with heat." He sagged against the wall, what breath he could pull in with his still-weakened body wheezing into his lungs. "The pain your father suffered when he denied me—will pale by comparison."

Lauren found the strength in her arms to push herself upright, to stand. She concentrated, focused, laved away Blaine's spell like dirt from her skin. *I am stronger.* She gripped the thought, held it like a safety line in white water. *I am stronger.* She took one step, another and another, until she ran. Through the stinking dark to the stairs, up and up and up, Blaine screaming after her.

As she mounted the third flight, the air rippled, the stench of death like a wave of foul water. The remains of Leaf Cateman met her at the top, rotted arms reaching for her. She barreled into him, tried to push him off balance, but he had been strong in life and just enough of that power remained.

Help. Lauren punched and kicked. Bandages and cursed flesh fell away from Cateman's arms until only sinewy muscle and bone remained. Skeletal hands gripped her throat. *Anyone out there. If you can hear me. Anyone?*

Anything?

"Now." Blaine came up from behind, pressed his face to hers. "Let us begin again." Sweat glistened, and blisters had formed on his forehead. "Let us—" He stopped. Turned, and looked back down the stair.

The corpse emerged from the dark, a sere shamble that pushed Blaine aside, grabbed Cateman's wrists, and wrenched them apart. Cateman's hands tore loose and he staggered, then toppled down the stairs.

Eyeless sockets settled on Lauren. The body from the cellars, the pleading voice like the click of beetle's wings. "Help me, too." Then it collapsed against Blaine, slowed him just enough.

The doors to Cateman's office glistened black in the half-light, a gaping maw. Lauren reached them and flung them open just as Blaine caught her—he pushed her inside, pulled the doors shut after him.

Lauren's lungs burned, thigh muscles twitched and cramped as Blaine's spell fought her every move. She worked to her hands and knees as he grabbed her from behind, dragged her upright, crooked his arm around her neck. "I will squeeze the words out of you, one by one, and the last will be the last thing you ever say." He whispered in her ear. "And then I will call you back, and we will play this game again, over and over and over—"

Lauren stomped down on Blaine's instep, shoved her elbow into his stomach—his grip loosened just enough, and she pushed against him, drove him back. He bounced off the painted wall, slid across the drawings made by a young man so many years before, then slumped down, sweat coating him like rain and the stink of smoke rising from his clothes.

Lauren leaned against the wall opposite, and pulled in one gasping breath. Another.

Blaine fought to stand, heels scraping against the floor. "I will bring him back, your Dylan Corey. I will set him on you like a bull, and your screams will be as music." He laughed, a high-pitched, manic chortle. "Give me a child for its first seven years, and I will give you the witch. I've always been fond of children. Eager little sponges." He struck the floor with his fist, eyes sharpening, then dulling, as the pain took hold. "It would have me as teacher, whatever you birthed. And you to practice on. And you—"

A sharp knock sounded. Lauren and Blaine both looked toward the door as it opened.

"We heard you call, child." The battered form of Dilys Martin stepped into the room. The cellar corpse followed, dragging a twisted leg. "We witches, we hear forever. We answer the call." She closed the door, then turned to look at Blaine, and her smile turned into something from a nightmare. "I know you. I saw you before I died. In the road. In the rain."

"Go back where I sent you." Blaine sidestepped her. "Go back." But Dilys moved in a flicker of light, took hold of Blaine's left arm, and held him while the cellar corpse took hold of the right.

"Hang on to him, Tom," Dilys said to the corpse. "He's a slippery one." She looked back at Lauren. "Have you met Mr. Barton, child? He knew your father well."

"Dilys?" Lauren dragged in breath after breath through an aching throat into searing lungs. "You'll burn."

"We're ready, child." Dilys nodded. "Say the words."

Lauren pressed against the wood panels, ran her hands over them, felt the burn marks, the scars of long-ago flames. "Do you know what this is?"

Blaine struggled in his captors' grasp. "It's wood, you stupid bitch."

"What kind of wood?"

Blaine stilled. It mattered, but he didn't know why, and the realization gave flower to the first hint of uncertainty. "From the Great Fire."

Lauren shook her head. "Something else burned before that." She touched the wood panels again, more gently this time, fingertips reading the pound of hammers and the rasp of saws, releasing the scent of herbs and the prayers of men. "On the twentieth day of December in the year 1836." She looked across the room at Blaine, the faint light that shone through the Lady's eye the only illumination, coating the room with memories of ash. "You must remember. You were there." Then she felt it. The heat, locked in every fiber, every cell.

"You'll die, too." Blaine's voice, suddenly gentle, the murmur of a lover. "You can't leave. You are the conduit. The fire only burns if you are there to release it."

"I know." Lauren lowered to the floor. Blaine's spell had settled in her legs again. Or maybe it was fear, freezing her. Resignation, taking away her will to fight. "Let memory of fire burn you. Let air feed the flame." This time, she found the words. The fire burst out around her hand and she flinched away, watched it lick around the room like a fuse toward the thing it had killed once, so many years before.

"What do you want?" Blaine tried to pull away from the shades that held him as the flame flickered across his chest. "What do you want? Tell me and you shall have it."

"So many died trying to put you down. No more." Lauren pressed against the wall even as it grew too hot to lean against—more fingers of flame licked around, a lacy web of yellow and white, crackling and hissing and whispering in its own language.

"You walk into the flame with me, witch?" Blaine coughed. The fire worked from within as well as without, smoke curling from his mouth like breath on a cold day. "I will wait for you in the wilderness." His face had gone black and blistered, clothes charred away. "Tell me what you—"

Flame burst forth from the walls with a freight-train roar, cycloned upward. The oculus exploded and glass showered down, a rain that would never cool.

Lauren drew her knees to her chest, huddled as the heat grew, the flames filled the room. She watched Blaine burn, his flesh bubble and burst and his limbs contract. Watched the late Tom Barton die again, for real this time, his body no longer needed to fool anyone.

Then Dilys turned to her. The gentle smile. "Soon, child. It will be over soon." Then even she was gone.

Lauren felt no pain. Was it the fear, deadening her? The scant remains of Blaine's spell? Or had she died already, overcome by smoke that filled her lungs and swirled before her, her final partner on that last dance.

Lauren?

Lauren squinted through slitted eyes, saw the shape through the flame, walking toward her. The familiar outline. The voice. "Dad?"

The man who had called himself John Reardon, who had been born Matthew Mullin, stood over her. "I knew it would end like this, and I tried to stop it."

"You should have told me."

He crouched in front of her. "I know that now." He wore work clothes, a denim shirt and khakis, and carried with him the scent of fresh-cut wood. He grew more solid as the seconds passed, as the flames filled in behind him like a movie backdrop.

"I can see you better now." Lauren reached out, felt the cotton softness of old cloth. "I can touch you."

"That's because it's almost time." Mullin held out his hand. "It's not hard. It doesn't hurt. You can trust me on this. I speak from experience." His eyes filled. "At least I can help you with this. I can be here for you like you were there for me."

Lauren grasped his hand, fingers closing over skin and bone as real as any she had ever felt. Around her, the flames changed, from yellow-white to silver to something beyond color. She stood, the spell that had bound her legs as dead as the witch that had cast it.

They walked in silence, father and daughter, as Gideon unfurled before them, a ghost landscape. Questions formed in Lauren's mind, all the things she had wanted to know when she lived.

"Yes, I did."

Lauren looked at her father as she filtered all those questions, tried to figure out which one he had answered. "Yes, you did what?"

"Love your mother."

"I shouldn't have doubted."

"I would have." Matthew Mullin, child of Gideon, shook his head. "I would have hated me."

"I could never hate you."

"Cross your heart?"

"And hope to die."

They both laughed at that. Then Lauren felt her smile fade. "You left them behind."

It took some time for Mullin to find the words. "We were going to die together, Emma and I. Take care of Blaine once and for all. But I needed her. I didn't have the strength to release the flames by myself. It was just supposed to be the two of us in the house, but when I got here, I saw Leaf and Amanda carrying something wrapped in a rug, and I panicked. I knew it was Emma and that they had killed her and that they would either kill me, too, or make sure I was blamed for her death." He held out a pleading hand. "I tried to get Jimbo to come with me. Him and Connie." He shrugged. "They did all right without me."

"Not really."

They walked in silence as time passed in whatever increments mattered in the wilderness. Lauren recognized the blankscape, and wondered if Emma and Leaf were out there somewhere, settling their differences. She saw others, men and women in all manner of dress, standing at intervals, talking in groups, bowing their heads and touching their foreheads as she walked by.

Then Matthew Mullin stopped, and nodded to one of the older women. She stood off by herself, hands clasped before her, smiling softly. She wore old-time clothes, a long, dark skirt and matching shirt adorned with an embroidered lace collar, her white hair gathered in a net cap.

"I've been waiting here awhile, Matthew." A soft voice, the barest hint of a drawl. "I know what you're thinking. It's not your decision." She drew up straight, and steel shone in her eyes. "It never was."

"Yes, Mistress." Matthew Mullin released Lauren's hand, beckoned for her to step forward. "Good-bye, Lauren."

"Dad—?" Lauren started after him. Then something gripped her,

Blaine's spell the merest touch in comparison, and she turned back to face the woman. "Mistress Mullin."

Eliza Blaylock Mullin inclined her head. "Likewise."

"I'm not sure about that." Lauren stuffed her hands in her pockets, felt odd delight in the fact that she still could. "I let him get me."

"Well, he got me, too." Mullin beckoned, and together they walked along a path that formed before them as needed, lengthening with each step they took. "But I cleaned his goose, and you cooked it." She smiled, and the years fell away. "It took some time. But one thing a good witch learns is how to wait." She stopped and turned. Sighed. "There he stands, like a lost lamb."

Lauren looked back, and saw her father sitting on a nearby slope, watching them.

"He fears what I am about to tell you."

Lauren felt a jolt. She had already died. What could happen to make it worse? "What?"

"That this isn't your time." Eliza Mullin pointed toward the lighted horizon. "That there are greater dangers, and you're the one who must meet them. This wilderness has many paths, many door-ways, and not all of them are well guarded."

Lauren looked down at herself. "I'm not dead?"

"You never were." Mullin eyed her sternly. "But if you keep pass-ing back and forth as you do, one day you'll find you've left too much of yourself behind in one place or the other, and you will have to make a choice." She pointed again to the light, like a teacher ordering off a wayward student.

"Wait." Lauren dug through her pockets, swore under her breath, ex-cused herself. "I just had it—" Her hand closed over the small, cold thing, and she pulled it out, then held out her hand. "I got this from Amanda Petrie. An ancestor of hers somehow got hold of it after the fire."

Mullin stared at the locket dangling from Lauren's fingers, raised her hand over her mouth.

"Did I do the wrong thing?" Lauren closed her hand. "Maybe you didn't want it, because of the memories—I'm sorry—" She quieted when Mullin held out her hand.

"Thank you." Mullin held the locket up by the chain, then fastened it around her neck. "I now feel as complete as I possibly can."

"Did you ever see him again?" Lauren nodded toward the locket. "I don't mean to pry, but I opened it and—"

Mullin shook her head. "I lived too long. If I had died within a few months of him—and I admit I was tempted to help matters along more than once—I would have. But if too much time passes, paths diverge. You travel so far in one direction that you can never find your way back." Her eyes dulled. "His name was Tom. He's in a different place. I pray he is content." She took Lauren's hand, and squeezed it. "You will never see your Mr. Corey again. I'm sorry."

"Is he in a bad place?"

"You make your choice, and you pay the price. On both sides of the divide." Mullin looked up at what passed for the sky, the tempered light like the inside of a lampshade. "You should go, Lauren Mullin. This isn't your place."

Lauren started for the horizon. As she walked, she scanned the hills, the paths, searching for the man in the denim shirt. But her father was nowhere to be seen, and she realized why he had said goodbye.

Paths diverge . . .

Lauren picked up her pace, her eye on the horizon.

CONNIE PETERSBURY LOOKED up at the sky. It flickered, like lightning behind cloud, and she felt the charge in the air. Ashley had vanished at the first sign of the light, screaming into the trees like the beast she had become. Then all had gone quiet.

She put her hand in the water, and felt a swath of warmth like she had never felt. It swirled around her knees and popped and danced as though a school of fish boiled past, tickling her toes. She laughed, and then she quieted.

She had gotten to know this river. She knew an invitation when she felt one.

Then she paused, and listened. Not just an invitation. A plea.

Connie slipped off her glove, her coat, and they fell atop the water and floated downstream for a time before vanishing beneath the surface. She looked down at her hands, and saw skin clear and smooth, like a young girl's. The water bubbled, warmer than it had ever been, and she felt the pain in her knees fade to nothing. Her right hip.

Oh, she liked this. She liked this a lot.

She plunged in, like she hadn't done since childhood. The water washed away everything it didn't need, and she flitted, mirror sides glinting, a shift of light and current.

Gideon. She could feel it drawing closer. She plunged deeper into the water, followed it into cracks and crevices and pipes old and new, underground caverns that no human had ever seen or dreamed existed, as other shifts of light and shadow greeted her and called her friend.

She refilled a cistern old as time, then pushed through dirt and rubble, layer after layer, as though they weren't even there.

Then she sensed it, all of it, the heat and the flame and the huddled figure in the midst of it all.

I know you! I know you! Connie pushed ahead, drilled upward, floor after floor, dousing flames that hissed and sparked as she drew close, swept them into nothingness with the back of her hand.

She was still Constance Petersbury. But she was also so much more.

She was the river.

41

Lauren felt it. Heat. Like standing in front of a bonfire.

Then she heard a roar like wind. All about her shook and the brightness changed to cool gray and silver, tiny mirrors, a million reflections of a single sun. She felt herself lifted, buoyed, carried along, around and across and down.

Hello. A quiet voice. Familiar. *Don't worry. It's just me.*

Light blared, so bright it struck like a blow. Lauren felt cold now, road roughness through her clothes. She opened her eyes. The Cateman house filled her view, a sodden wreck, charred and smoking.

Then she heard the pounding of booted feet, drawing closer. Voices.

"What in the name of hell—?" Zeke bent over her, stared at her, then at the house. "Whatcha been up to?"

Lauren sat up. Phil had already joined Zeke, and they stood over her, as Virginia Waycross and the others pelted toward them. "You're not dead."

Zeke nodded. "That's right, we're not."

"You're alive?"

"That's the opposite of dead, last I checked. Yes."

Phil grabbed her under the arm and helped her stand. "They almost caught us, just off Old Main by the intersection, and then we heard this roar like a tornado touching down and they all screamed and the sky sort of opened up like a clamshell kinda and all this light flowed out and pushed away the dark or ate it or some damned thing." He looked up at the sky, now normal, blue with a scattering of cloud. "And then it got all quiet and we looked around and we were the only ones there."

"Well." Waycross looked up at the Cateman house. "Looks like you've been busy."

Lauren started to smile. To laugh. To gaze up at the sky and wonder at the blue, breathe air free of murk and tension and the acrid taste of a warped soul.

Then she turned and headed up the walkway of the Cateman house and up the steps onto the porch. Found what she was looking for, and stopped.

"What do you think you're doing?" Waycross ran after her, grabbed her by the arm. "It's not safe in there—you could fall through the floor and—" She fell silent, and stared at the thing resting on the doormat.

Lauren knelt beside the sodden remains of Nicholas Blaine, fingered charred flesh rendered soft and pliable by the water of Gideon. "Memory of fire burn you. Let air feed the flame." She reached into the planter next to the door, took a handful of dirt. "Memory of earth bury you." She sprinkled the dirt over his face. "Let water erase your name."

Waycross knelt beside her. "I thought you didn't know the words?"

"Sometimes they just come to you, I guess."

"I guess."

"Wow." Zeke had crept up behind them, and removed his hat. "They've got a wood chipper for rent at the hardware store." He rocked his head back and forth. "Doubt anyone else is using it now." He flinched as a bird swooped down and landed on the porch railing. The crow regarded them first with one eye, then the other. Then it leaped down to the porch, walked to Blaine's corpse, and pecked it.

"Use the chipper." Lauren stood. "Scatter him for the crows." She turned and headed back down the stairs.

42

"Been one helluva week." Rocky stuffed the bundles of cash and credit-card receipts into a zipper bag, then closed the register. "I'll miss all these reporters when they're gone. Eat like there's no tomorrow. Good tippers, too."

"I won't. Damn snoops." Virginia Waycross took a seat in a booth in the near-empty diner, caught in the midafternoon lull. "They keep trying to talk to me, and I don't have time."

"It's in all the papers. They're calling it the Gideon Freeze." Brittany hefted a stack of plates under the counter. "One of the snowplow drivers said we showed up as some weird blob on the radar and folks just went crazy."

Lauren took her coffee and left her seat at the counter to join Waycross. The two of them sat in silence as Rocky and Brittany bickered about a meat order and tinny music sounded from the radio.

Waycross stared down at her cup, then set it aside. "Half the town is gone. Over a hundred souls. Somebody's going to want to know what happened to the bodies."

"Maybe there weren't so many." Lauren scribbled atop the table with her finger. The Lady's sign, again and again. "Maybe folks managed to get out before Blaine closed us off."

"I think we both know that's not true." Waycross drained her cup, then stood. "I need to get going. Plow finally cleared the road to

410

my place. I'm going to borrow Lois, check and see how things are."

"You want some company?" Lauren followed her outside, grabbing her coat off the rack along the way and putting it on.

"No, you stay put and rest up. I can handle my own—" Waycross fell silent, and stared in the direction of Gideon's square.

Lauren turned in time to see a horse amble across the bare lawn. Soon after, another followed, at a pace all its own.

"Oh, my Lady—oh my—" Waycross broke into a run, past a reporter heading up the walkway toward them. The man turned, spotted the horses, then waved to a nearby van and set off after Waycross.

"At least she got Bert and Ernie back." Brittany stood in the diner entry, dish towel in hand, as Waycross embraced one horse, then the other, and the reporter and camerawoman circled at a safe distance. Then she stepped outside, let the door close behind her. "I never said—" She blinked, kept glistening eyes locked on the scene in the square. "I tried to hurt you, and then you saved me, and I never said thank you or apologized or—"

Lauren shook her head. "It's okay."

"No, it's not." Brittany threw her arms around her, hugged her tight enough to hurt, then let her go and backed away. "So many people gone."

"We'll be okay."

"Promise?" Brittany tried to smile. "I need to get back." She looked back over her shoulder at the reunion in the square, then went back inside.

Lauren watched as Waycross took hold of one of the horses and ordered the reporter to grab the other. As they headed toward the cul-de-sac, she set out in the opposite direction.

"We survived the Gideon Freeze." Lauren tucked her hands in her pockets. "A lot of good people didn't." She hoped to visit one of them now.

THE WOODS HAD the clean smell that settled after a rain. The sense of dread had vanished, and the shadows were just shadows. Lauren walked until she came to the bend in the river, that place where she first saw the ruins of her father's house. Stood for a while, and imagined, and remembered.

Then she heard a horse nicker. As she walked, a small bay emerged from the trees and paced her along the other bank. He looked real enough, well fed and gentle. But scar tissue crisscrossed his flanks and marred the corners of his mouth, and though he seemed tame enough from a distance, something told Lauren that she had best not try to get too close. "Kermit?" His ears perked at the sound of the name. Then he shook his head and vanished into the brush.

She walked along the bank, stopping every few steps to get a sense of the place. When she felt warmth drift through the chill, she sat on the nearest rock, and waited.

After a few minutes, she sensed movement in the air. A flicker of light.

"Hard to tell the difference between your world and mine now." Connie Petersbury sat on the rock next to Lauren. "It's the sun—it's leaking over." She squinted up at the sky. "Not complaining. Just not used to it." She squinched her toes into the snow, then buried her feet to the ankles.

"Aren't they cold?" Lauren shivered on general principle.

"It's all water to me." Connie shrugged. "Hot or cold don't make no never mind."

Lauren took off her earmuffs so she could listen to the crows, and heard rustling as Kermit rummaged among the low branches of an old apple tree. "Is he alive or—"

"He's here, with me. That's what's important. When you tell Virginia, tell her that."

"I will."

"Not his fault, poor thing. He's been demon-rode. He'll recover eventually, go back where he belongs, but it will take a while." Connie shrugged. "In the meantime, folks walking through the woods might sometimes see a horse following them. Better than some of the things that we've had follow us around here."

"True." Lauren spotted a crow eyeing her from a nearby oak. Dug in her pocket for a few of the peanuts that she and the others now carried as a matter of course. "We can try to bring you back, if you want. Mistress Waycross thinks it's possible because you never went over all the way. There's still a part of you anchored here. Like with Blaine, but in reverse. In a way." She tossed the peanuts into the shrubbery; the crow graced her with a head-cocked side eye, then glided to the ground and hopped in after them.

Meanwhile, Connie sat quiet, and pondered the dappled water. Then she shook her head. "On thaw days, heat days, the sun shines, and it's calm. On ice days, I can shelter beneath, and it'll be quiet and still. Most peace I've ever known, being a river. And you know, I can get in places you couldn't imagine."

Lauren smiled. "I bet I could."

"Oh, no, I am found out." Connie's grin wavered. "I can look after him here. Kermit. Tell that to Virginia. Make up for the way I hurt him before."

"I never got the impression that she held that against you."

"Virginia blames herself. That's her way. I think knowing he's here and getting better might ease her mind." For the first time, sadness touched Connie's face. "When the sense is right, I can just see Jim, wandering. I like to keep an eye on him. Make sure he can return to the Lady, someday." She pulled her feet out of the snow, crossed her ankles, swung her legs like a girl. "I'm the last Petersbury. Ain't no more, after me. I like the thought that I can close out the family on my terms. Just dyin', that's the Lady's terms. Life's terms." She looked out over the river like a landowner regarding her domain. "These are mine."

Lauren didn't argue. If there was one thing she understood now, it was finding one's place. "I'll visit sometimes, if that's okay."

"I'll be here. Ain't going nowhere."

Lauren stood, and held out her hand. "Thank you. For saving my life."

Connie stared at the hand. When she finally took it, she watched Lauren as if she expected something to happen, for her to blow up and vanish or melt. Eventually, she smiled. "You're strong."

"I'm a child of Gideon. I learned from the best."

"Lady keep you."

"Likewise." Lauren headed out the way she had come. When she looked back, she saw Connie still seated, her arms and legs outstretched, like a child drying off after a swim on a summer's day. The next time she looked back, the woman was gone.

Lauren wandered back into Gideon along the Old Main Road, past the bustling hardware store, the diner's overflow parking lot. Across the square to the cul-de-sac, enjoying the smell of the sweet, sharp winter air, the warmth of the sun on her back. As she reached the Pyne house, the front door opened, and Zeke hobbled down the walk toward her.

"Mistress?" He touched the brim of his cap. "I think you need to take a look at some of Leaf's, well, things. There's books that didn't burn that we—well, Phil wanted to bring them into the house but I told him 'no the hell way' and so they're setting out in the driveway behind the house. Old. Big leather—" He inscribed a large square in the air. "Phil looked at one, and well, his daddy used to tan back in the day, hides, you know, and he said the book feels . . . not right, if you know what I mean."

Lauren shook her head. "I'm not sure I want to."

"Well, seeing as you're Mistress now—"

"I don't think that's been decided."

"Oh yes, Mistress, yes it has." Zeke bobbed his head. "Anyways, we think you should have a look, if it's not too much trouble."

Lauren nodded. Watched for a time as across the street the first bangs and rumbles of demolition sounded, backed by a chorus of crows.

"Mistress Mullin?" Zeke waited on the porch. Held the door open for the Mistress of Gideon, and followed her inside.

did take some liberties with the terrain and history of north central Illinois. Gideon is a fictional place; the River Ann does not exist. In addition, while the Sudden Freeze of December 20, 1836, did occur, details of the weather conditions in Gideon differ from those noted in historical accounts. I don't believe the sun shone anywhere else in Illinois on that day. It shone in Gideon so that the subsequent temperature crash would have that much more of an impact.

ACKNOWLEDGMENTS

This book was years in the writing, and there were times when I thought it would never be finished. Along the way, a number of friends and colleagues offered their support. Particular thanks go to Kate Elliott, Patricia Bray, and Michael Curry, who read and provided comments on the very first versions of the story, and to David Godwin, best beta reader ever. And finally, a special shout-out to Julie E. Czerneda, who provided moral support, critique, and encouragement every step of the way. Book buddies are the best.

Many thanks to my agent, Jennifer Jackson of DMLA, and my former editor, Diana Gill, for providing support above and beyond the call, and to my current editor, Kelly O'Connor, who helped me realize that sometimes the darlings do have to die and that the story is the better for it.

ABOUT THE AUTHOR

Alex Gordon resides in the Midwest. She is currently developing her next book, and is having too much fun doing research. When she isn't working, she enjoys watching sports and old movies, running, and playing with her dogs. She dreams of someday adding the Pacific Northwest to the list of regions where she has lived.